Hannah's Heart

JILLIAN HART

CHAPTER ONE

Colton Kincaid reined in the team of horses. Trepidation skidded over him like the fat chunks of falling snow. It wasn't much of a town. Just a couple streets, a handful of businesses, and a few unimpressive houses. But it looked quiet and safe. A real family place. A town where nothing went wrong, men were honest, and, he figured, there would be no need for a full-time sheriff.

Colton felt a tug on his sleeve.

"I'm hungry."

This child was all he had in the world. Colton studied the small boy's round face, and a trickle of hope filled him. Maybe he could find what he was looking for in this forgotten little town. A home for his son. The dream of living again.

Lights shone through the falling snow, warm like a beacon welcoming him home.

Home. Colton craved it like the feel of a hot, crackling fire. He'd been without one for so long. But this was the last leg of a long journey. After this, there would be no more traveling. He snapped the reins. The team broke into a trot as if they sensed the town might mean home, too, and the sled's runners squeaked on the loosely packed snow.

The main street was quiet, perhaps on account of the storm. Only one horse, a fine spotted mustang, stood drowsing at the hitching post outside the only hotel.

"Look at the lights," he told his son. "We can eat in there."

"Want beans."

"Me, too, little fella." Colton reined in the team and climbed from the sleigh, careful to keep cold air from slipping in beneath the thick blankets, careful to keep a tight control on his heart. It would be easy to start putting up dreams, building on them one by one, looking at a peaceful place like this.

Dreams, he'd learned, didn't buy a boy a hot meal and a safe bed for the night. Hard work did. And by God, that's why he was here—to start a partnership with his one-time friend and, in time, buy his own land.

Determined to right old wrongs, Colton lifted the child from his snug nest in the sleigh.

The hotel's front door popped open, and his gaze landed on the woman who emerged with one hand propped on the doorknob. She stopped in the well-lit threshold, her back to him as she laughed with someone inside.

"Rose Carson," she said, light as air, "you stop matchmaking for me. Maybe you should concentrate on finding men for the younger girls in this town. They're foolish enough to actually *want* husbands."

The woman turned, facing him. Lamplight filtered through the window, burnishing her uncovered gold hair. His breath caught at the sight. Her face was heart-shaped, her blue eyes kind.

"What a handsome son you have." Warmth. Gentleness. Those qualities filled her voice like melody and harmony, and she breezed closer.

"Thank you," Colton managed. If he had one pride, it was his son. The quiet, gentle-hearted soul who'd been left in his care after Ella's death. Colton set the boy on the ground, keeping a firm hold of him so his small feet wouldn't slip on the ice.

"How old is he?"

"Two," Colton answered.

Zac held up three fingers.

The woman's laughter made the freezing air feel warmer and easier to bear. "Well, little one, you'll have to come to my Sunday School class. We have two other children who are just your age. That is, if you're planning on staying in town that long." She tilted her face and looked up at him. His heart skipped five beats.

"We sure hope to." He found the air to speak, and noticed the shine of a gold band on her left ring finger. "I'm Colton Kincaid. And this little charmer is my son, Zac."

"It's a pleasure to meet you both. My name is Hannah." She reached into her cloak pocket and withdrew a pair of gray knit gloves. "You must be new to town."

"Yes, ma'am." What was he doing, talking to a married woman, far too fine for the likes of him? Colton took a step toward the hotel, holding on tight to Zac as the boy toddled and nearly slid.

Colton caught him, both hands on those small elbows, and kept him upright. Zac, the trust so deep, kept waddling.

"Perhaps you could tell us if this is the only place to eat in town?" he found himself asking, just to catch her gaze again.

"Yes, it is." Dream-blue eyes brushed his. She wasn't bold or flirtatious, just friendly, and it intrigued him, touched him.

How long had it been since he'd lived in a place where women could greet strangers with such a smile? Such complete faith in the goodness of the world?

All the more proof he was a duck out of water. A man like him, he didn't belong here. But for his son's sake, he would do his best.

Colton nodded his thanks and took a few more patient steps up onto the boardwalk, carefully holding Zac by the forearms so the boy could walk on the ice on his own.

"Rose Carson runs this establishment." Hannah rushed after them, her face pinkened from the harsh burn of the cold air. Despite the bulky winter coat and the care she took on the ice, she looked graceful and gentle. And as well dressed as a fashion plate. "Rose is a great friend of mine. I should introduce you."

So eager. Colton wondered at that. Then he realized she was watching after his son, the small boy determined to follow in his father's footsteps, sliding, but unafraid of falling. It was for the child her eyes shone and her voice rang like melody and harmony.

A knot tightened in Colton's throat. When he studied her now, with a careful eye, he saw the lines of sadness etched around her mouth.

"Thanks, but I think I can manage on my own," Colton said more gruffly than he intended.

Hannah froze, a stiffness settling along her jaw. In her eyes, he saw her own reproach. He'd embarrassed her, he realized. Worse, she must have thought she'd embarrassed herself.

But in his book, any woman who cared so easily over another's child, why, that was a good thing indeed.

"Yes, come inside and introduce me to this Rose." Colton let his voice soften. He felt bigger, better, when a small but sure smile brushed her soft lips.

"I hope she's a good cook," he added.

"I'm hungry," Zac grinned.

Hannah's heart caught. Such a dear child—she could see that about him already, this tiny boy who was the exact replica of his father, with the same dark hair and eyes. The same sense of stoic strength that made heroes of men. At least in myths and legends.

She'd never known a man who was halfway trustworthy, let alone one who could be called a hero.

But she did admire how this man, Colton Kincaid he'd called himself, held open the heavy front door to the hotel with a patience only a father's love could provide. Her throat ached, remembering.

How she'd wished things could have been different, that Charles could have looked with love like that so bright and alive in his eyes at his own child. But there was no changing the past. Certainly not now.

Her whole chest hurt watching the little boy as he ambled on short, chubby legs out of the bitter cold and into the hotel. Her arms felt empty. Her heart felt empty.

"I didn't mean to..." Zac's father paused, "embarrass you, I guess. I think he's something special, too."

"Then you're a good father." Hannah forced a smile. Loneliness wrapped around her as cold as the snow outside but here, in the light of this stranger's presence, she felt less alone. "All little children should be so lucky."

"Not so lucky." A single shake of his head.

Hannah wondered at the swift denial. Then wondered at the man. His chiseled face looked rugged, but handsome. His black hair was long, falling just past his collar to touch his shoulders. And the shadows in his brown eyes, they drew her. As if he, too, had lost hope long ago.

Remorse shivered through her. Small lines hugged his eyes, etched his face. Hardship had placed them there. And time.

And here she had been longing after his child like...like a kidnapper. Blushing, ashamed her feelings rose too easily to the surface, Hannah only took a step past the door he held for her. She caught a fresh scent of pine and outdoor air that clung to his coat, to him, and it was as rugged and as attractive as the man.

She cleared her throat, determined to leave before she

could embarrass herself further. It just hurt, being so alone. Having such empty arms.

"Rose," she called out into the warm and well-lit parlor. "You have customers."

"In this weather? Oh, my!" Rose bustled out from the back door of the kitchen, wiping her hands on her crisp, ruffled apron. "My, what a handsome little boy. Hannah, are these friends of yours?"

She felt the man's gaze on her, sure and steady, bold as a touch. Had she given him the wrong idea? "No, I just met them myself. I wanted to recommend your wonderful cornbread and baked beans."

"Beans," Zac repeated wistfully.

The big, powerful man, handsome as the devil, pulled off the tiny boy's knit woolen cap. A simple brown, nothing special, made with a mother's love.

Hannah wondered if they were alone. If Mr. Kincaid was a widower. Then she shook herself, determined to stop letting her dreamy nature get the best of her. Whatever Mr. Kincaid was, he wasn't her business. Never would be.

"I've got to get home, Rose," Hannah called out to her friend. But Rose was already kneeling down to talk to little Zac as his capable, broad-shouldered father unwound the boy's dark muffler.

"Thank you, ma'am." Colton's words rattled through her like a thunderstorm, low and dark and powerful.

"Good luck to you." She managed the words, thankful she sounded normal. Thankful her heart didn't show, for she was determined to hide it.

" 'Bye," Zac turned, lifting his mittened hand in a cute, childish wave.

Her heart collapsed. Would the pain always be with her? Lord knew she'd tried so hard to bury it. But there it was again, always raw and hopeless. She supposed she would have to try harder. More determined, Hannah closed down her feelings, dug a little deeper, and laid the yearnings in her heart to rest.

"Good-bye, Zac." She tried to smile through the words, but couldn't. Not really. So she stepped out into the cold and let the freezing comfort of the snow wash over her.

* * *

Mrs. Rose Carson's wholesome beans, honeyed ham, and fresh cornbread did the trick. It had taken the edge off his hunger and driven the cold from his bones. Colton sat down on the edge of the double bed, neatly made and the tick freshly stuffed—he could smell the clean straw—and gently tugged off Zac's shoes.

Tummy full, the boy's eyes had closed the instant Colton had laid him in the bed, more exhausted from the trip than Colton had figured. In truth, the cold ride out from Missoula had been a grueling one this time of year. He hadn't thought cold weather would come so soon in these mountainous foothills east of the Rockies, but he'd been wrong. Had he known, he would have started for these parts weeks earlier.

But in his letter, Charles had promised there was no hurry, that the job would be waiting for him—and the opportunity. It was too damn good to be true. The knowledge of what he stood to gain calmed the guilt of how hard the trip had been for little Zac. He was so young now, but if Colton played his cards right and worked for all he was worth, the boy would have land to call his own one day. He wouldn't have to make his living the way his father had, at the cold end of a gun.

A light knock on the open door spun Colton around. It was only Mrs. Carson, harmless in her blue gingham and ruffled apron, a smile lighting her eyes. "He's a precious one. Is he sleeping?"

"Hasn't even stirred." Colton set the tiny shoes on the hearth to stay warm and turned to pull the hand-crocheted afghan over his son. "Thank you for the meal. I know it was late, past dinner time. You were cleaning up your kitchen."

"I always have food for a weary traveler, especially one so small." There was no censure in Rose's eyes. Maybe a question. And he could guess it. What was a man doing out in such weather with a child?

Colton was appreciative that the woman didn't ask. "The town looks shut down because of the storm."

"It is." Rose leaned against the threshold. "Folks are used to the snows around these parts, but it's the blizzards that come up and can kill a man. Last winter ranchers in these parts lost most of their cattle. The winds were so cold and hard and the snow drifted so high it smothered entire herds."

That was not news to Colton. When Charles had written late last spring, looking for a partner and extra cash to help save his ranch, he'd written of the terrible storms. Of the tremendous losses that had sent him—as well as many other cattlemen—into neck-deep debt.

"The mercantile's open, though," Rose continued, as if his silence didn't bother her in the least. "The Bakers live on the second floor above the store, so it's good for business because they can stay open no matter the weather."

"Yes, ma'am." Although he wasn't by nature a talkative man, he rather liked this woman's pleasant chatter. He was hungry to know more about the town. "The lady I met outside today, the one who introduced us, mentioned Sunday School classes."

That had struck his interest. Zac needed to be around children his own age. And church sounded like the right place to take the boy. It felt like he'd landed on his feet this time. A small ray of hope burned in Colton's chest.

"Yes, Hannah Sawyer—she teaches the littlest ones every Sunday. She has a gentle hand with them."

"Hannah *Sawyer*?" Realization ran over him like a speeding train. The woman he'd met, with the angel's face and the ache for a child in her eyes, this woman was married to Charles?

His mind reeled. He hadn't put the pieces together. Couldn't even remember, in fact, if Charles had written his wife's name in his letters. Now he resisted the urge to dig through the small packet in one of the two satchels sitting on the floor and find out

"Charles Sawyer, why, he was killed just a few months ago."

"Killed?" Charles, who'd offered him a partnership in his ranch, was dead? "That can't be—"

"Terrible accident. Has left Hannah in difficult straits." Rose's voice dipped in genuine sympathy.

A terrible emptiness echoed through Colton's gut, and his hopes for his son faded.

CHAPTER TWO

"I'm not going to sell." Hannah fisted her hands. "Bully me all you want, Glen. I managed to make the mortgage payment. You go check with the bank if you don't believe me."

"I bet you barely scraped up enough money," the tall, dark man supplied. "But it's not something you can keep doing time after time. Don't deny it, Hannah. My brother would want me to have this ranch. He told me so."

Hannah bit her tongue against words a lady never said. But she thought them. Big, bad, nasty words that burned with an anger she didn't bother to hold back. "Glen, what your brother told you doesn't matter. He's dead, and that makes this land mine."

"For only as long as it takes the bank to decide to recall your loan."

"That hasn't happened yet." If her heart knocked against her chest and her limbs trembled with a light, cold sensation, she wasn't about to let her brother-in-law know. Or see. She'd suffered through a marriage that had drowned out every bit of happiness from her heart, and she was free of it. She hadn't prayed for Charles's death, but she'd found comfort in it.

She was free of that man's control over her life. And this ranch—this land—was hers. She'd worked alongside her husband to clear the timber and set the fence posts and helped him build the house. She had the scar from a machete cut and the winter ache from a broken ankle when she'd fallen from the roof to prove it. She'd sweated blood and tears for this land, and no man would take it from her.

Especially not Charles's equally arrogant brother.

Glen tipped his head back, jutting out his chin as if he'd already won the ranch from her, as if he'd already defeated her.

What was it about men who took pleasure in harming a female who was so much smaller?

"Now, Hannah, don't make the mistake of thinking you're safe because you made the payment." His narrow eyes flashed. He stood tall and straight, probably to show off the brand-new tailored suit he thought so fine.

But she wasn't impressed. "Glen, I *am* safe. No more discussion."

"It's just the beginning."

"No, it's not." The thought of losing her home, after she'd lost so much, could devastate her. Or make her fighting mad. "Beginning or end, I'm not going to listen to any more of your nonsense."

She pointed to the door, which was neatly situated between the parlor's two glass windows.

"I'll leave when I'm good and ready." Her brother-in-law drew himself up like a bear—and looked about as difficult to get rid of.

Blast! Double blast. It took every bit of her willpower not to lose her temper.

"Hannah, this could all be over if you would just accept my offer."

"Marriage? To you?" Her heart ached. Seven years ago she'd married the wrong man. She would not indenture herself further or set her heart up for more sorrow by marrying another.

"I'm not so bad." Glen reached out as if to lay his hand against her cheek.

She stepped back, avoiding the contact, but there was no mistaking the desire in his eyes. He wanted to possess both her and her land.

"One day you'll come begging for my help. And my wedding ring. You'll see." His gaze never left her face.

But she refused to look at him. Instead, she rescued the broom from the corner where she'd placed it when he'd interrupted her work. She held the worn handle tightly in both hands. "Good-bye, Glen."

His boots thunked against the floor. "Hannah, I'm just trying to help you out."

"Like heck you are." She wasn't fooled. "If you don't get your snowy boots off my parlor rug, you'll lose all hope of ever being anyone's husband. I can perform unspeakable acts with this broom handle."

His eyes narrowed. "No sense getting testy. I'll get off your rug." He headed toward the door, slow, sure. As if he were certain, in time, this home and everything in it would be his. "You know I want you. I've wanted you since the day my brother married you."

A cool chill slid down her spine. She looked up into his eyes. If only she could fight him back, physically and strategically. But she feared what he could do. "Glen, get out of my parlor so I can sweep up this snow you've thoughtlessly dripped on my floor."

Once he was out of her house, she could think, could try to figure out what hold he thought he had over her.

,Something to do with the bank, perhaps. She could smell it like smoke on the wind.

He opened the door and plopped his hat on his head. "Someone's coming."

She straightened. "What? It's nearly a blizzard out there."

She pushed back the lace curtain at the window, lace she'd crocheted herself, and peered out through the haze of white-gray falling snow. "Who would be foolish enough to travel in this storm?"

"Don't know. Whoever it is, they're coming down the road from town."

She could only see the dark shadow of two horses pulling a boxy sleigh and the shape of a man behind the reins, but she could not recognize him.

She hoped to high heaven it wasn't more trouble.

It hadn't been easy leaving Zac back at the hotel, even if Mrs. Carson seemed kind and eager to care for the boy, citing how she missed her grandchildren, who had moved far away. She'd reassured him she would watch over Zac until his return.

Between leaving his son behind—and Colton never left Zac with strangers—and this weather that had him half frozen, this trip had been one bad idea. But he had to know. Now. He could not sleep a single night not knowing what would become of his future, not after he'd traveled so far and risked so much.

Fierce winds battered him, drove ice straight through the layers of wool to his skin beneath. The house before him rose up out of the impenetrable wall of snow and wind. A light glowed in twin windows, a beacon telling him he'd made his way safely. Surely this was the right place?

He had expected a tiny shanty, like so many of the dwellings in this part of the country, but not this log home, roomy and well built. Fancy lace curtains hung in the glass-paned windows. He recognized the woman gazing out at him.

Hannah. So, this was her house. He was in the right place, had not been driven off track by the storm.

The door flew open and a man towered in the threshold. Tall. Powerful. Dark eyes met his, hard and

15

unflinching.

Colton's spine straightened. He met the man's gaze, leveling him with one as equally challenging. From his years working behind a gun, he'd learned to assess people. Could see right past their defenses to measure the man—or woman—beneath. This one was cunning, not someone to trust upon sight.

"Who are you?" the stranger asked as he towered above on the sheltered porch, just out of reach of the wind and driving snow. "What are you doing here?"

"I could ask the same of you." Colton kept his head up and climbed out of the sleigh, wincing at the stiffness in his limbs.

"I'm just paying a call on my sister-in-law." He clomped down the few steps and into the snow, waiting a moment before he extended his gloved hand. "Glen Sawyer."

"Colton Kincaid."

They shook. Glen's grip was hard. Almost bruising. As if the man wanted to act more powerful than he was.

Colton stepped back. "I knew Charles from Arizona. We were neighbors for a time before he came north."

"That explains why I don't know you." Glen tipped the snow off his hat and gestured toward the barn.

Colton led his team in the same direction. Curious. Maybe this brother of Charles's could shed some light on the situation. Colton needed to know if he had any chance here. If there was any way Charles's offer still stood.

Once out of the shelter from the wind the house provided, it was too difficult to talk. Or see much of where they were going. Colton kept tabs on Glen, nothing but a dark shadow in the furious snow, and kept tight rein on the team. The horses were cold, he knew it, and growing nervous over the ever stronger wind. It howled through the tree limbs, speaking with an eerie voice.

They'd reached the barn. The scents of warm horse and fresh straw met his nose. Colton gratefully followed Charles's brother into the shelter and out of the bitter cold.

He looked around. This structure was sturdy and of good construction. Colton spotted two empty box stalls close to the door. Deciding to stable his mares there, he knelt to work the ice loose from the harness buckles.

"I'll lend a hand," Glen volunteered, after shouting into the darkness for help.

Colton wondered at the man's motives as he knelt down and began work on the buckles that held the sleigh. "I was sorry to hear of your brother's death."

"Is that why you've come, to pay your respects?"

Those sharp eyes missed nothing, Colton thought, but he took comfort in the realization that not even Charles's brother knew why he was here. Maybe that was a good thing. It wasn't always wise to let just any stranger know the amount of money a man carried in his saddlebags.

"In a way." Colton said no more. His numb fingers worked a buckle free and he stood to lift the heavy leather harness from the mare's neck.

"I can take that from you, clean it up, and dry it off." An older man, gray-haired but sturdy, appeared out of one of the dim aisles and lifted the collar from Colton's arms. "Glen, you want me to get your gelding saddled?"

"That's the idea, Sean. I don't intend to walk back to my place."

Colton lifted a brow at the man's tone. Whatever he was, Glen Sawyer wasn't kind. The way a person treated a hired hand told a lot about him. Colton decided he didn't like Charles's brother. He would not seek answers from this man after all.

"I don't recall seeing you around town." Glen's voice came gruff and hard.

Colton had seen too many men of Glen's nature when he wore a badge—and more in his life without the badge. "Just rode into town today."

"And you've come to pay your respects to a widow in this storm?" A raised eyebrow, but the gaze beneath spoke of a deeper curiosity.

Colton freed the second collar. The bay tossed her head, glad to be rid of icy burden. The old man reappeared.

"I'll be glad to rub down your horses, sir," he said.

"Thanks." He regretted leaving the mares. He believed a man ought to tend his own horses, but the weather was cold and he was on a quest.

"Excuse me, Glen." Colton lifted his saddlebags from beneath the seat of his sleigh.

"You have business with Hannah?" Those dark eyes sharpened. "Or have you come to court her?"

Colton saw a warning, a signal that something was wrong. He decided to say nothing further and headed out into the storm, the saddlebags slung securely over his shoulder, facing the cold head-on.

Colton felt watched. He looked up at the house and saw the glow in the window, thought of the warmth inside, of a fire crackling brightly, and of Charles's widow.

She stood at the window—he was close enough to see her. Lamplight shimmered in her gold hair, and her blue eyes squinted through the storm as if watching for him. Then the curtain fluttered into place.

Colton's teeth chattered in the cold, and he clenched his jaw.

The door opened before he could knock.

"Mr. Kincaid. I can't believe..." She hesitated. "Come in before you freeze."

Colton strode into the room, not at all surprised by the coziness of her home. A fire burned in a gray stone hearth. A green rug warmed the polished wood floors. Comfortable looking furniture invited a man to come inside, put up his feet, and dream. It was snug and warm, a good home for a child.

"You have a beautiful place here."

"Thank you." Her eyes warmed like morning light. "You look half frozen. Please, let me take your coat. You need to get those boots off and go warm yourself at the fire."

Before he could protest, her slim hands were reaching out for his coat. He lifted his stiff fingers and began unbuttoning the garment, regretting the speckle of falling snow and ice that rained down on her perfectly polished floor.

"Where's that little boy of yours?"

The last button came loose and he slipped out of the jacket. "In town with your friend Rose. She swore up one side and down the other she would guard him with her life."

A twinkle glimmered in Hannah's eyes. "That's Rose. She has a soft spot for children, now that hers have grown up and moved away. Why, she's never even seen her newest grandson." Hannah turned to hang his ice-covered coat on a wall peg. "I bet she's spoiling your boy something terrible."

"That's fine by me." Colton tried hard not to think of the past. "Zac could use a woman's affection."

Hannah stared hard at the floor. Then her chin came up. He could see it in her eyes; she wondered, but she wouldn't ask.

"His mother died last year." The quiet words tore through him.

"I'm sorry."

"Seems we both know what grief feels like."

Her eyes shadowed. "You're freezing. I have a pot of coffee on the stove. Let me get you a cup. You must thaw out before you head back into that storm to wherever it was you were headed."

As if she'd set her feelings aside, Hannah lifted one hand and gestured at the fire. He stood rooted to the floorboards and drank in the sight of her. She'd changed into a soft blue checked work dress, the skirt trimmed with ribbon and a ruffle. There was a cameo pinned at her throat. She was a very pretty woman.

What had Glen Sawyer said? *You have business with*

Hannah ? Or have you come to court her?

"Make yourself comfortable." She gestured toward the divan and then the chair with the footstool closer to the fire. "I'll be right back."

Colton watched her go with a graceful swish of her light blue skirts. Charles had married this woman? Colton wondered about her as he tried to remove his boots where he stood, but neither came loose. Too full of driven snow and ice, he figured.

By the time he reached the fire where he hoped to thaw out a bit more, Hannah returned with a steaming blue enamel cup balanced in her small hands.

Hands that were red from hard work. His gaze didn't miss those details. In fact, he noticed many things about Charles's widow. Like the kindness shining in her eyes—it was heart deep. And she wanted a child of her own, at least judging by the way she'd watched Zac.

Hannah stepped close.

"Thank you." He took the cup from her, amazed by the lighter blue flecks in her eyes. She smelled like honeysuckle, light and sweet. The scent tickled his nose and stirred his blood.

It had been a long time since he'd so much as looked at another woman.

"I apologize for dripping snow and ice all over your clean floor," he said, because he knew women cared about such things. "My boots are frozen on."

"Then let me help you. You need to warm up your feet. A lot of ranchers around here have lost toes and more to frostbite. Come, sit here." She knelt and patted the upholstered footstool.

He watched her in amazement. Was she so used to doing the same for her husband? Colton remembered how Charles could be when he drank. Mean as a cougar after a few sips of whiskey.

He set his cup on the mantel and sat on the stool. "I want you to know I'm not in the habit of allowing women to play with my feet."

The hint of a smile danced along her mouth. "So, you think I'm the kind of woman who can't keep her hands off a man's extremities?"

Colton laughed. "I knew you were that sort when I first laid eyes on you."

Her smile warmed her face. "You're lucky you look so cold, or you wouldn't be enjoying such liberties."

"And a firm grip." He winked when she laid one hand at his heel and the other at his ankle. "A man likes a firm grip."

"You're terrible." Merriment burned in her eyes. "And here I thought you were a nice man, what with your sweet little boy."

"You like children?" he asked as she wrestled with his boot. To make it easier for her, he pulled against her. His foot gave. Snow and ice tumbled out on her pretty rug.

She set the boot on the stone hearth to warm. "What's not to like?"

His heart twisted. What, indeed? "You have no children of your own?"

"No." A simple answer, light and plainly spoken, but he wondered at the emotion she hid. He remembered the look in her eyes, so bright and adoring, as she'd admired his son.

"Brace yourself. We still have one more to go." Her hands settled over his other foot and pulled.

Looking down at her, Colton studied the delicate part in her spun-gold hair and the fine bone structure of her shoulders and arms. He didn't miss the blisters on her palms when she lifted her hands for a better grip.

"This boot is being stubborn on purpose, I think," she teased.

"Maybe I'd better thaw out a bit in front of the fire first. Then it will come right off."

"I can get it." The weight of her hands, one on his toe, the other on his heel, teased him.

"It would be better to wait."

"Why wait? Brace yourself."

He laughed. "As if a little thing like you could pull me off this footstool."

"I'm tougher than I look. Since my husband's death, I've been doing his work around this place." She puffed air at the gold wisps falling into her eyes. Then she yanked. Surprisingly hard.

His boot slipped, then stuck. Colton braced himself. She pulled harder, and he did, too. He felt the boot give but could do nothing to stop Hannah as she toppled backward, his snow-bound boot clutched in her small hands.

Panicked, he sprang up, fearing she'd hit her head. But then he heard her laughter, like sunshine bright enough to warm every part of him.

"Do you believe I did that?" she said and laughed.

"Are you all right?" He reached down and held out his hand.

Hannah looked up at him, mirth glimmering in her eyes. Then she laid her slender fingers in his palm and accepted his help. "As right as I've ever been, I guess. At least I got the boot off."

"You sure did." More unruly blond locks had escaped from her fancy knot and fell in eye-catching curls around her face.

He swung her up to her feet, her checked skirts swishing at her ankles. Her honeysuckle scent drew him nearer, made the blood thicken in his veins.

What was he thinking? Angels were out of reach for a man like him.

"Well, at least now you can relax and get yourself warm." She breezed away, clearly unaware of her effect on him, and set the second boot beside the other on the stone hearth.

"I'm much obliged, ma'am." Colton turned away and reached for the mug, still steaming where he'd left it on the mantel. He took a warming sip. "You make a good cup of coffee."

"I'm glad you think so." Brushing off the compliment, she'd already crossed the room to grab up a broom he hadn't noticed before. "It's my one indulgence."

"Coffee?"

"With white sugar and fresh cream." She bent her head as she set to work sweeping up the trail of melting snow he'd left across her floor. "I hope you don't mind—I took the liberty of sweetening it for you."

"Not at all." Actually, he preferred his coffee black. "Let me do that."

"No." She held the broom possessively. "You're a guest, and I don't get many of them."

Colton watched her efficient movements as she guided the broom across the floor. "No, I bet you don't," he said quietly. "You seem pretty isolated out here."

"Were you headed up to the Mullens' ranch? They're just down the road two more miles. You must have taken a wrong turn." She stopped sweeping.

The truth closed up his throat. One look into her gentle blue eyes had him hurting. Had him remembering another woman, quiet and more plain, who once made him hope, once made him believe.

"Mrs. Sawyer!" The door banged open. Alarm rang in the old ranch hand's voice.

A jolt charged through Colton. His hand jumped, straying to his hip. No gun. It took his mind a moment to remember he didn't need one. He wasn't a deputy, not anymore. Old habits died hard.

"We got trouble."

CHAPTER THREE

Hannah felt the broom slip from her hands, heard the clatter as it hit the floor. "What kind of trouble?"

But Sean had already turned and dashed out the open door into the bitter wind and snow.

It couldn't be. She didn't even glance back, didn't stop to grab her coat or slam the door shut behind her. Only one thing flashed into her mind and stayed, big and fearful and enough to ruin everything. *Fire.* Just like last month.

Snow so cold it burned slapped against her face, driven by the wind. She fought the restriction of her skirts, then finally grabbed them up to her waist. Ice hurt her nose and throat, but she kept running.

A shout behind her told her that the newcomer to town, Colton, had followed her out into the scouring snow. She ignored him. She didn't have time to explain. It could already be too late.

Dark, thick smoke billowed out the open barn door and melded with the falling snow. Too much smoke. Hannah fought against the helplessness knotted in her breast. She kept running.

She spotted a water bucket left beside the well pump

and snatched it up. Snow had already fallen, covering the bottom, inches deep. She filled it as she ran.

"I'll get more buckets," Sean shouted to her as she stepped out of the storm and into the smoky barn.

Horses neighed, made frightened by the fire. She saw no flames. Where the hell was it?

"The haymow," Sean choked before he disappeared.

Fear beat in Hannah's heart. The hay was tinder dry. Eager flames would consume it—and her barn—in no time. Her legs were carrying her to the far side of the barn before she could think.

The smoke thickened, choking her. Tears ran down her face, and she blinked hard against the sting. She kept running.

The haymow was black with smoke. The crackle of flame filled her ears and jangled her nerves. The fire was huge, growing bigger, and so fast. How could they stop it?

She charged straight into the smoke. Everywhere she looked, a blaze of orange licked at the eight-foot-high pile of hay. The loft above would soon be engulfed as well.

Hannah gritted her teeth, hefted the bucket upward, and tossed the five gallons of snow as far as she could. It melted and sizzled but had little effect.

"Stand aside," a man's voice called. Not her hired man, but Colton emerged out of the clouds of smoke with two buckets and began spilling the contents on the thickest patch of flame.

"Get Sean to let the horses out," he shouted above the crackle of fire.

Hannah bit her tongue. At Charles's funeral, she vowed never to let a man order her around again, but this time she needed help. She ran back through the barn, tossed open the rear double doors, and filled her bucket a second time.

"Sean!"

Somewhere there had to be another bucket. There, by the feed sack. She filled that one, too, before the old man darted out of the smoke-filled aisle.

"I tried to stop it from spreading, Miz Sawyer."

"I don't care about that right now." She grabbed both full buckets and gritted her teeth against the weight. "Open the stall doors and let the horses out."

"But they'll run off."

"Do it." She didn't have the time or patience for an argument. If she led every horse out of this stable by the halter, then she would lose her barn and every scrap of feed in it.

As she ran down the aisle back toward the flames, Colton ran at her, his buckets empty. He tossed them, and they hit the board floors with a clatter.

"Give those to me!"

Hard-jawed, strong-armed, capable. She saw his determination. Whatever reason he'd wandered across her land, she was grateful.

His big hands covered the bucket handles before she could let go. Then he was off, a man of such powerful strength it made her eyes tear.

Thank, God, she wasn't alone. She couldn't fight this fire by herself with only an old man's help.

She retrieved the buckets and ran as fast as she could, coughing from the smoke, and plunged outside into the snow.

A dappled mare galloped by, eyes wide with fear, and disappeared through the thick curtain of driving white flakes and black smoke. So much smoke.

They couldn't stop the fire. She knew that in her gut. Cold wind scoured her face as she ran, her hands already so numb she could not feel her fingers grasping the metal handles.

Horses neighed their panic and kicked their stall doors, the sounds of their fear rising above the smoldering smoke and the snap of flames. Hannah fought her own fear as she dodged a bay kicking his heels high as he dashed toward the open double doors.

Hannah fought for breath, even as she breathed in smoke, and coughed. She met Colton at the entrance to the haymow. She handed him the buckets, knelt to grab for the empty ones he'd tossed on the floor, then turned and ran.

Horses bolted past her. She filled the buckets with her bare hands.

"It's useless, Miz Sawyer," Sean shouted above the chaos.

She shouldered past the old man in the aisle. "You've got to release all the horses."

"Can't. It's the smoke." The old man covered his mouth and nose with a handkerchief. "Gotta get out of here."

"Sean, I need your help," she screamed as he walked away.

How could he leave her like that? His smelly old cigars probably started the fire. Anger tore through her, hotter than an inferno. Well, she would not lose this barn. She would fight until there was nothing left inside her.

"We're not making enough progress." Colton's grim face, smeared with soot, met her in the aisle.

Behind the strong line of his shoulders she could see the flash of flames glowing orange in the pitch-black smoke. She coughed. "I have an idea."

"Wait!" He caught her arm.

She pulled away and snatched up the pitchfork lying forgotten against a stall door. The horse inside ran in circles, eyes rimmed white, neighing a high, ear-splitting sound. She snapped open the door and let the animal free.

As if Colton read her intentions, he snatched the pitchfork from her and headed back into the thickest smoke.

"Colton!"

"Bring in the buckets." His shout rang over the growing scream and panic of the aisles of trapped horses.

She grabbed the buckets and headed straight for the

spindles of crackling flame. Seeing how much the fire had grown in just the last few minutes, panic skidded through her veins. She had mown that hay herself.

She squinted her eyes against the stinging flame. Colton was nothing more than a shadow in the darkness, but she could see him work the burning hay with the steel-tongued pitchfork.

"Hannah, I need some of that snow over here."

She hefted one bucket and ran. Her chest felt ready to burst. Then Colton tore the bucket from her hands and dumped it on the hot, writhing fire.

"Watch out!" his voice called.

Greedy flames roared higher, like a living thing, reaching toward the loft overhead. No. Tears from the smoke ran down her face. She grabbed the second bucket of snow and hefted the heavy load as far into the inferno as she could.

"It won't do any good," Colton's voice vibrated in her ear, ricocheted down her spine. "It's too late."

"We have to keep trying. Please." Her heart beat thick in her chest.

Then he moved away. With pitchfork clutched in his hand, he headed straight for the roaring twist of deadly flames.

She watched heat lick at his clothes. Hannah held her breath, terrified, as he climbed onto the crumbling stack. He towered close to the inferno, then stuck the tines of the pitchfork into the pile and began separating out the unburned hay.

He wasn't going to stop fighting! Hope arrowed through her heart. Hannah snatched up the buckets and ran. They could beat this, the two of them, working together. There was no other choice. She could not lose this barn.

Hannah returned with the buckets, took one look at his work, and tossed her snow on the edge of the greedy blaze. The flames beneath sizzled and died.

She turned around, running past the piercing shriek of the terrified horses. She couldn't afford to stop. Her muscles screamed with exhaustion.

Hannah returned and emptied her buckets, for the little bit of good they did. Her hopes failed. Fire was everywhere, licking up the wall, snaking across the floor, shivering across the bare boards of the loft overhead.

The sight of Colton sent a bolt of awe straight through her. She saw him with the pitchfork on the other side of the burning haystack, working hard to take as much fuel from the fire as possible.

Heat blistered his arms and hands. Sweat sluiced down his face. But he kept working, climbing around the burning circle of hay, beneath the dangerous loft overhead. He kept turning the burning hay over on itself.

Then the flames flared up and his shirt caught fire. He took it off and kept working. There was nothing but flame cutting him off from the only exit.

"Colton!" She ran, looking for another pitchfork, found it, and began tearing her way through the building flames. Her skirt caught on fire and she beat the fabric until it died. "Colton!"

His head snapped up.

"The loft's on fire!" She jabbed her arm straight up.

How long did they have until the wood gave way and flame rained down on them both?

Panic made her knees weak, but she lifted her fork and faced the wall of flame, disbursing the clumps of burning hay. Heat roared up in her face, snapped painfully across her hands.

Colton was trapped.

"Get out of here!" he shouted.

She couldn't leave, not without him. "There has to be a way—"

"Find a hammer!"

The pitchfork fell from her hands. Fighting for air, her lungs spasming from the smoke, she tore down the aisle and snatched the mallet from the tack room. She caught sight of a hammer against the wall and took that, too.

"Watch out!" She tossed the mallet through the flames. Please, she prayed as she glanced up and saw the burning bits of hay falling down from the loft above.

She ran past two horses; both had managed to escape, and she circled around back, battling the freezing winds and blinking hard against the snow.

There. The sound of Colton's mallet thudded against the outside wallboard. Hannah fell to her knees in the snow and tore at the edge of the board with the hammer's claw. It gave just enough. From inside a blow knocked part of the board loose. She moved aside and worked on the adjacent board. It came away in her hand and Colton tumbled through.

"I didn't think I was going to make it out."

"Neither did I." Her knees had never felt so shaky.

"How many horses do you have in that barn?" Colton plunged his hands in the snow.

Her heart fell. Had he been burned? "Maybe fifty."

"Then we'd better get them out"

"You should go back to the house. Are you burned anywhere else? Let me see your back."

Only then did she let her gaze stroke across the red angry pucker of a nasty burn marring the smooth skin covering the ridge of his ribs.

"We don't have much time, Hannah." Colton lifted one hand. "The roof is on fire."

"Oh, Lord." Prayers would not help her now. "You need medical attention."

A grin curved one half of his mouth, etching a dimple in his cheek. Night-black eyes flashed. "Don't worry. I'm tougher than I look, angel."

Smoke ribboned on the wind, smarting her eyes as Hannah ran back into the barn.

It was a maze of smoke and panic. She lost sight of Colton but did stop to tear off a piece of sagging petticoat to tie around her face.

She'd never worked so hard in her life. Or felt so frantic. The fear of the horses became palpable as the interior of the barn turned black as hell and just as hot.

She tore open stall door after stall door and let the animals run. They milled in the aisles, desperate for escape. Some were too panicked to find their way, so she tossed her petticoat over their heads and pulled them outside by their halters and by the very strength in her arms.

Snow fell, and outside, away from the ignited barn, the world felt peaceful, fresh and new. Hannah sank to the ground and buried her face in her hands.

* * *

Colton staggered out of the barn and saw Hannah collapsed in the snow. Ashes mixed with the falling flakes and tumbled down on her. She rubbed a chunk of ice against her hand.

His guts clenched. The burning wood cracked behind him, the snap of the fire now licking along the supports of the structure.

"We saved the horses," he began, uncertain what else to say.

She looked up. Only then did he see dthe burn along the edge of her palm. "That's important I'm just glad you weren't trapped in that haymow. I'm still shaking from being so afraid for you."

"And not yourself?"

She lifted one shoulder.

His heart fell. She looked vulnerable. Her dress was scorched and stained. Her delicate gold hair hung in soiled tatters around her sooty face. Even while exhaustion and loss weighed her down, something inside held her up. Fascinated, he could do nothing more than stare at that hint of light glowing deep inside her.

Colton held out his hand. "I notice you have another barn downwind. We need to watch the falling embers and make sure nothing ignites, just in case."

"And I need to round up my horses." She laid her cold hand in his. He felt the blisters on her palm, saw the smear of blood after she stood and moved away.

A woman who did the work of a man. Probably because she couldn't afford more than that old coward to help out around here.

Colton thought about that and took a step forward. "Hey, do you have a shirt I can borrow?"

Hannah's gaze widened, focusing on his chest. "Up at the house. In my bedroom." She tucked her lush bottom lip between her teeth, then added, "I haven't gotten around to packing up Charles's things."

"I'll find it on my own, if you don't mind."

"Go ahead. Please bring my coat back with you. It's hanging on the peg closest to the door." She stepped away, and the curtain of snow and smoke engulfed her.

"You should let me take you to a doctor," Hannah scolded just as the clock a room away donged the hour, echoing through the house. Four in the morning. "This burn is serious. How much does it hurt?"

She watched him grimace as her fingers brushed over his left shoulder blade and swept down toward his spine. "Not much."

"You're a liar, Colton Kincaid." Really. She'd never seen a burn this bad. Remembering how he'd been trapped beneath the loft, ignited hay dripping directly onto him, he was darn lucky it wasn't worse. She spotted a few small sores along his neck and arms. And when he tried to hide his hands, she saw even worse damage.

"That's good enough, Hannah." He tried to move away.

"No, you don't." She caught him by the shoulder and pressed him back into the chair. "Now, stop acting tough and sit back and let me tend you."

"Well, I suppose it's not often a man gets an opportunity like this, being alone with a pretty woman."

Despite the pain and exhaustion lining his face, he winked up at her, a teasing light glimmering in his eyes. "But this isn't exactly what I had in mind."

She laughed. Oh, he was a charming devil, no doubt. Strong as the day was long and handsome enough to gaze at forever. "Looks like I have you just where I want you, half naked in my kitchen. How the gossips' tongues would wag."

"They would be shocked at you. You can't keep your hands off me."

She dipped her fingers into the grease and herb mixture she'd simmered on the stove. Despite the burned skin, badly blistering, her gaze kept returning to his back, to the fine sculpted muscle that rippled when he moved.

She spread more of her rancid-smelling balm across the edge of his shoulder blade.

His body flinched. "I should go out and check on the fire."

"It was nearly out when we left it." It hurt to think of all she'd lost. "And with this snow, there's no danger of the other barn igniting."

"Still, I should check and make sure the embers are cooling." He groaned slightly as she spread balm on the ridge of his spine.

"I can do it." She wished...well, wishes never came true, not in her life. "Thank you for helping me. If you hadn't stayed, then I would have been alone with that horrible fire."

"I noticed your hired man took off." He twisted up to look at her, seated at her kitchen table, the length of his wet hair falling into his eyes. "It's not good for a woman to be alone."

"Oh, I don't know about that." She blocked her heart from feeling. Surely, the past was best forgotten. "At least my horses survived."

"If we can round them all up."

"We?" Hannah wondered at that as she turned to the

stove. "You've helped me enough, Mr. Kincaid."

"So formal all of a sudden." He stood, a big shirtless man who made her cozy kitchen shrink all the more. "Are you hoping to get rid of me, Mrs. Sawyer?"

Oh, it was the devil twinkling in those eyes. Hannah scooped more balm from the fry pan onto the saucer and tried to avoid looking at his chest. His magnificent chest. But she couldn't. "I rather figured you had your own life, Colton. That you wouldn't want to be burdened by my problems just because you became lost in the storm and wandered up to my doorstep."

"I came to see you." He leaned one hand against the table. So close she could reach out and touch that breath-stealing wall of chest.

"Me?" Why, she couldn't imagine. And in such weather. Only a fool would have traveled with the mercury below freezing like that. "Turn around, Mr. Kincaid. I'm not finished dressing your wounds."

"Ah, I love a woman who knows how to avoid a threatening subject." His mouth drew up into a lopsided grin. "Besides, you're safe for now. Go ahead and finish bandaging me. You just want to keep me half naked as long as possible."

"You're far too saucy, sir," Hannah laughed. Why would he come to see her? "Turn around. I can finish this up quick enough. I know you want to get back to your son."

"I shouldn't have left him alone like that." The way emotion weighed down his words said everything.

"You stayed here to help me. I'm grateful." She finished smearing the balm on the smaller wounds she'd spotted along the line of his shoulder and there, down his right arm. "But I know that's little comfort for your son."

She looked up, saw him wince. The emotion she read in his eyes stymied her. Love shone there, bright and true. She'd never in her life witnessed the evidence of a man's love, not for a woman, especially not for a child.

She felt ashamed, as if she'd invaded something intensely private. Hannah lowered her gaze and ministered to his burned hand.

"Zac doesn't handle separations well," Colton confessed, his voice low like a caress, troubled like a wound.

"Such things are hard for a boy so small." Hannah remembered the button face of the child, safe and snug as he'd been in his father's arms.

How would it feel to be held like that?

"His mother's death was terribly hard for him." Colton stared hard at the window.

And for Colton, too, Hannah wagered. Her chest ached wondering if the love she'd seen in his eyes was an emotion he carried for his deceased wife, too.

"Rose is wonderful with children." Hannah reached for the pile of torn, clean cloths. "Don't worry about your little son. He's in safe hands."

"I hope your friend doesn't think I've abandoned the boy."

"Rose would never think that," Hannah said firmly, even if the story of a father abandoning his children was not unfamiliar to her own life. "We'll get you bandaged and send you back to town. You'll be at your son's side before breakfast."

"Then I guess our talk will have to come at another time." Colton faced her with a saucy, flickering gaze. "I just saw one of my mares dash past your window. I'd better go catch her."

"But I'm not through with you—"

"I have no need of such care." He strolled away, snatching up the borrowed shirt and his hat from the table. "Save it for someone who's worthy."

Hannah stared down at the bandages still in her hands. The door clicked shut, and she was alone.

CHAPTER FOUR

Hannah stepped out into the cold, pulling on her warmest set of mittens. The snow was falling like tiny crystal teardrops now. It was cold and growing colder.

Her gaze strayed across her land, past the garden spot covered and turned for the winter, to the row of fencing beyond. Some of the horses were corralled there, dark spots of movement against the snowy world. Others dashed, still free. She and Colton had only managed to catch some of the more docile animals last night in the dying glow of what remained of the barn.

Only a dark scourge on the ground remained, still puffing gray-black smoke. The thought of the valuable shelter that building had provided and the loss of more than half her winter's feed made her knees weak, her stomach turn.

It isn't the end of the world, she reminded herself. She would figure something out. There was always a solution. She just had to look hard enough. Or work hard enough.

"Hannah!" Colton's voice.

She scanned the landscape and saw him standing amid

the smoldering ashes. "I thought you were going to catch your mares and head home."

"My tack was destroyed. And my sleigh." He gestured. Sure enough, there stood the burned-out rubble of his vehicle, which had been parked alongside the barn that used to exist.

"I guess I owe you a harness and a sled." She trudged through the snow.

"That's a generous offer." Even from this far away his grin was good-natured and sported twin dimples that made him look dashing.

"You can take what you want from the other barn." She gestured south, toward the latest addition to her ranch. Thank heavens it still stood, solid as ever, and the animals within safe and sound.

"Do you have any idea how the fire started?"

"No. Sean sneaks his cigars in the barn. I've chewed him out over it before." Hannah sighed. "I threatened to fire him the next time I caught him at it, but he's getting old and forgetful. He took off last night and it doesn't look like he showed up for work today."

"No, it doesn't." Colton gestured toward the remaining barn. The sound of hungry horses destroyed the peace of the morning.

"I'd better get cracking." Always work. The thought of mucking out that entire barn by herself exhausted her before she even started. And that was just the beginning of a workday without end.

"Wait." He reached out, curling his hand around her wrist.

Heat rippled up her arm.

"Look what I found." He stepped around the blackened scar in the earth and nudged at the edge of something twisted with his boot. "Do you know what this is?"

Hannah knelt. She shook her head.

He crouched down beside her, his dark, intelligent gaze

pinning hers. "I think it's the remains of a can. Probably kerosene."

"What?" She shook her head. "I don't allow kerosene to be stored in either of my barns."

"Well, I thought I caught a faint whiff of it when I was in your haymow fighting the flames." His hand snaked out and stopped hers from reaching. "Careful, the embers are still hot. You'll burn yourself."

"But what is a kerosene can doing here?" The question burned through her, hot as flame. "What—"

"This fire wasn't started because of a single cigar, or a match." A world of trouble flashed in his eyes.

"It wasn't?"

"Let's face it, kerosene doesn't ignite by itself."

A chill trembled down her spine. "No, of course not." She just didn't want to think of the alternative. That the fire was deliberately set.

"I figure it started here, in the center of the haymow."

"How do you know?"

"It's the blackest spot. It burned the hottest, probably aided by fuel of some kind. Kerosene."

Hannah thought about that. Her heart knocked against her ribs. Everything felt so wrong. She was only one woman. How could she keep fighting on her own against one problem after another?

She stood and turned suspicious eyes to him. "You never told me why you were here."

He straightened up, towering over her. The frown of his brow, the squint of his eyes deepened into harder lines. "You think I might have done this?"

Hannah shivered. "I hardly know you."

"So, you think because I was in this barn before it burned, and then I situated myself in front of your fire so I could come out and lend you a hand, that I have something to gain from all this?"

The sound of anger tense and low beneath his carefully controlled words spun ice through her veins. Angry men frightened her. But she held her chin firm. "All I know is that you are a stranger to me, to these parts, and my barn burned."

"You are accusing me."

"No." She met his gaze.

"You're considering the possibility." A muscle jumped along the tense line of his jaw. "Look, I'll admit you don't know me, but I'm not a destructive man. If I want something, I just say it. I don't burn down a poor widow's barn instead."

"Poor? I don't want your pity." Her throat ached. She'd had enough pity to last her a lifetime, and she could stomach it no more.

"I mean broke. Facing financial ruin." He took a step back, away from the ugly black scar of the earth and smoldering embers. "I came here for a reason, Mrs. Sawyer. And it wasn't to get myself nearly killed in your haymow. Do you want help with your morning chores?"

His eyes were almost hard, his jaw so tight it looked ready to snap in two.

Hannah shook her head. "I've had enough of men and their anger to see me to the moon and back. Take your horses, help yourself to my tack, and get off my land."

"Fine." His big hands fisted, but not in a threat. Hannah had learned to recognize that. The wind breezed through his hair, rumpling those too-long locks, black as night, against the formidable width of his shoulders.

Her fingers tingled, remembering the feel of his male-hot skin and the hard layers of muscle and bone beneath.

"But make no mistake. I'll be back."

She watched him walk away, a dark shape against the purity of the snow. What did he want? Had he set fire to her barn?

No, her innermost heart told her. Colton Kincaid was not the kind of man to do a woman harm.

But that's what she'd thought about her Charles, and look how wrong she'd been.

* * *

"**M**r. Kincaid, come in." Rose swung open the front door of the hotel, a crisp white apron tied around the front of her dark dress. "I worried about you out in that storm, but I figured a man as smart-looking as you would do just fine."

"Thank you, ma'am." Colton eased through the door, near to freezing, grateful for the bright welcome in the innkeeper's eyes and for the radiating heat from the crackling fireplace. "How's my son?"

"Little Zac is doing just fine." Rose locked the door behind him and then scurried on ahead toward the kitchen. "He was a bit fretful last night when you didn't return. I had my worries about your safety, but everyone knows around here if a man gets caught in a storm, he finds shelter and stays there until it lets up. That's what I told him, and after a good night story and a few lullabies, he drifted right off to sleep."

Colton's throat ached. "You're a kind lady, Mrs. Carson."

"I have a warm spot for little ones." Rose waved off his words but beamed with pleasure nonetheless. "Let me pour you a nice hot cup of fresh coffee. It'll be just the thing to warm you right up."

"Thank you, ma'am."

"Rose," she corrected with a smile, then breezed through an open doorway and disappeared.

Zac was fine. Relieved, Colton set his saddlebags on the floor, eased into a plain blue wingback chair and set his feet close to the fire. It was cold out there, probably ten degrees or so. The heat from the fire felt damn good.

"Papa?" Such a small voice, yet it was everything. Colton held out his arms as a little figure in blue flannel flew into his lap.

"I hear you were a good boy while I was gone," he said, snuggling close.

"Good boy," Zac sighed.

It felt right, holding his son tight in his arms. No matter what, they were still together. But what would have happened to the child if he hadn't managed to escape from Hannah's barn? Colton hated having no family, just as Ella had none. Who would raise the boy if Colton couldn't?

"Look who's up," Rose's voice rang like a happy song in the quiet parlor.

Zac burrowed against Colton's chest, and Colton cuddled his son more tightly, treasuring the moment.

Rose set a steaming cup on the nearby decorative table and clasped her hands together, her gaze fastened on his child.

"I was just wondering if a big boy like you would help me make pancakes for breakfast."

"Could."

"How many do you think you can eat?"

"Three." Zac held up four fingers.

Rose's delight lit up her face. "Mr. Kincaid, you have a treasure there in that boy."

"Don't I know it." It was luck, and Colton knew it. And Ella's gentle love and care throughout Zac's first year of life.

That's what the boy needed. A loving hand. A mother's love. Now that Colton knew Hannah Sawyer would need his money more than ever, he could start thinking ahead, building a future for his son.

A mother meant marriage. And marriage was something he wasn't ready for. But who would care for Zac while he worked? A housekeeper? No matter how kind the woman, a housekeeper was not a mother.

A mother ought to be forever, a gentle woman who baked cookies and fussed over everything and always had a hug to give. That's what he had to find.

Hannah Sawyer's cozy home, warm and inviting, flashed through his mind. The way her kitchen smelled like cinnamon and apples. And the quiet sadness in her eyes when she'd looked at his son.

* * *

Hannah thought of Colton Kincaid every time she walked past what remained of her barn, and she felt...confused. A little angry. And regretful. She'd been unkind to a man who nearly lost his life trying to help her. His courage of that night remained with her, haunting her movements.

Why had he come to see her? How were his burns healing? She felt responsible for the wounds, a little panicky that he was in town at all.

Money. Had Charles owed him money?

As she guided her mare around the slick mud that comprised the roads—the snowstorm had already melted—Hannah worried over the meager funds at the town bank. Meager wasn't the word. Puny. Embarrassing. How was she going to afford to feed her horses through the winter?

Well, she couldn't. That was painfully clear.

Colton Kincaid's face eased into her mind, his voice reverberating through her memory like thunder. I'll be back.

Was it a threat or a promise?

* * *

He didn't think of himself as a church-going man, and as he started down the narrow hallway, Colton doubted he'd ever feel at ease in this place. He heard the chatter of women, happy and comforting, and glanced past an open doorway into a room of Sunday-best dressed ladies with Bibles open in their hands.

The second door on the left, the minister had told him when he'd inquired after Hannah Sawyer's class. Yes, there she was, standing in the sunlight with the small window behind her, her golden hair gleaming like satin, her gentleness warming the room.

"All right, you two," her voice smiled as she knelt down to join her tiny pupils seated on the floor. "Help me decide which hymn we should sing."

"All the children!" the boy shouted out loud enough to echo in the room.

Her eyes laughed, even as she gently admonished him to remember to raise his hand.

Colton could only stare. Zac tugged at Colton's trouser leg, reminding him why they'd come. Colton knocked on the open door. Her gaze flashed upward. A frown tucked between her eyes when she recognized him, but her smile was warm, even warmer when she saw Zac.

"I'm so glad you could come join us this morning." She swept through the room. "We are going to have so much fun."

Colton looked down at his shy son. The boy wrapped both arms around Colton's knee and held tight.

"Go on," he said gently, ruffling Zac's dark hair.

The boy looked up. Colton nodded.

Hannah held out her hand. "We're going to sing songs. Would you like that?"

She still smelled of honeysuckle, sweet and light. Like everything he didn't deserve to have again.

"He's a little shy," Colton explained.

"That's all right." Nothing but acceptance in those eyes. He remembered how fragile she'd looked sitting in the snow as her barn was burning, and later that night as they watched to keep the other outbuildings safe. And in her kitchen, those fingers soft against his skin.

Zac's grip on his leg eased. Colton watched his son take Hannah by the hand and approach the other children.

He felt lonely as he watched Zac take this first big step away from him, safe at Hannah's side.

* * *

"He's the best-looking man I've seen in a long time," Paula Sutcliff said as she leaned close to whisper despite the minister's fervent prayer. "Not since the Parker boys moved in."

"But they were terrible farmers, remember," Rose

added, leaning across Hannah to conspire with Paula. "Lost their homestead the first year out."

"This one looks smart," Paula whispered, then bowed her head out of respect for the ongoing prayer.

Hannah tried to duck her chin, but why did her gaze stray across the small church to a pew on the other side of the aisle? Blame it on temptation. And the memory of the man who'd stayed up an entire night in the bitter cold just to protect her outbuildings and round up some of her horses.

"Amen," she whispered, her heart heavy. Why had she accused him like that? He had no reason to torch her barn.

Colton turned. His gaze snared hers, ricocheting like a lightning strike down her spine. He smiled, and the chiseled angle of his face softened, the shadows in his eyes eased.

How many men would take such care of a tiny boy? None that she'd ever seen.

"I heard he spent the night at your place," Paula whispered. "You must know what everyone is saying."

"What?" Hannah stared at her friend. "My barn burned down. It's not like we had time to...well, be inappropriate."

The minister's voice blasted through the near-silent church. His topic, Hannah noted with a falling heart, was the follies of sexual temptation.

Rose nudged her. "See? Even Reverend Hardy thinks you and Mr. Kincaid were...inappropriate."

Hannah remembered Colton's bare chest. And the tingly feeling that skidded across her fingertips when she'd touched his naked skin.

"I wouldn't mind being tempted by that man," Paula whispered. "Well, if'n I didn't already have a husband. One man is more than enough for any woman."

The service was painfully long. When it was over, Hannah tried to avoid Colton's gaze as she filed into the aisle behind Paula.

"Hannah." Colton's voice rumbled down the back of

her neck.

She turned. "Zac did a great job in class today."

The tiny boy leaned against his father's knee and gave her a shy, dimpled grin.

"We need to talk." Colton's voice brought her gaze upward, to his face. He was so handsome, half the women in church probably hadn't heard a word of the sermon.

"Perhaps in a more private place," she said, aware of the crowd and the curious ears around them.

"The hotel, then." A hint of a smile sizzled along his mouth.

"I'll whip up some sandwiches," Rose decided at once and took off down the aisle.

Hannah followed her friend out into the brisk air and crisp sunshine. The din of adult conversation and the shrill laughter of children punctuated the solemn day.

"I know what you're doing, Rose Carson," she accused, lifting her skirt with both hands as she picked her way across the muddy road.

"I'm not doing a thing."

"Trying to match me up with Colton Kincaid."

"Why, the thought never entered my mind." Rose hopped up onto the safety of the boardwalk.

"Rose, you shouldn't lie on the Sabbath."

Rose laughed. "All right, I am trying to match you two up. But he is a fine man."

"You've only known him a few days."

"I know from Mr. Drummond at the bank that your Mr. Kincaid—"

"He's not my Mr. Anything."

"—opened an account with a substantial amount of cash." Rose tipped her head forward to fish through the contents of her reticule. "Ah, there's the key."

"I'm glad Mr. Kincaid has adequate funds to provide for his son," Hannah said, seeing at once where her friend was going. "I am not looking for a man to pay off my debts, Rose."

"Never said you were." Rose unlocked her front door, left her closed sign in the window, and stepped into the parlor. "I'm just saying Mr. Kincaid is no bum. He'd make a woman a good husband, with that little boy needing a mother and all."

"Don't even say that," Hannah warned, heading straight for the fire. "My, I think autumn has abandoned us and we've gone straight to winter." She knelt before the embers and grabbed the poker to stir the fire.

"Go ahead and change the subject—it doesn't matter." Rose headed straight toward the kitchen. "Here he comes."

The door handle turned and Colton Kincaid, broad-shouldered and looking fine in his black jacket and trousers, stepped into the room.

Little Zac grinned shyly and toddled her way.

"Look, I have the fire started," she said to the boy. "We'll all be toasty warm in a minute."

Colton studied this woman and mulled over all he'd heard from Rose, the man in the feed store, the banker, and the clerk over at the mercantile.

Hannah was holding onto her ranch by a thread. She was out of money. Colton knew she'd lost a sizable amount of winter feed in the fire, not easily replaced even with enough funds this time of year. And she was alone.

He'd come to buy into a partnership with Charles, because he hadn't been able to purchase the kind of ranch he wanted—not yet, anyway.

But now he saw another opportunity.

"Do you still think I set fire to your barn?" he asked, seeing the answer already in her eyes.

"No." A small blush crept across her face. "I'm embarrassed that I lashed out at you. You were good to help me. You didn't deserve my suspicion."

She was fair and pretty and kind. Not that he would ever love a woman again. He lacked the heart. And faith. Life was too damn fragile. "Did you contact the sheriff?"

"I spoke to Baker." She unwound the knit scarf from

around her neck, mussing her hair. Gossamer curls of gold shimmered in the lamplight.

Colton swallowed. "And?"

"Did you used to be a lawman?"

"Yes. And no." He eased down on the knee-high hearth where she sat with his son, her pretty gray calico skirts spread out around her. How did he say it? He couldn't. "I don't talk about my past."

"I see." She ducked her chin. "I notice you didn't take my sleigh when you left Friday morning."

"It was your only one."

Her gaze came up to search his. Colton could feel the question, big as the sky. "But yours was ruined."

"I don't care about the sled, Hannah." How did a man begin to say the things he had in mind? How did he know she would even listen?

"I wish I could afford to reimburse you, but I can't."

Colton ached to reach out and brush the unhappiness from her face. It didn't belong there. She didn't have to be alone.

Footsteps interrupted what he was going to say.

"Look what I have for you, Zac," Rose called as she carried a tray before her.

"Choc'lit?"

"Just like I promised." Rose set the beverages on the sturdy shelf of the hearth. "I brought coffee for you two. Ought to warm you right up while we wait for my bean soup. It won't take but a few minutes."

Rose bustled away while Colton thought. He knew there was no other way to say it.

"Hannah, marry me," he said, just like that.

And watched the smile fade from her face.

CHAPTER FIVE

"**D**on't jest with me, Mr. Kincaid. I don't think that's terribly funny."

"I never joke, Hannah."

Zac leaned against her knee and reached for the cup of chocolate.

"Careful, it's hot," she warned, grateful to concentrate on the task of helping the child. Her heart drummed in her ears when she felt Colton's gaze, intimate and assessing, rake over her face as she held the cup for the little boy.

Zac stretched for the steaming mug and took a careful sip. She hated seeing her hand tremble. She wasn't rattled. Really. Colton could not be serious. He couldn't think that she would—

"So, will you?" Deep and stroking, that voice. Enough to make her shiver from head to toe.

"You *are* serious." How could that be? Her heart skipped five beats. "You don't even know me. You don't even know that I would never marry again."

She set down the cup when Zac moved away.

"I know that you came to Paradise answering an advertisement for a governess, but Mr. Drummond decided to hire a relative from back East."

"How do you know that?"

He lifted one shoulder, straight and strong. It was not hard to remember the power that lay there, dormant in muscle and bone. She'd witnessed his strength the night her barn burned. Felt wonder as she'd run her fingers across his injured back.

"I know that you were courted by many men, since there aren't too many pretty, eligible women in this county." Colton reached across her, the solid heat of his arm pressing against her knee as he worked at Zac's coat buttons.

Tingling sensations skidded up her leg. Hannah blushed, but there was nowhere to go. The fire behind her and the little child at her other side trapped her.

"I know when you married Charles Sawyer, he made promises he never kept." Colton's gaze narrowed.

Her throat filled. "My marriage is none of your business."

"I know that you're sitting on one of the best ranches in this county. And the prettiest, too. Two whole sections of land, half prime timber and large enough to graze the breeding horses you have in your barn."

"You've been asking Rose about me, haven't you?" Hannah clenched her fists. "Rose may be my friend, and she thinks she's acting in my best interests, but she had no right to tell you—"

"She didn't tell me anything I didn't already know." His gaze narrowed. "I learned that you made a payment on your mortgage, but there isn't enough money in the bank to see you through the winter, let alone meet the next payment."

"How can you—"

"I know they are thinking of recalling the loan because it's against their policy to let a woman have a mortgage."

"Colton, you have no right. You're a stranger—"

"I'm a friend of Charles's." Colton lifted his son's tiny

wool coat and laid it on his knee. He kept reaching past her, his arm against her leg, far more intimate than he had the right, as he unwound Zac's muffler and plucked off his little hat.

"Charles had no friends other than those he met in the saloon."

"I'm not a drinking man, Hannah. Nor a gambler."

"I really don't care what you are. I really—" She pushed past Colton's arm and stood. "Stop asking questions about me, do you understand? I'm not what you think. I'm not looking for... I'm never going to trust another man with my home and my life again."

She kept walking. She didn't want to see him standing there, so big and gentle with his sweet son at his side. Surely he'd heard about Charles's death and come, hoping to charm her into marriage. To get whatever it was he thought she had.

Hannah burst out onto the sidewalk, his marriage proposal playing over in her mind, his voice deep and sincere.

But then Charles had been sincere, too. And so infinitely kind. It was impossible to have known the true nature that hid so carefully beneath the polite mask.

It was impossible to know that about any man.

* * *

"I heard what Colton Kincaid said to you in my parlor last Sunday." Rose's eyes burned with curiosity as she pushed the threaded needle through her side of the blue and green log cabin quilt.

"You eavesdropped?" Hannah's needle stilled. "Rose, you're my friend."

"Which is exactly why I kept my ear to the door, but I couldn't hear much. Not without stepping back into the parlor with more coffee or some such." Rose bent over her work, but the smile warming her face was not hidden. Nor her glow of approval.

"You heard him propose to me?"

Four gasps rang out from around the full-sized quilt stretched tight on the rack. Hannah lifted her gaze and realized she'd spoken too loud. The women who'd been gossiping about what the schoolmaster had done now had fallen silent, mouths agape.

"Mr. Kincaid proposed to you?" Paula burst out. "Oh, Hannah. He's a dream."

"And he's the nicest man." Holly Pruitt nodded her approval. "He came in to order a new harness in our shop and he was terribly polite."

"And ain't it a shame about his poor motherless boy," Abby Drummond added.

The women clucked.

"Wait one minute," Hannah objected. "You're acting as if Colton—Mr. Kincaid," she corrected herself, "is the best thing to come to this town since the stagecoach."

"Kincaid's surely one I wouldn't mind riding," Paula winked.

Hysterics burst around the room. Hannah blushed.

"Paula, you know I'm not—"

"Interested. So you say." Paula's eyes laughed. "But face it. A woman has needs. You just need to have a real man bed you, not one who liquors himself up first."

"Poor performance," Rose agreed.

That sent the women into more laughter.

Hannah felt the heat increase across her face. "I'm not going to marry him," she interrupted. "Really. You are my friends. You ought to know at least that much about me."

"But how could you say no?" Holly leaned across the quilt and gathered up a handful of straight pins. "All I know is that if he looked my way, I'd roll over for him in the street"

"Well, *you* would," Abby teased.

More laughter.

Hannah didn't feel like laughing at all. "A dog rolls over in the street, not a woman."

"Well, if a handsome man wanted to scratch my

belly"—Rose winked—"I wouldn't care."

This time, even Hannah couldn't hold back a chuckle.

"When's the wedding?" Abby's eyes shone. "Are you going to have attendants and lots of flowers?"

Holly reached for a spool of white thread. "Really, where would she get flowers this time of year?"

"Well, a pretty dress then."

"Yes, what are you wearing?" Holly's excitement rang in the small room.

"Wait one minute." Hannah held up both hands. "You're all acting as if I've said yes. As if it's already arranged."

"But—" Paula stopped.

The women fell silent, and Hannah stared at their faces, a mix of misunderstanding, shock, and disbelief.

"We heard he spent the night with you last week," Paula began, serious as her brother the minister had been on Sunday morning. "Hannah, the whole town is abuzz about it."

"My barn burned down. It's not like we were...doing *you know* while the hot embers were raining down on my other barn and the roof of my house."

"Well, it really doesn't matter," Rose agreed, the mirth gone from her face. Friendship burned there, a steady shine in her eyes. The concern of a friend, and Hannah didn't miss what was unsaid.

"You can't tell me everyone—even you, my friends— thinks I would, well, become intimate with a man I don't even know."

"Well, no." Abby stared down at the half-finished quilt. "But my father opened Mr. Kincaid's account at our bank, and he liked the man. And learned from him he was a friend of Charles's. That he'd only just learned of his death upon arriving here."

"Yes, I know Colton, er, Mr. Kincaid, came to see Charles." Hannah leaned back in the chair, its wooden spindles cutting into her spine.

"And he asked my father about the market value of your ranch, Hannah." Abby cut a length of white thread.

The spool rolled to the floor.

Hannah didn't know what to say into the silence. Her ears drummed. Colton had asked how much her land was worth?

Abby blushed. "Y'all think I was listening in, but honest, I was in the vault counting Mr. Kincaid's deposit funds and I accidentally overheard. You know I wouldn't normally say a thing, except...maybe Hannah ought to know."

A chill flitted clown her spine. "I'm glad you told me, Abby." The girl was young, probably never thought such information should be given in private, but she was grateful nonetheless.

"Do you still think I should marry him?" Her gaze met Rose's.

Rose blushed. "Now, I'm certain Mr. Kincaid would never mean any harm. He was probably being sensible. He has a little boy's welfare and future to think about."

"Men only think of their own." Hannah reached for her sewing scissors. "I've learned that from hard experience."

No one in the room could argue with that.

The talk turned to Holly's nuptials, scheduled for the spring, and pride that the quilt, intended for her marriage bed, would be completed ahead of time.

* * *

Hannah endured the long, cold ride home from town. Her sewing circle meetings always left her feeling warm and connected. She lived a lonely life. But tonight, she felt ready to explode.

So, Colton Kincaid had been asking questions about her land. Before he'd asked her to marry him. She still hadn't answered him, refused to give it a single thought.

Yet the way his capable hands had unbuttoned his tiny son's coat that day in Rose's parlor before the fire only proved to her that Colton wasn't a bad man. Right?

"Hannah." Glen stepped out of the barn, dark as the shadows.

"You scared me near to death." Catching her breath, Hannah slid from the saddle and gave her mustang a reassuring pat. "What are you doing here?"

"I thought you and I should talk."

"About what?" Hannah took the mare by the bit and walked her into the barn.

"About the rumor I heard about you and Kincaid."

"You know I don't put much store in rumors." Hannah loosened the animal's bridle.

"This particular one interests me." Glen's footsteps tapped behind her, then stopped. "Did Kincaid ask you to marry him?"

"What does it matter?" Hannah unbuckled the bridle and slipped it up over the mustang's ears. "You know better than most why I'll never marry again."

"Charles was good to you most of the time." Dark eyes bore into her, deeper than the shadows.

Charles was far from good. Remembering the nights he'd come home smelling of whiskey and cigar smoke made her stomach curl. The control he'd had over her life...well, no one would understand.

"Go home, Glen. I'm not going to marry Colton." She patted the mare gently and bent to release the cinch.

"Maybe you should marry me." He stepped closer. Hot breath, smelling faintly of cigarettes, fanned across her face.

Hannah's stomach turned. "Maybe you should get out of my barn."

"The way I see it, this will soon be my barn."

"You're entirely too sure of yourself." Hannah shouldered the saddle off the mare and across the aisle to the tack room. "Glen, don't just stand there. Take this brush and help me out."

His fingers closed over hers. "I'd be happy to take over, Hannah. Go inside and I'll do everything."

"That's not what I meant and you know it." She grabbed a second brush.

"I want to know if it's true." His hand snared her wrist. "Are you interested in this Kincaid fellow?"

"Let me go." Hannah pulled back. "Maybe if you weren't such an oaf, you wouldn't need to go around trying to strong-arm women into marrying you. Try being polite."

He laughed. "Next thing you know I'll be saying *please* and *thank you*."

"Wouldn't hurt." Hannah laid her hand along the mare's withers and began brushing with even, gentle strokes. "You've been pressuring that banker friend of yours, haven't you?"

Glen ducked his head. "You want me to ease off?"

"I want you to stop harassing me."

"You can't keep up this work, not by yourself." His voice dipped.

"I'm doing fine."

"Look at your hands." He caught her wrist, lifted the brush from her fingers, and ran his thumb across the raw band of sores open on her palm. "A woman wasn't meant for this kind of work. I'd be happy to relieve you of all your troubles."

"At what cost?"

Their gazes met.

"You're tired, Hannah." Glen took over the brushing. "We'll talk about this later. Tomorrow."

"There's nothing to talk about." Hannah turned her back, hands shaking, and chose a rope halter from the tack room. "Good night, Glen."

He handed her the brush. "As you wish, Hannah. But how long is the hay in this barn going to last you? Another month? What are you going to do then?"

He strolled out into the night as if he owned it. Good riddance.

Hannah laid her head against her mare's velvet warm neck. The mustang leaned against her, and Hannah held close this small piece of affection.

* * *

"Looky!" Zac tipped his head back and lifted his chubby fist toward the sky.

"That's a hawk. See how he glides." Colton settled a hand on the tiny arm to insure he wouldn't topple off the rented wagon's wood seat.

Zac watched, spellbound.

Hannah's only remaining barn rolled into sight around the next corner. Percherons grazed in the neatly fenced meadows. It was a beautiful sight. And so was the log house on the hill, smoke curling from its stone chimney.

Would she be in the house or the barn?

The barn. Colton remembered the blisters on her hands, the kind earned only by hard work. With her husband gone and no hired hands, there would be no one else to do the heavy manual labor required to tend to so many fine animals.

"Hannah?" he called out as he climbed down from the wagon.

No answer.

Zac held out both arms and Colton lifted him high just so the little boy would giggle, then swept him down safely to the ground.

"Kitty." Zac took off toward the marmalade feline crouched in the barn doorway.

The cat took off in a startled run down the aisle as Zac waddled as fast as his tiny feet would allow.

Colton stepped into the barn after his son, checking for any danger. Every stall door safely shut, no pitchforks or other dangers visible. Zac stretched out both hands and ran, calling, "Kitty, kitty, kitty." The poor startled animal took off like lightning.

"Zac." Hannah stepped into sight. "What a wonderful surprise. What are you doing in my barn?"

"Kitty," he sighed with frustration.

"I bet you can find last summer's kittens right here in

this stall." She smiled when she spoke, but the warmth faded from her face, from her voice, when she lifted her gaze. "Colton."

He stepped forward. "Hannah, Zac wanted to ask you something."

"He did?" She pushed back gold curls that tumbled across her face, tiny gossamer strands escaped from her chignon. "Right now he's sitting on the floor with three kittens in his lap."

"Then I'll ask you for him." Colton strolled closer. "I brought a picnic basket from Rose's kitchen. Would you join us?"

"It's forty degrees outside." She lifted her chin. "It's far too cold for a picnic."

"There's always your kitchen. What do you say? Don't disappoint Zac."

Her gaze narrowed. "Colton, you're trying to use that boy against me. You know darn well I have a weakness for children."

"Yes. It shows in your eyes." He might as well lay it all out for her to see. Let her look at his motives and decide for herself the type of man he was. "You would make a good mother."

"Oh, I don't know." She bowed her head, ducking his gaze. "I was never blessed enough to find out."

No sorrow tolled in her voice, at least none that he could hear. But he sensed it. She leaned over the top half of the stall door, where Zac sat on a fresh bed of straw. Half-grown kittens, all play and fire, tumbled back and forth over the little boy's outstretched legs, making him giggle.

"He doesn't look like he'd miss picnicking with me." Hannah's eyes twinkled.

Colton laughed. "Well, I thought it would work, considering the way you left things between us on Sunday."

"Stooping to manipulating, huh?"

"Well, I'm a desperate man."

"Who isn't these days?"

I'm never going to trust another man with my home and my life again. Colton remembered Hannah's vow, an obstacle to everything he wanted.

"You've been speaking to the bank president about me." Not accusing, but she didn't sound happy either.

He turned to watch his son, giggling happily as a kitten nuzzled that chubby little hand. "I wanted to know about your ranch."

"You came here to see Charles. Why?"

He felt her gaze on him. He doubted his old friend had told her much of the financial problems or of his intended solutions. "How many head do you have?"

"You didn't answer my question, Colton."

"No, I didn't." He pulled wide the stall gate. "Come, Zac. Let's show Hannah all the good things Rose put in that basket."

"Chicken." The tiny boy gave a flat-handed pat to the eager kitten and stood. "We got pie, too!"

"Well, how can I resist that?" Hannah asked, all warmth.

Colton liked her for it. This woman, too fine for the likes of him, had nothing but kindness to show his son. "Let's face it. You can't. Leave the barn work. I promise to help you later, after we've eaten."

She knelt to scoop up the friendly kitty, who'd been nuzzling Zac, and hugged the furry bundle. "Why would you offer to help me?"

A thin veil of suspicion, but Colton figured he could handle that. "Because I'm interrupting your workday. Livestock need to be tended regardless of a rancher's social obligations."

"Oh, so you consider yourself my social obligation, huh?" She laughed at that, sweet and light, the cat trustingly limp in her arms. "As in, I'm obliged to have dinner with you?"

"No, as in, you're delighted I came to call." He decided he liked the way her eyes smiled. It made him feel warm down deep in his chest. "Well, at least you could look at this as a free meal."

She laughed. "If only free meant without obligation."

"So, you've figured me out." Colton stepped through the door and out into the daylight. "You know what I'm up to."

"And then some." She bent to set the kitty to the ground, but stopped to let Zac get in one final, delighted pat. Once freed, the kitten ran circles around the boy, then took off toward the warm barn. She straightened, fastening her gaze on him. "I'm not going to marry you, Colton."

He reached to release the buckles holding the whiffle-trees to the harness. "I didn't come here to pressure you, Hannah. I'm not a man looking for romance."

"Good thing." She lifted her chin. "Because I've learned it doesn't exist. I won't be sweet-talked just so some man can get his hands on my land without paying for it."

He laughed. "So, you think that's where I want to put my hands?"

A blush stole across her face. "I know you've been speaking to the bank about my finances."

"I've made no secret about it." He met her gaze, determined to let her see what he was. "I would have told you that and more if you'd given me the chance on Sunday."

"Why should I give you a chance?"

"Because I don't have a weakness for drink and gambling like Charles did. I'm not a brute of a man like his brother." Colton pushed the wagon out of the way. "And I have a little boy who needs a mother, someone to take care of him in the event I can't."

"Why would you say something like that?" She lifted the heavy collar from the bay's neck.

He reached over her, the sweet scent of woman and

59

honeysuckle filling him up, and rescued the bulky leather collar from her grip. "Because things happen. Life is fragile." *And a man with a past like mine is never safe.*

"True." She grabbed the bay by the bit and led the animal into her barn.

It was dark and warm and comforting inside, out of the bite of the wind. She heard the pat of feet behind her. Zac scurrying after the kitty.

She ran her hand down the bay's flank. Cool. He'd been gently walked from town, she guessed. And led him into a fresh stall.

Colton came right behind her. He found the grain and water barrels, and she knelt down to hold the kitty for Zac to pet.

The young cat's tongue darted out to lick Zac's hand.

I have a little boy who needs a mother, someone to take care of him in the event I can't.

"Thinking over my offer?" Colton's voice. His hand out, palm up.

"No." She lied.

His eyes sparkled as if he knew it.

He smelled of man and mountain air and fresh sunshine.

She laid her hand against his and stood. A smile tugged at his mouth, that sexy, lopsided smile.

They were so close she could see the individual stubble along his jaw, see the flicker of warmth in his eyes. Her instincts shouted a warning, but heaven help her, she felt helpless to move one inch away from this man of strength and gentleness.

Colton leaned closer. His mouth covered hers and took possession.

CHAPTER SIX

Velvet flame skidded across the surface of her lips. Hannah knew heaven would never taste this sweet. Colton's mouth dominated hers, hot and demanding, drawing the air from her lungs. She couldn't breathe. She couldn't think. Sensation buzzed through every part of her body. All this from a single kiss.

Colton's hand cupped the side of her face, his touch infinitely tender, wondrous. Tiny flickers of heat popped across her skin where he touched her.

Then he moved away. Cool air whispered across her lips, damp from his kiss, and she trembled.

"Let me put away the horse." His big fingers curled around the leather reins she held, brushing her hand.

Her heart hammered. He towered over her, so close she could smell the wood smoke and pine scent of him. How could she pretend he didn't affect her? "Use the empty stall there, near the aisle."

"I will."

Dreams were made of kisses like that. Hannah wrung her hands as he walked away, his stride powerful and confident. Unlike Glen, Colton radiated a masculine strength, and it wasn't domineering. It wasn't brutal.

But that didn't mean he was a man to dream of. Colton Kincaid was a man, flesh and blood, bone and muscle, far superior in strength and value in the eyes of the world.

The bank would never revoke his loan.

A tug at her skirts. "Hannah?"

"Zac." She knelt down and brushed those fine dark curls from his eyes. "Do you like my kittens?"

He squeezed the marmalade feline tight against his chest. "My fav'rit."

"Zac, tell Hannah you're hungry," Colton's voice called out from behind wooden walls.

The boy tilted his head. "Hungry, Hannah."

Her heart twisted. "Then we'd better have that picnic your father is trying to bribe me into. We can't go around starving little boys."

Colton's laugh rumbled. "See? I knew Zac could talk you into anything."

"This isn't fair, Colton," Hannah warned, far too charmed by the little boy to do anything more than lead him toward the gaping barn door and the world beyond. "I'm not going to forget this."

"I'm shaking in my boots."

Laughing, Hannah snatched the basket from the wagon's floor. Just because Colton thought he could kiss her didn't mean he could have anything he wanted.

Colton Kincaid was about to learn how wrong he was.

* * *

"Rose Carson makes the best fried chicken I've ever tasted." Colton pushed away from the table, satisfied with the heaviness in his belly. He was warm, full, and he was ready to grab hold of his dreams. "Of course, I bet your fried chicken is better."

"Ah, so now you think flattery will change my mind." She whirled from the work table, backlit by sunshine through the kitchen window that tossed lemony rays across her hair and fragile shoulders.

"Flattery. Hope. Call it what you will."

"I see." She plunged her slender hands into the dishwater. Water sloshed onto the wooden work table. "Well, if you're hoping to taste my cooking, then you're out of luck."

He watched her closely as he approached. "Why's that?"

"Because I will never cook a meal for you, Mr. Kincaid."

He chuckled. "You sound awfully sure about that."

"And why shouldn't I?" She scrubbed hard at a blue enamel plate. "This is my house. I decide who visits and who stays for supper."

"Sounds like you don't plan on marrying me."

"Exactly." She slipped the plate into the clean rinse water.

He reached for it and began to dry.

"What's this?" She swept the length of him with her amused blue eyes. "A big, tough man like you lowering yourself to woman's work?"

"My grandmother believed a man ought to know domestic skills."

"Smart grandmother." She slipped soapy flatware into the rinse water. "Do you sew, too?"

"I can manage a respectable stitch."

She laughed at that, tipping back her head. Honey gold tendrils brushed along the nape of her slim neck. "I see what you're doing. Your flattery doesn't work, so now you're trying to impress me with your imagined domestic prowess."

"Exactly. Think how handy it would be to have a husband who can help out with the dishes."

Amusement flickered in her eyes. "Right. As if a husband would do the dishes instead of sitting before the fire patting his full belly."

"Have a little faith, Hannah." He set the plate aside and reached into the rinse water for a second. "I can rope a wild horse at a dead gallop. I can repair fence posts and guard a property line better than any man in this territory. I can do those things and do right by you, too."

"You'll not be repairing my fence, sir."

He laughed. "See? I can't show off my dazzling skills with that kind of attitude. I'm doomed to trying to sway you with my domestic abilities."

"You aren't dazzling me."

"Do you need any seams mended?"

Hannah laughed, light and bright, the sound filling the room and brushing against his lonely heart. "Stop teasing me. And put down my plates."

"So, am I changing your mind?" He had to know. Too much was at stake.

"No." She plunged her hands up to her elbows into the wash basin and came up with the last fork. She scrubbed it thoroughly, then dropped it into the rinse water. "I appreciate the meal, Colton. It was thoughtful of you. I know you mean well, but I just can't—" She sighed, heartfelt and deep.

Silence.

Colton remembered how whiskey could transform Charles into a harsh man.

"Then you'll lose your land, your home, your horses."

"There has to be another way."

"What way?"

"I don't know—I'm still working on that." She circled around him, averting her eyes, and gathered up the clean dishes stacked at his elbow.

Colton took a step back and studied the worry cutting a deep frown across her forehead. "I have money. I can buy the winter's feed. I can take over the work. I can build you another barn."

Her spine rigid, she lifted the stack of plates up onto the top shelf of her hutch. "I don't need another barn."

He stepped forward to lay a hand on her shoulder, feel the vulnerability of fragile muscle and bone. So small.

"You need protection."

She turned. So close, he could see the flecks of lighter blue in her luminous eyes, feel the fear and confusion. "You think you can protect me? From what?"

"From Glen's greed. From homelessness."

She bit her lush bottom lip, and sparkles of fire exploded in his gut. Kissing her again would be no hardship. "I'm not brutal, Hannah. I'm no saint, either."

She met his gaze. He felt her measure him, sweeping like a touch clear through to his heart.

"Few men are saints," she said.

"And few women."

Her chin jutted, but it was a nice stubbornness. One that told him of the core of strength down deep, solid as iron. He liked that.

She took a shaky breath, the color gone from her face. "You think you can persuade me and charm me and impress me into changing my mind. You're dead wrong."

He stepped back. "Fine. Then lose everything. Be homeless. Stay lonely and childless. I'll take my basket and my son and leave."

He strode away. Her hand caught his arm, stopping him. He turned to look down into eyes filled with unspoken fear. A fear she would not admit to, he'd wager. A fear he knew too well.

"I'm sorry, Colton. I wish I could accept your help."

"Why can't you?"

She tucked her bottom lip between her teeth, thinking. "I know you want the land. I know how easy it is to love the meadows and the forest and the mountain tops so high they touch heaven. How much money do you have?"

He stopped, considered. "That's a personal question. I didn't think you wanted to get personal."

Her lovely face clouded. Anger sparked blue flame in her eyes. "If and when I can't satisfy the banker, I'll ask for every penny you have. I'll sell you the land, Colton, if I have no other option. If you have money enough to cover the mortgage."

Pride lifted her chin. Strength held her up. "I don't have that much, Hannah. Don't you think that would have been my first offer if I had enough to buy you out?"

Her eyes clouded. Her hand dropped away. "I see."

He sensed his opportunity, knew she was in more trouble than he knew about, than she would admit. Exhaustion rimmed her eyes, purple like bruises against the soft porcelain skin of her cheeks.

He took a deep breath. "There is no other solution, Hannah. Think about what I'm offering you. I have a son. You have no children. You have a ranch, and I have no home. I am honest and hardworking and I swear I will never show you violence. You could do worse."

"I know." Blue eyes looked up at him, filled with something he couldn't name.

But he could feel it. Hannah Sawyer's defenses were weakening.

"Come say good-bye to Zac," Colton said as he scooped up the handled basket. "I think we're going to have to pry that kitten from his grip."

"I have a crowbar," Hannah teased, light as song. Pain nothing but the slightest shadow in her voice.

His heart ached. He'd forgotten the gentle feelings a woman could put inside a man's heart. He'd forgotten the beauty a woman could bring to a man's lonely life.

* * *

Colton sheltered the match from the cold night's wind with his left hand and waited for the cigarette to catch. He'd learned from his years wearing a badge that if he wanted to find out information, he'd better treat himself to a drink.

With Rose keeping watch over his sleeping son, he strode across the muddy street and wandered down the row of dark buildings, businesses closed up for the night. At the far end of the boardwalk, lights shone through unwashed windows.

He pushed open the solid wood door to find a room lit just well enough to play poker by and just dark enough for a man to lose his troubles. Heat blasted from the potbellied stove in the center of the room, surrounded by tables.

"You the newcomer to town?" The saloonkeeper's gaze was direct but friendly.

Colton tapped the ashes from his cigarette. "Whiskey."

"Comin' right up." The rail-thin man wiped his hands on his stained apron and grabbed a shot glass.

Colton settled down to the bar next to Eaton Baker. "Howdy, Sheriff."

"Good to see you again, Kincaid." The portly man gave a curt nod, dignified in his fancy black vest and white dress shirt. Dark trousers hugging his rounding form were made from fine fabric.

Colton had never seen a lawman look so soft. It was a good sign—there wasn't much call for a peacemaker in a town like Paradise. And it was a bad sign—he doubted this merchant, who'd won the town's last election for sheriff, knew the first thing about tracking a criminal.

The barkeep slapped down the shot of whiskey. Colton tugged two bits from his pocket and tossed it on the scarred wooden bar. "Heard Hannah—Mrs. Sawyer—talked to you about the trouble out at her ranch."

Baker leaned back in his chair, a shock of gray hair falling across his glossy eyes. "Yep. Seems she thinks that fire in her barn was set on purpose. Hard to tell about something like that, though."

"Why's that?" Colton lifted the glass and swilled a sip of whiskey around in his mouth.

"Bein' a lawman's a tricky business." Baker downed his shot in one toss. "Seems like it could be a crime—there ain't a doubt there's a few men around these parts who would kill to get their hands on a free piece of land that nice and a widow that pretty, but the truth is, the woman probably set the fire herself."

Colton swallowed. He'd seen Baker's type before. "You think so?"

"Sure." Baker flicked his glass across the width of the counter, a signal to the barkeep for another round. "A woman like that, trying to do a man's work. It's too much for her. She gets tired. Leaves a can of kerosene in the barn, drops a match when she lights a lantern and boom, instant fire. It ain't hard to figure out."

"You said yourself there's a few men who'd kill to get their hands on that land." Colton took another drink. "Maybe there's some who wouldn't go quite that far."

"But torch a barn?" Baker straightened, his brow dark, his voice sharp like a knife. "No, the pieces don't fit."

"You're the law." Colton shrugged and tipped back his glass, downing the remaining whiskey in one long draught. Fire licked through his belly. "I was just wondering, was all."

"Son, it's best not to stick your nose in where it don't belong." Eaton Baker wrapped his soft, pudgy fingers around the width of the shot glass, newly filled. "I'm the sheriff around these parts, and I know what's best."

"Fine." Colton nodded at the barkeep. He'd never been much of a drinking man, but whiskey loosened tongues like nothing else—in the right circumstances. He was a man who knew how to bide his time. And get his point across. "Tell me about Glen Sawyer."

"Now, there's trouble. I wouldn't have no work at all if it weren't for that one."

"Why's that?" Colton asked patiently. A man fishing for information had to be patient.

"It ain't so bad now that his brother's dead." Baker relaxed, encouraged by another shot of whiskey and his over-inflated sense of worth. "Some nights he gets out of hand, but I can handle it. I heard you were a friend of Charles's."

"I was. Once."

"I've got my eye on you. I don't stand for trouble in

these parts. Just like I don't stand for a greenhorn trying to tell me my business."

Colton nodded and ground out his cigarette. So, that was the way the wind blew. An incompetent rich man who couldn't overpower a violent drunk if he tried. A man who probably didn't know how to handle a gun despite the polished gleam of the new revolver holstered at his side.

Hannah had been right. There would be no help from this sheriff. Eaton Baker wouldn't know how, even if he wanted to.

Colton scanned the room. He already knew Tom Pruitt, the tanner, hunched around one of the tables deep in a poker game. And Andy Drummond, the banker's son. He'd heard young Andy, hardly more than a boy, had a crush on Hannah.

Colton thought of her soft beauty and the tempting heat of her lips. His pulse jumped.

"Mr. Kincaid." A hand clasped on his shoulder, hard, unyielding.

Colton wasn't surprised. He'd recognized the sound of the man's gait. "Glen Sawyer." He turned to face the man.

"The drifter new to town." Glen lifted his chin in a superior smirk. The man was too damn cocky and full of himself. "Will you be drifting on out of here?"

"The tavern, yes. I'm not much of a drinking man." Colton curled his fingers around Glen's wrist. "But no, I'm not leaving town."

"I suggest you do." Unflinching eyes, dark and flat.

Oh, yes. Colton knew exactly what kind of man he faced. His guts clenched. Conflict. Anger. It wasn't the life he wanted to live. Not now. Not anymore.

Colton wrestled Glen's grip easily from his shoulder and stood. He knew his Colt, scarred and well used, was plainly visible, snug and unsnapped in its holster. "I don't want trouble, Sawyer. I just came for a few peaceable drinks."

"Too late. You have trouble. More than you can

handle, most likely." Alcohol fumed his breath and exaggerated the big man's motions.

Colton watched Glen's eyes. If Sawyer planned to jump him, his eyes would give the first signal. "Maybe I can buy you a drink. Barkeep, bring that bottle of whiskey down here."

"I don't want a drink." Both meaty hands fisted.

Colton relaxed his muscles and readied himself for whatever might happen. And hoped it wouldn't. "Then what do you want, Sawyer?"

"Hannah." One fist shot out.

Colton deflected the punch, knocking Glen's hand harmlessly to the side. Silence. Not a sound rose in the saloon. Not a cough, not a whisper. "Have another drink, Sawyer. There'll be no fighting tonight."

Red-faced, Glen glanced around, measuring the staring gazes. Colton knew the man was judging the cost to his pride on backing down against the cost to his ego if he lost a fight. And he would lose. Colton, stone sober, could best him without a doubt.

Glen relaxed. "This ain't over, Kincaid. If I see you sneaking into Hannah's house again, it will be the last time you're seen around these parts."

Colton heard the sheriff behind him release a pent up breath. The barkeep sloshed two shots of whiskey on the counter. The poker game near the stove resumed with Drummond's risky bet.

All Colton wanted was peace. That's all. No fighting. No violence. No checking his back to make sure there wasn't a man standing there, gun drawn.

All he wanted was a safe life for his son. Some mean-spirited bully like Glen Sawyer wasn't going to stand in Colton's way.

* * *

Hannah's head bobbed, startling her awake. The parlor clock counted the hour—two bongs. Two in the morning. Exhaustion hugged her skull, weighed down her body. The picnic with Colton and Zac, however pleasant, had stolen valuable time from her day and put her behind.

But the memory of tiny Zac licking his fingers after eating Rose's fried chicken filled her with warmth. A child at her table, in her house. Her arms and her heart no longer empty.

Colton Kincaid. He could charm the socks off the Devil, no doubt. Just as easily as he'd stolen a kiss from her.

She sighed, opened her account book, and studied the ledger. A heaviness lodged beneath her ribs. How was she going to make it? She could not hold onto her ranch.

There is no other solution, Hannah. Think about what I'm offering you.

She shouldn't even be thinking it. She ought to get herself up to bed and grab some sleep before dawn came.

What for? Another day of backbreaking labor awaited her. How much horse manure could a person stand to shovel? Hannah liked a clean barn, but if she had to lift one more shovel full—and that stuff was heavy—then she'd run screaming for Canada.

Well, at least then she wouldn't have to worry about the mortgage.

I am honest and hardworking and I swear I will never show you violence.

It was easy to make promises. Harder still to keep them. Remembering Charles's same vow made Hannah's stomach turn.

A woman who trusted a man was a fool. She'd learned that the hard way. But she needed help. She couldn't do this alone. Running a ranch took money and physical strength, knowledge of animals and breeding and medicine. All the things she didn't have, didn't know.

I have a son. You have no children.

Hannah closed the ledger and reached for the light. The emptiness of the house echoed around her. Outside the window, starshine brushed the newly falling snow like fairy dust.

She had no magic in her life, no hope.

But that didn't mean she should trade her freedom for security, her loneliness for a son.

CHAPTER SEVEN

"**H**annah!" Rose Carson's voice rose above the sounds of town and the toll of the new schoolhouse bell. "Wait up!"

Hannah rubbed the wet lumps of freezing rain from the edge of her bonnet brim. "I thought you'd be busy cooking for your guests."

"Colton and Zac are well and fed." Laughter twinkled in Rose's merry eyes. "Speaking of those two, did you enjoy the picnic?"

Hannah blushed as she fell in step beside her friend. "Now, don't you go gossiping to everyone about the meal Colton brought me. You have to promise, Rose."

"Fine. All right. I'll give you my word." Rose leaned closer. "But only if you tell me everything. Is that man as gorgeous-looking without his shirt?"

"Rose!" Hannah halted outside Paradise's only bank. "What's got into you? I can't believe—"

"There's nothing wrong with a little romance."

"There's everything wrong with a little romance." Hannah remembered the bleakness of her marriage, of the control she'd freely given her husband. She'd freely given it, right there in the ceremony promising to honor and obey. She'd said the words, and Charles never let her forget them.

Romance. She didn't need romance. She needed Drummond to let her keep her mortgage.

"Come stop with me at the mercantile," Rose invited, halting outside the glass storefront. "I've got a hankering to make me some new curtains for my bedroom window. They're as old as the hills and thin enough the moonlight shines right through."

"I'd love to, Rose, but I've got an appointment at the bank."

"What kind of appointment?" Worry crinkled around Rose's kind eyes. "Now, you're not hoping to still keep hold of that ranch on your own, are you? I've told you my fears, Hannah." She lowered her voice when Mrs. Kinny strolled by, bid her good day, and waited until she was safely inside the store. "That Glen Sawyer is a mean galoot. There's rumors he nearly killed a man down in Missoula over a gambling debt and the injured man's too frightened to go to the authorities."

Cold shivered down Hannah's spine. "Glen is capable of a lot of things. I ought to know—I was married to his brother. But he wouldn't hurt me. I'll be fine, Rose. Please, don't worry."

"What about that nice Mr. Kincaid, the one you spent the night with?"

Hannah tried to hold back her smile at the sparkle in Rose's eyes and failed. "What about Colton? He wants my land, but that doesn't mean I'll mortgage my heart to keep hold of my home."

"So, that's how you look at marriage—a loan to be counted and tallied and owed on? Hannah, that's not—"

"It's obligation and duty, and little else." She thought of Charles's hand raised, his palm flat, anger trembling in his voice. "Rose, I know you're concerned about my reputation—"

"Everyone's saying—" Rose paused. "Hannah, I have to tell you this. I kept an eye on little Zac last night so young, gorgeous Mr. Kincaid could visit the saloon."

"What? He left his son alone so he could go off and drink?" The very idea drove a chill straight through Hannah's bones. "And he told me..." *I'm not a drinking man, Hannah. Nor a gambler.* She could hear his voice playing in her mind, rich and deep, rumbling with sincerity.

"He and your brute of a brother-in-law got into an argument." Rose leaned closer. "Glen started it. Colton finished it. Even the sheriff was impressed. Some say he was a coward not fighting Glen right there in the saloon, but others said he didn't back down, kept the peace. That's a good sign, don't you think?"

Hannah opened her mouth, but no sound, no words formed. Colton had been in a tavern drinking? When he'd given her his word he wasn't that kind of man?

Her heart fell and her hopes along with it. "I'm glad you told me, Rose." She squeezed her best friend's hand. "I have an appointment with the bank."

"I didn't mean—" Worry crinkled over caring eyes. "Hannah, what Colton did was good and honorable."

"No, it wasn't." He'd lied to her. He'd deceived her about who he was. The memory of his kiss still buzzed across her lips. She thought of his strength, how he'd looked like a noble warrior fighting the flames. She remembered the true concern for his son as he held the child, like a gentle giant, on the ice so Zac could walk without falling.

No man had that much honor. Not her own father, who drank his nights away before a fever took him. Not her uncle, who worked her like a slave. Not the men in the families she'd stayed with through her years as an orphan. She saw anger, violence, and fought a few off her bed in the dark hours of the night.

Beneath the polite charm, Colton Kincaid could not be much different from Charles.

"I'm going to be late," Hannah managed through a too-dry throat. "I've decided to make Mr. Drummond take a chance on me."

Rose wished her luck, worry bright in her eyes.

As Hannah watched, the rain turned to snow.

A chance. It was all she asked. It was all she needed.

* * *

"Snow." Zac pointed as they stepped outside.

"Come stand on the step and watch it fall," Colton said to the boy, holding out his hand.

Tiny fingers curled tightly around his. Colton sat down on the top wooden stair and cuddled his son on his lap.

Zac sighed, wistful.

Colton readjusted the boy's cap so those little ears were better covered. "We'd need to get a lot of snow before we can make snowmen again."

White crystal flakes tumbled down on the peaceful town. Hope. It was a fragile thing. Colton felt it build up inside him, one piece at a time. His gaze landed on a familiar woman across the street. Bundled against the cold, fragile as an angel, she pulled open the door to Drummond's bank.

The hope inside him burned.

A woman's presence in his life. A woman's cooking. That's what he missed most of all. Maybe not *most*. Colton remembered Ella's loving touches, the warmth cozy in his heart as he cuddled her close. The belief he would keep her safe.

Don't think about it. Colton closed his eyes and willed the memories away, the feelings of failure.

"Zac, would you like to see Hannah?"

A vigorous nod. Colton lifted his son until he stood safely on the slush-slick boards and stood himself, then took the tiny, trusting hand in his.

The sturdy brick building looked pleasant with its only window lit against the day's storm. Colton held the door while Zac took small steps out of the snow and into the warmth.

"Hot."

Ignoring the sighs of adoration from a woman behind a nearby desk—Drummond's daughter, Colton remembered—he knelt down and tugged off the boy's hat, loosened a few of his coat buttons. "Better?"

A grateful nod.

Colton turned to the pretty girl at the desk who was looking up at him with curious eyes. "Is Hannah in there with your father?"

Abby swallowed. "Yes. I—"

Colton scooped Zac up into his arms and headed for the closed door. He heard Hannah's voice through the wooden door, the soft lilt of her words sharp with emotion.

"Mr. Drummond. You know if I were a man you'd give me more money—"

"You aren't a man, Mrs. Sawyer. And this morning we've had another default on a mortgage. We aren't a large bank, and these are tough times. I can't afford to finance risky ventures. I am going to recall the loan. If you can find a way to pay the entire amount due by the end of the month, then the ranch will remain yours. Otherwise—"

"You can have my horses as collateral."

Colton opened the door. Drummond looked up. Hannah twisted around, her mouth curled into a surprised "O."

"Drummond, I thought you and I had an agreement."

"We do, Kincaid." The man stood, smoothing the well-cut coat around his thick waist, a nervous gesture. "Sawyer was in here earlier. I'm not bowing to his threats."

"Good." Colton felt Hannah's gaze on him, accusing and angry. He faced her. "I have nothing to do with Drummond's decision on your loan, Hannah. I only told him if he decides not to work with you, I wanted to be first in line to take over the mortgage."

"You can't have it without marrying me." Her chin

lifted, stubborn and vulnerable all at once.

"Exactly."

"You have three choices, Mrs. Sawyer." Drummond's eyes squinted with apology. "It's not an easy decision, believe me. I know Charles wasn't the easiest man. He made some damn bad decisions and frankly, I worried over giving him that mortgage. But you pose a greater risk. You either marry Colton or Glen to keep your land, or I take your ranch and your home. It's up to you."

Hannah popped out of the chair, fists curled. "You men have every detail figured out as if I were nothing more than a piece of property myself." Anger sparked in her eyes.

So, the angel had passion. Colton decided he liked that. Very much. "Not a piece of property, Hannah."

"A possession, then." She reached for her reticule. "Good day to you, Mr. Drummond."

Pride. It steeled her spine. Held her up as she walked. Colton saw it, measured it. She might be fragile, but she was strong. Strong enough to protect his son, raise Zac if there came a time when he couldn't.

"Hannah, have you made a decision?"

"Don't talk to me. Don't you ever—" Tears glinted along with the anger in her eyes. And the helplessness. "I'd rather be homeless than marry another drinking man like you."

Colton watched her stalk off, curls bouncing, shoes stomping.

"Hannah." Zac held up his hand, calling her back.

She turned with a sweep of ruffled skirts. "Hello, little one."

"Kitty." Zac hugged himself, as if remembering the fun he'd had with her tabby kitten.

Hannah's lower lip trembled. Her gaze collided with his, dark with emotion, and Colton regretted trapping her like this. He knew she would hate him for it. But there was no mistaking the adoration in her eyes when she looked at

Zac.

He knew then what her decision would be.

* * *

She wouldn't marry him. She wouldn't. She wouldn't marry anyone. Hannah pitched another forkful of soiled straw into the wheelbarrow and stopped to swipe the sweat from her brow.

She'd been shoveling ever since she'd returned home from town. Light drained from the day, casting webby shadows in the corners of the stall. The only good thing about the barn burning down was now she had half the shoveling to do.

The horse crosstied in the aisle gave a friendly nicker and lipped at her shirt. Impatient for his grain.

"I'm almost done, you big lug." Hannah turned to pat the colt's strong neck.

Charles would never have approved of how she treated the horses. He believed it was best to rule by the back of his hand and the end of a whip. Her throat tightened.

A man who spent every available dime gambling and drinking in town, who came home so drunk and mean one night, he beat his horse right here in this barn. She'd found Charles the next morning, dead from a kick to the chest.

She'd cried from relief at his funeral, not from the grief others had assumed.

A thud echoed through the barn. Somewhere a horse's neigh, agitated and trumpeting, reverberated through the rafters. The colt in the aisle swung his head around and scented the air.

A chill inched down her neck. Hannah tightened her grip on the pitchfork and started down the aisle, listening. The normal sounds of horses shifting in their stalls had vanished into silence.

Something was amiss. Perhaps she had a visitor. Hannah hurried to the big double doors and found them open just as she'd left them.

Along the aisle of stalls, every horse's head was

79

uplifted, turned toward the gently falling snow, nostrils flared.

Her stallion kicked the door of his stall, agitated, then let out another trumpeting neigh.

The house. Someone was at the house. Hannah couldn't see a horse tied out front. She had no idea who could be visiting her.

She laid the pitchfork against the wall and headed out into the snow, brushing straw from her hair and skirt. The patchy gray of twilight cloaked the sky and a crust of snow and ice crunched beneath her boots.

The house stood silent. Nothing amiss. Maybe...

A light flickered to life inside her house, a faint glow through the parlor window. Someone was in her kitchen.

Hannah circled around back. She saw two horses, a bedraggled bay gelding she recognized and a red roan she didn't. At least there was no real threat. Sean had probably come for his paycheck, what little of it there was.

Besides, she wanted to wring his neck for running away from the fire, leaving her horses in danger.

She pushed open the door. She scowled at the two men seated at her table. "Sean, what are you doing in my house? Why didn't you come to the barn?"

The grizzled man stood. "Didn't seem right for me to come surprise you at your work."

"But it did seem right letting yourself into my house?"

Her gaze flicked toward the second man, a stranger. He was tall and brawny. The wide brim of his hat shadowed his face. A flicker of warning licked her spine. "I'd like you both to leave. Please." She held open the door.

"Think again, Hannah." Sean strolled forward, passing through the lamp's glow. "I've come for what's mine."

"I always intended to give you your rightful pay." Her spine bit into the wooden door. There were two of them. Did they mean her harm? Or did they just want to frighten her out of a few dollars? "Of course, with the way you ran off like a coward that night, I didn't know if you would return."

"I want what's mine." Grim. Determined. His voice hollow.

Hannah's heart fell. Her gaze flicked to the second man. Unlike Sean, this man hadn't been drinking. And, unlike Sean, he was clean-shaven and freshly dressed, radiating power and danger.

Sean had brought this man to strong-arm her into paying him if she tried to refuse.

Well, such brute force wasn't necessary.

"Let me count out your earnings, Sean." Hannah gestured toward the door. "I'd like you and your friend to wait outside while I tend to it."

"I got more coming to me than that." Sean wrestled the door from her grip and easily slammed it shut. "I worked on this land when it was wild, nothing but wilderness. You ought to remember. Your husband hired me first. And made me promises."

"He made everyone promises. And broke them." Hannah pushed hard against the wall.

"I know. Never saw that no good son of a bitch keep his word once. Not while he was alive, nohow."

Her heart kicked in her chest. "What do you mean?"

"I mean it's time that bastard kept his word." Sean's breath blew across her face, sour with alcohol.

Her stomach rolled. Sean had her trapped; she couldn't even overpower him to open the door and flee. And he'd brought the man with that flat, lethal gaze who strolled closer, with the uncaring ease of one without conscience.

Sean had never done her harm before, Hannah reminded herself. He probably just wanted some kind of restitution. Maybe one of the horses Charles might have promised him...

The nameless man paced closer. Sean's drunk gaze flickered.

There was a handgun in the safe. The last time she'd checked, it was loaded. If there was any trouble, maybe she could distract Sean and his dangerous friend with promises of money. If she could open the safe and get her hands on the gun...

No, surely it wouldn't come to that.

"Everyone's been saying that uppity Kincaid's gonna marry you." Sean's voice vibrated with threat. "Now, that's not something I like to hear. I was in the saloon. I saw how that cheatin' Glen Sawyer thought he could have you. And how Kincaid figured you was his."

What did he want? Hannah tried to guess. Fear quivered in her limbs, turned her blood to ice. The nameless man pulled back his long coat. Two battered revolvers were holstered at either hip, strapped to his massive thighs.

The threat made her cold, stopped her heart.

"As I see it, the man who marries you gets this ranch."

"And gets the debt, too." Hannah lifted her chin. "Mr. Drummond isn't going to let just any man keep this mortgage."

"That ain't true."

"He told me he had another default just this morning."

"Don't try to confuse me. I ain't gonna let you talk me out of my plan. I deserve this ranch."

"Drummond isn't going to gamble on the weather, not if it's another winter like the last one. He isn't going to trust you to pay him back the money, Sean."

"I cleared the meadows while your goddamned husband sat there puffin' on his cigars." The old man turned red. A vein pulsed in his temple. "I split every bloody fence post for the entire first year until Charles broke down and hired more help. I cleaned the barn and I handled the horses. I showed that buffoon you married how to break a horse and how to drive cattle and how to stack hay so it sheds the rain."

"I won't marry you, Sean." Hannah hated the wobble she heard in her voice.

"Rex is here to make sure you do." Sean gestured

toward the desperado towering in the room, the walnut handles of his holstered revolvers gleaming in the faint light. "He's going to accompany us to a preacher. Better get yourself a coat. We have a long ride ahead."

The gunman's hollow gaze punched her, and her stomach soured.

"I have money—"

Sean laughed. "Not enough, princess. Get ready to say 'I do.' "

* * *

Colton reined his mare to a stop at the crest of the last hill. Dusk edged the horizon, casting a haunted tint to the gray light. The sky was clear and cold, the world silent. His heart rocked as he looked at the ranch below. Solemn and peaceful and safe, a haven from his violent past.

In the corrals surrounding the barn, big Percherons huddled in small groups, their rumps to the wind, drowsing in the cold. Remnants of hay littered the newly white ground.

Hannah's defenses were weakening. Tonight he'd come with the intention of changing her mind. By tomorrow this would all be his. His son's.

Pride bubbled in his heart, strong and honest. It had been a long time since he'd felt good about his work, about the money he earned.

There was no smoke rising from the log cabin's chimney. It was the first sign. This time of night Hannah ought to be in the house, stoking her fires against the chill and fixing her supper. Even the barn looked dark, both doors gaping wide open.

That was no way to leave horses for the night, where the cold north wind could blow right down the main aisle.

The second sign was the mess of tracks leading around toward the back of the house. Dark windows reflected his image back at him as he dismounted his mare and left her, reins wrapped around the saddlehorn. Well-trained, she stood, waiting.

He circled to the back of the house and saw the two horses, tethered and saddled. A faint light and long shadows fell across the snow-crusted ground.

A man's shadowed profile shivered along the frozen back steps. Trouble. Colton had lived long enough to smell it, to feel it. He'd spent too much time knowing men on the wrong side of the law.

Hannah's voice. He couldn't make out the words; he was too far away. But he could hear the fear in her tone and her struggle not to give in to it.

Colton checked both revolvers, loaded and ready, then crept along the dark wall of the cabin.

Hannah's voice—he could recognize the words now that he was closer. "You can't force me to marry you. You can't put a gun to my head. A minister isn't going to stand for that."

"But if we put a gun to *his* head, he will." A familiar voice, gravelly and slightly slurred, as if drunk. "With the threat of death, a man of the cloth will let a no-good old coot like myself marry a pretty young thing like you."

Colton saw the second man, standing in the doorway, guns holstered but ready. The look of a professional. The cold kind of bastard who murdered without conscience. Colton weighed his options.

"I've got a bad feeling," the hired killer said. "Get her coat and let's go."

A shadow moved. Colton recognized a length of rope. Hannah protested. His heart thundered in his chest. A loud, resounding smack of fist against flesh. Hannah cried out.

Colton could wait no longer. He sprang into the threshold, both guns drawn. Sean whirled, too startled and drunk to draw. Colton's arm extended, the revolver spit fire and the gunman crumpled to the ground with a shot through his left arm—Colton kicked the second gun from his reach before the hired man could get off another shot.

Then he spun around, prepared to deal with the old man.

"That leaves just you and me, Kincaid," Sean rasped, his old Colt drawn and shaking, pointed at Hannah's jaw. "Drop the guns."

"Whatever you say, Sean." Colton watched stress flash bright red across the man's face. Saw the white knuckles gripping the revolver. Read the plea in Hannah's frightened eyes as she sat hunched on the floor. An angry red handprint marked her cheek.

The old man didn't move, and Colton softened his voice. "Just relax, Sean. I don't want any trouble. I have a small son I'm responsible for. I don't want to get myself shot."

"You're a sensible man, Kincaid." Sean's hand still shook, but some tension eased from the tight lines of his face.

Colton knelt. "I don't like violence."

"Of course you don't. A man like you walks away." Sean's sneer was swallowed by the thud of the first revolver Colton laid on the floor. "Lily-livered. Chicken."

Colton laid the second Colt to the floor, but didn't let go of it.

"I'm going to hate to shoot you anyway—"

Colton pulled the trigger and Sean fell forward, blood spattered against Hannah's papered wall. Colton jumped to cover the gunman, who was climbing to his feet. Unarmed, he surrendered.

"You've got a hell of a draw for a ranch hand," the hired gun growled.

"I'm not a ranch hand," Colton said, wishing to hell he could close the door on his past. "Hands up. Hannah, let's get these men to the sheriff."

"Sean's dead." She hadn't moved—she was nothing but a fragile, frightened woman huddling in the corner.

He'd wager she'd never seen a man killed, never imagined he could pull a trigger on a man without thinking, without regret.

He bound the injured man's wrists tight with the rope, pushed him over the table, and left him there to groan.

"Colton." Her gold curls had tumbled down from her knot and framed her face like an angel. A fragile, good woman who'd never seen such an ugly side of a man's nature.

Overcome by the step he was about to take, Colton held out his arms. Fear launched her against his chest and he held her tight, close to his heart.

CHAPTER EIGHT

"I've got Hannah soaking in a hot tub," Rose said in a low voice as she swept down the dim hallway. "She's pretty shaken up."

"She has every right to be." Colton's hand rested on the glass doorknob. "She trusted Sean. Sounds like he worked on her ranch for years."

"Yes." Rose clasped her hands. "The sheriff told me, well, I overheard him say that the man you shot was a wanted man. A real bad character."

"So I understand." Colton thought of the price on Rex Roland's head. Two thousand dollars. He hoped this bounty would be his last.

"Sheriff says you must be some kind of expert, able to take down two men like that. You saved Hannah's life."

Colton took a breath. He didn't want to talk of what was past. "Seems to me Sean would have had to let Hannah live if he'd wanted to gain legal right to her land."

"Strength, courage, and modesty, too," Rose laughed, brushing a light touch on his arm. "You are some man, Mr. Kincaid. Hannah's one lucky woman."

He shook his head at Rose's wink, but his chest felt

empty as she walked away. The distaste in his mouth, the memory of the ugly violence tainted the hope he had for his future—and his son's.

Zac's room was dark and toasty warm. Orange flames glowed and shivered in the stone hearth, casting dark shadows across the bed. The tiny boy slept, his thumb in his mouth. Judging by the looks of things, Rose had tended to the child well. Colton's throat tightened.

The boy was safe. It was all that mattered.

He closed the door and headed down the hall. He knocked only once and heard the startled splash from the woman in the bath.

"Hannah?" He opened the door.

"Colton!" Those big blue eyes in her pale face caught his gaze. Beneath the chin-deep water, she crossed her arms, hiding her breasts.

"Don't worry. I didn't come to gape. Or grope." He closed the door and leaned against it. "It's late, but you and I have a score to settle."

Steam rose from the water's surface, curling her loose blond waves into sunshine gold ringlets. The sleek surface of her skin—her neck, her shoulders—gleamed like fine satin and would feel twice as rich, he wagered.

"I didn't thank you for what you did tonight." She looked down as her mouth formed the words. "For coming along when you did. And for—"

"Shooting two men?"

She nodded, eyes round.

"I scared you." His chest ached at the knowledge.

"I've never known anyone who could shoot like that. Not even the outlaw you wounded—"

"I'm capable of great violence," he conceded, crossing the room. With every drum of his footstep on wood, Hannah's eyes grew wider. "But on my honor, I would never harm a woman. Never hit her. Never threaten her. Never dominate her."

Her eyes clouded. Her beautiful mouth tightened into a

doubting straight line. Wordless, she hunched in her bath.

A fire snapped in the hearth, the flames roaring, and he thought about how to tell her. How to frame the words so she would not run away. He needed her. Worse, Zac needed her.

He reached for one of the white, fluffy towels Rose had piled close to the tub, then knelt down so they were nearly eye level. Angels had eyes like those, clear blue all the way to her soul. She was the antithesis of what he stood for, everything he'd been.

"Petty men have need for control over others. Was your husband such a man?"

"Maybe you could leave." Her gaze flicked toward the closed door. "I'd like to get out of my bath."

"I'm not leaving, Hannah." He stood, grimacing at the ache in his knees, and snared the green dressing robe lying over the back of the wing chair.

"Right, Colton." She sighed. "Of course you don't dominate others."

He laughed. "I never said I was perfect. I just want you to listen to me. It's important"

"I listen better when I'm dressed." The lines crossing her forehead relaxed a little.

He held out the robe. "Go ahead. I won't look."

"I don't believe you." She laughed. "You have a pretty good view of me from where you're standing."

He looked down through the soap-clouded water and easily saw the delicious curve of full breasts, the slope of her belly, the outline of inner thighs. "True. Like I said, I didn't come here to grope."

"So, I can trust you to look away?"

He turned his head.

Water splashed. He heard the brush of her movements, the rustle of cloth as she slipped the robe around her slender body, the light pad of her wet feet against the wood as she walked away.

He looked in time to see her tying the sash. "I kept my

89

word."

"Once." Color pinkened her cheeks, brightened her eyes. She was naked beneath that robe. They both knew it.

"I will always keep my word to you." He sat down on the wing chair and stretched out his legs.

"Easy for you to say now." She hugged the robe close to her body. "I haven't forgotten what you did to Mr. Drummond."

He thought about the line of anger crinkling between her eyes. "I didn't pressure the banker. I didn't threaten him."

"No, you just dangled your money in front of his greedy nose." That angry line eased a little. "That's more effective than putting a gun to his head."

"True." Colton wouldn't lie to her. "I want you to understand, Hannah. I have a past I wish I could change."

She bit her lip, considering his words. He remembered kissing her, the sweet taste of rich velvet and heat. "That's why you could... kill Sean."

He nodded. "I've been hunting bounties for nearly three years. I bring criminals to justice and I collect the reward. And I collect enemies, too."

She stared into the fire, leaning forward. Her wet breasts pressed against the cotton. He could see the rise and shape of her nipples. Nice. Very nice.

Then she rubbed her forehead. *Hell, she's going to say no.* Colton's heart thumped. His dreams for his son faded. And dreams for himself. "I hated the work. But it made me a good living. I had a young wife to support, then a baby. A future to think about. Ella saved every penny she could. I wanted my own ranch. One day, I wanted to leave the violence behind."

"Can a man do that? Leave violence behind? Leave it out of his nature?" Pain so deep in those eyes.

Colton knew he'd been right guessing how Charles had treated her. "I believe so."

Tears welled, glimmering like diamonds in the light "I

don't have a lot of choices, Colton. Times are tough. Last winter was so severe, the blizzards so unrelenting, men lost everything they'd worked for. How can I hold on to what's mine?"

"If you don't marry, you can't."

"I know." Her gaze met his, direct and honest. He could see the kind of woman she was—not just her beauty, but the heart of her. Sincere. And lonely. "But when a woman marries, she gives up her freedom. She has to obey."

"Not my wife." This was another thing he could give her, something she wanted. "I was married to Zac's mother for nearly ten years. I never lied to her. I never deceived her. I never made her cry, never stooped to violence. Nor did I expect her to obey me."

Hannah's lower lip trembled. So vulnerable. He remembered the naked image of her in the bath, cloaked by the distortion of the water. His blood heated. He could take care of her, protect her.

He leaned forward and brushed the satin heat of her chin. "I only want to work with you, by your side."

"Dreams. I know the sound of them. I can hear them in your voice."

"I can't have them without you. Well, certainly not as easily." He laid his hand along her cheek, felt the fragile cut of her jaw and cheekbones, felt the wondrous silk of her skin. He wanted to touch a woman again, to know this woman's passion. "Hannah, I need you to raise my son."

"Because of your past?"

"And because he deserves a mother." He would not think of the men who hunted Ella down, killing her for retribution, for revenge. Colton knew he could leave it all behind him where it belonged. The past could not touch him—touch her—here. "I know I couldn't find a better woman. Besides, Zac already likes you. He wants to come live with you and the kitty."

"You're not playing fair, using my affection for that

little boy."

"Do we have a deal?" He offered her his hand.

She laid her palm against his. "As long as you follow my rules." Her eyes shone, luminous in the glow of the lamplight, in the heat from the fire.

"Rules? I don't remember anyone mentioning any rules."

That made her smile, made the worry lines fade from her beautiful face. "No drinking. I mean, never."

"Fine. I'll suffer, but I'll keep my hands off a whiskey bottle." He wasn't a drinker anyway. "That's not much of a sacrifice."

"Don't you ever raise your hand to me." Her chin jutted, stubborn and strong. "Or I'll take my frying pan to you in your sleep."

He swallowed his chuckle at the image of her standing in her nightgown, black pan raised up to bean him in the head. "Fine. I'll control myself." Really, he shouldn't laugh.

Hannah frowned, but her eyes glimmered. "There's one more thing."

"Only one?"

"No intimacies."

"No sex?" His jaw dropped. "A husband has a right—"

"You have no rights." She smiled, sweet as candy, pure as an angel. "Not if you want my ranch, that is. Being my husband will give you a lot of power over my life. I'm not happy about that. Not at all. But there's one thing you can't have, and that's me."

No sex. He thought about that. Now that was a sacrifice.

"Deal." He leaned forward and caught her mouth with his, felt the satisfying lick of desire kick through his blood. She tasted like coffee and passion. He broke away, met her gaze. "Of course, you never said I couldn't kiss you."

She laughed then, tipping back her head.

The worries inside him eased. It would be all right. Colton knew it with the same certainty as the sun rising each morning, as the birth of spring from each winter's darkness.

Their bargain was sealed.

* * *

Hannah stood before Reverend Hardy in her best dress and said her vows. She took it as a good sign that Colton had spoken to the minister before the ceremony and asked him not to use the word obey.

It wasn't even nine o'clock in the morning, yet Colton caught her lips with his in a brief kiss of heat and promise. She was a married woman again.

Rose embraced her. Paula kissed her cheek. Hannah tried to smile, but felt cold inside, hollow. How could she be glad? She only had Colton's word and his honor. She'd seen far too many men break their word and live without honor to put much faith in Colton. But what else did she have? He had risked his life for hers.

A tug on her skirt. She looked down into Zac's button face, sweet with innocence. All men started out this way, as trusting little boys who did not hit, did not control, did not inflict harm.

"Cake." Zac grinned.

"Not yet, little one." She knelt and brushed back those flyaway dark curls from his eyes. She could touch him now, love him. It was her right. "After dinner we'll have cake."

A plea in those moon-round eyes. "Kitty?"

Colton's rich, rumbling laugh vibrated. "That boy's already figured out how to play you. Cake and kitties. What's next?"

"Candy?" Zac tried.

Laughter bubbled in Hannah's chest right along with a big chunk of happiness. At least she was gaining something from this marriage and it was more important than land, than any material possession. For years she'd ached for a child to love, to fill her empty arms. Now she had a son.

* * *

"Rose, you shouldn't be doing this." Hannah swiped the curls from her eyes with the back of her wrist. "You have a hotel to run."

"And my only customer moved out this morning." Rose glanced up from Hannah's kitchen floor, scrub brush in hand. "This is your wedding day. You're not going to clean up this bloody mess by yourself."

"Or make your celebration dinner," Paula added, bent over the stove. "Remember when I was married, you and Rose snuck out early and had a ham meal all ready when Arnie and I walked through the door. Now it's your turn, so I don't want to hear one word of protest."

"This isn't the same." Hannah doused the wash rag into the bucket of hot, soapy water. "Colton and I aren't..."

Exactly how much did she want her friends to know? Then again, it was no secret Colton had only married her for the ranch, for the land he coveted.

"A wedding is a wedding," Rose declared as she scrubbed her way across the muddy floor, wiping away all traces of the gunman's boot prints from the night before. "Besides, Zac wants fried chicken and cake. How can you say no to that little boy?"

She couldn't. Hannah dipped her chin. When they'd arrived home after the ceremony, Colton had deftly convinced Zac to search for the kittens in the barn, knowing full well the mess inside the house remained from last night. That was one reason she trusted Colton at all: the unwavering concern and care he showed his son.

The other was not so simple. He'd left her in the barn with Zac, insisting she watch over him, as he led Rose and Paula to the back door. When he arrived later with a determined smile on his face and the quiet strength that characterized him, she knew what he'd done: cleaned up the dried blood in her kitchen so she wouldn't have to relive last night's fear.

She cleaned anyway, scrubbing hard to rid the wall of that stubborn stain.

"The cake is out!" Paula announced. "I can't believe it didn't fall after I banged the door shut the way I did."

The kitchen sparkling, all but the tiniest traces of last night's violence washed from the room, Hannah joined her friend at the table and admired the cooling layers of white cake set on twin racks to cool.

"Paula, let's see what you've done." Rose bustled away and Hannah could only stare, only realize the importance of the cake, of the satchels crowded against the wall in the living room, just in view through the arched doorway.

"All we need to do is set the table, put the potatoes on to boil, and frost the cake." Paula smiled, friendship lighting her eyes as if she understood Hannah's worries.

"You two will stay, won't you?"

"Oh, Hannah. You won't need us." Rose chuckled. "We're just going to make certain you have enough food. You must have energy for your wedding night."

Paula laughed. "That's right. Colton is quite a man. He could wear a girl out."

"Oh," Rose cooed. "I can't remember the last time my man wore me out."

"Rose!" Hannah tried not to laugh. Really, the image of Colton, so virile and attractive, naked in her bed—

"She's blushing." Paula folded her hands over her stomach. "That's a good sign. Rose, I'll put the potatoes on to boil if you whip up the frosting. I think Hannah and her delicious new husband need to be alone."

Hannah sat down at the windowseat and shook her head. "I can't believe you two. You think that I would—"

"I would," Rose winked.

Colton's rich laughter rumbled from the threshold. His dark eyes latched on hers, flickering with amusement. And heat. "Ladies, that cake smells like heaven."

"We aim to please," Rose added. "I don't want you to think I'm happy you've moved out of my hotel and taken that adorable little boy with you."

Zac leaned against his father's knee and hugged the orange tabby kitten tight. His strangling hold elicited a loud, contented purr. "Kitty."

"Hannah." His gaze felt so hot it could burn right through her. "Come upstairs and show me where we should put Zac."

"Kitty." The boy toddled forward, his hold unbreakable on that kitten.

Hannah knelt before him. "You want that to be your own special kitty?"

A serious nod.

"Well, we don't have a house cat. We really need one." Her heart ached at the happiness in those clear, little-boy eyes. Life should be just this simple. "Come upstairs with me and we'll make up your room."

Zac toddled behind her. Hannah turned to see Colton still standing in the doorway, his jaw set, his gaze watching her as if he expected her to explode.

Hannah took Zac's hand as they climbed the stairs, but inside, she felt troubled. Colton had hardly mentioned his wife, and she wondered now. Was he unhappy to marry again? Did he have regrets?

"This will be yours." She pushed open the door of the small room tucked under the rafters, the dormer window inviting warm, southern sunshine to skid across the wood floor.

She'd always meant this room to be the nursery for her first baby.

"It won't take me long to build him a bed," Colton's voice spoke in her ear, his presence a radiating warmth at her back. "I saw extra lumber in the barn."

"I only have a crib, and it's much too small." She tried to joke, but it failed, especially when she measured the sadness in Colton's eyes, a sadness for her and her dreams that never happened. "I'm so glad there will finally be a child to fill this room with happiness."

He nodded, more than just agreeing. He was giving her his approval.

"I have an extra tick, brand new. I made several last winter and never had use for more than one at a time. Unless—"

"No." His hand curled around her forearm, hot like fire, reassuring like sunshine. "We are going to share the same room, Hannah. I agreed to no sex in our marriage, but I would like the comfort of lying beside you."

"But you said—"

"And I meant it." It was there in his eyes, the shine of honesty, of honor.

It brought tears to her eyes, pain to her throat. She believed him. God help her. She was in trouble now.

Zac's giggle brightened the empty room. The kitty was licking his hand.

"I'll put my clothes in our room."

Her heart kicked. "Fine."

Trouble shadowed his eyes. This wasn't easy for him, she realized. "I'll need your help stuffing the tick."

"No problem. I can manage that." His mouth dipped, and her gaze followed the movement. "Your neighbor up the road saw to your livestock this morning."

"He's a nice man, always ready to help out." Last night had been restless with worry and nightmares, this morning busy with the arrangements she saw no sense in putting off. "I should bake his family some of my cinnamon rolls as a thank you."

"I'd best head back out and start cleaning the barn. I have a feeling that's the real reason you agreed to marry me." Those dark eyes sparkled with humor, with a warmth she wanted to reach out and touch. "You were just plain tired of shoveling horse biscuits."

"That's the only reason," she laughed, the tightness in her chest gone, the laughter easy. "Not for Zac, not for your money, but because I look at you and see a man capable of shoveling manure all day."

"Such a compliment." His smile broadened until those twin dimples showed, charming as a rogue's. "I'll try not to let your praise go to my head."

He left her laughing in the room that had been empty for so long.

CHAPTER NINE

Colton liked the feel of the pitchfork in his hands, even welcomed the burning ache in his back from hours of barn work and the dank scent of the soiled straw.

The horses watched him with a careful eye, some protesting, others difficult. They weren't ready to trust a stranger in their midst yet. Half wild, he figured as he untied a sturdy Appaloosa and led her back into her stall.

Satisfaction filled him. This land was his now. Just as its debt would be. No matter. The horseflesh in this barn was valuable. Hannah had taken good care of her stock after Charles's death.

Not that there wasn't work that should be done. Every wall in the place needed to be scrubbed until it shone, the tack mended and washed, the water troughs cleaned.

The rustle of the horses, discontent in their stalls, hushed. The air somehow changed. Colton bolted the Appaloosa into her stall and headed down the aisle.

He recognized the tall man standing in the open doorway. "Sheriff."

The rotund man knuckled back his Stetson. "I thought

I'd come by and tell you what I found."

"Trouble?"

"Maybe." The sheriff glanced through the open doors toward the cozy log house beyond. "I know this is your wedding day and all, but I figured you'd want to know."

Colton leaned against the pitchfork, waiting.

"I got an eyewitness who says Sean was the man who set your barn on fire." A cocked brow.

"Is that so?"

"Yes, sir."

Colton considered that. "Who's your eyewitness?" Although he already knew.

"The same man who drank himself into a temper after hearing how you married Hannah out from under him." The sheriff began to stroll toward his horse, waiting patiently outside in the crusty snow. "Right now he's in the jail, sleepin' it off. I'll let him go when he actually pays what he owes the saloon owner for destroying personal property. I'm not relyin' on that no good son of a gun's word. This ain't the first time he's been behind bars for raisin' a ruckus."

Colton faced the wind, scanning the lay of the land, the rise of meadows and forests and foothills to the craggy mountain peaks beyond. *His* land. "Sawyer."

"Yep." The sheriff slipped his boot into the stirrup and mounted up, the leather saddle creaking beneath his considerable weight. "I see it one of two ways. Sean was a bitter man, no one's denying that, and he ain't the first in these parts wantin' to marry Hannah for her land. You just outfoxed him."

Colton heard the questions Eaton Baker didn't ask, felt them all the way to his soul. A man with secrets always had to wonder. A man with a past could never forget.

"Sean either set that fire himself, just like Sawyer says, or Sawyer set it himself. Nothing like a little financial disaster to make Hannah's situation bad enough for her to need his help."

Colton hid a smile. This was the same man so unwilling to discuss arson a few nights ago. "Sounds like two solid theories to me, Baker."

The sheriff nodded. "You may be right, Kincaid. And if you are, then watch your back. Sawyer ain't none too happy with what you did, marrying Hannah, outsmarting him. But if Sean set the fire all on his own, then I guess there's no danger. Only time will tell which it is."

Colton's guts twisted. Instinct told him the trouble with Sawyer was far from over. "I appreciate it, Sheriff. That you took the time to ride out and tell me."

The sheriff gazed up at the house. "Congratulations to you and your new missus. Hannah must be pretty happy to be mothering that little son of yours."

"I guess she is." Colton didn't miss the glimmer of caring in the old man's eyes. "I hope this marriage is a happier one for her."

The sheriff nodded, tipped his hat, and rode away.

The back of Colton's neck prickled. He knew Sawyer was locked away, sleeping off his drunken binge, but he felt unsettled.

Until he dealt with Sawyer, Colton knew there would be no peace.

* * *

Eaton Baker headed into the bitter north wind, something eating at his craw. Colton Kincaid didn't handle himself like a drifter—or a rancher, for that matter. Too confident. Too hard-edged. Too damn intelligent. Something lurked behind those jet black eyes, as if the man was measuring and calculating.

Colton Kincaid wasn't what he seemed.

Eaton thought of Sean, dead with a single shot through his heart. Of the hired gunman, Rex Roland, so dangerous the bounty on his head was a staggering sum. Kincaid had handled both men single-handedly. Neat as a pin.

And today, Eaton had visited more to make a judgment on the man than to tell him about Sawyer. There was a solid integrity about Kincaid, Eaton decided. But that dangerous edge, it lurked in his eyes, hid in his voice.

All in all, this was a peaceful town. Always had been. Eaton figured it was his duty as the sheriff and as a businessman to make sure it stayed that way.

He would write a few friends, men he could trust, and ask what they knew about this Mr. Colton Kincaid.

* * *

"It looks good." Colton's voice, low and whisper-rough.

Hannah jumped. She hated the way her heart pounded cold fear through her blood. She wrapped her arms around her middle and tried to smile at the man shadowed in the upstairs hallway. Her husband. Leaving the sleeping child safe in his bed, she stepped out of the room and quietly closed the door.

Colton's nearness dizzied her.

"I had the quilt already made," she explained, uncertain. "It's not exactly for a little boy."

"It looks nice." Colton's nod of satisfaction reassured her. "I can't believe you got him down for his nap. He's had an exciting day."

"I read to him." Hannah thought of the Mother Goose stories, the treasured book she'd bought long ago as a new bride with too many foolish dreams. "He finally gave up the fight and drifted off."

"Another sign I made the right choice." Colton stepped closer. She could see the attractive stubble of his whiskery jaw and smell the horse-and-straw scent clinging to him.

"You have doubts?" She shrugged, slipping past him, needing distance to feel safe. "It's a little late."

"True." He strode closer. "Don't you have doubts?"

"A thousand of them." She turned and pushed open the bedroom door—then regretted it. Her bed—their bed—dominated the center of the room, the wooden headboard snug against the end wall, the window showing the shadowed mountains beyond.

But there was no mistaking that bed, just wide enough for the two of them. She shivered at the thought of his hot male skin next to hers, even in sleep.

"I unpacked your clothes." She tugged open the wardrobe, where he could see his shirts and trousers neatly stacked, the space where Charles's clothes had been on the night of the fire.

It was damn strange being married. He'd pushed her into it, no doubt. But still, the responsibility weighed on his shoulders, cold and hard. He'd failed one wife. He would not fail Hannah. He'd already saved her from Sean's violent intentions. Colton felt good about that.

"Maybe I should have asked first before I unpacked your things." So much vulnerability in those eyes.

His heart kicked. "No. It's just nice to have a home again and a place to put my clothes."

She tucked that lush bottom lip between her teeth, her eyes shadowed. "It's dark, nearly suppertime. I should go set the table—"

"We ate dinner late. I'm not hungry yet." He caught her arm. She felt delicate beneath his fingers, yet her skin was hot silk. "I thought we could talk."

"Talk?"

"About the ranch." He watched the uncertainty. He wondered just how much agreeing to marry him had cost her pride. "About us."

She wrapped her arms around her slender waist, a protective gesture. Worry marked her pretty face, twisted her soft mouth.

Just looking at her lips made him remember the fiery way she tasted, how that bottom lip felt soft and yielding beneath his. Blood thrummed in his veins.

"Did you manage to clean most of the barn?" She averted her eyes and paced to the far wall where the window gazed out at their land.

"Every stall."

Surprise flashed across her face, then she smiled. The

reward of it warmed the coldness in his chest. Hannah turned to the window, still holding herself. "And the horses?"

"Fed and watered." Twilight swept through the window, washing her in a blue-gray glow. "I plan on having enough time to start exercising them tomorrow. I thought maybe you might tell me what you've been doing."

With a rustle of cotton skirt and petticoat, she faced him. But her gaze was guarded, lacking trust.

What was it about him that put that look in her eye, made her pull away from him?

"What do you want?" She hugged herself more tightly, and he ached to stride over to her, wrap her in his arms, tell her it would be all right. "You want to know each horse's routine, of course."

"Well, that. And more." He sat down on the corner of the bed and looked up at her. She was such a small woman. "I thought we agreed to work together. I'd value your help, Hannah."

"Are you suggesting I should offer to help shovel out the barn?" A small twinkle in those eyes, an attempt at humor.

Colton breathed out. He hadn't realized the tension tight beneath his breastbone until it was gone. "No, no I'll be more than happy to shovel out the barn."

"Happy?"

"It's part of the job." He rubbed the flat of his hands along his thighs, framing his words. "Hannah, I know you're afraid of me. You know the violence I'm capable of."

She blushed and looked away.

"It's not every woman who watches her husband-to-be kill a man less than twelve hours before he weds her. When you look at me, is that all you see? The violence?"

She swallowed. No, she saw the man. A complex mix of physical power and strength, and a rare tenderness. She'd seen the gentleness he showed toward his son. But what lurked beneath that controlled gentleness? She'd been foolish to think—

"I never should have married you." She looked down at her hands, stared hard at her rough skin and split nails.

"Charles controlled your life." Such a rich voice, honey-sweet and rum rough. Tempting enough to make her think he cared. "You told me once that a man was never going to control your life or your heart again."

"I mean it." Stubborn pride made her lift her chin. Uncertainties coiled in her stomach. Had she been blinded by fear? By the relief of seeing Colton Kincaid, powerful and confident, bursting into her kitchen, guns firing? Seduced by the idea that she could depend on someone who wouldn't let her down?

"I don't want your heart, Hannah. Just like you, I don't believe in romance." Clear eyes, dark as midnight and twice as compelling, fastened on her with the power of the man, of his honesty. "But as I see it, we're in this marriage and this ranching business together. I don't want to run your life, Hannah. Or take it away from you."

He looked like he meant it, there was no mistaking the honesty shining as true as the northern star in his eyes— immovable and forever.

It was so much, too much, to believe. "Then tell me what you want."

"Just your opinion." He leaned forward, this big man dwarfing her bed, shrinking the size of the room with his unmistakable masculinity. "Tomorrow, come and ride the fences with me. We'll take Zac. Maybe a picnic dinner."

He wanted a picnic? Hannah tried to smile, tried to forget the image of this man and his gun, killing as if it were nothing.

A bounty hunter. A man so tender with his child. She could not reconcile the two sides of him. Part of her wanted to run. The other part wanted to believe that a man could treat those he loved with gentleness.

Those were the same hopes she'd had when she

married Charles. Just the memory sent fear through every part of her.

* * *

Colton had spent all evening trying not to remember another woman, soft and gentle, his wife he'd failed to protect, who'd been killed because of him. Every time he looked at Hannah he was reminded of his guilt and his responsibilities. She'd warmed the leftovers from their wedding dinner, setting a fine supper on the table to Zac's delight. The kitten darted around the kitchen floor, chasing imaginary prey, as Hannah leaned close and tied a bib around the boy's neck, brushing back those unruly curls with a caring hand.

Colton's guts turned cold remembering how Hannah had avoided his gaze, purposefully focusing all the attention on the child. Oh, he was glad Hannah was obviously so happy with a little one to fuss over and coax adoring smiles from—that wasn't the source of his worry. Colton feared her purposeful distance from him signaled a deeper problem.

He set down the soapy cloth and reached for a fresh one, dampened it a bit, then swiped the horse collar clean. His concern over Hannah wasn't the only thing troubling him this night. A faint scent of cigarette smoke tainted the wind. The nearest neighbor lived two miles away, too far to smell smoke from their chimney.

Someone was out there in the dark, watching.

Colton sat in the faint shadows of a lantern, the wick turned low. That way he could work, but still see the shades of darkness outside—the move of shadow upon shadow in the yard beyond. See the house where his son slept, tucked safely into the bed Colton had fashioned from new lumber, between the sheets and beneath the quilt Hannah had lovingly placed there, brushed by her gentle hands and graced by her loving smile.

Yes, the scent of cigarette smoke troubled him.

Sean, now dead, his body lying in the undertaker's back

room awaiting burial, would have kidnapped Hannah and forced her to marry him at gunpoint for this ranch, for the prime land and valuable horseflesh and the nicest home he'd seen since Missoula.

By marriage, Hannah had made him one of the wealthiest men in the county. How many men had wanted to do the same? How many men as ruthless as Sean had been?

The upstairs light in Hannah's window still burned. This late at night, she might be changing for bed, slipping out of her pretty calico dress, unlacing her corset, sliding off her undergarments. Colton's groin kicked. He remembered the sight of her in her bath—all creamy skin and tantalizing curves.

It had been over a year since he'd been with a woman—his Ella. Colton's heart thumped. Maybe Hannah and her no sex rule was for the best. How could he so easily step into another marriage? How could he ever set aside the past to love another woman he didn't deserve?

He spent the long hours after midnight watching and listening, waiting for the scent of cigarette smoke to fade.

* * *

Hannah heard his step, heard the turn of the knob. Her heart flip-flopped. She squeezed her eyes shut and curled up on her right side, as close to the edge of the mattress as possible.

He wouldn't touch her. He'd said as much. He'd given his word.

But the blood cold in her veins was about a bigger fear. She knew some men said one thing and did another. Was Colton one of those men, despite his courage in saving her, despite the tenderness he showed his son?

The door whispered open on its leather hinges. Colton's weight squeaked on a loose floorboard. She jumped, cursing herself for moving. If she pretended to be asleep, if he believed her to be asleep, then maybe he would simply lie down.

In her heart she knew a simple pretense on her part would not determine his behavior, determine if he would keep his promise to her.

Tears knotted in her throat, and she fought to keep her breathing even. Colton's steps stopped before the wardrobe. A cabinet door squeaked open, and she heard a rustle of cloth, then the muffled thunk of a belt buckle.

Charles had such an impact on her life, on her beliefs, even now. She tried to set aside memories of another wedding night when she'd come to this bed as a bride expecting love and learned the pain of a man's touch, of a man's invasion into her body. That first pain had been the worst. The blood had washed away, the tearing of flesh had mended, but the brutal experience always left her feeling cold and used and horribly empty.

Another floorboard squeaked. Colton was approaching the bed, moving slowly in the dark. A thud, the bedstead shook, and he whispered a curse. Hannah closed her eyes. He'd stubbed his toe, most likely. She could only hope—even if she'd never seen him act less than honorably—that he would not take his anger out on her.

She'd learned on the same night she'd become a wife that men took what they wanted. And she knew Colton was no better. He wanted her land and he found a way to possess it. Even if he was her best choice, even if he had saved her from homelessness or a cold marriage to Glen.

The mattress shifted, the ropes beneath adjusting to his weight. Hannah felt the heat of tears on her face. Heard the thud of wetness against her pillow.

He stretched out, his big body taking up every inch of remaining space on the bed. His heat, his maleness, changed the chilly atmosphere in the room and burned away the memories of another who'd lain on that side of the mattress and taken pleasure in making her cry.

"Hannah?" Whispered warmth, not the voice of a man who hurt women.

Still, it was so hard to trust. Only his word stood

between them. If he broke it, there was no way she could fight him, no way she could stop him.

"Hannah." His voice again, tender as morning.

She tried to swallow away the pain bunched like a knot in her throat, stubborn and unyielding.

"You can relax." His hand touched her hair.

She jumped.

"Hannah." He wrapped a curl around his forefinger. "I'm not Charles. I'm not going to hurt you."

She knew that, deep down. Tears of relief spilled down her cheeks. She knew Colton would keep his word; it was just so damn hard to believe.

His fingers brushed her hair, slow like a breeze, intimate and gentle. "I'm never going to hurt you."

She squeezed her eyes tight. Still the wetness brimmed, hot and aching. Gratefulness burned in her heart. Whatever Colton wanted of her from this point on, she would try her best to do, try to be the best possible wife to him and mother to his son.

He'd kept his word. He would not hurt her the way Charles had, holding her down, claiming his rights, shaming her afterward for her barren womb.

"Good night, angel," Colton's voice. Colton's respect Even after he'd bunched up the pillow and his breathing changed in sleep, she couldn't stop crying.

CHAPTER TEN

"Good morning." Colton spied Hannah in the aisle as he pried the lid off the grain barrel. "I hope you didn't mind. I lit the fire and came out here to get a jump on the chores."

"No." Her clear blue gaze mirrored the surprise in her voice. "It was nice to come down to the kitchen and find the room warm and the fire roaring. Thank you."

"No thanks necessary." He remembered her curled up, stiff as a frightened child on the mattress beside him last night, remembered the tap of her tears against the pillowcase. "I'm your husband. I consider it part of my job."

"I have breakfast nearly ready. I hope you like pancakes. Zac told me they were his favorite."

"I love pancakes." Truth was, this cold morning air combined with hard work made the idea of a hot meal sound better than anything. "I'll be in as soon as I finish tending the stallion."

She clasped her slender hands, red and callused from work she never should have had to do. "Did he give you any trouble?"

Colton grabbed an empty pail and dunked it into the barrel, the sweet scent of grain and oats filling his nose. "Not if you call a few bites trouble."

"Oh, are you hurt?"

"It won't kill me." Colton grabbed another pail. "Just broke the skin."

"Colton, you're bleeding."

"I'm fine, Hannah."

"Let me look." She caught his arm and unrolled his sleeve. Scabs dotted the skin on his forearms, wounds still healing from the burns he'd suffered fighting the fire in her barn. The nip from the stallion was superficial, but enough to bleed. "I should bandage this before you get an infection."

He pulled his hand free. "I'm tougher than any infection. Where's Zac?"

"Sound asleep." She stepped back, somehow stung.

Colton's voice came warm, his face handsome and calm. "Snuggled up with his kitty?"

"He'll be up the minute the sun rises."

Colton flashed her a quick grin. "I'll be in as soon as I finish feeding the horses."

Hannah watched him walk away, this powerful man of muscle and bone, of controlled strength. This man was her husband. She shivered deep inside, remembering the heat of his body beside hers last night. The barn was neat, so clean, the animals tended with care.

Maybe marrying Colton hadn't been a mistake after all.

Without a word she hurried through the thin morning fog to her snug log home and the little boy safely asleep upstairs.

* * *

With Zac on his lap, held with a firm hand, the ride down the south side of the property line proved a challenge, only because the boy cooed and grinned, trying to catch Hannah's attention every minute.

Zac was no fool. He knew a good thing when it smiled at him, sweet as an angel, pretty as heaven.

As for Hannah, she rode her mustang mare astride, even though she had a sidesaddle in the tack room, polished and brand new looking. Her riding outfit, a dark blue, hugged her figure in just the right places, cupping her soft breasts, nipping in at her tiny waist, curving over the slim contours of her fanny. It made it hard for a man to concentrate. Damn hard.

As they rode, he listened to the call of the winter birds, the squawk of a hawk high above the meadow land, and the rustle of wind through the boughs of the tall stands of pine and fir. All was well. Still, Colton felt unsettled.

The sheriff had brought a warning. And Colton knew the feel of trouble, had known it all his life.

Hannah's voice, like a song, drew him in, kept him listening as she told him about the Percherons, the giant workhorses with the gentle eyes. She knew each one by name. She catalogued the horses in the barn, their training schedules, their exercise schedules, told him about the little mare in the end corner stall who'd survived a bout of colic.

Colton kept his tongue and listened, determined to ride out whatever troubled her. Like last night, so rigid in the bed beside him, waiting for him to break his word to her. Waiting for...well, for whatever Charles had taught her about men and women.

A bitter taste soured his mouth, drew a rank smell to the scent of the mountain air and fresh meadows. Let her treat him like a business partner, a man who'd brought money to her ranch and nothing else. She would find out soon enough he was a man she could trust.

"Cake," Zac said, tugging at Colton's shirt.

One look into those little eyes tore at his heart. Damn, it was hard to say no to Zac.

"Are you hungry, Zac?" Hannah twisted around in her saddle, gold curls falling around her face, gleaming in the cool sun. So much concern and so easily given.

"Hungry," Zac sighed.

Yep, the little tike knew exactly how to twist a woman's heart. Colton laughed and hugged his son tight.

"I know a place." Her eyes sparkled. "It's the best spot for a picnic. It's not far."

"Lead the way." Colton couldn't take his eyes from her. The cool wind burned a rosy hue into her cheeks. It was hard remembering her fear last night looking now at this woman of gentle caring. His heart ached, and he wished he knew what to say.

She avoided his gaze, as she'd done most of the day, their second day as man and wife. She flashed him a smile that could rattle a lesser man and chirruped to her mare. The mustang leaped into a smooth canter.

He tried not to think of her thighs, slender and creamy, and the strength in them, gripping the horse's flanks like that.

His heart kicked. He might not be looking for romance, but he did have a wife. A wife who didn't want him.

"What do you think?" Hannah's voice, lilting upward with excitement, soft as a bird's trill.

Colton scanned the land—his land—and nodded. Mountain peaks, craggy and snow-capped, reached into the sky, the forests of pine and fir guarding the glen's edge. Meadow land sloped downward toward a shallow, frozen creek.

"It's stunning."

"So, you like the land you married me for?" She flashed him a teasing grin.

He didn't answer. He didn't feel good about how he'd pressured her. But he wanted a mother and a home for Zac. And she needed help. Yet she looked at him and wondered what promises he would break. She feared how he might treat her.

Could she look at him and see his past, etched so deep into his soul?

"I brought an extra blanket to sit on." Hannah dismounted with the ease of a cowboy, as if she'd done it hundreds of times. "The ground's pretty darn cold. Only a fool wants to picnic in this weather."

He grinned at her teasing. "I've been called worse."

"That doesn't surprise me one bit." Her blue eyes laughed at him as she reached up for Zac.

He handed down the boy and felt her take his small weight, folding the tiny child into her arms and listening carefully to his childish words.

"Yes," she chuckled. "I remembered to bring slices of cake. I wouldn't forget your favorite, Zac."

The little boy sighed, contented, nestled beneath her chin.

Colton felt lonely as he dismounted, lonelier still as he fetched the saddlebags and extra blanket rolled behind her saddle. Zac's happy giggle was answered by her warm words, a warmth she didn't seem to have for him.

Well, he hadn't married Hannah for love. He doubted he would ever love again. But a man didn't mind a touch, a kiss, a roll between the sheets.

His mare nudged him in the shoulder, bumping him back into awareness. The wind had died, the birds silenced. He felt a prickle along his spine, a coldness against the back of his neck.

He scanned the edge of the forest, stretching as far as eye could see. No movement. Nothing out of place. Yet...he couldn't shake the uneasiness.

"Colton," Hannah smiled up at him, opening up the basket. "Come sit with us. We're ready to eat."

"Ready, Papa!"

"Zac, don't you eat my piece of chicken," he teased his son.

Zac looked up and giggled. "Breast."

Colton tipped back his head and laughed. "Yes, Zac, I like the breast. You're right about that."

Hannah blushed, pretty as a picture, and his heart

warmed. He sat down on the blanket, the abundant food spread out before him, and tried not to remember the image of her in that tub, the curves of her body, so soft and sweet.

"Hannah," he teased, unable to resist, "pass me the breast."

"Maybe you'd better help yourself."

"Is that an invitation?" He wriggled his eyebrows so she would know he was only joking.

The pink staining her face deepened. "No. Just eat your chicken and be decent, Mr. Kincaid."

"I still want the breast—of course, I also like thighs."

"That's enough." Hannah fisted her hand and he ducked just in time. A napkin sailed through the air and knocked his hat right off and into the grass.

Zac clapped his little hands.

Colton straightened. "Hey, I just wanted a little brea—"

"Don't push me, Colton Kincaid, or that will be the last breast you ever get your hands on."

"You'd deny my son fried chicken?"

"No. Just you." She laughed then, light and easy, and when her gaze met his, sparkling with humor, he saw a glimmer of trust.

Taking that as a good sign, Colton reached for the breast and didn't say one more word about it, even though Hannah couldn't stop giggling.

* * *

At least Colton was a hard worker, Hannah thought with a stab of satisfaction as she peeled the potatoes for supper.

She could just see him through the small window over the work table, a strong, towering shadow of man and muscle as he worked the new little palomino on a lunge in the southernmost corral.

"I'm hungry," Zac sighed, then leaned against her knee. So much little-boy trust. So much innocent need.

"Supper isn't far away. We're going to have roast beef.

Do you like it?"

"Roast beef." Zac considered the possibility with a furrowed brow. "Okay."

Charmed, Hannah knelt to brush some of those rowdy dark curls from his eyes. "Would you like a slice of potato?"

Zac's eyes lit at the offered chunk of raw vegetable. His chubby little hand stretched out. "Thank you."

It felt so good to feel this child's happiness in her kitchen, satisfying to hear the thud of his feet against her floor.

She dumped the potatoes in a pot, filled it with water, and set it on the stove to cook. She set the table as Zac dangled a length of red string for the orange tabby kitten. Adorable giggles punctuated the contented warmth of the room and transformed her lonely little house into a home.

"Hannah." The door flew open and Colton stood in the threshold, dependable, strong-shouldered, handsome as sin. "Come look."

"Is something wrong?" Her heart flipped over at the urgency in his voice.

"Papa!" Zac tottered across the floor, still dragging the string, the kitten happily chasing.

"Just a ten point buck." A smile broke across his face, deepening the intimacy of his gaze.

She felt touched. Then his words sunk in. "You want me to get a hunting rifle." Disappointment slipped through her. She thought of Charles, who killed wild animals for the sport of it, for the pleasure.

"No." Colton lifted her wool cloak off the wall peg behind him. "I thought you might want to see it."

"I have my potatoes on—"

"Take 'em off."

Why did that jaunty grin make her heart skip? Hannah thought to argue, but no words came. Only the lure of his twinkling gaze and the intrigue of his invitation.

She grabbed a dish towel and lifted the pot from the

stove.

"Come on, Zac," Colton's voice, gentle and yet excited. Hannah turned to see him unwinding the red yarn from his son's little fist. "You can play with your kitty later."

The kitty meowed in protest.

Hannah hesitated. Colton held Zac in his arms, snug against his chest. Their heads bent together, father and son. She wasn't part of this intimate bond. A sadness flitted through her chest, cool and lasting.

She'd married Colton to be a mother, but really, she was only a caretaker. As much as she adored the little boy, he didn't need her, didn't look to her as the constant source of love in his life.

She hadn't assumed marrying Colton would solve her loneliness or forge a bond between her and Zac. But she hoped in time...

Colton held out his hand, palm up, a silent question in those eyes as dark as night.

Hannah stepped forward and slipped her hand on his. Big, blunt-shaped fingers curled around her own, trapping her with his sure, powerful grip.

"Your cloak." Why did his voice make her shiver? Make her heat all the way to her toes? "It's already freezing out there."

"Did you make sure the horses have enough water?" She freed her hand and took the heavy cloak, slipping into it. "Animals freeze if they don't have enough water to insulate them."

"I know that, Hannah." Easy words, not censuring and not arrogant, either. "I know one end of a horse from the other."

"Rump." Zac giggled.

"Rump?" Colton shook his head, scattering ebony locks against the breadth of his jacketed shoulders. "Did you teach this to my son?"

Hannah grabbed her muffler. "No, I believe you're the expert on body parts."

Colton tipped back his head and laughed. "I guess I am. Did you learn that word from me, Zac?"

"Yes."

More laughter.

Hannah secured the length of wool tightly around her throat, but she could not take her eyes off Colton. He'd been hard at work in the barn before dawn and had spent most of his day shoveling and hauling and scrubbing. Exhaustion rimmed his face and drew lines around his mouth and eyes, yet there was only laughter and affection for his son.

And kindness toward her.

This same man who'd admitted to killing men for the price on their heads, who'd burst into this very room and saved her from harm.

How could she reconcile the two parts of him?

"Come." Colton stepped out into the gray-blue evening, the light nearly gone from the sky. "Be careful. The steps are frosty."

He caught her by the elbow, ready to guide her.

Hannah shook him away. "Thanks, Colton, but I'm no child. I don't need any help."

"Fine." His smile remained, but felt shallow, superficial.

What should she do? Act helpless so he would feel manly helping her down the same steps she descended for years in all kinds of weather? She didn't need to lean on him—on anyone—the way Zac might, so small and unsteady.

She had her independence. No man would take it away this time. At least not without a fight.

"Look, he's still there." Colton's whisper rose like fog in the chilly air. He cradled Zac in one arm and pointed to the corral beyond.

A heavy moon hung low in the sky, casting just enough light to see the silhouette of the elk, his ten pronged antlers held high, scenting the air. The elegant animal stood poised for flight, thick neck extended, long legs tensed.

Zac sighed. Hannah forgot to breathe.

"He's a bull in his prime," Colton said, his low voice blending with the coming night, soothing, just above a whisper.

Hannah moved closer to this man, spellbound by his words. She wanted to hear more. "Why is he here?"

"It's mating season." Even in the dark, Colton's eyes glittered with a quiet mirth, a joke at her.

"Don't get any ideas, mister. We've made a bargain."

He chuckled, low, rich as rum. "I know. The poor fellow should be enjoying the attentions of his females about now, but he's without a herd."

"Enjoying?" Hannah lifted a brow.

"I'm sure mating is pleasurable for an elk, too." His words rumbled with humor. "I noticed a limp, and I spotted his tracks earlier in the paddock. He's injured, I'm guessing. And he spotted those horses you've been spoiling and figured he might as well help himself to some hay and seek safety from predators in the herd. If he's injured, there's mountain lion, bear, and even wolf in those mountains that would love to make him dinner."

"You won't shoot him?" She held her breath.

The moonlight, faint and silvery, brushed Colton's handsome face, and she could see the pinch of his eyes, the disappointment. "What's wrong? You think I'm the kind of man who would kill an animal that beautiful? When we have food enough to see us through the winter?"

Her throat filled. She sensed his anger, felt the stab of temper in his words. She closed her eyes, thought about how best to right the situation. "No, I just wondered if you—"

"Would kill an animal that can't run away from my gun?"

"—liked to hunt," she finished lamely, though her words rang false and empty. She hadn't fooled Colton.

His jaw clamped shut. His body, all steely muscle and

bone, tensed. "You're wondering if I can kill without reason, aren't you? Without conscience. If I can just end a life, especially a human being's as easily as I did in your kitchen."

"No, this isn't about that night—"

"Then it's about my past." Anger. It cut through the night, echoed in her heart "I wish you hadn't seen how well I handle a gun."

"Me, too," she said quietly, hating her fear, hating the wobble in her voice.

Bitterness lined his face. "Look, I want to forget Erase my mistakes, what happened to Ella, and leave my past behind."

Zac sobbed once. The wind stilled, the night silenced. Hannah watched regret fill Colton's eyes. And so much sadness. He kissed his son on the cheek and then handed him over to her.

"I have work to do," he said, his back already to her as his boots struck the frozen ground. "Leave supper warming in the oven. I'll be working until late."

Weakness trembled through her limbs, swirled in the pit of her stomach. Hannah gave Zac a squeezing hug, and the worry ebbed out of the boy. He started chattering about his kitty, still inside the house, and so they headed back toward the warm kitchen. The lamplight spilling through the windows lit their way.

What kind of man was Colton? Beneath the easy charm and solid competence, there was a darkness and an anger. How great a darkness? How fearsome an anger?

Hannah unbuttoned Zac's coat and hung it on the wall peg. She worried what effect Colton Kincaid would have on her life, on her heart.

* * *

Glen Sawyer struck a match, cursing the damn wind blowing out the flame and driving a chill straight through his bones. He dug out another match and lit the cigarette, satisfied only when the rich smoke filled his lungs.

Colder than hell frozen over, that was Montana. It had been Charles's idea to come here, going on about cattle barons and millions of acres of free land. Turned out Charles hadn't known what he was talking about, nothing unusual there. His older brother couldn't whistle and walk at the same time.

Now the bastard was dead and gone on to his punishment, and Glen had a problem he couldn't do anything about. Not right now. Not with the sheriff keeping an eye on him. Even that old fool Baker could figure out that if another man died the same way in the same barn, then both deaths might not be coincidental.

A light flickered to life in the second story window. Curtains hid the room from his sight, but he was a patient man. A silhouette passed through the light, tossing a shadow against the curtains. Hannah crossing the room. Her hair was loose; he'd seen the tumble of curls down her slender back.

Heat kicked in his groin. The silhouette returned. She must be standing between the lamp and the window. Plain as if she was standing before him, he watched her unbutton her bodice, then slip the dress down her slim body, over those curvy hips. She was all shadow, but he could see the rise of her breasts as she climbed out of her underthings.

His erection surged. Her breasts would be creamy white and pink-tipped. He'd imagined them so many times, asked his brother about them. Unfortunately, Charles hadn't been of a mind to share. That was all Glen had asked, just to share the woman. Well, that and the ranch's profits.

Charles always had been a selfish bastard.

The shadow moved against the curtains. Hannah lifted her arms so he could see the silhouetted profile of her breasts perfectly, imagine the taste of her skin. As she lifted the nightgown over her head, his erection pulsed, trapped in the confines of his trousers.

Yes. He would be in that room right now, making her strip for him, forcing her over the edge of the bed, pressing her thighs apart, if Sean hadn't gotten greedy. If he'd kept to the bargain and hadn't tried to take Hannah for himself.

Now, matters were worse.

The nightgown shivered down over Hannah's breasts, concealed the flatness of her belly and the curve of her hips. Glen could almost taste her, the heat of her mouth, the silk of her breasts, the dew between her legs. He could almost—

His heart kicked in alarm. Glen scanned the black relief of night where shadows shivered over one another to see what had startled him.

Colton Kincaid stood in the open barn door, the lantern at his back, shoulders set, hands fisted.

There was no way that drifter was going to wind up with everything Glen wanted. No, sir. Some things were worth fighting for.

He glanced up at Hannah's window. She sat on her cedar chest at the foot of the bed, brushing her hair. Long strokes, steady and practiced.

Blood thrummed in his groin. He would watch. And wait.

CHAPTER ELEVEN

Colton shivered into his trousers, teeth set against the chilly morning air. It was still dark, and his big toe stubbed the corner of Hannah's cedar chest at the foot of the bed. He bit down against the shot of pain, but managed to make no other noise.

She slept beneath the covers at the edge of the tick, curled tight into a protective ball.

They'd been married two weeks now, and he'd kept his promises. He hadn't touched her. He'd been to town, paid off her debts at the feed store and the mercantile, and made arrangements with Drummond at the bank. The mortgage was secure in his name.

Yet everything about Hannah and concerning Hannah remained the same. She smiled at him, but the wariness shadowed her blue eyes. She cooked and cleaned and watched over Zac with a loving warmth Colton envied.

His life felt cold in comparison.

Colton eased the door closed and padded down the hallway to push open the second door. Zac's relaxed breathing, even and deep in sleep, reassured him all was well. Somewhere in the dark, huddled beneath the covers, slept the orange kitty Zac couldn't part with.

Downstairs he lit both fires, one in the parlor, the second in the kitchen, and fed the flames, dampers open, until heat chased away some of the iciness from the rooms. Soon Hannah would be down and he wanted her morning to be easier, warmer.

She did so much for him and for Zac. It had been a long time since someone cared enough to mend a tear in his shirt or knit him new socks. Moreover, Colton couldn't remember the last time Zac's smile came so easily, so genuinely.

Yep, he owed a lot to Hannah Sawyer. Well, Hannah Kincaid, now. She'd given them all a place to belong, a real home, and a future for his son.

Colton grabbed his coat off the wall peg and stepped into his boots. Outside snow fell in airy crystal flakes. It was close to five, maybe ten degrees at the most. His breath hung in white clouds in the still air. The frozen ground crunched with every step.

He pushed open the barn door and slipped inside. The air was warmer. Horses stirred in their stalls; nickers and neighs welcomed him.

"You're not fooling me," he said to the waiting animals. "You look at me and see breakfast."

The stallion flung his head, nodding violently.

Colton's chuckle died in his throat.

Something was wrong, disturbed. Warning buzzed through him. His blood stilled as his hand strayed to his hip. No gun.

The stallion's bedding was disheveled, as if he'd thrashed around his stall. Flecks of lather shone gray-white against his dark neck.

Footsteps crunched outside, light and quick. The door squeaked open a fraction. "Go back to the house."

"I have to milk the cow." The handle of her pail rattled. The sweet scent of her, light and intoxicating, teased his nose, but he didn't turn around.

"I told you to go back to the house and bolt the door."

Silence. "What's wrong? What happened?" Her boots tapped on the floorboards.

He spun to face her. "I don't know. I just want you in the house where I know you're safe." He reached for the pail. "I'll bring in the milk."

"Patches will never let you close enough to milk her. She's a little ornery." Hannah tucked her lip between her teeth, so small and fragile. So damn vulnerable.

Colton remembered another woman, pretty and trusting. Death had come easily to her. She'd been too small and weak to fight.

"I don't care about the ornery cow." He tossed the pail on the floor, his instincts punching out a warning. "Come with me." He caught her hand. "I'll take you there myself."

"Colton." She tried to shake his grip.

He only squeezed tighter. Until he knew what he was dealing with, he'd make damn certain she was safe. He wasn't going to make another mistake. He wasn't going to be responsible for another woman's death.

"There's been a disturbance in the barn," he bit out, tugging her out of the barn, fear and old memories fueling him.

"What do you mean?" She dug in her heels, the stubborn woman. "Why—"

Alarm shadowed her eyes, so round and half afraid of him. Colton's conscience kicked.

"It's my barn, too." She set her chin, defiant and ready to fight.

Ready to fight him.

Colton's heart sank, all his hopes falling, too. Before he'd asked her to marry him, he had stayed up most of the night trying to work it out in his head. Trying to see how they could live together without love and how he could keep hold of his heart.

He spent all that time worrying, when now he could see there would be no affection between them. Not with that fear of him shadowed in her eyes.

"I just don't want you hurt. That's all."

Her chin lowered a little. She uncurled her fists. "Are my horses all right?"

"Your horses are fine." He sounded weary.

She was weary, too. "I'm glad. I—" She paused. "I feared a wild animal had somehow snuck into the barn and—" She shivered at the brutal image.

Colton's hand covered her shoulder. Heat burned through the layers of wool and flannel to scorch her skin. His touch transformed her—made her warm inside. It was the one thing about him that she could trust

Every night for two weeks he'd crawled into the bed beside her and gone to sleep. And she was grateful to him. If he wanted his touch to hurt her, he'd have done it before now.

Those broad shoulders, such strength. The powerful beauty of his body drew her. And frightened her, too. Not the terrifying kind of fear she'd felt in her marriage to Charles when he lost his temper. But a fear of being more vulnerable than she'd ever been before.

"If it's not a wild animal, then what could be wrong?"

"Let me do my job." Square jaw tensed, dark eyes determined, there was no weakness to him, no vulnerability. "I can't do that while worrying about your safety, Hannah. Do what I say. Please."

"I didn't promise to obey you."

"Well, I guess you win." Anger sparked his eyes, tensed the muscles in his shoulders. "Just keep out of my way."

Hannah's breath caught, sensing the power in him, not just from his well-built body, but from him, from the man he was. It dizzied her, intoxicated her. Somehow she managed to follow him back into the barn.

"Ashes." Colton knelt to study the floorboards.

Sam, the rambunctious stallion, tossed his head and trumpeted.

"Cigarette ashes." He stood, knuckling back his hat.

The normal sounds of livestock filled the barn. If there was a threat, then it was from a man the horses knew.

"Someone was here, smoking in my barn?" Hannah's knees wobbled.

"Looks that way."

"Only a fool smokes in a barn. Only a—" She wanted to wrap her hands around the scoundrel's neck and give him a shaking he'd never forget. "There could have been another fire."

Grim, Colton nodded. "Whoever it was, wanted us to know that. There are too many ashes. He wasn't just walking down the aisle, he stood here and smoked."

"If the barn caught fire in the night, then—" Her throat closed. Then all the horses would have burned with it. All her beloved friends. All her spring profit.

They would be ruined. She would lose her home.

Colton grew silent and dark. Hannah knew he realized the same, that he had just as much at stake. He marched down the aisle, every muscle tensed, as capable and in control as the night he'd rescued her from Sean.

Her heart hurt. He'd done so much for her. How dare someone—anyone—break into this barn and light matches, smoke less than a foot away from ignitable hay? How dare they take anything from this man who worked so hard?

Colton disappeared down the aisle. She heard his boots thud to a stop, a final sound that lingered in the rafters.

He'd found something. Dread thudded in her chest and she ran to see. She tried to stop the images of disaster from filling her mind.

"It's ruined." Colton rubbed his hands over his face. "Over two month's worth of feed has been destroyed."

Hannah's knees wobbled as she stepped forward. "What—"

"The hay's as wet as if it had been outside in the rain." He kicked at the edge of the mow with his boot, and the scent of wet hay drifted upward.

"Who would do such a thing?" Hannah couldn't imagine. The hard months of work to bring in the hay, to mow it and dry it and load it and haul it and stack it. She'd done it herself, after Charles's death. So much work, so much sweat.

Angry tears bit behind her eyes. "How can we possibly afford to replace it?"

"Don't worry." Colton pushed out the back door and knelt to study the ground.

Seconds ticked like heartbeats in the tense silence.

Hannah stared at the damage in her mow. Someone must have hauled water from the well. Or emptied the horses' buckets from their stalls.

What would happen now?

"The snow's obliterated any tracks." Colton rubbed his hands on his knees, then stood. He strode closer, controlled power, harnessed fury.

Hannah watched him closely, studied the curl of his fists, the tense line of his jaw. He wasn't a violent man, she told herself. But she knew he could be.

But not to her. His eyes softened. "I'm going to find out who did this, Hannah. Don't worry. I'm your husband now. I'm not going to let anything hurt you, my son, or our future."

He meant it, this man of honor. Tears bunched in her throat, admiration she couldn't let herself express.

She didn't understand him, but he hadn't disappointed her, hadn't let her down. Colton Kincaid was different from any man she'd ever known.

* * *

Hannah squinted against the cold flecks of snow as Colton guided the team through town. The wagon wheels skidded slightly at the corner—the skiff of snow frozen to the ground wasn't enough to warrant the use of the sleigh.

Zac, bundled tightly on her lap, twisted to look up at her, those dark eyes shining. "Candy."

Sunshine bubbled through her chest and she chuckled, squeezing the boy in a quick hug. "Do you think I'm going to buy you some candy?"

"Red candy." Zac clapped his little mittened hands.

"The red candy is your favorite?"

"Fav'rit." The boy nodded.

Above the knit cap hugging the child's head, Hannah felt Colton's gaze. She looked up to see sprinkles of warmth sparkling in his eyes, the secrets there shuttered, so only the charm of the man remained.

"Good thing I set up a charge account." Colton winked. "Zac is going to put me into debt buying red candy."

"And lic-wish."

"Licorice, too?" Colton shook his head. "I'm doomed."

Hannah watched his gloved fingers handle the reins and draw the team to a stop right in front of the mercantile. Despite the tragic morning and the ruined hay—impossibly expensive to replace—Colton hadn't lost his temper.

Unlike Charles, he hadn't used her as a target to vent that anger. At least not yet.

Maybe not ever. Hannah dared to believe it. Colton's smile widened, genuine and true. He set the brake and hopped down.

"I don't need you to help me," she murmured quickly when he reached up to lift Zac down.

"I want to help you." The smile remained, handsome and dashing. He set his son safe on the boardwalk and then extended his hand.

Leather glove touched yarn mitten. Yet the tingle of sensation, of awareness, licked like fire through her veins. He caught her by the elbow as she descended, and the scent of him—pine and wood smoke—filled her senses. The sheer size of him left her dizzy.

"Buy anything you need, Hannah." His voice dipped, intimate and caring. "I know you're proud, but my money is your money, too. Remember, we agreed. Get what you need and don't worry."

"But with the ruined winter feed—"

His fingers brushed her lips. Wild tingles danced at his touch. "I can take care of it."

"But—"

"Trust me." Oh, how that jaunty, rakish grin could charm her into nearly anything. Then Colton raised his voice, the devil shining in his eyes. "And don't let Zac have any candy. Especially any red candy."

"Papa!" Zac's eyes twinkled with merriment. "Red candy."

"Maybe the yellow candy. But not the red."

He rode away, leaving Hannah warm inside.

"He's such a hunk of man."

Hannah spun around. "Rose. I was hoping to see you today."

"Shame on you, spending time with that delicious new husband of yours and this adorable little boy instead." Rose's eyes teased, comfortable with old friendship. "Are you headed into the mercantile?"

"Yes." Hannah picked up her skirts and hopped up the few steps. "I need a few things for Zac."

"Candy."

Rose laid a hand to her bosom, charmed. "I see you aren't sparing the rod with this one."

"I've decided not to spoil him," Hannah joked back, and reached for her stepson's hand. Her stepson. It was the first time she'd thought of him that way.

Rose held open the mercantile's glass-framed door. "Think you can make it to our sewing group this time?"

"Truth is, I'd love to." Hannah made certain Zac stepped over the threshold without tripping. "I'm not sure what to do with this one."

"Have you asked Colton to watch him?" Rose stopped beside the pickle barrel. "Hannah, you aren't training this husband right."

"Well, I don't think it's a matter of training." Hannah reached for a basket.

"Think of it as gentle guiding. You know, don't spit in the house. Leave the muddy boots outside. Obey my every command." Rose winked. "Especially in bed."

"Rose, really. This is a public place." She blushed, thinking of Colton's hard body beside hers, radiating heat. "I'll ask him and see if he'll keep an eye on Zac."

"Candy." The wistful little boy gazed at the front counter where the bright candies were stored in glass canisters.

"We're starting a new project. I'll count on you to be there. That is, if you can drag yourself away from pleasuring that new husband of yours." Rose tapped over to the canned goods, stopping all argument.

Hannah wasn't fooled. She caught her friend's laughing smile across the aisle and shook her head. She studied the skeins of yarns, piled neatly on a low shelf.

Pleasure. Certainly the only one who had pleasure from such an act was the man. Hannah's stomach went cold remembering Charles, his rough touches, the way he made her feel used.

But Colton... She'd seen his bare chest, delineated with muscle, lightly dusted with dark hair. He always undressed at night before the window. Sometimes she could see the amazing shape of him—hard and lean where Charles was soft and roundish—broad shoulders, flat abdomen, sculpted thighs.

Her fingers buzzed, remembering. Once, when she'd rolled over in bed, awake from a disturbing dream, she looked at him beside her, lying flat on his back, sleeping soundly. The covers had fallen away and moonlight from the window brushed his skin with a silvered, attractive glow. He'd looked like a marbled god or a Grecian hero of old, still as stone, so handsome it made her heart hurt to look at him.

She'd wanted to touch him. Even with only the tip of

one finger. Just to feel the male heat of his skin, know the feel of this flesh and blood man she'd married.

Maybe, in touching such a man, there might be pleasure.

Blushing at her bold thoughts, Hannah reached for a fat skein of red yarn. "Do you like this, Zac?"

"Red." He sighed his approval.

"We'll get you enough for new mittens, too." She calculated the amount of wool she'd need. Two extra skeins would make him a cute little sweater. With stripes. On impulse she snatched up another skein of dark blue.

"Candy now?" Hopeful eyes.

Hannah felt love for this little boy beat in her heart. "Yes, let's go pick out your candy."

"And lic'wish, too."

* * *

"Do you think it's Sawyer?" Eaton Baker lifted one hand to signal the barkeep.

"I don't have evidence. But yes." Colton dropped his hat on the wooden bar. "Ale, please."

The barkeep poured another shot of whiskey for Baker, then filled a clean mug from the handy keg. Colton counted out the nickel and dime and a generous tip for the man.

"He's been in the saloon gamblin' near every night." Baker knocked back the whiskey. "But he's been leaving early."

"I'd appreciate it if you could keep an eye on him." Colton looked at the ale, but didn't drink. "I'd appreciate it if you could find the man determined to see my ranching efforts fail. If that's what he wants."

"I'll do all I can." The sheriff slammed his shot glass on the counter. "I wanted to tell you your bounty money will be comin' on the next stage."

"I'm glad to hear it." Cold rage crackled inside him. Colton gripped the mug and tried not to hate the fact that he'd made more money off another man's death. "Truth is, if I keep sustaining losses like this one, I'll need that money."

He thought of the hay, ruined. No good for the horses, not even for the floor at their feet.

"I checked up on you." Eaton pulled out two cigars from his vest pocket and offered Colton one.

He shook his head. "What did you find out?"

"That you were the best damn bounty hunter this side of Arizona. That outlaws with a price on their heads trembled if they heard you were huntin' them."

"Too bad I didn't enjoy my job." Colton set down the mug of ale, hard enough so foam sloshed over the rim onto the bar. "Look, Baker, I'm not ashamed of my past, but I don't cherish it, either. I came here to start over, to build a good life for my son. I want to keep it that way."

"I understand. A man has a right to his privacy."

"I appreciate that." Colton pushed away from the bar. "Good day, Sheriff."

He felt watched as he strode out the door, felt burdened by a past he'd never wanted and wasn't proud of. If Baker had sent telegraphs inquiring about Colton's past, then he'd know about what happened in Arizona, no doubt, about the day Colton lost his badge and spent seven years in jail.

A man like him, maybe he didn't have the right to build dreams. He stood on the boardwalk, peering through the lightly falling snow to Baker's Mercantile across the street.

The window, crammed full of displays, drew his eye. Hannah was in there with his son, the best part of himself.

He would do anything—anything—to keep them safe.

Colton pushed open the door to the feed store, turning his mind back to business. To the life he was determined to build for his family. Nothing—and no man—would stop him.

* * *

"How much did it cost?" Hannah asked with a furrow to her brow. "I thought you were buying hay."

Colton watched her carefully studying the load piled high and tied securely to the back of the wagon. "Leslie said he'd bring out a load today. He gave me free delivery, considering how much we're buying."

"But this lumber." She didn't look happy. "We didn't discuss this kind of a purchase. Colton—" She looked around, scanning up and down the street, then lowered her voice. "I don't think you should have spent the money. You promised you would speak to me first before you—"

"I told you I was going to rebuild the barn. I didn't think there was anything to discuss." He knelt down and gave his son a wink. "Got any candy in there for me?"

Zac opened up one of his three small paper sacks and peered inside. "Lic'wish." He opened another. "Red." He opened the last "Yellow."

"Ah, butterscotch. My favorite." Colton popped a candy into his mouth and pressed a kiss to his son's cheek.

Zac rewarded him with a broad, merry grin.

Hannah began lifting her purchases into the wagon bed and Colton hurried to help her.

"Looks like I'm back in debt." He winked as he set one package behind the seat, safely out of the wind.

She didn't laugh, didn't even crack a smile. Snowflakes clung to the brim of her bonnet, caught in the curls at her shoulders. Cold pinkened her angel's face and drew his gaze to the cupid's bow shape of her mouth, lush and soft-looking. He knew just how she would taste, how she would make him feel.

His lips buzzed in anticipation.

"I bought some things for Zac. And for you." All business, polite and distant, she handed him a heavy bag. "And some foodstuffs. You've consumed nearly all my coffee stores."

"You're mad at me. About the lumber."

"Damn right I am." Fire sparked in her eyes, pure blue flame that dazzled him, made his heart thud.

He wanted to taste that fire, stroke her until it burned only for him.

Colton took a hard breath, drawing the cold air deep into his lungs. It cooled his body, but not his thoughts. Lying next to her every night was tough, knowing she was his wife, all creamy skin and fascinating curves, and he couldn't touch her. He was only a man, and it was killing him.

He lifted the last package from her arms, light and bulky, and weighed it down with a wedge of wood. "I thought we'd already came to an understanding about the barn. I did mention it to you."

"But now we need to buy more hay to see the horses through the winter. I don't see how we have enough money for both, even with your mysterious bundle in the bank."

He deposited Zac on the wagon seat. "Maybe we'd better take back some of that yarn, then."

He waited for understanding to dawn across her face, so pretty it hurt him to look at her.

"Stop teasing me. This isn't a joking matter."

She grabbed hold of the frame with her slender, gloved hand, but he was quicker. He caught her by the elbow and helped her up to the seat. Her honeysuckle scent tickled his nose and her lustrous blond curls brushed his cheek. Colton's heart twisted.

He would move heaven for this woman, his wife.

She squinted down at him, always a bad sign. "Tonight I'd like to resume my social activities. You'll need to watch Zac for me since I'll be attending my sewing group."

Yep, she was still a little miffed over the lumber. But once she saw the barn, she would forgive him. He knew what it was like to worry about money, about not having enough to see to the most basic of needs. In time, she would see he could take care of her, that he was a man who provided for his family.

"Do I have to cook supper, too?" He swung up into the wagon.

"Don't be cheeky," she scolded him lightly with almost a smile in her voice. "Of course you'll have to cook. You'll make sure he does the dishes, right, Zac?"

"Right."

"Are you going to side with her against your own father?" Colton asked his nodding son. "Are you going to tell on me if I don't do the dishes?"

"Yep." Merry eyes, happy smile.

Colton's heart felt happy, too. He'd done the right thing marrying Hannah. She might refuse his touch, but she lovingly cared for his son.

She wasn't cold. And in time, he knew, she would come to trust him enough to show him her passion, share with him mutual comfort in the night.

CHAPTER TWELVE

Hannah shrugged the snow from her hat and shawl, standing beneath the porch roof to Rose's back door. Even though it was early evening, it was dark in this part of the country and Hannah disliked being out by herself at night. Maybe if Mrs. Mullen, her neighbor, came tonight, they could ride back together.

She knocked at the door, then rubbed her freezing hands together to stay warm.

The knob turned, the door squeaked open. Rose's welcome gaze met her. "Hannah, I'm so glad you could leave off pleasuring that simply edible man to come spend a little time with us."

"Pleasuring him? I left him doing the supper dishes," Hannah teased back, stepping through the threshold. Then froze.

"Surprise!" Ten women, all friendly faces and joyful smiles, stood up from around one of Rose's dining room tables.

Holly moved away and gestured toward the table where a pile of gifts, the folded quilt they'd just finished, and a wonderful white frosted layer cake crowded the surface.

"Congratulations," Rose trilled, helping Hannah off with her wraps. "Abby brought the coffee—her father ordered it from back East. Doesn't it smell wonderful? And Paula made the cake—you know she's the best baker among us. And Holly thought, well, we all thought the quilt should go to you."

"What?" Hannah caught her breath.

"It's from all of us," Holly said and stepped forward to hold out her hand. "You deserve it, Hannah. You deserve to be happy in this new marriage."

"But the quilt was made for you, for your wedding." She couldn't believe the generosity, the sweetness of such a gift.

"Holly isn't getting married until June. Stop arguing." Paula grabbed Hannah by the elbow and pulled her down into a chair. "Now, open my gift first. I started it the instant I suspected Colton was hot for you."

The women tittered.

Rose returned with a steaming pot of coffee.

Hannah blushed. "He isn't hot—"

"Sure." Blanche Mullen winked. "That man's lukewarm and mediocre. A real dud."

Nine women chuckled in agreement.

Hannah's fingers trembled as she unwrapped the decorated paper from Paula's gift. "Oh," she breathed, fingering the delicate work, the elegant lace edging the pillow cases and the edges of the top sheet, and the elaborate embroidered rose bouquets in white thread against the cream flannel fabric. "Paula, I can't accept—"

"Yes, you can, because it's for love." Paula's eyes filled. "That's what I wish for you and Colton."

So impossible. Hannah looked longingly at the precious gift.

"Open mine next," Abby chimed above the din. "Actually, it might be something more for Colton than for you, Hannah."

The women oohed in anticipation. Hannah's fingers

shook as she unfolded the paper. She held up a delicate silk nightgown edged with machine-stitched lace.

"Colton will love this," Paula announced. "He can see right through it."

See right through it? She could never wear this for him, standing before his eyes, letting him see... He was a stranger to her, even if he was her husband.

Really. She and Colton had a different arrangement. A business agreement. Hannah thought of his hands on her body, hot against her skin and it made her feel...very warm.

"Look, she's blushing," Rose teased.

Delighted laughter filled the room.

* * *

The clomp of horse hooves against the frozen ground echoed in the yard. Colton straightened from his work, swiped his brow, and glanced through the open barn doors into the starlit night.

Hannah's mustang. Hannah's shape, elegant and slight, sitting astride that horse. The worries that had knotted him up all evening eased. He hadn't liked letting her go to town alone, but the night was too cold to haul Zac to Rose's and back twice in an evening. Besides, the suggestion had made Hannah mad.

Remembering the way anger darkened her eyes and scrunched up her pretty face made him smile. He considered it progress. Anything was better than the wary distance she'd kept from him over the past weeks.

"What do you have there?"

"Gifts." She drew back on the reins, halting the horse just outside the barn doors. "They're tied to my saddle, tied behind the saddle, hung over my saddlehorn."

"Some people believe this is a real marriage," Colton commented as he took the bundle she offered him. A big blanket. He set it on the clean, new hay, for the floor was in need of sweeping.

"Shows you what some people know." Lantern light danced across her face, showing the sparkle of humor in her eyes.

She dismounted, and he caught her elbow, helping her down. The feel of her slim arm felt right in his hand. The luxury of her so close made him catch his breath.

"Did you finish the dishes?" Curious eyes, not laughing.

Colton wondered at that. "Zac will be my witness. I washed, dried, and put them away."

"Thank you." She dipped her chin, then spun away from him. "I had a nice time tonight."

"I'm glad."

So close, he wanted to reach out and pull her against him. Feel the heat of her in his arms. He was tired of being alone, tired of being lonely.

"How's Zac?" She lifted a bag down from the saddlehorn.

He jumped to help her with the others. For purely selfish reasons. They worked side by side, and he inhaled her flowery scent, breathed in her nearness. She made him want what he could never deserve again.

"He's sound asleep, snug in his bed with his kitten." Colton lifted down the last parcel. "I just checked on him."

"He's safe alone in the house?"

"I locked the door. He's not going to wander off into the night." Or no one would be wandering in. "Zac sleeps straight through til morning, once he's down."

"He's a good boy." So much affection in that voice. Hannah reached for the mare's reins. "You've done an admirable job caring for him, Colton. Most men would not have done so much."

"He's my son." Colton never understood what made a man walk away from his own flesh and blood. His own father had. "And caring for him—" He cleared his throat.

Hannah paused in the wide aisle, waiting.

"Well, I know Ella would want me to do my best. She died suddenly, before she could ask that of me." He ground his jaw, fighting hard against the rise of memory. "I know it's what she would want."

"Such loyalty." Even in the shadows there was no mistaking the wonder in her eyes. "How you must have loved her."

"I didn't deserve her." *Just like I don't deserve you.* But he would keep Hannah safe. He wouldn't let anyone harm her. "Go ahead and leave your mare. I'll tend her."

"I don' t mind." Hannah opened a stall, and the mustang disappeared from his sight.

Stubborn. Independent. She didn't need him. Colton knew it. He wandered out into the night and breathed deep, scenting the wind. No cigarette smoke. No sound of trouble. Everything was as it should be—the chomp of the still-injured elk in the south corral, the whoof of one of the giant workhorses bedding down for the night, the hoo-hoo of an owl perched on the peak of the barn roof. And the house, safe and dark, where his son lay tucked beneath his blankets.

"What was she like?"

"Who?" He turned. His pulse jumped at the sight of her, so pretty with her hair down, wearing the blue checked dress he liked so well.

"Your wife."

"You're my wife." He grabbed up his pitchfork and stepped around her packages. "Let's see. You're a damn good cook and pretty as a picture and—"

"That's not what I mean, and you know it." She tossed him a grin as she produced a second pitchfork. "Do you really think I'm pretty?"

"Absolutely. I would never marry an ugly woman, not even for her land." He winked, only teasing, and her musical laughter, sweet and light, eased the tightness in his chest.

"What was Zac's mother like?" She caught a forkful of hay and tossed it into the mow with a neat, well practiced flick.

"Hannah, I don't expect you to do barn work." It didn't sit right with him. "It's my job, just like caring for Zac is yours."

"You took care of Zac tonight." She filled her fork and pitched again.

"Yeah, well, I didn't have a party to go to."

"So I'll help you with your work tonight." She paused to swipe sunshine gold curls from her eyes. "Besides, I'm too worked up to go right to sleep. And I like barn work."

"I thought you hated all the manure shoveling."

"Well, yes, that. But I love working with the animals. And I love the fresh smell of hay." She resumed pitching and he joined her, amazed by her, by everything about her. "You promised we could work the ranch together. I've had so much to do, fixing up Zac's room, but now I'd like to start working with the horses again."

"What about Zac?"

"He naps."

She worked hard. He had to give her credit for that. She forked the hay quickly, with a light, sweeping touch. She was even more competent inside the house. The meals were always wholesome and tasty, her house sparkling; his clothes were not just clean, but smelled good like sunshine.

He owed her much. "Do what you want," he said, because he knew she'd like him for it.

And she did, rewarding him with a sizzling grin that made his knees weak.

"You still haven't answered my question." She set down her pitchfork and rescued the blue and green quilt, laying it carefully on her discarded coat.

"Which question?"

"The one about your first wife." She was careful to be specific this time. "I'd like to know."

"What?" He kept his back to her, moving with athletic grace, a powerful ripple of eye-catching muscle. A thin sheen of sweat glistened along his naked, sun-browned back, caught in the touch of the lantern's light. "There's nothing to know."

"Do you regret having to marry me, because of her?"

Hannah had always wondered since the day he'd brought his son to live with her.

"Why would I regret marrying you? Aside from your third rule." He tossed her a flashy grin.

Her heart wedged in her ribs. She thought of that silky nightgown, hardly more than a chemise, and wondered what it would feel like to have real silk against her skin.

Silly thought.

"Maybe you weren't ready to marry again." She watched his bare back stiffen. "Maybe you wish you didn't have to replace her memory with someone like me."

"Someone like you. What does that mean?" He twisted to catch her gaze. "You work hard. You clearly adore my son. I have no regrets."

Hannah didn't believe him. She saw the shadows in his eyes, dark and unreadable. "You said she died suddenly."

"And I buried her." No emotion in his words, yet his sorrow felt as deep as the night. "She was good and kind and honorable, and it's my fault she's dead. Is that what you want to know?"

"Colton, I'm sorry. I just—" She'd only wondered about love in a marriage, if such things—pleasure and pleasing—could happen between a man and a woman.

"Yes, I loved her." He threw down his pitchfork and wiped the sweat from his brow.

"Charles didn't love me. He never loved me. I've learned enough to know that there are more important things than love. Like a husband who never loses his temper, who solves problems rather than rant and rave over them." Her heart broke, unable to tell him how much it meant to her that she didn't have to be afraid. "You haven't hurt me, Colton, just like you said. It means everything to me."

He chucked the last of the hay into the mow, then set aside the pitchfork. "Hannah." He approached her deliberately, a powerful man with tender understanding alight in his eyes. "I'll never hurt you. Not with my anger or my temper or my fist. I'm glad you believe that."

"I do." He towered above her, so close she could see the flecks of black in his eyes and the stubble of a day's growth along his jaw. She longed to lay her hand on his face and feel that wondrous texture against her palm.

He bent to retrieve her quilt and slip her cloak over her shoulders. "You're wrong about one thing. There's nothing more important than love."

Her chin wobbled. Her heart stilled. Every wish she'd ever made as a foolish girl teased her now.

"Come on." He gathered up her gifts. "Since you helped me with my work, I'll do something for you. I'd love to draw you a nice, hot bath."

"I'd like that." She wanted him to kiss her, to feel the brush of his lips against hers one more time.

"Me, too." He smiled at her, starlight dusting his handsome face, changing him from man to hero.

"But I bathe alone," she reminded him, waiting while he grabbed his shirt and the flickering lantern.

"I've seen you in a tub before. Are you sure you won't change your mind?"

"Positive," she lied.

* * *

Steam fogged the kitchen windows as Hannah slipped through the threshold, closing the inner door behind her. "Zac's still asleep with his kitten."

"You've done a fine job of fixing up his room." Colton emptied the last bucket into her washtub, vapor rising from the water's surface.

"It was my pleasure." She went straight to the bread box and lifted the lid. "I hope to make him a little quilt as soon as I finish the new clothes I'm planning."

"You should have bought some fabric for yourself." Colton set the bucket on the floor near the bright red stove. "After all that sewing, you ought to have something for yourself."

"I have plenty. Besides, Zac comes first." Hannah

thought of the little shirts and trousers she had in mind. "I've always looked forward to sewing for a child."

He leaned against the work table. "That cake sure looks good."

"There were two pieces left over tonight, and Paula insisted I take them home." Hannah's heart fluttered as Colton's finger reached out and scooped a luscious dollop of frosting from one of the slices. "I brought them for you and Zac."

Colton's eyes darkened as he held his finger, loaded with frosting, to her lips.

Her stomach flip-flopped. She opened her mouth and reached out with her tongue. She tasted sweetness and salty male skin. Before she could catch her breath, his mouth covered hers, demanding and hot. His lips caressed hers with a wondrous friction. Little sparks of sensation fired along her mouth. Hannah tipped back her head and sighed. Her entire body tingled.

Colton's tongue dove into her mouth. Pleasure swept along her tongue, across her teeth, and deeper. Everywhere he touched her, she felt alive, on fire. Nothing had ever felt like this.

She took a ragged breath, unwilling to move away. His hands cupped her face, his kiss deepened, exploring as she clutched at his shirt, spellbound by such feelings.

Maybe Rose was right. Maybe there was some pleasure to be experienced. She opened her eyes to find him watching her, passion dark in his gaze, his mouth damp from possessing hers.

Don't let it end. Long, breathless seconds passed. His hands, locked against either side of her face, slid downward. Delicious heat swirled in her belly. Tantalizing sensation curled around her spine. Colton's thumbs rested at the base of her neck. She could feel the fluttering thumps of her heartbeat, see the corresponding excitement flickering in his eyes. The length of his arousal felt hard against her thigh. They were far too close. These feelings far too dangerous.

She ought to stop him, move away, find her sanity. But as his kiss grew tender, infinitely gentle, all reason fled. There was only this delicious melting sensation of her bones, of her will. And the heat of his hands caressing lower, then lower still, over the curve of her breasts.

It shouldn't be like this, like fire licking through her veins, then a tug of twisting ache, powerful and strange, deep in her abdomen. Sweet heaven. It was too much, she felt too much. Hannah tore her mouth from his and struggled to breathe.

His fingers fumbled against her bodice. Buttons opened. Her knees wobbled while she waited through long seconds. Then one hand dipped beneath the layers of her undergarments and covered the bare skin of her left breast.

Hannah moaned deep into her throat. Her eyes fluttered shut, her head fell back. Her hands found his shoulders, broad and solid beneath her touch. She clung to him as his hand kneaded her flesh, scorching her with need and want His thumb found her nipple and she bit her lip for fear of crying out again. Desire clamped tight in her belly, desire for him.

Somehow he'd pushed her dress down to her hips with his free hand, and the garment fell to the floor. His lips nipped the arc of her throat. Soon she was bare, her corset unlaced, tossed away, her chemise puddled at her ankles, and she stood only in her drawers before him. But instead of feeling shy, she only wanted him to keep touching her, keep brushing sweet, blessed sensation through every inch of her body.

She'd been lonely for so long. Hungry for a man's touch. And for far too long, she hadn't believed a man's strength could be in his tenderness, in the gentle affection of his touch, in the kindness of word and deed.

Tears crowded her eyes as his mouth closed over one bare breast. Her breath caught as his tongue laved her nipple over and over again. Hannah fought to breathe, but all she could manage was a moan. So much pleasure, it engulfed her, threatened to drown her; it invaded and overtook every bit of her body, every part of her mind. All she wanted was this, this way he was suckling her, touching her. She never wanted it to end, even if it was too much. How could she bear so much pleasure? So much wondrous sensation? She didn't know if she could endure more without exploding into a million parts.

Colton's hands brushed over her ribs, exploring, caressing, and so he couldn't move from her breast, she caught his head with her hands and held him there, pressing kisses across the length of his brow.

They felt it at the same time. She knew from the way he stiffened. His touch at the scar cutting across her abdomen, ridged and rough, reminded her of all that could never be.

"What happened?" Colton gazed up at her, his mouth damp, his eyes still bright with passion.

She reached for her chemise and held it up to cover her body from his gaze. It was a flimsy barrier. Still, she struggled into it, the only decent thing to do.

"Are you going to tell me what happened?"

She pushed away from the counter. "It doesn't concern you."

"Is that the reason why you're barren?" Colton watched the light fade from her eyes, as if all the hope had left her.

She hung her head, staring at the floor. "Maybe." Her quiet words shivered, low like harmony without melody. "If you knew Charles, you know how easily he could lose his temper."

"When he drank." Colton nodded. He'd worked as a deputy in Arizona when he'd known Charles, a man who a few times ended up sleeping off the effects of his temper and too much whiskey in the jail. "I've seen that side of him."

She pulled one pin out of her hair. Blond curls fell free. She reached for another pin. "He was terribly angry I hadn't become pregnant right away. He wanted a son. It was all he wanted. All he talked about." Tears shimmered in those words.

Colton waited.

"Two years of marriage, and I hadn't conceived. He was furious with me. So furious." She swallowed.

Every cell inside Colton vibrated with anger. Anger at any man who would treat a woman so.

"He drank more and more. He lost his temper often. He made my life a living nightmare." Hannah lifted her face, revealing the fearful memories in her eyes.

"Did he beat you?"

In answer, she laid a hand over her stomach, flat and empty. Tears glistened in her eyes, rolled down her face. "What I'd been praying for finally happened. I was going to have a baby of my own. Finally, I was going to have an infant to hold and nurse and sew for and love."

She released a shaky breath. "Charles told me it had better be a son, but I knew in my heart it wasn't. I loved that little girl with all my heart, because it tore me apart that Charles would never value her. She was going to be everything to me, my own precious baby. But one night, Charles came home very drunk and in a foul mood. He'd been cheated at a card game or so he believed, and he took it out on me. I was too fat and ugly to lay with. He wanted to..."

She hesitated. "I was so angry with him. I never should have talked back to him, I never should have opened my mouth, but it made me so angry that he valued the life within me so little. In a rage, he pushed me down the back steps. I fell hard and cut myself pretty badly." She sobbed, just once. "I went into labor and lost the baby."

Colton's heart ached. He reached out to comfort her, but she shook her head, moved away.

"I just can't" Her mouth crumpled. "I can't—"

He stepped forward and pulled her into his arms anyway. She buried her face against his chest and silent tears wet his shirt.

It would be too easy to care, too simple to involve his heart. Colton pressed a kiss to her forehead and wished he could be the man she needed, the one she deserved.

"Let's get you into your bath," he said.

She nodded and moved away from him. Not just in body, but in spirit. Colton knew without asking she would not let him that close again, close enough to see the lonely sorrow in her heart.

Helpless to do more, he left the room.

* * *

Images of her beautiful, naked body felt burned into his eyes. Every time he blinked, there she was, lush breasts and sweet thighs and endless vulnerability.

Colton leaned back in the chair and stretched. Tightness bunched in his neck and shoulders, for the length of wood was heavy. He'd finished the last tongue and groove, and now he could lay the pieces out on the barn floor in the light of the lantern to judge how best to begin.

He lifted his gaze, scanning the darkness outside the barn, listening to the normal sounds of the night. No scent of cigarette smoke.

Colton thought of the guns strapped to his hips. He wasn't taking any chances. Not this time.

He studied the wood before him, pieces that when fit and glued would make both a head and a foot board for his son's bed. The wood frame holding the small mattress tick was adequate, but not special. Colton knew how the boy loved animals. He planned to inlay carved kitty and puppy faces along the top edges of the wood, happy faces that would please Zac.

Dissatisfied with the slightly imperfect fit of one board against another, he lifted the piece, settled back into his chair, and deftly scratched his knife over the carved edge.

He'd been a fool to touch Hannah tonight, to take liberties with her. It wasn't as if he could give her a heart whole and loving.

He would not be sleeping next to her, teased by the light fragrance of her silky skin and tempting hair. At least not until the intruder who intended harm was caught and dealt with. It was just as well.

Colton felt the darkness, sensed the threat even if it wasn't close tonight.

Whatever happened, he would be ready for it.

CHAPTER THIRTEEN

Colton woke with a start. The dream swirled around in his head, still gripping him, as bright as reality in his mind. Ella sprawled out in the bed, a spray of blood against the wall, the pool of it turning black on the quilt beneath her. Sightless brown eyes staring up at him, silence, the emptiness, his heart shattering. *Where was the baby?*

Horror rocked through him. Colton jumped to his feet. The chair clattered to the floor. His pulse pumped in his chest. Sweat dripped off his brow.

The peaceful world stared back at him. The sickle moon hung low in the sky, the pines like dependable sentries guarding the edge of night, the whisper of an owl gliding by, hunting field mice. Cold winter wind breezed through him, pure and cleansing.

Yet the ugliness—the guilt—remained. Colton took a breath and rubbed the sweat from his forehead.

Every night for the past three weeks he'd dreamed of Ella. Since the night he'd drawn Hannah's bath and undressed her and tasted the sweetness of her breasts.

The truth was simple: Hannah wouldn't have married

him but to keep her ranch and home. She had little choice. And while he knew he needed to marry for Zac's sake, to provide the tiny vulnerable child with a mother, Colton knew better than to involve his heart.

Life was fragile. He'd been the cause of Ella's death. He could never face such loss—and such responsibility—again. He could not risk coming to love Hannah. He did not have the right or the heart.

* * *

"So you're the man who's stolen my snow broom," Hannah teased as she strode nearer over the crunching snow, shivering despite her layers of wool and flannel.

Colton shrugged, a man of power and strength with shadows in his eyes. "You caught me. I'm guilty as charged."

"Snow broom," Zac agreed, pointing with one little red gloved hand. "Papa."

The sight of the cute little boy could warm her straight through even on this frigid January morning. Hannah squeezed his little hand within hers. "Your papa thinks he can just take anything he wants without asking first."

"Trouble." Serious eyes wide, Zac shook his head.

"Are you saying I'm in trouble?" This time Colton managed a grin, adoration alight in his eyes.

Zac nodded. "Trouble. Big trouble."

Amusement brought out those rakish dimples. "Is that true, Hannah? Are you going to punish me?"

"No cookies for you." She held out her hand. "I thought I'd sweep off the front steps if you'll hand over the broom."

"I'll be more than happy to do it." Colton knocked at the flakes clinging to the brim of his hat. "I'm trying to get the snow off these new boards so I can lay more of the floor this morning. When I saw you coming, I thought you might want to help."

"If the barn work is finished."

"Absolutely. I even fed our pet bull elk." Colton scooped Zac up in his strong arms. "Do you see him?"

Hannah reached for the fallen broom rather than reach out for father and son. Ever since the night in the kitchen, Colton had kept his distance. Always polite, always good-natured, always complimentary, but never affectionate.

She didn't blame him. It wasn't as if he married her for love. What truly mattered was that she was safe from harm, for now she'd come to believe Colton would never hurt her. She had a home and a son to care for, a little child dependent upon her for his happiness and well being. She couldn't ask for more.

"That bull elk is still limping," Colton reported. "With hay so expensive, I don't want to feed him. But on the other hand, he'd never make it on his own until he heals. I don't think he'll be here much longer, by the look of that wound."

Hannah gave the broom a good shake. "That elk knows he has it good. He doesn't have to forage for food by digging up all this snow. You walk over to him and give him hay. Why should he leave?"

"He's still a little shy, but he lets me come up to him." Colton's eyes shone as he turned to study the thick-necked animal penned up with the prized Percherons. "I always dreamed of something like this. Hawks and eagles hunting in the skies overhead, a moose wandering through the yard, a herd of deer bedded down near the house for the night. This is the kind of life I want for my son."

"Snowmen." Zac pointed at the ground, not at all interested in the breathtaking display of nature, the snow-covered virgin forest, or majestic white-capped mountains so close they felt touchable.

Laughing, Colton lowered his son to the ground. He tugged the new red cap a little lower to better cover those little ears and sent Zac on his way. The boy fell to his knees and began scooping up snow.

Colton turned to watch his wife, his fair Hannah,

vigorously sweeping the remains of last night's snowstorm from the new barn floor. She worked hard—he admired that. Yet she always had a smile ready for Zac. Always put him first in her life.

Her affection showed in a dozen little things, in a hundred different ways. Colton recognized it because he'd known the lack of caring in his own childhood, and it made him all the more grateful for her efforts concerning his son. She made cute red gloves, hat, and scarf, and a warm striped sweater to match. She sewed trousers and underthings and adorable flannel shirts, all made with care. Every stitch just so, sewn with love.

"Fiddle!" Zac's joyful protest rang in the still air as the little orange cat darted into the path of his growing snowball. "Silly kitty."

"He wants to help you, Zac." Hannah's voice smiled, warm and sunny.

"Silly," Zac laughed. So much glee.

Colton grabbed up the saw. He would cut the boards to length while Hannah nailed them into place. He took his time, for when the sawing was done, he would join Hannah on the new floor and work with her side by side until she needed to head indoors to start the noon meal.

Being close to her riled him up, made him remember how sweet and passionate she'd tasted—and acted—beneath his touch.

He couldn't have her. Wouldn't involve his heart. But his body, thrumming with desire, wanted more. He closed his eyes against the images in his mind—of her head thrown back, eyes closed and mouth open, her breath quick and shallow, her breasts filling his hand, the tantalizing nub of her nipple in his mouth.

And he wanted more. He wanted to know all of her, the silken curve of her thighs, the damp wetness that welcomed him in, the tight grip of her body, the sound of her surrender.

Considering it was barely ten degrees in the sun, Colton

felt damn hot.

* * *

Hannah glanced at the sleigh flying up her road and then at the dark clouds crowding the northern rim of the horizon.

"Glad I thought to come out early," Paula's voice trilled from the kitchen doorway. "It's hardly light yet and there are twelve men standing around jawing in your barnyard."

"Soon to be thirteen. Eaton Baker's just pulling up." Hannah couldn't hide her surprise.

"My, my, the upper crust of Paradise." Paula tapped up to the parlor window and peered through the lace curtains. "Baker must think a lot of your Colton to come help him like this. I don't know if Eaton knows how to hold a hammer."

"Maybe he's come to supervise." Hannah rubbed her forehead. "I should have asked Rose to bring her coffee pots, too."

"Now, I brought two from my kitchen, and they're boiling away on your stove as we speak. We'll have those men warmed up with enough coffee to get those walls raised and a roof on before that storm gets here."

"I hope you're right. It looks like a nasty one on the way." They'd had their unfair share of blizzards last winter, one after another, deadly and frightening. "I'm really glad you're here. It's beyond the call of duty."

"My pleasure." Paula glanced over her shoulder at the little boy on the floor before the hearth, playing with his toy horses, the kitty nearby, stretched and asleep, absorbing the fire's heat. "It does my heart good to see you've made a real family, Hannah. This house has been too long without children. I'm happy for you."

"Thanks." Her chest tightened. She thought of all the distance between her and Colton, the scars too old and deep to mend. Yet they had at the same time forged a mutual respect. That was more than most marriages had. Certainly she'd never had half as much with Charles.

155

"Now, I know you're worried, but I'm used to cooking for a lot of hungry people." Paula trotted back to the kitchen. "With that huge roast you've got in the oven, and the sliced ham I brought from my kitchen, why, all we need is a soup pot full of potatoes to boil. You made two pots of baked beans like I suggested?"

Hannah knelt to brush her hand over Zac's curls. He tipped his head back and smiled. He would be all right playing by himself. She stepped over the kitten and headed toward the kitchen. "Yes. The beans only need to be warmed on top of the stove for a bit. Colton set up board tables in the barn because that many men just aren't going to fit in my kitchen."

The back door blew open with a puff of cold wind and he filled the threshold, all wide shoulders and muscled man. "Hannah, come walk with me. I have to talk something over with you."

Excitement flickered in Colton's eyes, but the curve of his mouth remained grim. Leaving Paula in charge with a promise to watch over Zac, Hannah lifted her cloak from the wall peg and followed him outside. "What is it?"

"Baker came today with an offer. I'd like you to consider it." He laid a hand on her shoulder, such a comforting and undeniably possessive touch.

Hannah's heart stalled. Would he ever kiss her again? Ever make her lose control the way she had that night before her bath, naked and craving him?

"What offer?"

"He wants to buy six of our Percheron mares."

"Six?" Hannah took a step back. "No. They're breeding stock. It would jeopardize the ranch's future profits."

"But Baker's brother in Missoula is the mayor and he's looking for six more workhorses to pull cars for the city. They'd be well cared for and not overworked. It's a good opportunity."

"No. Besides, prices are low right now like they are every winter. I don't want to sell at a loss."

"Those six mares eat an enormous amount of hay in a week. We can save that money if we sell them now and consider it a profit." He lifted one dark brow. A half smile haunted his mouth. "What do you say?"

"No. It's a bad decision. I won't sell my brood mares."

"But the sale will help us out."

"Colton." She tried to ignore the charm of his smile and the way his hand burned heat straight into her blood. "They're my horses and I say no."

"They're my horses, too, remember." He rubbed his brow. "Look, we have enough money to see us through, but Hannah, it could still be a mean winter ahead. We could lose stock we'd have to replace come spring. Think about it."

"I can't." Buying the Percherons had been her decision, and she'd pushed Charles until he thought the investment sound, too. She adored those gentle giants and firmly believed they would bring more profit than cattle would have, even from the sale of the other horses. "Besides, I love those mares. They're mine. I raised three of them from foals born right here on this land."

He cocked his chin. "Are you always this stubborn?"

"No." She caught his hand. Tiny frissons of awareness telegraphed over her skin. "You won't sell them without my permission?"

"I'm thinking of it." He didn't blink, didn't flinch. Yet where she always expected anger, only kindness shaped his face, crinkled in the corners of his eyes. "It will be my decision, Hannah. You have to understand. I will do what I think best to provide for my wife and son."

"And my decision doesn't matter?"

He covered her mouth with his before she could protest, before she could back away. The distant ring of hammers, the call of a sparrow, the bite of the wind all ebbed and flowed until there was only Colton, only the firm, demanding pressure of his lips to hers, the caress of his tongue. Hannah's pulse jumped and she leaned on tiptoe into him, knowing darn well she should pull away. His iron-strong arms enfolded her, binding her to him.

She moaned against his mouth. He breathed in her kiss. Amazing tremors rippled through her body. Lord, her insides would melt if they kept this up, so hot and sweet.

Colton moaned low in his throat. His tongue laved her bottom lip in a slow, sensuous caress, then his teeth nipped her lower lip and drew it into his mouth. Dizzy, breathless, Hannah could only hold onto the muscled steel of his arms.

She shivered from the cold, and he drew her closer. She started when she felt the hard ridge of his arousal against the inner curve of her thigh, so amazing and wonderful the air squeezed from her lungs.

Dazed, Hannah looked up to meet his gaze. Saw the invitation, the want. Being touched by him, by this man of honor, was so different than she expected, so different from the cold duty Charles had demanded with his quick, rough touches and hard-mouthed kisses.

"Colton, I—"

She only had time to catch her breath before his mouth covered hers again. He towered over her, and she melted against his solid chest. A building, coiling need pumped through her blood.

The back door banged open, and Hannah startled from Colton's arms. He let her go. She looked up in apology, her senses ready to explode, her heart hammering. Passion snapped in Colton's dark eyes. A passion that said he wasn't finished with her yet.

She shivered, whether in anticipation or fear she didn't know.

"You're becoming a temptation I can't resist." He touched her cheek. Gentle. Tender. Then he smiled. "I better join the men. They'll have those walls up and the rafters started without me."

His hand brushed her jaw, compassion in his eyes so bright it could light up the lonely places in her heart. Then he simply walked away.

"Hmm. Looks like someone won't need a cup of coffee to warm him up," Paula said and winked from the top step. "Rose just breezed in and is making a mess in your kitchen. Why don't you help me take all this coffee out to the men?"

Hannah nodded, unable to lift her gaze from Colton's retreating figure until he was nothing more than a shadow against the sun-dusted snow.

* * *

Colton perched on the peak of the trusses, hammer in hand, a row of nails tucked between his lips. Nearly two dozen men from town and neighboring ranches crawled around the structure of the new barn—bigger than the original, yet still only a skeleton. Frigid cold blasted him. And he looked up, studying the sky, darker than lead.

A movement along the road caught his eye. A lone rider astride a dark bay, spine straight and arrogant. Glen Sawyer. The bastard dared to show his face? Colton's mouth soured. He knew without a doubt this man posed a threat to his family.

"Came to lend a hand," Glen called out, sounding amicable.

Colton climbed to the ground and wasn't fooled.

"Thanks, Sawyer, but I don't need your help. We already have enough men on the job."

"Looks to me with the storm moving in, you could use me."

Colton saw the cold flash in Sawyer's dark eyes and the holstered revolver strapped to his left thigh. "A man doesn't need a gun to build a barn."

"No, but a man never knows what vermin he's going to come across." Glen didn't blink, dead calm and calculating. "Or when a man will need to fight for what's his."

The ring of so many hammers had ceased. Colton looked up and judged the faces of the men—some concerned, some curious—and waved them back to their work. The sheriff met his gaze. Trouble.

Colton turned back to Sawyer. "Glen, Hannah was never yours."

"She would have been if you hadn't stepped in my way." Flat eyes, black with warning, hard in the way of a man who lacked conscience.

"A man can't own a woman. She isn't a possession."

"That's rather liberal thinking, isn't it?" Dark mirth twisted across Sawyer's face. "When Hannah is my wife, I won't be sleeping in the barn."

"Hannah will never be your wife." Colton smelled the man's threat, read it in the empty hatred of his eyes. "Even if I hadn't come to town, Hannah would not have married you. We both know it. She doesn't want another man like Charles, a drunk and a brute."

"I'm nothing like Charles, and Hannah knows it." Fury glittered, bright and lethal, but his words came whispered, not meant for the men hard at work on the new barn less than twenty feet away. "Too bad you won't be around, Kincaid, when I make Hannah mine."

"I don't kill easily, Sawyer." Colton's hand itched. He thought of his gun belt rolled up in the top shelf of the tack room, away from a tiny boy's reach. "Then again, a coward like you, preying on a man in the dark, can't have much of a draw."

"Really?" Glen lifted one mocking brow. "Haven't you wondered why that bull elk didn't show up in your corral this morning? You thought he was well enough and left to join his herd, didn't you?"

Colton watched, his stomach sick, as Sawyer lifted a wrapped package from his saddlebag.

"Care for any venison?" The triumphant laugh cut like a knife, gouging the pleasant afternoon into pieces. Glen dropped the meat to the ground. It landed with a sickening thump on the snow.

"Watch your back, Kincaid," Sawyer warned before he

reined his horse around and headed back down the road.

And to hell, for all Colton cared.

"I heard what he said," Baker murmured, reaching into his coat pocket for a cigar.

Colton declined with a shake of his head when the sheriff offered him one. "I can handle Sawyer. I've run into his kind before."

"I bet you have." Baker struck a match, cupping the flame to protect it from the brisk north wind. "I'm going to go talk to him tonight, remind him when a man makes a threat the way he just did, he'd better watch his step. You wind up dead and I'll have his neck in a noose so fast, he won't be able to catch his breath."

"I appreciate it, Eaton." Colton knew without a doubt Sawyer was the man in the dark, smoking his cigarettes. The waiting was over.

He caught sight of Hannah, carrying a huge silvered tray balanced in both hands, refreshments for the men working so hard. She walked with an easy, unassuming grace that drew his gaze. Her skirts snapped in the wind, whipping tight around her slim body and hugging lean legs and smooth hips. His groin kicked at the memory of how light and sweet she'd felt in his arms. How eagerly she'd kissed him back.

He had no heart for love, but comfort was another thing. One day he would lay her down in that bed they no longer shared because of Sawyer, because of the threat he posed, and Colton vowed to show her how comforting it could feel to be pleasured by a man.

"Apple pie?" Hannah smiled up at him, her eyes as bright as they'd been after he'd kissed her this morning, wrapping her in his arms and claiming her as his.

"Where's Zac?" He lifted a plate off the wide tray. A melting dollop of whipped cream, crumbling crust, cinnamony apple slices. He couldn't remember the last time he'd so much as looked at a dessert this good.

"He's napping with his kitty." Hannah's smile filled his

entire heart with the love she carried so quietly for his son.

She offered the sheriff a slice of pie, then hurried off toward the eager men climbing down from the height of the rafters, men who were already offering compliments on her fine baking.

Hannah blushed, shy, such a tiny thing. Her vulnerability touched him, soft and gentle and so sweet he wanted to believe in it. To let her change him, make him new.

* * *

Colton thanked Lars Johanson, one of the last men to leave, and offered him the packaged venison. He knew Johanson had eight small children to provide for and could use the fresh meat. Lars thought to reject the offering, but Colton insisted. The kindhearted Swede had been the first man to arrive and the last to leave. It was the least Colton could do.

As Johanson rode away on his big workhorse, the snow began to fall in earnest from the night sky. The light in the windows of the house shone warm and sustaining like a promise in the dark. Colton thought of his wife and son, snug and safe and trusting him to protect them, to provide for them. He thought of Glen Sawyer's bold threats and the gun the man wore strapped to his thigh.

Colton turned the lantern low in the barn as he worked. He would not make himself an easy target for Sawyer. Tonight, the hunt would begin.

Colton sat down on the porch to tug off his boots. His belly rumbled. First he needed supper and a full pot of coffee to chase away his hunger and the chill in his bones. Tender thoughts turned to Hannah. She was there, in the house, the lamps burning. He knew the kitchen would be hot, food and a full pot of coffee waiting just for him. That, and the warmth of her smile.

Colton pushed open the back door. Home. It was beginning to feel that way. Warm and welcoming. All Hannah's doing. She'd left a lamp, wick turned low, burning on the table. A single setting, flatware, a covered basket of bread, the butter pot, the sparkling clean blue enamel mug and plate. The scent of honeyed ham and her sweet molasses baked beans teased his nose, made his mouth water.

But Colton had a greater hunger. He crossed the room and followed the path of light to the parlor, faint and low. A fire snapped in the hearth—he could hear the pop of flames needing fuel.

Hannah. He froze in the threshold. Every bit of his defenses, of the bitter memories of his past faded at the sight of her cradling his son in her slender, protective arms. Longing ached deep in his chest—the need to touch and be touched, hold and be held.

The fire glowed deep orange in the hearth, nearly embers, casting a red hue to the shadows in the room to caress the hem of a woman's dress. Hannah's dress. A blue knit afghan covered the tiny boy she cuddled in her lap.

Zac slept soundly, his head nestled beneath Hannah's drooping chin. A book had fallen closed in her hand, gripped tightly even in sleep, her precious volume of children's nursery rhymes. His heart flipped over. Tenderness for his son, for her filled his chest.

"Oh, Colton." Her voice was as soft as a snowy morning. "I must have fallen asleep."

"Intolerable." Just seeing her smile made his heart thud faster. "Want me to take him upstairs?"

"Yes."

He knelt closer. The faint scent of honeysuckle brushed his nose as he lifted the sweet, light weight of his son into his arms. Zac mumbled, fast asleep, and settled against Colton's chest.

"He's worn out." She rose with a rustling of skirts. "He was so excited watching the barn go up. He loved seeing his papa on the roof."

"Well, I'm glad someone had fun today." Colton started up the stairs, into the dark second story. "I about wore my arm out doing all that hammering."

"It looks fine to me." A light, teasing voice, and something deeper.

"Do you like my arms?"

"Not at all." There came a glass clink as Hannah grabbed a lamp, and the flash and dance of light licked up the steps behind him. But the lie in her voice—he could recognize that even with his back turned, even so exhausted he could hardly stand up.

Colton smiled to himself. "I appreciate all your work today. I'm now the envy of half the men in Paradise. They figure you're one of the best cooks in the county."

"That was Paula's doing." Hannah slipped around him in the hall. Her shoulder brushed his arm. He ached at the nearness. Oh, to feel a woman's touch against his bare skin.

Hannah pushed open Zac's door and set the lamp on the little stand beside the bed still missing the headboard— he hadn't finished carving it. She pulled back the warm down comforter and he knelt to lay Zac gently between the soft blue flannel sheets.

Colton's heart twisted as the little boy snuggled against his pillow, lost in sweet dreams.

With a meow, the orange kitten hopped up on the bed and curled up against Zac's shoulder. Hannah pulled the comforter snug beneath the tiny child's chin, above the sounds of the kitty's happy purring.

Colton thought of Sawyer's threat and of the past when he'd almost lost his son. His throat ached with what he didn't know how to say.

"He's so cute," Hannah whispered, tilting her head to one side, a cascade of blond curls falling against the curve of her soft face. She was courageous enough. Her heart was big enough.

Colton drew her to his side. "Promise me," he said, although with the closeness of her slender body against his, he did not want to speak of sad things.

"Promise you what?" A certain amount of happiness sparkled in Hannah's blue eyes.

He felt good about that. A woman who treated his son so well, who worked so hard and earnestly, deserved to be happy. Regret twisted through his chest. He opened their bedroom door and walked straight past the four-poster bed to the wardrobe along the far wall. He dug behind his socks to pull out his second holster, the Colt Peacemaker unloaded, but cleaned and oiled.

"What do you want with that?"

"I have a feeling I'll need it." Colton pulled out a box of cartridges. The rattling of the bullets made Hannah's eyes widen as he shoved them into his shirt pocket. The truth of what he might have to do sobered him. "I need your most solemn vow, Hannah. I need to know now, before I leave this house tonight."

"What?" She held her fists tight as he strapped the gun to his hip. "Colton, has there been more trouble?"

"I just want your word, Hannah." He took her hand, cool to the touch. He was frightening her and he knew it. Damn. "If something happens to me, you will protect Zac with your life, won't you? You'll raise him as your own son. You'll make certain he grows up to be a good man, one who is everything I'm not."

"Colton, you're a fine man." Breathless, she gazed up at him. "Something is wrong. You must tell me. I have to know—"

"Keep Zac safe and the doors bolted." Colton grabbed a thick flannel shirt from the shelf. "I plan to put an end to all this worry tonight. I'm tired of sleeping in the barn trying to protect it and our animals. Now there are two structures and I cannot watch them both at the same time."

He laid a hand aside her face, her dear face, and pressed a quick kiss to her mouth. To his surprise she tipped her chin upward, deepening the caress of her luscious satin lips against his. Colton's groin kicked. His blood beat fast and hard through his veins. He wanted to lay her across that bed and undress her, to join them as man and wife.

"I'm tired of sleeping in the barn," he murmured in her ear and felt a tremble ripple through her body. "I have better things to do than guard the hay. Like showing my beautiful wife how to break rules."

"Rules?" Her eyes glistened like topaz, clear and deep.

"Hell, I'm not going to just break your rule number three." He snatched another kiss from her succulent lips before he turned toward the door. "I've waited long enough, Hannah. I'm your husband. I'm going to smash rule number three all to hell."

CHAPTER FOURTEEN

Colton's words pounded through Hannah's mind as she cleaned up the plates and flatware left for his supper. Prowling around the kitchen in the flickering lamplight, she could think of nothing else.

Hannah locked the door and turned down the wick. Darkness descended. She hesitated before the window, black from the storm outside. She could feel the tensed power of charged air. They would have a blizzard before midnight.

She pushed open the door. Thin light brushed over the tiny boy cuddled in his bed, sound asleep and safe as a child should be. Love ached in her chest.

She thought of the secrets in Colton's eyes. And of the dark, hard edge of power she'd seen tonight as he'd strapped on his second gun.

* * *

Colton heard the footsteps long before the door pushed open. A light gait. Hannah's step. The stallion nickered low in his throat, recognizing her, too. Lantern light shivered over her as she stepped into the barn.

"Hello, you big baby," she cooed, catching the horse's head in both hands and planting a kiss to his nose.

The stallion's nimble, velvety lips kissed her in return.

"I have competition." Colton coiled the last length of rope.

"Only for my heart." She tried to step away from the stallion, and the great beast gently caught her long gold braid with his big, sharp teeth. "Oh, Sam."

The stallion seemed pleased with his victory and accepted another pat of that slender hand.

Colton couldn't blame him. "I thought I told you to stay in the house."

"You did." She lifted her chin, a challenge veiled beneath that small confidence. And a risk, too. "I wanted to tell you to string up rope from here to the house so you can find your way once the blizzard hits, but you already have."

"The storm hasn't hit yet." He hung the rope from a nearby peg within easy reach.

"Are you going to stay out here all night?" Concern so huge in those words. "Will you be safe?"

"I'll be safe enough, Hannah." He felt warm inside, tingly and wanted, knowing she cared enough to ask. "The barn is snug and safe from anything that blizzard has to offer."

"I wasn't afraid of the blizzard." She wrapped her wool cloak more tightly around her and pulled tight the belt at her waist. "You left with your gun strapped to your thigh. You're expecting trouble."

"No, I'm ending it."

"How are you going to do that?" She said it quietly, but she had to know.

Light danced across his face, lined with strength and hiding something dark. "I'll do what I have to. I believe whoever burned down the barn and destroyed our winter feed is the same man. A man I intend to turn over to the sheriff as soon as I can catch him."

How could she voice her concerns? Colton was made of honor, she'd seen it, but the deeper layers of him, those she could not easily see, made her uncertain. Like the way he'd killed a man and wounded another. He had saved her and she would always be grateful, always be glad he broke through her door when he did. But he'd been a bounty hunter. A man who hunted and killed other men, criminals or no.

There was so much she didn't know about Colton. So much she needed to know.

"Hannah." His hand, at once comforting and unsettling, laid against her jaw. "You care."

So much power in that touch. So much gentleness. She couldn't deny it. "I don't want to see you hurt. I don't want—"

"I can take care of myself. Don't worry. I'll keep my promise."

"Which one?"

"All of them. Then I'm going to make love to you." Promise glimmered in his exhausted eyes.

Hannah's pulse jumped. His nearness burned through her like fire. She wanted to lay her hand against the flat of his chest and feel the beat of his heart and the amazing texture of male skin and muscle.

Blushing, she pushed past him, intent on returning to the house before she could act on her inappropriate notions. Better to think of business and of the purpose of their marriage. "I'd better not leave Zac alone too long. But I wanted to make certain you weren't planning anything rash. Anything dangerous." Her heart skipped a beat.

His eyes shadowed, unreadable. "No. I'm just protecting my family, Hannah. That's all. Let me walk you back to the house."

Colton held out one hand. His fingers twined through hers, palm to palm. Hot sizzles of desire flashed through her stomach at his touch, at being so near to him.

The cold night felt expectant. All of nature stood silent. Colton walked beside her, a tall, dark figure of a man, head up, studying the shadows.

For the first time in her life, she could see how a marriage could work. Happiness threatened to break loose inside her, to carry her away with its enormity. Her ranch was prospering—the new barn, the well-tended horses, the neat stack of wood piled out behind the house. Enough feed for the livestock. A pantry piled with foodstuffs. Enough pretty yarn to keep her busy all winter. And a family—her family. She had laughter in her house, a child to hold and care for, and pleasant meals around the kitchen table. Colton had given her all this.

Her gloved hand hesitated on the doorknob. She looked up and there he was, towering over her, so breathtaking.

"Sleep well, Hannah." His deep voice rumbled through her.

She craved his touch. The feel of his arms enfolding her. The comfort of being held against his solid chest.

His mouth caught hers, then he stepped away before she could draw him back, leaving her standing alone in the glow of lantern light from the window, aching for more of him. He didn't look back and he blended into the night, intent on his duty, determined to keep their future safe.

* * *

Colton bolted the kitchen door from the blizzard at his back. It was nearly five in the morning and yet with the storm, it felt as dark as night. He shook the ice from his clothes, but it was driven deep into the fabric. Snow scrubbed at the walls like sand. The room was cold, but thoughts of Hannah warmed his blood.

He wanted her. Yet how could she ever want him? If she knew of his past, learned of what he'd done, would she still gaze up at him with desire in her eyes?

He knelt to build a fire in the stove. He watched the embers catch hold of the kindling and flame. Watching, he thought of himself. When he lost Ella, he'd lost his heart, his life. Yet here, living beside Hannah, she stirred the embers inside him, long buried, and made him feel again, made him want. And that desire for her, like fuel added to a fire, burned.

Colton padded through the unlit room to the window and stared out into the storm, seeing nothing but blackness. Sawyer hadn't been out there last night. Colton had waited, guns ready to hunt him down in the dark. It would have been best for them all. Glen would be cooling off in Baker's jail right now, and an arsonist—maybe a killer—would be behind bars.

"Colton?" Hannah breezed into the room, so beautiful she pulled at his heart, made him care. "I thought I heard you rattle the stove lid. Zac woke up with a small fever last night. I don't think it's anything serious, but I want to brew up some honey and lemon tea and see if that will help his throat."

"Was it a rough night?"

"I rocked him for a while and he fell back asleep. It wasn't too tough." She flung open the pantry door and rummaged through the canisters. "Was it a quiet night for you?"

Too damn quiet. "After the blizzard hit, I figured we were pretty safe."

"Did you check on my mares in the north corral?" Hannah clutched a jar of honey as she turned around.

One look into those concerned blue eyes and Colton knew he was in trouble. "You didn't see Eaton Baker take those mares with him yesterday?"

"You let Mr. Baker take my mares?"

"Well, we discussed a price first. Promised to have Drummond deposit the funds into our account at the bank." Colton took the honey from her and set it on the table.

She stood very still. "You sold my mares even though I told you not to?"

"I'd already made my decision. I did tell you that." He pulled out a chair and sat down, rubbing his hands over his face. "I knew you'd be angry, but I've been up all night and I worked hard all day yesterday. I'm not going to fight about this."

"You're not even sorry. Colton," she began, then paused. "You promised before I agreed to marry you that we would run the ranch together."

"I remember, Hannah. But making this place prosper is my job, just like raising Zac is yours." He did look tired, the circles beneath his troubled eyes black and bruised. "I made a decision. I'm sorry it's one you didn't like. I talked Baker into the other mares, the ones you didn't raise by hand. He wasn't as happy, but he didn't argue. Be grateful for the money. It was a fair price considering the season."

A knot began to pull tight in her chest until she could hardly breathe. "I thought I could trust you. To listen to me. To keep your word." A terrible shaking began deep in her stomach.

"Hannah." Colton stood, his hand on her arm.

She grabbed the honey jar and twisted open the lid, ignoring him. Her jaw locked tight, anger bottled in her throat, his horrible words ringing in her ears. *Be grateful.*

"Hannah, don't be mad. I told you what I was going to do. I listened to your opinion."

"And ignored it." Be grateful, he'd said. Hannah grabbed the teakettle and dropped it with a clank on the stove top. "I think I hear Zac. Excuse me."

She couldn't look at him as she stormed through the kitchen and up the stairs. She hated seeing the exhaustion on his face and the solid look of a man trying to do his best.

She wanted to be angry at him. He'd sold her horses, and maybe he was right. Those draft horses ate an amazing amount of hay in a day, the last thing they needed when they were purchasing expensive winter feed from town. But she was truly angry with herself. She'd let down her guard, let herself pretend she could trust him.

His actions only proved the power he had over her life. *Be grateful.* Charles had said the same when he'd come home drunk and violent, intending to remind her that she had more than she deserved.

Be grateful.

Zac's door was shut, all was quiet. She'd only used him as an excuse to leave Colton. Hannah stepped into her room. Alone in the dark, she closed her eyes. Yesterday in his arms, so safe and wondrous, she'd wanted a dream that didn't exist. There was no man worthy of complete trust. No matter his honor. No matter his kindness. He still had power over her life.

Hannah thought of how eagerly she'd kissed him, of how she craved the snug shelter of his arms. She'd come damn close to making an enormous mistake. She'd foolishly wanted to make love to him.

Colton was her husband. He controlled her life. She would do best never to forget it.

* * *

"How are you feeling, little fella?" Colton knelt down beside the boy bundled in an afghan in the chair before the hearth.

"Bad." Zac rubbed his throat. "Hurts."

"I know it hurts." Colton rubbed a hand over his son's dark curls. "I bet Hannah almost has that chocolate ready for you."

"Like choc'lit." Zac held out Hannah's precious book, sticky with little fingerprints. "Read to me."

Who could resist the plea in those sweet eyes? "Only if I can get a hug first."

Zac stretched out his little arms and Colton leaned close enough to hold his boy close. Love squeezed his chest. He looked up to see Hannah standing before the fire with a mug and a saucer, one in each hand. Her blue eyes looked cool, yet she smiled.

"Here's your chocolate, just like I promised." Hannah

waited until Colton sat down and settled Zac on his lap before she handed over that steamy mug of chocolate. "Be careful, it's hot. Let's let your papa hold it."

Colton felt Zac's light weight against him, felt the bob of that head in an eager nod. Hannah had so much love for the boy. The loneliness in his heart ached, deep inside where he remembered what it was like to be loved by a woman—truly loved.

"Thank you." Zac covered his mouth with his hand and coughed twice.

"And I have a saucer of warm milk for Fiddle." Hannah knelt to set the plate on the hearth. The kitty jumped from his perch beside the chair, pink tongue showing.

Zac slurped the chocolate, happy, and Colton watched Hannah sink onto the sofa. The little lines drawn tight around her eyes told him she hadn't forgiven him.

The lonely part of him wished she would reach out to him. Offer him the comfort of her bed.

Wind howled at the walls. Snow scoured like sandpaper. As long as the storm remained, Colton knew the barn and the horses—their very future—were safe. No way could Sawyer risk losing his life just to seek a little revenge. No, as long as this weather held, Colton could rest, spend some time with his family.

She looked up and their gazes locked. His lips tingled. His blood heated. How he wanted her, only her. To cup the firmness of her breasts in both hands, to press kisses along silken curves of her inner thighs, to discover the tight, glowing heat of her body.

He looked away. The blizzard trapped him inside the house, here, inches away from her beauty. And it kept him from stopping the man who threatened them.

Colton opened the book of nursery rhymes and began to read.

* * *

Blood stained the dusty walls of the sheriff's office, spattered across the papers on his desk. The deputy's lifeless body was on the floor, eyes staring sightlessly, mouth twisted into a frozen state of surprise.

"How should we do him?" Max Varney rubbed the butt of his revolver against the graying temple of the still-alive sheriff. "Right through the head, quick and bloody? Or should I go for the gut?"

"Don't look at me, Pa." Tom's stomach turned. He never had the guts for killing. "Make him tell you where he keeps his strongbox."

"Money. It's all you ever think about." Max shook his head. "I think I'll gut-shoot him. Let the bastard who tried to lock me up lay there and suffer. I like makin' a man suffer."

"Here it is." Tom turned his back, thankful he'd found the gray metal box all on his own, without further bloodshed, in the lower drawer of the sheriff's desk.

A gun blast echoed in the office, rang in his ears. Just like the old man's groan of agony. 'Course, it was hard to do more than groan with a broken jaw.

"Suffer, bastard." Satisfied, Max knelt down with a thud.

Tom glanced over his shoulder to see his father pawing through the dying man's pockets.

"Got twenty bucks in his billfold." Max tucked the greenback into his vest pocket.

"Come over here and blow off this lock for me."

"Do it yourself."

Tom swallowed. He worried about upsetting Pa when he was like this, bloodthirsty and in a rush from killing. He hated guns but pulled the one from his holster with trembling hands and fired it. He winced at the sound. God, he hated guns.

The box lid, blown half off, opened easily. Inside there was money—not a fortune, but several hundred dollars. Splitting it with Pa would still leave him enough to add to his savings.

"Look what I found. Can't make it out, though." Pa tromped across the blood-slick floor and shoved the paper into Tom's face. "Read it."

"It says here, *Dear Elijah.* That must be the sheriff you just shot."

"Go on." No remorse in those eyes.

Tom sighed. He didn't want to read on. He didn't want it to lead to more trouble. Hell, he guessed it would happen anyway. Pa made trouble wherever he went, and took pleasure in it. And there wasn't a thing Tom could do about it. He couldn't stand up against his father.

"*I have a favor to ask of you. Seems we got us a newcomer to town. Stop. I just want to know what I'm dealing with, a criminal come to harm us or a man seeking peace. Stop.*"

"Peace," Pa snorted.

Tom kept reading. "*The name's Colton Kincaid. Stop. Tell me whatever you can find—*"

"Kincaid?" The bitter words twisted from Pa's throat. "The bounty hunter?"

Tom's stomach felt cold. Here we go. More trouble.

Pa grabbed the telegraph and stared at it. "Where is he? Where the hell is that rotten, no-good bastard who dragged in my son?"

"M-Montana." Tom tried to hold back his fear. When Pa got started on Al's death it was always a bad thing.

A bad, bitter, killing thing.

God help Colton Kincaid.

* * *

The house shrank with his nearness. Everywhere Hannah went, everything she did, she could feel his presence. Maybe because he'd spent so little time at home and slept in the barn. She took the noon meal from the oven, and he was there to lift out the roast and slice it for her. He grabbed a towel and dried the dishes while she washed. His elbow brushed her shoulder once and she forgot how to breathe.

When he left to check on the animals in the barn, the house felt empty without him. She wanted to hold tight to her distrust. The storm was fierce. Relentless, it beat at the walls, powerful enough to tear away a man's hold on a guide rope, deadly enough to confuse him so he would wander, lost and freezing.

The rope he'd tied from the back door to the closest clothesline pole to the back door of the barn was tight, right? Hannah glanced at the clock as she kneaded her bread dough. He'd been gone a long time.

She patted the soft, mealy dough and examined the tiny blisters bubbled along the surface. Trying not to think of Colton, of his voice light and low as he'd read nursery rhymes to his son by the fire, of his black gaze that drew her closer to him, drew her in.

She rolled the dough into a bowl and set it in the warming oven to rise. The back door flew open with a chill of winter and shower of snow. Colton burst through and pushed the door closed against the bitter wind.

"That's the worst damn storm I've ever seen." He tore away his muffler. Ice tinkled to the floor. He was white everywhere. His eyebrows. His eyelids. His mouth.

"You look like a snowman." She pulled a chair up to the stove. "Come sit here where you can thaw out. You must be cold."

"Cold? I'm frozen clean through. Frozen solid. I might melt like an icicle on your clean floor."

Even frozen and uncomfortable, a touch of gentle humor twinkled in his eyes. Hannah's chest tightened. She didn't want to care. She really didn't. "If you melt to a puddle, then at least I'll be rid of you."

"Once you started shoveling out that barn, you'd miss me." Colton tugged off his hat and gloves with frozen fingers, his movements awkward.

"Here. Let me." She crossed the room in time to slip the second glove from his hand. His blunt-shaped fingers were red. She reached up to unbutton his coat.

He stood still, his gaze fixed on her face. "Are you still mad?"

"Maybe." She slipped the jacket over his broad shoulders. More ice rained like glass shards to the floor. "I have fresh coffee waiting."

"You're a good wife, Hannah." He managed stiff steps.

"Because I couldn't stop you from selling my horses?"

"Because you haven't held it against me. Much." Again that tad of humor, bright and dazzling. Colton winced as he settled into the chair.

"Maybe you'd better dress more warmly the next time you go out in a blizzard." She grabbed a towel and lifted the pot from the stove. Rich, aromatic coffee steamed the air and filled the mug she held.

"You're not just a good wife, but a smart one, too." He held out his hands for the coffee.

"Any fool knows to wear more than a coat out in that weather."

"Hey, I wore a hat. And a scarf."

"I know—you're too tough to let a little cold bother you." She shook her head, unable to do anything but smile at him, even when she wanted to frown. "Those chilblained fingers will be enough of a reminder next time."

"Pain." He tried to flex one fist. "I see what you mean." Happiness curved his mouth.

His grin devastated her, blew away all the anger and distrust she wanted to hold tight to. "Good. I'm glad you're hurting. That's the least you deserve for not respecting my wishes."

"We're back to the horses again."

"Yes." She wrapped a towel around the stove door and turned. Flames popped as she added wood. "I don't want you doing anything like that again. This isn't a real marriage, Colton. You can't do anything you want."

"I'm not." Colton sipped the coffee, staring at her. Not blinking.

She wanted to argue, but closed the stove door instead and moved away, her face flaming from the heat. He didn't understand. She startled when his hand caught her wrist. He smelled of snow and man, and the scent filled her up, made her dizzy, made her want.

How she wanted.

"I'm not ever going to hurt you, Hannah. You know that."

She nodded. Not physically. And maybe...looking into the depth of his eyes to the honor she'd always known was there, she saw her answer. He was a man who always did what he thought was right. And he attracted her like no other.

But he had a past and so many secrets. She knew so little about him. Only the way he smiled, the determined competence in his every movement, the comfort of his touch, the patient love he showed for Zac.

Her heart pounded. Desire—pure and physical— punched through her veins. She wanted him. She wanted to feel the powerful combination of his strength and gentleness. She wanted him to hold her and chase away the doubts in her heart.

CHAPTER FIFTEEN

"Oh, it's you rattling my stove lid."

Colton straightened in the near darkness as Hannah swept into the kitchen, her voice light, her long nightgown glowing like a ghost.

His throat tightened. She'd fallen asleep in the rocking chair in the nursery. He waited, but she'd never come to him in their bed. "How's Zac?"

"Fine. He has nothing more than a sniffle." She breezed close.

Need for her crackled through him. Being cooped up in the house with her flowery scent and gentle smile and the way she chuckled low in her throat was affecting him, consuming him. He wanted to kiss her again, to cup the weight of her breasts in his hand. And more. He wanted to undress her and touch her everywhere until they were both breathless, both out of control.

"Some scoundrel is walking on my clean floor with his wet boots." She tilted her head. "After I scrubbed up the mess you left when you came in from the barn last."

"I'm a cad, a molester of clean floors. Do with me what you will."

"Ah, you sound like you'd enjoy that too much." The lightest trace of a smile glittered along her mouth.

The clock in the parlor struck one.

"The silence is eerie." He lifted his still-damp coat from the wall peg. "I thought I'd better get out to the barn. Make sure the animals have enough water."

"Good. Here, take my scarf. It's dry."

Colton looked at the length of knit wool she offered, saw the emotion burn in her eyes like a lamp turned low. It was a steady light. She cared.

The enormity floored him. He accepted her offering and wrapped the scarf around his neck. It smelled flowery and light, just like her.

Cold air seeped through the cracks in the door and drove through the walls of wood. He shivered. Truth was, he'd slept hard for the first time in a long while. And it felt damn good. If only she'd been beside him, a woman's warmth in his arms.

"I shouldn't have slept so long."

"It's been quiet not even for an hour." Hannah's eyes didn't hold censure. "It would take nearly that long for someone to ride the roads from town. I don't think you need to check on the barns."

Something didn't sit right in his guts. "No, I'd better get out there and keep watch. We can't afford any more losses." Although he wanted to stay inside with Hannah and his son.

But he faced the bitter cold instead. Breath froze to his face as he plowed through the enormous drifts to the silent barns, the new one not fit for occupation, the farthest one shut against the weather.

When he saw the doors standing wide open, Colton didn't need to guess at what he would find. The tracks gouging the snow told him everything. His hand went to his guns, holstered beneath his coat. But the barn was empty. No enemy. No animals.

The bastard Sawyer hadn't needed to light another fire

to destroy everything Colton had worked so damn hard for. All Glen had to do was set the horses free.

How could he tell Hannah? How would she feel, knowing he'd let her down?

She heard the back door slam. Colton had only been outside a few minutes, not enough to check on the stock and make sure they had water.

"Hannah!" His voice echoed through the house like anger. Except it wasn't anger.

Her pulse jumped and she set down her hairbrush. She was on her feet, but already he was pounding up the stairs. He burst into her room, still in his coat and snow-covered boots, eyes dark and jaw set.

"I'm going to ride to the Mullens'. We've got trouble and I need some help."

"What kind of trouble?" she asked, but she knew. The horses. "What—"

"They're out." He tossed off his coat and grabbed a thick sweater from the wardrobe. "I can trust the Mullens. I know they're good people. You need to stay here and watch over Zac. With that fever he had, he can't be exposed to the night air."

She caught his arm. "I can't just sit here. I have to help."

"This is a man's job, Hannah." He grabbed his coat, all stubborn and steely man, and charged back down the stairs.

She ran after him, hiking up her nightgown so she wouldn't trip on the ruffled hem. "All the horses?"

"Every damn one of them."

"Even my Percherons?"

"The draft horses are hanging around the house. They're too tame to go anywhere, but those half wild horses took off for the mountains at a dead run."

Hannah saw their hopes slipping away, dreams dispersing like dust in the wind. "Ask Mrs. Mullen if she'll watch Zac. I'm going with you."

"Hannah, it would be better—"

"They're my horses, too." Her determination felt like steel. "We're in this together, Colton. Don't even think about arguing with me."

"Fine." His eyes glimmered with an emotion that penetrated the fog of panic clouding her mind, spurred faster the beat of her heart.

Respect.

He closed the door and was gone. But the warmth in her chest for him, the begrudging trust she kept fighting, bloomed a little more.

With so much to lose, with their entire financial future at stake, she knew Colton would ride like the devil to the neighboring ranch and bring back help and Blanche Mullen to watch over Zac. She knew the man she'd married would do no less.

* * *

Colton rode his bay hard. The obedient mare had not wandered far from the shelter of the barn and trotted up to him when he'd whistled. He hadn't even taken the time to do more than slip on a bridle. Barebacked, he made the two-mile trek in record time, despite the snows. He pushed the horse too hard, and she lathered during the final stretch toward home.

The house looked dark except for a single lamp burning in the kitchen windowsill. He rode out into the yard and saw Hannah astride her mustang, riding toward him from the barn.

"Rousted the Mullens out of a good night's sleep." Colton knuckled back the brim of his hat. "They agreed to help. Blanche is coming to care for Zac. The youngest boy of theirs—what is he, about sixteen? He's going to ride to the other neighboring ranches and round up more help. One of the other Mullen boys will stay behind to guard the barn."

Hannah, breathless from the biting cold, drew her mare alongside his. "I've kept a close eye on the house. I want you to know I'd never leave Zac in any danger. But I just couldn't sit still and wait. I had to do something. Some of the mares didn't take off with the herd. They probably took one look at all this snow and decided my barn was a better place to live."

"I know I did." The world was a cold place, but a woman like Hannah, warm and drawing as a home fire, could melt away the frozen edges of his heart. "Are those my trousers?"

"Mine." She lifted that determined chin. "I altered some of Charles's old clothes because my petticoats and skirt always startled the less tame horses. It was too dangerous to have them bucking and rearing just because the wind shook my dress."

"How many mares did you bring in by yourself?" He shivered in the bitter wind. Stared off toward the barns.

"Probably about ten." Hannah patted the coiled rope hanging over her saddlehorn. "I had to lasso them because they wouldn't come unless I drove them, and that would be too hard on my mare. It's going to be a long night."

"Yes, it is." Colton studied the woman before him, bundled against the cold but radiating a new competence that surprised him. He'd seen her exercise her workhorses, the gentle giants she guided with the lightest hand as she made them pull the sleigh around the meadows within sight of the barn.

He'd known, of course, that she had cleaned the barn and cared for all the animals, but he'd assumed Charles had handled the wild horses that now ran free. Colton had assumed that Hannah knew so much about them because she'd taken an interest and watched.

Maybe, he now realized, she was a far more accomplished horsewoman.

"I couldn't track the horses far." Hannah knuckled back her small brown Stetson. "Most of them headed northeast toward the mountains. Driven by the stallion, I think, judging by the tracks."

"He's driving them away from civilization, from ranches." Colton faced east, the snow-capped peaks of the rugged and dangerous mountains barely visible in the night, faintly dusted with a handful of starlight. "He's a smart bastard. He'll be hard to catch."

"But I will catch him." Fierce, that voice. Strong as iron.

"You mean, *we'll* catch him," he corrected her.

"You don't want me here." She said it suddenly. "You don't think I belong out here with you."

"That's right," he said quietly. "Those mountains are no place for a woman. But I trust you, Hannah. If you thought you couldn't do the job, you wouldn't risk slowing us down."

I trust you. His words echoed in her heart.

"There's Mullen and his sons now." Colton swung his mare toward the barn. "I'll need to change horses before we head out. Maybe you want to leave instructions with Mrs. Mullen."

Hannah nodded, watching him ride toward the men, lifting a hand in greeting.

* * *

Frigid wind knifed through Hannah's thick layers of clothes and teared her eyes. With every determined step of her mare, Hannah saw her future crumble. They needed those horses to survive. Colton may have money, but the money those mares could bring in once they were well trained could mean the difference between foreclosure and a successful continuation of the ranch.

The deepest time of night made it impossible to see. Hannah could only make out the faintest trace of tracks against the shadowed snow. Hank Mullen was tracking ahead of her.

It was slow going once they hit the line of trees, the start to the forest that stretched to the highest rocky peaks of the Continental Divide. Branches stuck out in the dark, lashing her in the cheeks, slapping her in the arms, punching her thighs. Still, they kept north, driving hard.

"We're going to have to dismount," Colton said as he pushed past her to speak to Mullen in the lead.

"You're right." Hank Mullen dismounted. "The forest is too thick and these tracks are hard to follow. We walk from here."

"Are you all right?" Colton's hand on her elbow.

"Yes." Her feet touched the ground. Her knees creaked. "How about you?"

"I'm damn tough." She heard the smile in his voice, even if she could see no more of his face than shadows. "I'm sorry."

"For what?" She lifted the knotted reins over the mustang's head. The animal nudged her gloved hand, asking for affection. She patted the velvety neck.

"I should have stayed in the barn. This is my fault." He sighed. Troubled, he lowered his voice, leaning close enough so she could smell the fresh-air scent of him and feel the heat of his body.

"You belonged in the house, Colton. If you had tried to stay in the barn, I wouldn't have let you." Her hand found his and she squeezed his fingers, meaning to offer him comfort. "It seems whoever wants to harm us isn't from town. It's a neighbor. A friend."

Her heart thudded. "Mullen's moving. We'd better go."

He nodded and said nothing more.

* * *

It was a grueling trek through the nighttime forest. The light thinned as dawn edged nearer, making the journey only a bit less difficult. Colton gritted his teeth against the bitter cold that chapped his face and numbed his hands. Steely determination drove him. Glen had outwitted him—but never again. Colton vowed to bring the horses in.

By dawn's light, they'd found fresh sign of the herd. By the time it took for the thin disk of the sun to lift above the rim of the mountain peaks, they overtook the stragglers. Hannah spun her mare around and caught his gaze.

"Do you think we have enough men to turn them?"

"Maybe." He drew up alongside her, close enough to see the touch of the frigid air to her nose and cheeks. Exhaustion bruised her eyes. "You're not getting too cold, are you?"

"I'm fine." The lie crinkled in the corners of her eyes and rang hollow in her voice. "We'll probably be lucky to turn only half the herd."

"But they're trying to run." Colton could see the stallion nipping the mares. "They're tiring."

"That's in our favor." Hannah reached out and caught his gloved hand. So much was said by her touch. She didn't blame him for failing to be there, for guarding the livestock. She didn't blame him at all.

The knowledge glowed warm in his chest.

"Let's bring these horses in," he called out to Mullen and rode hard into the bright flares of light from the rising sun.

* * *

Hannah thought she'd never seen anything more beautiful than home. The snowdrifts marked the line of neat fencing and barns, made cozy the snug log house on the rise. Lamplight shone in the windows and gray smoke rose from the chimneys. Zac was warm and safe inside. How was his fever?

The Mullen boy left behind had already dug out the gate and left it opened. He waited now until the riders had driven every last horse into the corral, then dashed to close them in.

Hannah wheeled her mare to a halt. Her gaze latched on Colton. He looked exhausted. The deep frown lines around his eyes and mouth told her he still blamed himself.

"I'm going to check on Zac." Hannah dismounted beside Colton. "I'll see how long it will take to heat up the stew I made for supper last night. We ought to at least feed the men before they head home."

"Hank intends to see this through, Hannah." Colton took the reins from her numb fingers, the shock of his touch like an arrow to her heart. "And so do I. You're not alone anymore. You don't need to worry."

"I'm worried about imposing too much on my good neighbors." Hannah edged away from his accusation. But there was more. They'd sustained a serious loss of nearly fifty horses. And the stallion.

She laid a hand on Colton's solid arm. So strong, so determined to make right his imagined wrongs. "Thanks for taking care of her for me." She patted the mustang.

"Give my son a hug." Colton gazed up at the horizon, at the wilderness where the stallion had escaped them. "And stop being so damn independent."

She might have taken offense if he hadn't grinned at her.

Hannah turned and hurried toward home.

* * *

"There's no doubt about it," Hank Mullen said as he led his cooled gelding to an awaiting stall. "Someone deliberately let these horses out. Do you have any guesses?"

"Maybe." Hedging, Colton guided Hannah's mustang into the fresh stall and shut her in. He grabbed a pitchfork and swept in a small amount of hay, then did the same for the Mullens' horses.

Hank followed after him. "You know, the Sawyer brothers came out here with enough cash to buy up two neighboring ranches. I remembered the way they treated the Jacobsens, who couldn't hold onto the land. I never held much respect for Charles Sawyer after that. I heard he was a friend of yours, but you seem to be cut from a different cloth, Kincaid."

"You don't have to worry about insulting me, Hank." Colton leaned the pitchfork safely out of the aisle. "I was never close to Charles. Tell me what I don't know."

Hank started for the door. "Glen bought a section and Charles bought a section, side by side."

"How did Glen lose his acreage?"

"Poker game. About a year ago now." Snow crunched beneath the rancher's uneven gait. "Big stakes. Glen was losing big time. Word is he had a full house, a sweet, sure win. He pulled out the deed, hoping to get the hand up on his brother."

"The two didn't get along?"

"Not with Charles always telling Glen what to do. He was bigger, older, meaner. Always had been, I guess." Mullen stopped to knock the snow from his boots before he climbed up onto the back porch. "Everyone figured Glen saw the chance to pay big brother back by winning his land fair and square and tossing him out. It was no secret from anyone but Hannah that Glen carried a torch for her."

Colton wedged his foot in the bootjack and pulled. "Glen has an awfully strong motive for wanting his land back."

"And more." Hank looked up when the back door flew open. "Hannah, is that your good coffee I smell?"

"You'd better hurry on in before your sons eat me out of house and home and leave nothing for you." She smiled, and she took Colton's breath away, like she always did, despite the loose men's clothes she wore and the bedraggled gold curls framing her beautiful face.

His heart stumbled. Images of her today flashed through Colton's mind, images of her riding hard, strong as any man. Yet he knew her fragility. She could fill him up with a smile. She could see a piece of goodness in an unredeemable man.

"Come in and warm up." Hannah reached out for his hand, and the past vanished until there was only the saving grace of her touch.

Hannah didn't know how she could begin to repay the Mullens' help. Blanche insisted on staying with Zac, allowing Hannah to head off with the men, intent on scouring the mountain hillside for the rest of her mares.

Without them, they could not turn enough of a profit to keep the ranch. Colton hadn't said so with words as much as the tight white line of his lips and the grim set of his jaw. Hank Mullen left three of his sons behind, one to tend to his own ranch, the other two to keep guard over the Kincaids' barns.

He blames himself. Her heart ached watching Colton. He rode with a stoic determination, his Stetson low over his eyes, his voice rough and steely. He didn't speak much, perhaps because of the cold or maybe because of his need to make things right. As daylight bled from the sky, they'd roped less than three mares, stragglers that had fallen behind the herd and looked lost and hungry and tired and gave little fight when a lasso's loop settled around their necks.

Mullen sent one of his sons back with the horses, and they agreed to keep hunting. The temperature dropped steadily as night came and they climbed higher along the mountainside.

"Hannah." Colton drew his bay alongside her mare. "Mullen thinks we need to turn back, and I agree. Those clouds coming in, they don't look good and the last thing we can afford to do is get caught without shelter if another blizzard blows in."

True, thick clouds were blotting out the rising moon, diminishing the visibility in the forest. "Take the Mullens back to the ranch. We're getting closer, and I'm not ready to quit."

His gaze locked on hers and held. The entire world silenced. "No. Hannah, you're exhausted and probably frozen clean through. I'm not going to let anything happen to you over a few renegade horses."

"A few? It's nearly half our herd."

"Fine, then I'll keep searching. But you go back with the men. I need to know you are watching over Zac."

"But you can't stay out in this forest alone. It's too dangerous." Hannah's gaze caressed the broad line of his shoulders, unyielding in the descending darkness.

"Blanche will care for Zac. We'll search together."

"No." His eyes darkened. "I've let you ride with us, but it's over. You're going back with the men."

There it was. The power he had over her life. As if he could issue an order and she would have to obey. Be grateful for a home and shelter and everything he'd given her. The image of Zac enfolded in Colton's arms, safe and snug and loved, burned behind her eyelids, made her heart hurt in a new way.

"You're right, Hannah." Colton lowered his voice, intimate and more caring than she'd ever heard him speak to her before. "This is dangerous country and I just can't let anything happen to you."

He said the words as if she were so precious. What did she say, how did she feel about an order issued out of concern instead of anger and the need to control?

She blinked hard, the tears freezing along the rim of her lashes. "Please, don't tell me what to do."

His eyes widened at her whispered words. Perhaps he heard the anguish within them.

Finally, he nodded. "Fine. We'll send the Mullens back to the ranch. Are you certain you're up to this?"

"Certain." Hannah crouched into her coat, wishing her wraps were thicker. Her insides tightened and she shivered from the cold—a dangerous sign—but she couldn't stop. "Besides, you need me. I can handle a rope better than you can."

"I've always wanted a woman who could tie me up," he teased.

"Colton." She meant to scold him, but his name lingered on her lips, more sweet and precious than she was prepared to admit.

"I don't want you hurt, Hannah. If I think it's getting too dangerous or if you're becoming too cold, then we both turn back. Is that understood?"

She nodded.

"I care about you, Hannah. I don't want anything to happen."

Even in the darkness, shades of gray upon black colored him. She could see the snap of emotion in his eyes, feel the way his heart drew her no matter how stridently she denied it. It was there, whispering of desires and foolishness she'd long ago refused to believe in.

"Come, let's send the Mullens home."

His gloved hand covered hers. Despite the numbness in her fingers and the layers of leather and wool, his touch felt intimate. She blushed, aching for that precious sweetness again, a sweetness she would never give herself.

Love didn't exist. She knew that. Had learned it from her husband's hand. She thought now of the nights she'd cried without comfort. The days lived with a loneliness so great it could swallow her whole.

She was foolish to think the dreams of a once-innocent girl could survive in a world as tough as stone.

CHAPTER SIXTEEN

As the night deepened, the temperature fell. The clouds parted to allow a small glow of silvered moonlight, but little of it seeped through the thick evergreen boughs to aid him.

If only the horses had kept to the meadows, he thought as he dismounted. The hours of falling snow had covered their tracks well enough so that following them proved difficult.

"Look." He caught sight of the tracks in the shadows along the forest floor. He swung off his mare and crouched low to the ground. He struck a match and it swelled to life. "Yep, it's our stallion, all right. About thirty or so mares."

Hannah swung down, too. Her gaze joined his, reading the tracks cut into the frozen snow. "How many hours ahead of us are they?"

"Not more than a few." The flame's light brushed her face briefly, and his heart kicked. He felt cold and exhausted and lonely. Oh, so lonely. "It's too cold for the horses to run for long, and there isn't much to eat in these parts."

"Then we can catch up with them tonight." Hannah shivered. Her face was white above the slash of the scarf covering her mouth. "If we keep going."

He caught her hand tight in his grip before she could mount her mare. "It's too cold, Hannah. It's too cold to run the herd hard, and it's too cold for you."

Her chin shot up. "I'm fine."

"It's got to be ten below, more with this wind, and the temperature's still falling. Your mare is exhausted, and only stubbornness is keeping you in that saddle. You'll do better to search tomorrow when it's daylight."

"If we turn back, we'll lose valuable time tomorrow." She swung up on her mare. "By tomorrow morning, they could be lost to us."

Tiny flakes of snow shivered to the ground between them, catching on her lashes and on the fabric of her coat and the brim of her hat. The match burned low. Colton tossed it to the ground, regretting the loss of light.

"We'll find us another stallion." Colton laid his hand on her knee.

She towered over him. "We need the mares, too."

"No horse is worth our lives, Hannah. We have to think of Zac."

Hannah winced. She could think of nothing else. This was the first night since he'd come to live with her that she hadn't tucked him into his bed, pulled the covers up to his chin and turned the light low, but just bright enough for her to read by. The kitty would curl close and she would read until those thick, dark lashes began to droop and he'd slipped away into the land of a little boy's dreams.

Holding onto the ranch now meant something else—something greater. It had always been her home. Now, it was a home she would fight to keep for Zac. She would not give up her fight to find her horses, to make sure the ranch was profitable. Even if she hadn't felt her toes since sundown.

Colton stepped into the silvered light of a moonbeam

reaching down between the dense trees. "See this here?" He pointed to a hollow in the snow.

"It's a creek bed."

"The tracks we're following separate right here." He leaned close. Smelled of snow and horse-warmth and man, a scent that twisted tight in her belly.

"Oh, Lord." Hannah slid off her saddle and dropped to her knees. She was so numb, she couldn't feel the cold snow seep through her wind-frozen trousers. Tears squeezed into her eyes. "I would have missed this."

"You're too tired. It just proves my point. We have to stop for the night." Colton gripped her collar and turned her toward him. She read the caring in his determined eyes.

"It's too much to lose." She wanted to go on. But how could she? Every inch of her body radiated pain. She'd never been so cold in her life.

Then he drew her against his wonderful chest, so iron-hard and strong. Exhausted, she rested against him, tears burning in her eyes.

"Just for once, Hannah, just this one time, lean on me."

* * *

The shack was where she remembered—an old miner's shanty long abandoned, but she'd ridden past it early last spring. She felt grateful it was still standing and that she'd been able to find it from memory.

Colton took the reins from her clenched fist, then reached up to help her down.

His touch felt solid. As her numb feet hit the earth, she stared hard into his broad chest. His solid dependability made her ache inside.

"I'll get a fire started." Colton's voice rumbled in her ear, igniting tiny tickles of want.

She shook her head. "I have the matches. I'll do it. If you care for my mare. It's too cold to leave these horses standing. I think I remember a shelter of sorts in the back."

"Hannah, you can't light a fire. You can't move your

fingers." He took her firmly by the arm. "I'll do it."

"But my horse." Hannah's heart kicked as her loyal mare nudged her shoulder, as if worried over her condition, too. In this mountain country, the care of one's horse came first.

"Don't worry. I won't leave her standing for long."

She found herself resting against his iron-hard chest as he carried her through the shanty's door. He stumbled across the plank floor in the filtered dark and set her down on a rickety chair.

"Where are your matches?"

"In my saddlebag." Weakness poured through her like water. Tears of frustration and anger at her own helplessness burned behind her eyes. She wanted to take care of herself, but everything they stood to lose frightened her.

She watched Colton haul in chunks of snow-covered wood and she wished she didn't need him so much.

Colton stirred the steel fork through the steaming beans.

"I'm amazed at your culinary expertise, Colton."

"It takes real skill to open up a tin can." He cracked a smile, only because the color had come back to her face and hands. A hot fire crackled and popped, spilling warmth into the single-room shanty. "I've cooked more meals than I can count over a campfire."

"When you were hunting bounties?" Emotion flickered in her eyes, part curiosity, part trepidation.

"That scares you, doesn't it? My past."

"Maybe." Her hand stilled. "The notion of anyone killing, especially for profit."

"They were killers themselves, Hannah. Men who had taken innocent lives for the pleasure of it. I took them in alive when I could, and only used force when I had to."

Her eyes searched his. "I believe that of you."

Colton's heart cracked a little. How long had it been since anyone put faith in him? Not since Ella.

"Why did you decide to become a bounty hunter?" Her question came quietly, soft as the light from the fire. "Most men take up something like farming or ranching or maybe working as a clerk."

"I didn't know how to do anything else." He tried not to remember, but there it was, the plea shadowed in her eyes. He'd told her so little about himself, so little of his past. Maybe she deserved to know what he'd truly asked of her.

"Most boys have a father to teach them a skill, to help them become men."

"You didn't have a father?" Such big eyes.

"No."

"Neither did I." Her lower lip trembled. So vulnerable. "I was orphaned when I was very small."

"So was I. My grandmother cared for me, but her health was poor. She died when I was thirteen. Not the easiest time for a boy to be without a family."

"No." She waited. "What did you do?"

"I was placed in a home for boys. When I was fifteen I got into a little trouble in town. The local sheriff caught me, tossed me in jail for the night, and come morning, when I wasn't nearly so cocky, he set me straight. Took me under his wing. Paid me to sweep and clean the jail, taught me everything I needed to know. By the time I was on my own, I landed a job as a deputy in a neighboring town with his recommendation. He changed my life, that man."

Hannah watched the past flicker in his eyes, shadowed but warm. He looked so far away.

"Of course, that was a long time ago. A lot has happened since then." Colton cracked a smile, a little lopsided, a little sexy. Enough to make her heart stop.

Silence settled between them. Questions buzzed on her tongue, but she didn't ask them. Instead she filled her spoon and ate while the beans were still steaming, letting the food warm her from the inside out.

"How are your feet?" Concern rumbled in his voice.

"Painful."

"That's a good sign. You won't lose any toes." Colton poured more coffee into her tin mug. "I'm worried about you. You should have stayed home."

"I had to come. We didn't have enough men to turn the herd." She gladly breathed in the steaming aroma of the hot coffee. Despite the fire, the thin shanty's walls were little protection against the bitter cold outside. "If I hadn't helped, then we would have lost even more horses."

The grueling ride trying to drive the half-wild herd back to the ranch still ached in her muscles. Shifting her weight on the floor did little to alleviate the pain.

"They are only horses. You are harder to replace, Hannah." Colton offered her one of the two last pan biscuits.

"But without the mares, we're ruined." She broke apart the warm, doughy roll with her fingers. "Or we might as well be. I know you don't have enough money in Mr. Drummond's bank to keep financing a losing venture."

"Making the mortgage payment come spring could be a problem. But you and Zac come first. Always." Colton's voice was full of so much sincerity, she could close her eyes and believe the scars in her heart could be healed by his touch.

"Tomorrow we can keep tracking what's left of the herd. We can bring them back." She finished off her biscuit. "We can't stop trying."

"We'll talk about that in the morning. For now, it's late. Well past midnight. Let's get you a bed made right here in front of the fire." He stood.

"I don't think I can sleep."

"Then at least try." He set the plates aside and unrolled a wool blanket with a flick of his wrist. "You need to keep warm, Hannah. Here, I have an extra pair of socks in my saddlebag."

She couldn't remember the last time she'd been pampered. She settled herself on the blanket as he rummaged in his pack, then smiled when he knelt down before her and gently slipped bulky wool socks over her feet with such care. The luxury of such an act burned in her eyes, knotted in her throat.

He was a good man. She knew it in her heart, despite the distrust learned over a lifetime. He was a man larger than life, strong enough to show his tenderness, better than anyone she'd ever known.

"Here. Lie back." He'd set one of his saddlebags down for her pillow. She was surprised at its softness. He folded the blanket over her and covered her with a second one.

"What about you?"

"I wasn't the one who tried to turn herself into an icicle tonight. Now sleep. You need the rest."

His footsteps rose above the snap of the fire and the moaning of the mountain wind outside the shanty. Awareness shivered along Hannah's spine as he circled around to lie behind her, sheltering her from the cold draft from the door.

She heard his every movement. Every breath. The rustle of wool as he settled himself beneath his single blanket.

"I can't sleep." Her admission drew a sigh from him.

"Neither can I. Too much at stake, I guess."

"With this storm." She paused, hating to say the words. "The snow could wipe out the tracks. We would have to search blind through these forests. We'd never find the horses."

"I'm more concerned with who's trying to ruin what you and I are working for."

"Do you know who did this?" She turned over, clutching the blankets close.

"I don't have any physical proof." He hesitated. "I have reason to believe it's Glen."

"No." The response was automatic. She thought of times past—when Glen had interceded on her behalf, had even told Charles to stop hitting her, and it had helped.

Glen was no prize, but—"He wouldn't hurt me."

"Maybe not physically."

"You think because he's a bully, and he was pressuring me and Drummond before you came to town. I thought—" She swallowed. "I thought he could have burned down the barn, but it doesn't make sense. If he wants the ranch, he wouldn't destroy valuable property. He wouldn't ruin feed or jeopardize profits."

"Then you tell me what he would do, Hannah. What he's capable of doing."

"He's obnoxious and crude and a brute, I know. I don't want to defend him. I can't." She thought of the nights when he'd brought Charles home when he'd been too drunk to find his own way, and Glen had kept Charles from those terrible violent rages. "He wouldn't. Glen has some terrible flaws, but he always protected me. I can't believe anything less. I just can't."

"Oh, Hannah." Colton's heart melted like snow to sun. She seemed to know that a man was both darkness and light, goodness and shadows, for better or worse.

Despite the bitter cold, he wanted to love her. Want, physical and emotional, beat in his blood, pooled in his groin. No doubt about it. He wanted to strip her naked so the fire's glow could kiss her skin, bury himself in the tight heat of her body, ease the loneliness and find the comfort he so longed for.

"Do you realize there's so much I should have told you, but I couldn't?" He tried to swallow past the painful knot of truth lodged in his throat. "You have every right to be afraid of my past. Of me."

"Never you." She believed it. It rang clear like a bell in her voice, shone like dawn in her eyes. In eyes as blue as heaven.

She could make him feel new. As if the past could be washed away and he could stand free of it. Free of the shame and guilt, regret and hardship.

The fire licked and popped, tossing dancing shadows

across Hannah's slender form. She lay on her side, gazing at him, her face shrouded in darkness.

"I spent seven years at the Federal prison in Yuma, Arizona. For second degree murder." Colton knew his voice sounded flat.

She let out a breath. Not a gasp, but still, a sound of surprise.

"Maybe you should know." He waited for her to stiffen in fear or grab her things and run away from him. She did neither.

"You didn't harm anyone." Her voice. Her belief. "I know you wouldn't."

"There wasn't enough evidence to hang me, but enough to put me in prison." It was too hard to talk about, the long nights in a cell, the days of hard labor. "I'd just stumbled into the bank, minding my own business, and walked right into the middle of a robbery. My problem was that I recognized a set of eyes above a bandanna. My boss. The town sheriff. He was going to kill the bank clerk who didn't have the safe combination."

Colton paused. "Women in line were crying, afraid for the lives of their children. And the sheriff, he thought his disguise protected him. He pressed a revolver to the clerk's temple and cocked it, ready to fire. The man pleaded for his life, spoke of his wife and newborn son. The sheriff would have killed him."

"What did you do?"

"I intervened. I took a bullet in the stomach and one in the thigh, but I stopped that bastard who used his badge as protection so he could kill innocent people."

The dark light from the fire caressed his face, half lit, half shadowed. "I paid for it with seven years out of my life."

She ached to touch him, to pull him close and kiss away the pain, hard and hopeless in his voice. But he tossed back his blanket and set more wood on the fire.

Tears burned in her eyes. "Did your Ella wait for you?"

"She did." He sat down on the hearth. "She endured the humiliation, and when I got out, there she was, waiting for me. There were lines of strain around her eyes. She'd taken in washing and somehow scraped by. Life wasn't easy for her because of me. But she took me in her arms without blame, and I knew she never doubted me. Not once. I believed that we could be happy together."

"Were you?"

He rubbed his hands over his face. "Yes. I couldn't go back to being a lawman. I didn't have enough land to try to farm. So I started hunting bounties. It was the only job I had the skills for."

Tears spilled down her cheeks. Hot, painful. They blurred her vision. Ached in her throat. She couldn't stop them. Tears for him.

"It wasn't an easy life. I was gone all the time. I wasn't even home to see Zac born, although I rode like the devil trying to make it in time." He looked sad. So infinitely sad. "A man who hunts down criminals the law can't find, he opens himself up to a lot of danger. I came home one day, thinking to find Ella cooking at the stove or tending to her wash, but I found her shot through the heart. Some murderer I brought in and banged up pretty good—I should have just killed the bastard instead of trying to bring him in alive—escaped Federal prison and wanted me to pay. But instead of killing me, he took my wife's life and kidnapped my baby son."

"He took Zac?"

Colton hung his head. "I tracked that bastard down and I killed him. When I had Zac back in my arms, crying and neglected, but alive and unharmed, I vowed that was the last bounty I would ever hunt. As long as I had someone depending on me."

"Oh, Colton." She laid her hand on his arm.

"I'm not the man you thought you married, am I?" A little bitter, and so much grief.

Her heart twisted. When she looked at him, she saw the

pieces of his soul. Goodness, honor, and strength.

Hannah leaned to press a kiss against the back of his hand. He drew in breath. His gaze fastened on hers. She saw nothing but the light shining warm and welcoming in Colton's eyes. He brushed her lips with his, gentle but possessive. A kiss that claimed her as his, that made her heart stammer in her chest.

She tilted her head, and he deepened his kiss. Hotter, harder, faster. His demanding mouth molded to hers and claimed her very breath, leaving every surface of her lips tingling.

Oh, yes. She'd dreamed of being close like this. Hadn't stopped thinking about the wondrous feeling of being held by him, kissed by him. Hannah melted against his chest and wished she knew how to give him more, how to ease the pain in his heart.

But Colton only held her more tightly. His tongue traced her lower lip, laving, caressing, demanding entrance. On a sigh, she parted her lips, opening to him. With a moan, he plunged inside. The velvet heat of his tongue stroked along the surface of hers and left her weak and wanting more.

"You taste like sugar. And coffee," he whispered, his lips brushing her mouth.

"So do you." She felt better. Brighter. "You smell like wood smoke. It's nice."

"You smell fresh, like snow." He buried his face in her hair. She felt his arms enfold her and she leaned against the wide, solid expanse of his chest. Nothing had ever felt so good, being sheltered against him, feeling the warmth of this wondrous man.

"I want you, Hannah." His hands brushed over her shoulders, whispered down her back. Everywhere he touched she felt on fire. Pleasure tingled, bright and sharp, a beautiful, exciting feeling she'd never known before.

"Oh, Colton." She sighed his name as he pressed warm, wet kisses down her throat.

"We just might have to break one of your rules." He tipped his head back and their gazes met, held.

"You mean the one where we agreed not to have any sex?"

"That's the one." His big hands cupped her breasts. Even through the layer of flannel her nipples pebbled, responding to the magic of his touch. "Any objections?"

She couldn't think of one.

His fingers tugged the buttons free at the front of her long Johns. Air breezed across her exposed breasts. Colton's eyes widened. Anticipation flickered in his dark eyes.

"Make love to me, Hannah. All I need is you."

CHAPTER SEVENTEEN

C olton could not look away. Firelight licked across her bared breasts, pebbled from anticipation and the cool air. Creamy and firm and generously pink-tipped.

Perfection was an inspiring thing. Blood beat in his veins. His manhood surged against the constraining fabric of his long underwear. He dared to lean forward and catch the tip of one pearly nipple with his tongue.

Hannah threw back her head and sighed.

This beautiful woman sitting on his lap, this angel he was afraid to touch, wanted him. The impact rocked his soul.

Her hands curled around the back of his head and tangled in his hair. With a sly smile, she drew him back to her breast. He opened his mouth, rolled his tongue around the puckered bud, laving and licking. Such creamy, silken skin. He felt lost just touching her. His pulse kicked as she wrapped those slender arms around his neck and held him there, tenderly at her breast. He closed his mouth over her erect nipple and suckled.

Colton could feel pleasure ripple through her body.

Her spine arched. She moaned low in her throat. Her head fell backward. He lifted his mouth to nuzzle, then suckle her other breast.

Heaven. She was like nothing he'd ever known. And it frightened him. But he could not pull away. Her sweetness filled him, pounding through his veins. He craved her like air, breathed her in, wanted to be a part of her. Every instinct within him wanted her now, and he fought to keep from rolling her onto the floor and burying his hard, aching shaft deep inside her. There was no rush. She was his wife. He had the entire night. He had forever to make this right. For her.

She trusted him—he knew that now. It felt like a reward he'd never earned, one that amazed him. He'd been lonely for so long. Hurting with no way to find comfort, no one he could trust or need. Now, he had Hannah. And how he needed her. Rich, hot desire drummed through his veins as his hands touched her back, then her arms, then her ribcage, tracing each rib.

He lifted his mouth from her breast, and she smiled. She lowered herself onto his lap, bringing them closer. His pulse surged as her inner thigh pressed against his groin. Hot, bright fire shot down his spine at her boldness. Already he was breathless, ready. But locking his gaze with hers, he saw the shadows in her eyes, a small piece of worry crinkling her brow.

He brushed at those anxious lines with his fingers. "You're afraid."

"No." Her chin came up.

She was torn, as he was. Desire also shone like a faint, flickering star in her eyes. A hope.

"You don't need to be afraid. Do you know that?" He had to ask. He, too, had a lot at stake. Now, if Hannah were willing, he could step beyond the loneliness and the grief. Step into the circle of light she'd brought to his life.

"Yes." Certainty. A little worry. So much trust.

Colton's throat tightened. He shared her need. And

how he wanted her. Her creamy skin beckoned him. Beautiful like satin, brushed by firelight. Warmed by his hands.

Heart pounding, Colton touched the first button at her waistband. Watched her dreamy eyes darken. A slow smile curved the corners of her mouth. He fought for conscious thought—but one look at her straddling him, half naked and glorious, and his mind shut down. With a tug, one button gave way. Then another. Hannah's eyes turned the color of midnight.

He shivered when her fingers smoothed across his shoulders and chest. Everywhere she touched, flares of heat sizzled beneath her fingertips. Excruciating need arced through his body. His hands brushed her thighs, removing the muslin drawers with a single stroke. She straddled his thighs, naked and exposed.

The fire crackled. Heat from the hearth radiated over her skin. Hannah managed a ragged breath, then gasped as he pressed his mouth into the hollow between her breasts. She clung to him as his strong arms encircled her and laid her back on the fire-warmed softness of her blankets.

His dark gaze searched hers. He was breathless, too. He was strong, steely hard. Everywhere. Hannah splayed one hand against his chest, amazed at the luxury of him, the texture of his skin and the light dusting of hair, the way he filled her senses and left her wanting.

His fingers brushed her intimately, and she reached to stop him, but already he was spreading heat and dew. Sensation coiled beneath his touch. Bold jolts of pleasure had her gasping. Hannah's hands curled. Her spine arched. Sharp spirals of desire twisted hard in her belly. So much unexpected feeling. She snuggled to breathe and Colton kept touching her, his fingers circling and caressing. White-hot sensation burned and spread. Bigger. Brighter. Consuming.

Hannah tried to move away, but there was his touch. Sharp pleasure coiling tighter. How could she endure more? There was nothing but pleasure, the tight rippling tension of every muscle. And she wanted more. She groaned when his kiss grazed her neck. Moaned when his tongue found her nipples, one at a time. It felt as sweet as heaven and twice as powerful. She planted her feet on the floor and pressed against Colton's hand.

His mouth closed on her breast. Hannah struggled, unable to let go, to let herself surrender to him completely. He kept caressing her most private place. She couldn't breathe. She couldn't lie still. She couldn't fight the amazing bolts of unbearable pleasure sizzling through her body.

"Oh, Colton." He had to stop. She couldn't bear more. Hannah struggled to sit up.

"Relax." He pressed her back to the floor with a kiss to her stomach. His tongue laved her belly button.

Oh, he'd gone much too far. A bubble of heat popped low inside her. His wet, thrilling kisses inched down the lower slope of her belly.

"Relax?" She sat up, entirely uncomfortable with the direction his tongue was heading. "Colton, I don't think you should—"

"Don't think at all, Hannah." His hands brushed her inner thighs, wedging her open to his eyes, to his touch.

No. This was too much. He dipped his head between her legs. Hannah felt a hot, sweet sensation burst beneath the forbidden brush of his tongue. She ought to push him away, but couldn't. Glorious, intense pleasure pulsed and faded, only to pulse again. Every muscle in her body tightened. She felt ready to break apart, to shatter uncontrollably. She had to stay in control. She couldn't let him—

"Relax." His voice.

He'd left her wide open and aching, thighs weak. His gaze locked on the sight of her. Breathless, he waited. Her pulse jumped at the feel of his erection hard and wondrous against her inner thigh. She thought about that hard part of him. Trembling desire bubbled through her. Want doubled with every beat of her heart.

His gaze collided with hers, far too intimate. She wanted to close her eyes and couldn't. His hardness nudged against her, against her hot, moist center, aching for him. She'd never known desire like this before. He filled her and there was no pain, only Colton, only trust and tenderness and pleasure. Hannah closed her eyes, amazed at how wonderful it felt to have that part of him inside her. He moved, and she gritted her teeth at the weightless pleasure. He withdrew, then filled her again. She sighed, pulsing around his thickness. Luxurious sensation trembled through every part of her.

"Oh, Hannah," he breathed.

Magical. That's how she felt. As if she'd discovered love for the first time, this heat spearing through her, warmer than affection in her heart. The drowning of herself in his arms until there was nothing but him—his skin against hers, his steely body moving counterpoint to hers, the aching tenderness of his kisses.

She felt Colton's thrusts deepen, opened her eyes and saw him looking at her. So much need, so much tenderness reflected in those eyes. His big, beautiful body stiffened. His hands clamped tightly on her hips, guiding her every movement, demanding more. A groan broke from his throat as he drove harder, filled her deeply, spilled his seed.

A groan tore from her throat. The aching sweetness started there, where they joined, and twisted higher, burned hotter. Tension drew her muscles tight, squeezed the air from her lungs, and left her helpless against the way her body tightened and tightened. The muscles gripping him began to throb, drawing her in, making her lose control.

"Oh, Hannah," he breathed, choked with emotion.

She couldn't look at him when release shattered her. A big, bright burst of sensation that tore a moan from her throat. A thrilling, heavy sweetness rippled through every muscle, every bone. Colton wrapped his arms around her, pressing a kiss to her forehead.

She snuggled against him, contented, and listened to the beat of his heart.

* * *

Careful not to wake her, Colton laid a second stick of wood on the fire. The pile shifted. Sparks popped. He heard the rustle of the blanket and her sleepy sigh.

"Colton?" She said his name with contentment.

He liked that. "I'm just feeding the fire. It's damn cold in this cabin. And you're naked underneath those blankets."

"You ought to know." She smiled, her cheeks still rosy from their earlier lovemaking.

"Is that an invitation?"

"Maybe."

Red light from the embers glowed along the silken expanse of her exposed skin, caressing her lean arms and slim legs. Colton's pulse thundered, remembering how those legs felt wrapped around his hips.

Tenderness twisted his heart. He set another stick of wood on the fire. "How are your feet feeling?"

"Fine."

"Liar." Colton turned his back on the fire and sat down next to her. "I've had frostbit toes before. Swelled up two whole sizes and hurt like hell."

"I've made up my mind my feet will be just fine. I have a lot of riding to do tomorrow...today." Those worry lines crinkled her brow. "What if we can't find my mares?"

"Then we face that together."

"Together. I like the sound of that." Her eyes filled. A smile warmed her mouth. Her beautiful, kissable mouth.

"So do I." He reached for the blanket and pulled it back. Orange light flickered across her creamy breasts and thighs. Blood jumped in his groin. His shaft throbbed, grew heavy.

Her gaze swept his naked body, and her eyes glittered. Colton took Hannah's hand. With a smile, she came to him. Kissed his lips. Ran her hands across his chest. Air wheezed out of his chest when she boldly straddled his thighs, then sheathed him inside her body.

Hannah woke with a start. Cold air seeped against her side where Colton had lain beside her throughout the night. Shivering, she hugged the blankets close, aware of her well loved body. She might feel cold in the frigid air of the cabin, but in her heart, she felt warm.

Footsteps crunched in the frozen snow outside. Through the poorly battened walls, she could hear his familiar gait. The door crashed open. He stood framed in the threshold. The gray of early morning haloed him like an archangel.

"Looks like a nasty storm is brewing." He stepped inside and closed the door against the bitter wind.

"Then I guess we'd better get going." She sat up, wrapping the top blankets around her bare breasts. "How much did it snow last night?"

"You mean while we were making love?"

Wonderful memories shivered through her. "Yes."

His eyes warmed, remembering, too. "About a foot. It's going to be a tough job finding those horses."

"But we're going to try?"

"I think you know the answer to that. Let me see how your feet look."

"They're fine."

He knelt down beside her and folded back the bottom of the blankets. "They're red and swollen."

"I can ride, Colton."

"Yes. And you'll be riding home." He probed her left foot. She jumped. "I'll be riding after the herd. Mullen said he'd bring a few of his sons and help."

"But still, you need me. I can ride as good as any man

and rope even better."

"I know." He brushed the curls away from her face with such tenderness. "But I care about you, Hannah. You can't let these feet get too cold. We can't take that kind of risk."

He cared about her. Truly cared. Firelight brushed his wide shoulders. He looked so immovable, a man of honor and will and steel. She wanted to touch him. To feel his kiss whisper across her lips. To lose herself loving him. "We'll see how my feet feel when I get them into my boots."

Colton shook his head. "Stubborn. I never met a woman like you. You could drive me to drink."

"Aw, but that's rule number one. Remember?"

"Well, I figured since we broke your other rule all to hell, it wouldn't much matter." His eyes twinkled.

Her heart stalled. "Just because I had a moment of weakness, don't think I've changed my stance."

"Weakness? You call your behavior last night weakness?" His lopsided grin was slow and sexy. "I call it sinful and wanton."

She wished she could argue, but he was right. Hannah shrugged out of the blanket and reached for her clothes. He handed them to her piece by piece, watching her dress. She blushed, but his gaze remained steady, unblinking, the smile wide on his face.

When she stood, sharp pain arrowed through her feet. She gasped and gritted her teeth.

"Still think you can ride with us today?" Colton laid her flannel shirt across her shoulders.

"Yes." *No.* She told herself the pain didn't matter, but how could she endure stuffing her swollen toes in those boots?

Hannah inserted her arms into the shirtsleeves and prayed for strength. Judging from the streak of pain when she took one step, she would need it.

Colton lifted her coat from the peg in the wall and held

it out for her. She avoided his gaze as she allowed him to help her into the garment.

"I really do care about you, Hannah." His voice stroked her like an intimate caress, tender and private. "The storm is going to get bad out there. These mountains are a dangerous place. I don't think both of us should risk our lives. You must go home."

"No, I'm fine, really I am—"

"For Zac. You promised me." Colton reached to lay his hand along her jaw. Tender. Affectionate. "Above all else, protecting my son is one vow I'm going to hold you to. If the storm worsens, all sorts of things could happen. Zac needs you in a way he'll never need me."

"But you're his father."

"You're his mother now." He kissed her, warm and gentle enough to drive any arguments right out of her head.

Her eyes teared because she knew he was right. If he followed the horses, terrible dangers could befall him.

"You gave me your word, Hannah." His gaze fastened on hers. "Will you keep it?"

"Absolutely." They needed to trust each other right now. She would believe he'd do everything he could to bring back the horses. Just as she knew he trusted her with his son.

She wrapped her arms around his neck and pressed her face against the solid wall of his chest. Felt the comfort he offered as his arms enfolded her close.

They were truly man and wife.

* * *

Colton rode the mustang, braced against the bitterly cold air. The new morning scattered pink-gray light across the silvery blanket of incoming clouds and across the blue-gray snow at the mare's hooves. He'd caught up with the Mullens and they were already riding hard, trying to pick up the stallion's trail.

Saddles creaked. Horses clomped through the drifts,

breathing hard. Peace and beauty surrounded him. Yet remembering Hannah's trusting gaze and the journey ahead of him, he couldn't enjoy the scenery.

He'd made a promise to her. And he would do nothing less than his best. For making love with her last night over and over again before the fire healed a place inside that had been empty and hurting for a long, lonely while.

* * *

Hannah clenched her teeth as she took the smallest step toward the back door. A fever pounded at her head. Her frostbitten feet screamed with pain. She grabbed the doorknob and twisted.

Zac launched himself across the kitchen, arms flung wide. "Mama."

Her heart bubbled over. She knelt down and wrapped him against her, breathing in the wonderful little boy scent of him—of cookies and sweetness and a hint of snow. Tears burned her eyes. It was the first time anyone had called her Mama, and he'd done so all on his own.

She brushed back those errant curls from his wide eyes. "I missed you so much while I was gone. Did Mrs. Mullen take good care of you?"

A serious nod. "We had pancakes."

"For breakfast and dinner, too." Blanche strode toward her, wiping her hands on her wide apron. "I'm glad to see you safe, Hannah. My, you look half frozen."

"That's because I am." She stood. Snow from her scarf drifted to the floor. She spotted the jacket hanging on the peg in front of her. A familiar coat. "Is he here?"

"Warming himself at the parlor hearth." Blanche's face darkened. "Came here offering to help with the roundup, but Hank, he turned him down flat. So Sawyer invited himself in to wait for you."

"I can handle it." Hannah unwound her scarf and slipped out of her coat. She stared at her boots, then sat down at the table to pull them off. Sheer agony. She looked up to see Blanche pouring her a steaming mug of coffee.

"It was wise of you to come home."

Hannah sighed. "I know." The coffee revived her, and she took several sips, then knew she could delay it no longer. Glen was in the parlor, listening to every sound she made. Her feet complained as she limped toward the front room.

"Hannah?" He sat in Colton's favorite chair closest to the fire, strong and masculine, but far different than Colton. Glen was sharp and overbearing. "I was worried. You shouldn't have been up in those mountains."

"Someone let my horses out. I had to go after them." She stopped before the fire and held out her hands to warm them, aware of Glen's assessing gaze. Colton's words came back to her. He thought Glen was responsible.

"What about your husband?" He stood beside her.

She stepped away from his nearness. "He's fine."

"You're not worried? A storm could blow in and strand a man. There are avalanches. Mountain lions. Those mountains are filled with too many dangers to name."

Hannah wondered at his point, if there was something darker, like a threat beneath his words. "You were there for me, Glen, when Charles was his cruelest. You took my side. You did what you could to protect me. I've always appreciated that."

"I only wanted to help you, Hannah. I care."

"Care? But you're angry I didn't marry you." She hesitated. "You wouldn't be the one doing this to me, would you?"

"Not to you, Hannah." Glen rubbed his brow. He sounded sincere. "If you need anything while he's gone, just ask." Glen laid a hand on her shoulder. It felt possessive.

"I'll remember that," she said, just so he would leave.

He tossed her a charming grin that reminded her of the man who'd defended her for so many years, then left her alone before the fire.

Colton heard the lone mountain lion's growl shiver like death through the clear afternoon forest. The mare beneath him tensed. She lifted her head and scented the air. The mare sidestepped, nervous.

"I don't think that cat is happy we're here." Hank headed his mount around the edge of the meadow. "Garth and Seth ought to be circling around into position by now. I say we get this show started and drive the rest of these horses home before that cat gets any ideas."

The hair on the back of Colton's neck bristled. "Good idea."

Silence echoed across the mountainside. The horse beneath him bunched as if ready to bolt. Not a good sign. Just in case, he slid the rifle out of its holster and checked the ammunition.

"The wind's holdin' steady. The stallion won't be able to scent us." Hank nosed his Winchester toward the silver-gray sky. "You'll follow behind me?"

"Count on it." The sooner they started to move, the better. Colton gripped the wooden stock, balancing the rifle with one hand. "That cat sounds close."

"Too damn close. I don't intend to be his supper. Let's go." Mullen pressed his gelding into the stand of trees.

Colton's mare sidestepped and he drew her around, carefully studying the small meadow tucked between the miles of mountain forest. Something didn't feel right Something felt off.

His instincts twisted hard, sharp.

Hank's double shot rang out—the signal to start moving in and forcing the herd south toward home.

Senses on alert, Colton drove hard into the forest, following Mullen's directions. He heard the crackle of breaking-branches. A stallion's shrill neigh tore through the forest. Hooves drummed the ground. Colton nosed his mare after them, boughs slamming into his arms and chest, his grip steady on the Winchester.

A scream in the branches overhead was his only warning. Colton looked up at the glistening-eyed mountain lion diving through the boughs, extended claws aimed at his throat. Lightning quick, moving with instinct beyond fear, he lifted the rifle, cocked and aimed. But the mare beneath him shifted, then reared.

Colton tumbled to the ground. The rifle slipped out of his hands. Before he could move, he felt the thud of the lion's front paws against his chest. Panic jammed through his blood.

He was going to die. Flashes of Hannah and Zac burst into his mind, fueling him. He struck the animal in the chest with all his strength.

Sharp teeth scraped along his neck. He landed a hard blow to the cat's throat and knocked it to the ground.

Colton spun. Reached for his gun. Blood stained the snow as he curled his fingers around the walnut stock.

Determined not to lose her fight, the mountain lion sprang.

CHAPTER EIGHTEEN

Hannah woke with a start. Maybe it was the pain in her feet. Maybe it was something else.

The men weren't back yet. There was trouble. She could sense it like the cold night air seeping into her room. She rose from her bed and crept on stocking feet to the gray stone hearth.

Zac murmured in his sleep, rolled over. He was so tiny in her double bed, he was hardly more than a wrinkle beneath the thick comforter and wool blankets.

Her heart warmed. The little boy had cried at the thought of another night without his precious papa to tuck him in. He'd clung to her, the need in his tiny grip so enormous, Hannah couldn't bear to do anything other than take him to her room and read him to sleep.

Now she knelt carefully before the fire, wincing with pain, and stacked more wood on the grate. The flames revived and crackled greedily. But her fears remained.

So many things could have gone wrong. Wild animals. Frostbite. They could have become lost or shot by mistake by any of the landowners struggling to hold onto their property in this rugged country.

She wasn't good at waiting. Yet with her vow to Colton, she could do nothing else.

Hannah stood at the window and stared out at her land. Clouds obscured the moon. She could see only shadows and shades of black upon black. Then a movement within the deep shadows drew her gaze. A light licked to life in the distance, in the barn. She saw the shapes of men. Four, she counted. And horses in the big corral.

They'd returned!

Happiness skidded through her blood. She ran through the door and down the steps, pulled on boots and a coat She dashed outside, breathless, snow filtering her view. A dark smudge rose in the distant night—a man's form. A wide-shouldered, steel-strong man. Her heart raced. How she'd missed him.

"Mrs. Kincaid?" Hank Mullen's voice.

She blinked. No, those weren't Colton's shoulders. Another chill shivered through her. "Where is he?"

"I don't know how to tell you." Hank shifted his weight from one foot to the other. "We went back to try to find him, but—"

Her heart stopped.

"There were cat tracks and blood. But not one sign of Colton. He's got to be dead."

☦ ☦ ☦

Light bled from the sky. Snow fell like rain. Hannah waited in the parlor, lit only by a low fire, all night. She'd watched the storm through the black window glass and prayed. Waited for first sight of him.

But Colton never came.

She fought with herself. She couldn't just sit and wait for him. Her every instinct cried out for her to head back up into those mountains and search until she found her husband, the man she'd made love to in that cold little shanty. Yet her promise to him kept her helpless at home. If she perished in the wilderness trying to find him, then there would be no one to raise Zac.

She could do nothing but wait. And try to hold close her memories of loving Colton. Of his strong bare chest against her hands, his arms holding her close, the amazing feel of his arousal buried deep inside her. Hannah's heart thudded. Those memories hurt because she wanted to love him that way again.

"Mama?" Zac ambled into the room, hugging his little blanket she'd knitted for him and followed by his kitten. "Where's Papa?"

"We have to wait for him to come." What would she tell the child too small to understand? What if Colton never returned? She held out her arms. "Come tell me what you want for breakfast."

"Pancakes." He trudged closer. "An' maple syrup, please."

He leaned against her, so loving and trusting. The weight of her responsibility struck her. And the sweetness. She would love this little boy forever.

"Kitty want pancakes, too." Zac squeezed her hard, then giggled.

Hannah blinked against the hopeless tears filling her eyes.

* * *

The day turned to night. Mullen's youngest boy came to tend to the livestock. With her feet still tender, Hannah was grateful for the help.

She kept Zac busy until bedtime, when he cried for his father. Hannah rocked him to sleep and read of cows jumping over the moon and children living in a shoe until exhaustion claimed his little body. She gently laid her son in his bed and tucked the warm comforter around Zac's little chin. The kitten's purr filled the quiet room and she left, her heart heavy.

Hannah retreated to the cold parlor and settled down at the window to wait. She looked out at the blackness—at the snow falling to mark the darkest time of night.

A shadow loomed overhead—tall and broad and so familiar, every piece of doubt shattered. "Colton."

"It's me." Low, rumbling, soothing as a lullaby. His voice shivered through the night and wrapped around her heart

She jumped out of the chair and into his arms. Oh, it was true. He was here, it wasn't a dream. Flesh and blood man so wonderfully solid in her arms.

"You must be glad to see me." He claimed her mouth with his. Demanding. Hard.

"No, not at all. I always sleep in the cold parlor." She laid her hand tenderly against his jaw. Her thumb circled over his rough whiskers.

"I got your stallion."

"You roped him?"

"And he fought me every step. I was lucky to get him in the barn. He's pissed." That half-smile wobbled.

"You look exhausted. Colton, what—" She saw a stain against his coat. She pulled back the collar to see the dark splash of blood against the flannel shirt and beneath that the angry lines of torn skin from the curve where his left shoulder met his neck down across the flat of his chest. "My God, you've been—"

"It's just a scratch." He winced as she pulled the blood-soaked bandanna away from the deepest part of the wound. "That cat almost had me. But I managed to get off a few shots."

So many words ached in her throat. Maybe she'd have time to say them later. He was pale. And sweaty. And probably far weaker than he was willing to admit. She took him by the hand. "This is serious, Colton. You've lost a lot of blood."

"I'm tough."

"Not that tough." She sat him down on the chair. "No, stay. I thought I'd lost you once. You're not going to do that to me a second time."

"Life's uncertain, Hannah." His hand curled around her wrist. "Especially for me."

"Life's uncertain for all of us." She remembered what he'd told her of his past. Of the enemies he'd made. Of the wife he'd lost. Fear beat through her and it was for more than the serious gash that tore through his skin and muscle.

She was afraid for him.

* * *

"Keep him warm and the bandage clean." The doctor snapped shut his black bag and stepped away from the bedside. Morning light seeped through the curtains and splashed across the green log cabin quilt. Colton's sleeping form lay quietly beneath, his breathing shallow. "He's lost a lot of blood. I'll be back after noon to check on his fever."

"I appreciate you coming so early." Dawn had barely lit the morning when Mullen's youngest son returned with the town doctor.

"You know I'd do anything for you." James Gable gathered his hat and coat from the edge of the cedar chest. "I'm glad to see Kincaid's good to you. And that little boy is sure something."

"Yes, he is." Hannah thought of the child still asleep in his bed, healthy and all hers. "Would you like to stay for breakfast?"

"No, I've got to get back to town and check on a patient. You look exhausted, Hannah. Take care of yourself, too. I don't want you needing my services next."

"Don't worry about me." Hannah led the way down the stairs. "I'm tougher than I look."

"That's what they all say." Warmly, the doc patted her on the back of the hand before he headed out into the cold morning.

She closed the door behind him, her thoughts turning to her husband upstairs, to the man who'd made a claim on her heart.

She couldn't lose him. Not now. Not ever.

* * *

Colton felt fiery pain arrowing across his chest. He tried to move his neck, but the blinding flash stopped him. His eyelids felt too heavy to open. The heaviness of sleep pulled him under, and he fought it. Dark dreams of loneliness, of blood spattered on the kitchen wall, of Hannah lifeless in his arms. And where was Zac? Panic shot through him. He had to find his son. He had to—

"Shhh. Just lie back and rest." An angel's voice, as sweet as song. A cool cloth at his forehead.

Hannah. He tried to reach out for her but couldn't swim to the surface of consciousness. The darkness of nightmares pulled him down.

* * *

Hannah sat in the bedroom, lit only by firelight, and tended her delirious husband. The deep wound where the mountain lion's claws had torn across Colton's shoulder and chest remained infected. She spoon-fed Colton broth and water and medicine and tea. She cleansed the jaggedly torn flesh and bathed his fevered body, carefully administering the laudanum and herbs as prescribed by the doctor. But there seemed to be no improvement.

Just Colton's labored breathing and his bouts with nightmares. He'd murmured incoherently, the words lost to her, but the fear and misery of his dreams haunted her.

Tears burned her eyes and she leaned her forehead against her fingertips. She'd never been so afraid. Nights without sleep were taking a toll on her. Thank goodness the Mullens helped with the barn work and hauling water and bringing in wood. She didn't want to lean on others— and she'd refused such help after Charles's death—but with Zac to watch during the day and Colton needing constant care, she couldn't do it all. She just couldn't.

"Hannah." His fevered voice, rusty and tormented,

whispered through the dark. "No, Hannah."

She reached out to him. His forehead felt so hot. She wrung cold water from a cloth and bathed his face.

He struggled against her touch. "Dead." His voice broke, lost in delirium.

"I'm right here, Colton." Tears knotted in her throat as she laid her hand against his whiskered jaw.

"N-nooo. N-not my Han-nah." Agony twisted his handsome face and he rolled away from her touch.

Hannah remembered what he shared with her in the shanty, the story of the wife he'd loved shot dead by a vengeful murderer, of his son stolen. She knew by the tears marking his face he was reliving that moment in dream. That he'd loved his Ella so very much.

Emotion hurt in her heart—sympathy for his loss, for him. An unnamable ache made tears fall from her eyes and a sob escape from her throat.

She'd been alone from her earliest memories—she couldn't remember her mother. On the outside of relatives' families, aching to belong, aching to be loved. Yet she'd seen nothing of love, only of duty. She understood duty. It was what she'd felt she owed the families who took her in and fed her, what she owed Charles no matter how he treated her.

But this terrible wrenching in her chest, it felt as if her heart was breaking into little pieces. Colton had changed her life the instant he'd walked into it, a man of beauty and strength and honor.

She loved this man. She loved him.

"N-no." Colton's head tossed from side to side on the pillow, restless, slipping farther away from her.

Hannah scrubbed tears from her own eyes and caught Colton's hand. His skin felt hot. She pressed her lips to his knuckles, laid the back of his hand against her cheek.

"Don't leave me, Colton. Please, don't leave me."

* * *

Colton opened his eyes. The dream lifted away like a shroud. No funeral, no gunfight, no helpless, crying baby. No grief so huge he didn't know if he could overcome it.

Just a green quilt covering him. Clean, sunshine-scented pillowcases. A woman's hand lightly resting on his chest.

He remembered the nightmares. He looked up to see Hannah, seated beside the bed in a chair, her head bobbing forward, the fall of gold curls obscuring most of her dear face.

His heart punched. Had she been up all night caring for him? He could barely remember coming home. He tried to move. Pain shot through his chest and neck. Weakness dizzied his head.

"Colton." She snapped awake. Oh, how tired she looked. Her hand brushed his forehead. He saw the worry pinched in the corners of her eyes. Concern for him so big and bright and beautiful he couldn't speak. Could only watch her as she released a slow breath. "Your fever broke. I shouldn't have fallen asleep like that."

He covered her hand with his, so cool and smooth. He remembered the feel of those hands caressing his forehead, his face. "W-water." His throat felt so dry. "P-please."

She moved away. He heard the clink of enamel. Felt the rim of a cup against his bottom lip. She smiled at him as he sipped. Cool water filled his dry mouth.

"There. Close your eyes." Her voice soothed him. Healed some of the hurt inside his heart.

Her footsteps tapped away. When he heard her voice again, she was still sitting in the chair beside the bed, her face just as tired looking, but the bright glow of affection in her eyes constant and unmistakable.

"Here. This will make you feel better." She smiled. The spoon at his lips tipped. Chicken broth filled his mouth. "We have to have you better by morning. Zac is very worried about his papa."

And so are you. He could read it in her eyes, in the quiet tenderness of her touch. No one had ever cared for him so much. Had taken such care with him.

He could see what she wanted—feel it as surely as the brush of her lips to his forehead, as the thud of his heart in his chest. But was he worthy of her? Could he be certain the past was buried? That the nightmares haunting him wouldn't come true?

* * *

"You must be very quiet." Hannah led Zac down the hall, his tiny hand within hers. "Your papa is feeling very badly."

"He got a big boo-boo." With a worried sigh, Zac stepped into the warm room.

The fire blazed. Drawn curtains let in the cheery morning sunshine. Colton lifted his head, and the little boy dashed across the room.

"Papa!" Zac stopped at the bed, uncertain. He'd come to watch his father sleep over the long days when Colton had been delirious. Eyes wide, the boy studied his papa seriously. "You sleepin' lots."

Colton's chuckle came weak, but as warm as ever. "Yes, I have. Come up here and give me a great big hug."

"Big hug," Zac agreed, crawling up onto the quilt and settling against his father's good side. "Mama promised pancakes."

"With huckleberry syrup." Hannah stepped forward, trying to hold back her heart.

Colton's eyes sparkled. He looked hungry. She felt relieved his appetite had returned. It was a good sign. Still, she would not stop fussing until she knew he'd regained full use of his arm.

"Maybe your mama will let me get out of bed and watch her make those pancakes." There was no mistaking the snap of hunger in his dark, gleaming eyes—he was wanting her, and no pancakes.

"Don't get too saucy," she warned as she snatched

Zac's book off the bureau. "Sit and read to your son. I'll bring up the meal and we'll eat in here."

"In bed?" Colton winked. "Then by all means, bring the huckleberry syrup. It could get interesting."

She blushed. The night in the shanty was never far from her mind. "You'll behave, sir, or I'll slip an extra dose of laudanum in your coffee and we'll see how frisky you feel after that."

He laughed, and while he was terribly pale and so very weak, it felt wondrous, luxurious, this closeness and warmth. They'd become a family.

"Fiddle." Zac giggled as his kitten hopped up onto the bed and snuggled into his arms. "Fiddle likin' pancakes, too!"

* * *

With food in his belly, Colton felt stronger, less shaky. He sipped his second cup of coffee alone in bed. Zac had followed Hannah downstairs to find his favorite wooden horse. Fiddle trailed the boy, as always.

Colton tried to move his left arm and failed. Pain sliced through muscle and bone. The injury was more severe than he'd figured.

His gaze strayed to the window where the sun glinted off the sheen of the snowy world—like peace and tranquility. The scenery touched him. His breath caught at the white-capped mountains so huge, they blocked the sky, the snow-blanketed forests, the gleaming white meadows.

Peaceful? Hardly. Sawyer was out there, waiting. Mullen's boys might be protecting the barn, but they were young. No match for a ruthless criminal out to steal what he could not buy.

Colton swore. He was no damn good to his family lying in this bed. He thought of the scorched earth beneath the new barn, the damaged feed, the bolt pins intentionally slipped out of over a hundred stalls. No, he could not afford to lie in bed. He could not risk leaving his family or

227

their livelihood unprotected.

Pain scorched him, dizzied his head, muddled his thinking. But Colton gritted his teeth and pulled on his trousers and shirt. He nearly fainted slipping his injured arm, mostly numb and useless, into the sleeve.

"Where do you think you're going?" Hannah turned from the washbasin, her hands dripping sudsy water on her clean floor. "Colton, you're far too weak. You can't risk that wound breaking open. You've lost too much blood."

"What I can't afford to lose is this family." Maybe it was just the delirium of fever, but the nightmare images of her dead in his arms, Zac taken, pounded through his brain, beat in his heart. "I'm not about to allow anyone to try more desperate measures."

He watched Hannah's gaze slide down to his hips. Her eyes widened at the sight of his holstered revolvers. He gazed out the kitchen window. "Are the Mullen boys still here?"

"I'm not sure. Hank can't spare them both, so they take turns when they can." She looked nervous as she wiped her hands on a towel, the dirty dishes piled behind her forgotten. "Colton, you look so pale. Please, sit down. Let me—"

"I've got to check on the barn." He'd learned to sense trouble, to smell it like smoke on the wind. "Stay in the house. And don't worry about me."

"I know. You're tough." Her lips pressed together in a thin line. "But I don't believe it."

He grabbed his hat. "Try."

The cold wind blew right through him. His knees wobbled, he felt so weak, but he shut the door and stepped out into the weather anyway. He felt Hannah's gaze through the window and was touched that she worried over him.

The barn was dim. Two identical sets of bootprints—one pair bigger and deeper than the other—had broken the melting snow in a track from the front doors to the nearby well. The Mullen boys had packed in water for the horses. He appreciated that. Hell, he owed the neighbors more than he could repay.

A different set of tracks, from a different set of boots. Bigger. And fresh. Colton gritted his teeth and stepped through the double doors of the barn.

Nothing out of place. The stallion, once again captive, lifted back his lips and showed mean, yellow teeth. Apparently the fellow wasn't happy with captivity.

But he wasn't agitated, as he'd been when someone had been in the barn and destroyed the hay. Colton relaxed. Maybe it was the Mullens after all.

He heard the scrape of a stall door, the clink of a door pin being bolted into place. "Seth? Garth?"

No answer.

He spotted a strange horse—the same black gelding the younger Mullen boy rode—and relaxed. No danger. He felt sick and weak, that was all. It must be affecting his brain.

Colton heard the whoosh before pain exploded against his skull. He staggered and reached for his gun. Weakness slowed his responses. Sawyer's pistol nudged Colton at the back of his neck.

"Step inside." The stallion's stall door opened.

The untamed animal began pawing the ground. Fury pounded in those wild eyes. Colton was lifted by his collar. The top button of his shirt choked him. His head spun. He was too damn weak to fight.

"I thought you were gone for sure when you didn't come back from the mountains." Sawyer tossed him into the stall.

Colton ducked as a rear hoof sailed past his head. The stallion, enraged and frightened, hit the back wall of the stall, then bucked again.

"People may say it's suspicious, that stallion killing two men the same way. Then again, he's a wild animal. Hard to control." Sawyer's laugh mocked. "But some will say you were too weak from blood loss to be trying to handle a horse as dangerous as this."

Sawyer's gun fired. The stallion's terrified neigh tore through the barn. Twin rear hooves rose up toward Colton's chest even as he dove out of the way. He hit the floor at Sawyer's boots. He looked up, despite the pain, and saw the man reach to close the door.

Colton didn't have time to grab his gun. Didn't have time to breathe. He wrapped his good arm around Glen's ankle and pulled. The stallion screamed. Sawyer tumbled into the stall. Twin hooves sliced through the air. Glen, not realizing the stallion wanted to be free, scrambled to his feet.

The bone-breaking sound of the lethal kick was unmistakable. Sawyer hit the straw-covered floor with a lifeless thud.

Bleeding, Colton tried to stand as Garth Mullen, skinny and armed with only a pitchfork, dashed into sight.

It was over. Colton took a deep breath. His family— and Zac's future—were safe.

CHAPTER NINETEEN

"Here's a cup of coffee, Sheriff." Hannah handed him a durable enamel mug. Steam rose from the surface in the cool air of the day. "Would you like a bowl of soup before you head back to town?"

It was dinnertime. She'd already quieted Zac with a small sandwich in the kitchen to tide him over until they could sit down to eat. If she could stop feeling sick inside. If she could stop feeling foolish.

On some level she'd trusted Glen. On another level she'd been afraid Colton was right.

Colton. Memories of making love with him hammered through her head, beat in her blood. There'd been true concern in his voice when he'd spoken to her, honest comfort in his touch when he'd sat her down to tell her what happened to Glen. She saw the blood from the cut above Colton's ear. She knew he was armed, yet had not used his guns. She believed in his heart he wasn't a violent man—but he was a man with a violent past.

"I've got the wife waitin' dinner on me as it is," Eaton Baker explained. "But I sure do appreciate the coffee."

Colton looked distant and grim as he strode from the barn. The undertaker's sled squeaked on the snow as it took off for town. The sight of the blanket-wrapped body in the back made her shiver.

Glen had been responsible for Charles's death. A part of her couldn't believe it. Another part cried for the awful truth. Violence was part of a man, etched in his heart, the way of his life. A part of every man.

Colton, magnificent shoulders set, strode toward her. His hat, tipped forward, shaded his face and hid the emotion in his eyes. "At least it's over, Eaton. I just wish it had a different ending."

"Couldn't be helped, Kincaid." The sheriff took a sip of his coffee. "Maybe you'd better let that wife of yours look after you. You're unsteady on your feet."

"I'm just fine." Colton's chin shot up. His gaze fastened on Hannah's. "But I could use a cup of that coffee."

"Then you'll have to come to the house." She lost her breath as she always did every time he looked at her.

He'd saved her in more ways than one.

"Now there's an offer I can't refuse." Colton's hand curled around hers, sure and strong. As if he belonged there, at her side. "Eaton, you don't need me to come to town?"

"Nah, I can handle it from here. No doubt Sawyer was the cause of your trouble." Baker finished the cup and handed it back to Hannah. "Looks like it's clear weather ahead for you two newlyweds."

He winked and left them alone, holding hands beneath the kiss of the bright sun.

"Don't even say it." Colton's grin sizzled. "I don't need a doctor. Don't even ask Baker to send him."

"You're bleeding." But it wasn't very bad. She thought of how easily she could have lost him, even a strong man like him, vulnerable with his injury. "You need—"

"You, Hannah," he interrupted, his voice rumbling straight down to her soul. "I need only you."

Colton halted in the doorway, the snap of the parlor fire behind him, the kitchen ahead. A kerosene lamp tossed a pool of golden light across the oak table and reflected in the black windows. Hannah lifted the coffee pot with a thick towel and carried it toward the table. The light brushed her with a warmth, an intimacy he longed for.

When she smiled, he felt brand new. He would fight one hundred villains for her, face a thousand blizzards. She was like a warm, steady light, beckoning him closer, bringing him home.

She dipped her chin as if suddenly shy. "How are you feeling?"

"Like a new man." He'd faced his greatest fears. The threat hadn't been from his past, after all. He'd protected his wife and son and now they were safe with a future solid enough to build on, with dreams to nurture.

Right now, he had only one dream. To lay her down on that polished wood floor and make love to her until neither one of them could draw another breath.

"I made the coffee fresh." She smiled a little. Lamplight brushed her sweet face.

"It's not coffee I need." He stepped closer. All he could see was the fire in her eyes and it drew him, tempted him.

"Colton, your arm—"

"Is fine." He claimed her mouth with his.

Demanding. Hard. His heart kicked when she melted like snow beneath his touch. He felt her hands splay across his chest. How welcome she felt in his arms. He liked the way her body fit against his. And he breathed in the scent of her, the feel of her. The heat of her kiss assaulted his mouth—she'd learned a thing or two up in that mountain shanty. So delicious and yielding.

"Are you strong enough?" Her whisper brushed his lips, spoken with his breath. "Maybe you should sit down?"

"It's good to have you worry over me." Damn good. It

made him feel wanted, more of a man.

In her eyes, he saw an admiration, a burning glow of a budding affection he could never deserve, certainly never ask for. But there it was, as steady as the North Star and twice as bright.

"If you didn't go off getting yourself attacked by mountain lions, I wouldn't need to worry at all."

Her eyes widened when he wound his fingers through her golden curls and gently pulled her head back. She sighed, a happy little puff of air as he nibbled and licked his way down her throat. Oh, how good she tasted, smelled. He breathed in the honeysuckle scent of her. Blood thrummed through his veins.

He pressed her back, catching her mouth with a kiss. Her tongue reached out to his. She bumped against the table, and the crystal lamp tinkled. His stiff fingers fumbled with her buttons. He pulled back the wool placket. Air rushed from his chest at the sight of her creamy breasts beneath. Her breath brushed his cheek, light and fast. He tasted the heat of her nipple. He rolled his tongue around the swollen bud, then filled his mouth with her sweetness.

"Do you like this?" he whispered against her damp skin.

She laughed, low in her throat. "No."

"Then I'd better stop."

"Don't you dare." She laughed again, wound her fingers through his hair, and held him close to her breast.

His blood charged when those sensitive fingers crept along his hairline. Desire flooded his chest as she pressed sweet, hot, tingling kisses down his throat.

He wrapped his tongue around her nipple, already moist from his mouth, and suckled. She sucked in air. He felt pleasure thrill through her body. An ache beat in his groin. Hannah threw back her head and moaned, low and needy.

That same need beat in his blood. He had to have her,

now, no matter how weak he felt, no matter how tough the day. She could soothe away the troubles, chase away the nightmares, this angel of his. He fumbled with her waistband. Slid down the first layer of her skirt. He was frantic to feel all of her.

"Zac's upstairs asleep." Breathless, her dreamy gaze searched his. "Maybe we should—"

"I can't wait." He untied her drawers. "Can you?"

"No." The last layer fell away. She stood before him naked in the shadowed light, shivering not from cold but from anticipation.

A slow, sexy, lopsided grin stretched his mouth. He unbuttoned his shirt. She reached to help him—he had trouble moving his left hand. Fabric fell away to reveal a perfect male chest—bronzed skin, a light dusting of curling hair, hard steely muscle upon muscle.

"Touch me," he whispered.

How could she keep her hands to herself? She ran her hands over him, over the hot texture of his skin, careful of his bandage, delighting in the feel of the hard muscle and bone beneath. So much power. So much strength. She thought of what he'd done, all that he meant to her. He both frightened and exhilarated her.

His touch undid her. Heated caresses over the rise of her breasts. Sweet, unbearable sensation skidded through her. Tension coiled low in her belly.

Her fingers found his trousers, and she tried to unbuckle him. Laughing, he caught her mouth as his hands closed over hers. He tasted like dark passion. Her heart caught when she heard the clink of his belt hitting the wood floor. His manhood surged against her inner thigh. Her mouth opened. Heavens, she couldn't breathe.

Colton's eyes darkened as he laid her back over the table. Oh, she craved him. She was so ready for him. Her inside muscles ached with anticipation. He splayed his palms on her hips. He filled her with one slow thrust. Inch by delicious inch his thickness stretched her. A shivery feeling twisted low and hard, a pleasure that was bright as a summer sun.

He rocked once, twice. His big body covered hers. His weight, wondrous. His kisses tender and tough and exciting all at once. She twined her legs around his waist and held tight, rocking up to meet him. He stiffened, release already pounding.

Hannah closed her eyes, pressed her face to his shoulder. All she could feel was him—moving inside her, taking her with him as if they were one. The crazy beat of her heart, the slick heat of his skin on hers, the fast, hot wave that rippled outward from deep in her abdomen all the way to the tips of her fingers. Spiraling white heat that tore a groan from her throat. Helpless, she held on as sharp pleasure tore through her, wave after wave.

"Colton." She breathed his name.

His lips brushed hers. "You liked that."

She caught his kiss. Returned it. "No. I didn't like it at all."

His eyes flashed. "You lie."

"Guilty as charged." Her hand laid tenderly against his jaw. Her thumb circled over his rough whiskers. Tenderness welled in her heart. So very much tenderness.

Still gloved inside her, she felt his reaction. Hard. Fast.

She tightened her thighs around his waist.

"I can't get enough of you," he murmured against her lips.

She kissed him, drew back. Saw passion glaze his midnight dark eyes. "You are some man, Colton Kincaid."

"Only for you."

She lifted her hips, taking him deeper. Pleasure twisted across his ruggedly handsome face. How could she keep from loving him?

He was a dangerous, powerful man, but a tender man, too. And he was all hers.

Hannah wrapped her arms around Colton's neck and held on as another wave of release crashed through her.

* * *

Tom Varney stepped off the stage at the Paradise stop and landed in a puddle. Slush and icy water rushed in through the hole in the sole of his boot. He bit back a curse and grabbed his two satchels from the driver unloading luggage from the coach's boot.

He hated doing his pa's dirty work, but it wouldn't be the first time. Pa was down robbing a few banks to the south. Figured they would be easy hits, that the peaceful towns on this side of the Rockies made the sheriffs lax. Why, some of the towns didn't even have lawmen.

Tom's stomach turned. He wished he knew a way to get out from under Pa's thumb. But one day, it could happen. It had to. Then Tom would be free to use the money he'd been saving to buy himself that ranch of his dreams. Nothing fancy, just something nice and peaceful. Something to build a life on.

"Excuse me." An angel's voice made him look up.

His jaw dropped at the sight of the woman, pretty as a picture in a light pink checked frock. He was standing in her way, he realized as she blushed, then shyly smiled.

This was the kind of life he wanted. And the kind of girl.

"Sorry," he managed to say with some polish.

"Have a good day." She breezed past and inquired something of the coach driver.

Tom took a wobbly step, but inside his heart raced, his blood pumped. He glanced over his shoulder, and the pretty woman's gaze met his, light and merry. She was much too fine for the likes of him.

If only things were different. If only he wasn't the son of a killer.

* * *

"You're looking paler all of a sudden," Hannah commented beside Colton on the wagon seat. "Do you want me to drive?"

"I can manage." Truth was, he hadn't recovered as

237

quickly as he would have liked. The gash from the mountain lion's claw along his neck had been deep. The muscles of his shoulder had been badly torn. Even now, his arm was stiff. He was damn lucky he could move his hand. "Besides, a man doesn't let his wife drive him around town."

"I suppose a man's reputation is important." Amusement twinkled in those dream-blue eyes. "Heaven knows, if people saw me holding the reins they would think you were nothing but the biggest wimp this side of the Badlands."

"Probably." He laughed with her. And it felt good on this early Sunday morning with the snow turning to slush beneath the wagon wheels—and spring in the air.

It was a time of change, of rebirth, of beginnings. Colton felt it deep in his soul.

"We gonna sing songs." Zac, cuddled on Hannah's lap, clapped his little hands together when they rode into town.

Colton's chest warmed, measuring the happiness shining bright in his son's eyes.

"Hey, Kincaid." Ira Griffin from the livery ambled up to the halted wagon. "I was wonderin' if you could swing me a deal."

"Depends on the deal." Colton set the brake, then climbed down.

"Got a new man in town lookin' to buy a horse or two. Now, you know I keep my stock low during the winter. And I don't have any good riding horses—not the kind he's looking for."

"You want to buy a few from me?"

"If that wife of yours will let me." Ira glanced at Hannah.

She laughed. "Well, Mr. Griffin, I suppose I'll allow it."

Colton smiled. All was right with the world. "I guess that means we've got a deal, Ira. Come out to the ranch any time."

Ira tipped his hat, pleased with his success and hurried

on as the church bell tolled.

"We're late." Hannah handed Zac down. "I swear, I don't know where the time is going."

"Don't you?" Cuddling his son, Colton grinned up at his wife. "I seem to remember what delayed us this morning."

A sweep of pink stained her face. "Mr. Kincaid, this is the Sabbath. Don't go mentioning that where anyone walking past can hear."

"It's sinful to work up that kind of a sweat on Sunday." He winked.

The blush deepened. "Colton, I—"

"Then again, a man likes to work up a sweat." He brushed a kiss to her lips, an outrageously indecent display of affection.

But Hannah's eyes shone, belying the prim angel's act. He wasn't fooled. He'd made love to her this morning until well after the sun rose, neglecting the hungry horses and all his chores just for the thrill of lying in her arms.

"Behave yourself," she whispered in his ear as he helped her down. "At least inside the church."

"I can't make promises. Reverend Hardy's sermons are mighty long." Colton looped the reins around the hitching post.

"Very long," Zac sighed.

"Then you'll just have to watch your papa and make sure he behaves, right, Zac?" Hannah laid her hand gently on the boy's shoulder.

Zac tipped his head back to grin hugely up at her. "Papa's trouble sometimes."

"He surely is." Laughter danced in her eyes, as alluring as paradise, and Hannah held out her hand.

He twined his fingers through hers. They walked together toward the open door of the church, careful of the mud-slick walk. His heart felt light, his burdens gone.

"Mr. and Mrs. Kincaid," the minister said as he met them warmly at the door, kindly bestowing praise on little

Zac.

Zac endured it bravely. He knew about those long sermons, too.

* * *

The church was crowded. Tom wasn't a religious man, but he wanted to be. Pa sneered at God. Said man's only salvation lay in the power of his gun and the accuracy of his aim.

Tom knew he was a coward by his father's standards. Knew he always would be. But maybe one day he didn't have to think about his pa. The pretty girl in the pink frock was sitting three pews ahead of him with her fine-looking family.

He'd spent only a little time in this town, but it was so friendly. The innkeeper learned he liked cinnamon rolls and baked them fresh for him just this morning. And treated him the way he imagined a mother might, with warm smiles and gentle words.

He hadn't met Kincaid yet, but learned he owned the best spread around. He hadn't scouted him out yet, because he didn't have a horse although he'd asked the livery man about buying two, but the land itself kept him captive. He went for a walk just north of town and took one look at the mountains, at the meadows, free and peaceful. His imagination overtook him.

He wanted his life to be different. One day. He wanted a real home. And a pretty wife to bake him cinnamon rolls and serve them with a tender smile.

As the sermon ended, the congregation stood. Tom hopped to his feet. He'd never attended a service before. He fumbled with the hymnal to find the right page. But he liked singing. He liked everything about this place.

Yes, maybe one day he could make a new start. This was the first time he'd been close enough to see what his dreams could be.

* * *

"**Y**our gorgeous husband looks pretty healthy for nearly being killed by a ferocious beast," Paula commented as she rolled a thread around her crochet hook.

"I count myself lucky he survived the mountain lion and found his way home." Hannah set the coffee pot on the small parlor table. Her heart skipped. The lonely nights of waiting for him—of not knowing if she'd lost the best thing that had ever happened to her.

Would she always worry that way, knowing of his past?

"I meant that beast Glen Sawyer," Paula said and set the needlework in her lap. "My, that coffee smells delicious. Oh, and your cinnamon rolls. Hannah, I'm going to burst my corset laces eating your goodies."

"Me, too." Hannah lifted her embroidery hoop from the seat of the wing chair and sat. "I keep baking so many cakes and cookies for little Zac, I'm going to need to let out my dresses."

Merry laughter rang in the air. "You look good, Hannah. The best I've ever seen you. You look happy."

"I think I am."

"Must be all that sweet lovin' from that man." Paula winked. "My, a good sex life can do wonders for a woman."

"I guess so." Hannah blushed and busied her hands pouring coffee. "Sugar?"

Paula tipped her head back and laughed. "Please. Did you see the newcomer to town in church today?"

"No. Although Rose commented on how Tom Varney was the best-lookin' man around except for my Colton."

"Your Colton." Paula reached for a cup of coffee, not at all fooled. "And it wasn't all that long ago you didn't want to marry him."

Hannah could only agree. She'd never felt this light before, this contented. As if she'd grabbed hold of a dream and couldn't let it go. The first-star-of-the-night wishes of a little girl without family, always on the outside looking in, yearning for someone to hold her close and love her.

She had that now. She had her own family.

Glancing out the window, she could see Colton beside the Boltons' wagon, tall with their monthly delivery of hay, supervising the unloading. Ira Griffin stood beside him. Apparently they were negotiating a sale.

She had a man she could trust, who would provide for them and made good decisions—even if she didn't always agree with him. She had a beautiful man who'd saved her life and livelihood, who'd shown her the gentle power of a man's love.

Her heart felt so full. She feared anything this wonderful wasn't made to last.

CHAPTER TWENTY

A gray drizzle misted the morning air as Colton set down his hammer. The last stall in the new barn was now finished—the door sturdy, the pin clean-fitting, the wood sanded smooth. Accomplishment burned in his chest—the outer shell of the building had gone up in a day, with the help of friends and neighbors, but the time-consuming work of laying the floor, constructing the inner walls, and finishing the roomy box stalls he'd done alone.

He rubbed his left shoulder, stiff, the wound healed, but the joint not fully recovered yet, and stood.

"Hey, handsome." Hannah strode toward him, her blue checked skirts littered with bits of straw. "I just promised Zac a ride on my mare. Do you want to come?"

"I've got work to do." Colton swiped his brow. He'd grown used to the cold Montana air. The comparatively warmer breezes of spring had him sweating. "I've got some horses to move into the barn this afternoon."

"Oh. Well, maybe another time." Disappointment hopped in her eyes. She brushed her hand across his jaw once, a brief touch. "You work so much."

"Not nearly enough. There's much to do." Colton

hooked the hammer in his work belt. "Let me help saddle the mare."

"I can manage." A quick smile.

"But I want to help." He pressed a kiss to her mouth. She responded with a parting of her lips. A deep kiss that seared his blood, left him craving more.

"Goin' riding, Papa."

Colton felt a tug on his trousers. He looked down to see Zac grinning up at him. Colton's heart skipped two beats at the happiness so vivid on his son's face. "Are you gonna be my little cowboy?"

"Already Mama's." Zac wrapped both of his arms around Hannah's knees.

Colton nudged back the brim of his son's tiny hat. "Then Mama's little cowboy had better help us saddle up." He swung his son into his arms. "You know what I've been thinking?"

"You, thinking?" Teasing glints deepened the blue of her eyes. "What?"

He set Zac down and hefted the saddle onto his good shoulder. "Now that this building is finished, there's going to be a lot more barn work around here."

"I don't mind helping out." Hannah smoothed every wrinkle from the fine blanket she'd spread along her mustang's withers. "I love working with the animals. And it's going to take both of us to get those horses ready for sale."

"Both of us, huh?" He set the saddle down gently, then bent to buckle the cinch. "We're money ahead from the deal I made with Griffin. I was thinking about hiring a hand."

"Now?" She dropped the knotted reins over the mare's neck. "We lost our stallion. With spring here, we're going to need—"

Colton kissed the blush streaking across the creamy skin of her cheeks. "Too bad he escaped when Sawyer jumped me. I wish—" He stopped. "Sutcliff has a stallion he'd be interested in selling me."

"You have everything figured out."

Was that a good thing? A bad thing? Colton couldn't quite guess as Hannah checked the cinch.

She swung up into the saddle. "We'll talk later. I'm taking my little cowboy for a ride."

"Yippee!" Zac reached up his arms.

Colton picked him up and deposited him on the saddle in front of Hannah. Her arms wrapped around the tiny boy protectively.

Colton's heart pounded loud as a brass drum. This woman was now a big part of his life.

"See ya later, Papa!" Zac's happy voice echoed in the rafters as Hannah headed her mustang toward the meadow.

Colton watched, his heart full. He picked up his tools and went back to work, humming.

* * *

With the noon meal dishes done and Zac a little sniffly, Hannah decided to keep him in the warm house the rest of the day. She'd wanted to help Colton with more of the training, but her son came first.

Zac climbed up on a chair to oversee her baking. "Little men cookies."

"Do you want to help me decorate them?" She laid the last gingerbread man on the greased cookie sheet with care. "They need eyes and mouths."

"I helpin'." Impressed, Zac leaned close to inspect the little faceless cookies.

"Here. Let me show you." Hannah laid two plump purple huckleberries for the eyes.

Zac clapped, delighted.

Over the crackle of the fire and the kitten chasing his tail on the floor, Hannah knelt close to her son as they decorated the cookie men. She used preserves to draw little collars at their necks and little buttons down their tummies.

It was all Zac could do to wait while Hannah slid the first cookie sheets into the oven, careful of the heat of the fire. He supervised, hands clasped and so eager, as she lifted the first sheet filled with half-baked men up onto the top shelf while she slid the second sheet into place. And it was so hard to wait until the first batch had cooled enough so those eager little fingers wouldn't get burned.

Hannah laughed as she lifted a cookie and blew on it. Then, deciding Zac might explode if he waited another second, handed it to him.

"Yummy," he announced with a full mouth.

He was too cute to scold for bad table manners.

The back door flew open. Colton burst in along with a blast of fresh, spring-scented air. He swept off his hat, and Hannah's heart knocked sideways when he grinned at her. He still favored his left hand. And he still wore his holster strapped to his thigh.

Again, she wanted to question him.

"Looky, Papa!" Zac held up his piece of gingerbread, already missing both hands and feet.

"What did Hannah make you?"

"Cookie boys." Zac rubbed a crumb from his lower lip. "Only eat one."

"Only one?" Colton studied the racks of cooling cookies. "Is that another rule of yours, Hannah? Only one cookie at a time?"

"Before a certain boy's nap."

True affection shone in Colton's midnight eyes. He laid his good arm across her shoulder and caught her mouth in a quick kiss.

Every inch of her body sizzled in response.

He leaned close. "How about for bigger boys who no longer need naps?"

Hannah reached for a gingerbread man. "You'd rather have a cookie and not a more grown-up treat?"

He took a bite of gingerbread. "Why not both?"

She laughed. It was so easy now that her heart was no longer troubled, no longer lonely.

Colton glanced at the ticking clock. "Isn't it time for Zac's nap?"

She didn't miss the message in those naughty, sexy eyes. She blushed, knowing full well Colton had not come in at nap time for a bite to eat. "Want me to take him up?"

"No, I will." Colton wrapped his arm around his son's waist and hefted him out of the chair. "How about it, partner?"

"Need more cookie," Zac decided after serious contemplation.

"We'll take it upstairs with us." Colton flashed Hannah a wink as he snatched another gingerbread man from the table. Any small bribe was apparently worth it to get the child up to bed.

Hannah laughed, watching him go. Her happiness was great, but always offset by the sight of his Peacemaker strapped to his thigh, even here in the safety of the house.

Colton watched her take the final cookies from the table, stacking them carefully in the big crock she used for a cookie jar.

She always kept it full of goodies for Zac. The boy was close to being spoiled, but in a good way. Colton figured a woman who could never bear a child of her own had a right to a little harmless indulgence. Besides, Zac was thriving on her loving care, the tenderness she gave to him daily.

He rubbed his sore shoulder before he stepped into the room.

The sound of his footsteps spun her around. She smiled, a vision of everything he'd never deserved, of everything that could possibly save him. She looked a little tired and pale, but her eyes sparkled with an unmistakable want.

She desired him. "So, you came back for a cookie?"

"No. I want a grown-up treat." He claimed her mouth

247

as they laughed together. A blood-tingling melding of chuckles and reaching lips and caressing tongues. She sighed against him, and he liked that. He liked that Hannah gave him this part of her.

"Are you certain he's asleep?" she whispered against his mouth.

"Absolutely positive." He breathed in the feel of her, so flower petal soft. Her body fit his as he found her mouth, laving his tongue against hers with a slow caress.

In answer, her hands splayed across his chest, then crept up to his shoulders to lock around his neck. She held on as he sat her on the table. In one smooth motion she parted her knees and he stepped between her thighs.

She flooded his senses—the scent of honeysuckle that clung to her skin, the new hint of sugar from the gingerbread, the silken threads of gold when he wound his fingers through her hair. The feel of her body—soft, yet firm, hot and pliable as he caught her hips with his hands and pressed her harder against him.

And her sigh. It whispered across his mouth and shivered in his soul.

Already she'd unbuttoned her bodice and the light chemise beneath. He bent to taste her nipple, to caress the creamy slope of her breast with eager fingers. She arched her back, contented. Her breath brushed his brow, light and fast. She wanted him the way he wanted her—completely. Immediately.

First he tasted the heat of her nipple. He rolled his tongue around the swollen bud, then filled his mouth with her sweetness. Her fingers curled against his neck, holding him close, encouraging him. He'd learned what she liked. He kept suckling, then laving that sweet bud. Hannah threw back her head and moaned, low and needy.

He couldn't wait. Neither could she. He heard it in her hot, quick breath, read it in her big, bottomless eyes.

"Don't make me wait" The words whispered across her lips and drew his gaze to her mouth, swollen and damp from his kisses.

He unbuckled his gun belt and set it within easy reach on the table. Then his trousers were next. His hardness surged against the silken length of her inner thigh. Colton watched Hannah's eyes darken. Watched her mouth open just a little. He moved to nudge against her wetness.

She relaxed back in his arms, her skirt bunched to her waist as he leaned over her. The crystal lamp tinkled as he laid her down on the table and sheathed his aching shaft inside her.

Heat. Tightness. A shivery feeling twisted around his spine, a sensation better than anything he'd ever known. Hannah gazed up at him, eyes glazed with something greater than pleasure, more lasting than affection.

Love. He knew it then, beating in his heart, heating his blood, building with every thrust within her gloving tightness. The way he felt about her was bigger and brighter than any other—and his obligation to her more precious.

He felt her release like a thousand rippling waves, and he lost all of himself. Climax tore through him so fast he couldn't catch his breath. All he could feel was the crazy beat of his heart and the heat of her sighs. Once wasn't enough, would never be enough. He came again, feeling the tide of her release.

Her eyes twinkled up at him. "I ought to make gingerbread more often if it affects you this way."

"At least once every afternoon."

Her smile saved him. Left him feeling whole, forgiven from a past he could not forget. "I love you," he said.

* * *

Colton ran his hand down the black's fetlock. Well formed. Strong. There was nothing wrong with this stallion. Big, gentle eyes studied him as he stood. The horse looked as if he were awaiting the decision, too.

"It's a deal, Sutcliff." Colton stood. "This stallion will do just fine."

"You won't be sorry." Arnie knuckled back his Stetson. "My wife told me I'd better offer you the best I had, seein' as how she's best friends with your wife."

Colton chuckled. "By the amount those women sew and talk, they could have quilted their way to New York by now."

"True." Laughing, Arnie signaled to his son, a boy of about ten, who ran out of sight. "Are you still looking for a hand?"

"If I find the right man."

"Had that newcomer to town, Varney, stop by and ask this morning. I didn't have any need with three sons of my own, but I thought of you." The boy returned with a fine rope halter and Arnie began slipping it over the stallion's head. "Now, I didn't want to send him on to you without your word first, but I think he's a good worker. He helped me split wood while he talked, and I was impressed. Not too many men will help out like that, not expecting to get paid."

"I caught sight of him a few times at church." Colton laid his hand against the warm flank. The stallion leaned against his touch. "You think he's a good man?"

"He seemed timid, like maybe he doesn't think well of himself, but he seems honest. Maybe you should judge for yourself. I can send him your way next time I see him."

Arnie snapped a lead onto the halter. "I told him to check back and see if I'd found something for him."

"You do that." Colton took hold of the rope and studied his new stallion. Friends, family, a prosperous ranch. It felt damn good. There was no danger from his past, no threat to his future. He could relax and let himself enjoy a little happiness.

* * *

"Have you seen him?" Abby Drummond made a little sigh as she poked her threaded needle through the taut fabric of the stretched quilt. "He's a dream."

"He's like a big chocolate cake," Paula agreed. "You just want to take a bite."

The women seated around the quilt frame giggled, many blushed. Hannah watched Abby's pink face darken and saw the girl's heart in her eyes. First love.

"Tom Varney opened an account at the bank. That's how I first met him. Of course, I saw him step off the stage when I went to fetch a bundle for Father, but I never thought—" Abby sighed.

"That you'd fall head over heels just saying hello?" Blanche Mullen finished. "That's how it was for me and Hank. Sure, you're thinking, what does a woman who's been married for nearly thirty years know about courtin'? A whole heck of a lot, I tell you."

"Blanche," Hannah scolded on a laugh.

"Blanche, you hot woman," Rose teased, and the room broke out in laughter.

Hannah thought of the pleasures of marriage. Thought of the way she'd fallen so in love with her husband.

"Tom is almost as handsome as your man," Holly added with appreciation. "Almost as handsome as my Robert. Sorry, Blanche," she added, blushing at her beloved's mother.

"What does your papa think of young Mr. Varney?" Rose asked as she unspooled a length of fine white thread.

Abby shifted in her chair. "Well, Father would like to see me marry well. I told him marrying a man I loved would be the best possible situation."

"Love is important," Hannah added, remembering the mistake she'd made in her first marriage, thinking of her happiness with Colton. Of the man who'd saved her life, who'd fought for everything she held dear.

He was a hero to her. And loving him? Nothing could be more heavenly, more right. They were truly partners now. Man and wife. Forged from the danger of Glen Sawyer's jealous greed.

Paula chuckled. "I stopped by Hannah's house

yesterday afternoon to pay a friendly visit and ladies, I want you to know our delicate and very proper Hannah opened the front door with her skirt askew and two buttons missing from her bodice and her hair tumbled down from its knot."

"Paula, you said you wouldn't tell." But Hannah found herself giggling with the rest of the women, safe and warm in the Drummonds' fine parlor.

"I just wanted to point out what a good thing a loving marriage is." Paula winked, inviting more laughter.

The talk turned to Holly and Robert Mullen's June wedding. Hannah, so full of happiness, tried to pay attention, but the image of Colton naked in the hay inviting her to love him taunted her.

That's how she'd left him, a rakish lover with a satisfied grin on his face as she rode off for her sewing meeting. Is that how he would be waiting for her when she returned?

The room was suddenly very hot.

* * *

Colton felt the change in the air, heard the silence of the spring birds. He crosstied the stallion in the aisle of the new barn and stepped outside.

Arnie Sutcliff, Paula's husband, and another. Colton recognized the brawny man right away. The tension eased from his spine.

Hell, what was he doing? Looking for danger when none existed? It was an old habit. A logical man knew there was no danger in these woods, in this forgotten corner of Montana. Colton had to start living, had to start believing he was a rancher, not a man surviving by the cold end of a gun.

"Hello, Arnie." Colton squinted up against the sunshine.

"This is the man I was telling you about. Tom Varney, meet Colton Kincaid."

The stranger's eyes widened. "Good to meet you."

His handshake was firm, but his gaze a little shy. Far

from forceful. Colton wondered about that. Still, Arnie had said Varney was a good worker. "Hear you're looking for ranch work."

"Hope to buy my own place one day." Dreams and something else, something darker, shaded those eyes.

Hell, hadn't he vowed to stop living in the past? To stop searching for the danger in a man? Colton gestured toward the barn. "Let me show you what I expect. It will be a lot of hard work."

"I ain't afraid of that." This time Varney's smile looked young, the way it should, and hopeful. "I want to learn the business. I don't mind cleaning barns."

"Good. Because that's what you'll be doing. To start." Colton knew about dreams. Admired a man who worked for them. "I came here with the same hopes."

"For a new start?" Varney couldn't be twenty years old, but he stood straight. Ambition burned in his eyes. "That's what I'm hopin' to find, too. I want to learn about the ranching business."

Colton held out his pitchfork. "Then this is the best place to start."

"With horse manure?" With an obliging chuckle, Tom bent to work.

* * *

A coolish breeze blew—the snows in the mountains had yet to melt. But spring had transformed the land. New grass sprouted in the field, painting the meadows a vivid, rich green. The winter sparrows had left and colorful bird song sweetened the air. Eager green buds hugged tightly to long tree limbs as if afraid to open. The sky shone as blue as heaven.

Hannah didn't fight the rising feeling of happiness as she rode the young mare toward home. The Appaloosa tossed her head, scenting the wind, perhaps remembering the days when she ran free.

The land was steadily being grabbed up by homesteads, taken in by ranches. The wild mustangs ran hungry. Come

June, when she and Colton had this batch of horses trained and sent by boxcar to the buyer near Miles City, they would round up more and start again to add breeding stock to their herd and training others to sell.

Their future shone brighter than the happy-faced sun.

"Hello, ma'am," a dark-haired young man said as he emerged from a box stall. He tipped his hat. "You must be Miz Kincaid."

"Yes." Hannah stiffened. Where was Colton? Why was this stranger in their barn? He was holding a pitchfork.

Footsteps knelled on the floorboards. Colton's gaze latched on hers, solid as iron and tender as love. "I've made a decision. I've hired young Mr. Varney full-time to help us out. I don't want you working so hard."

"Colton—" she began and dismounted. Tom eagerly took the reins, so polite she felt bad saying she didn't want him. Hannah marched toward Colton and waited until they were outside the barn to speak. "Full-time? I didn't know we could afford to spend that kind of money."

He cradled her hand within his. "You're more important than any amount of money, Hannah. You've lost weight. I'm just afraid Zac and I are working you too hard."

"How could you do this without talking to me first?" She took off toward the house, simmering anger hard in her step.

"You're mad at me," he guessed from the set of her spine.

"I'm contemplating serious physical harm." She didn't turn around, just walked right up onto the back porch and flung open the door.

He hurried after her. "You know this shoulder would probably heal the rest of the way if I didn't lift the pitchfork so many times a day."

"When I used that argument to talk you into hiring part-time help, you dismissed the idea." She tore off her cloak. "Hello, Zac."

"Angry." The boy looked up from the kitchen floor with huge eyes.

"Thanks for the tip." Colton grinned down at his son, who clutched his Union Pacific steam engine bought from Baker's store. "Hannah, trust me. I have a good reason."

"A full-time hand. You hired a full-time hand." She marched over to the pantry.

"We can afford it."

"We didn't agree to it together." She banged open the pantry door. "I'm not going back to that. I'm not going to start trusting a man only to find him disregarding my opinion and doing whatever the hell he wants."

"I'm not—"

"You are." She banged raw potatoes down on the cutting board.

Only then did he see the glisten of tears. Tears. He'd truly upset her. When he'd hired Tom, he hadn't thought it would make Hannah cry.

"He just showed up here. I liked him. I thought it would make life around here easier for all of us. Especially for you." He caught her wrist, small in his bigger hands.

"You've been so tired," he began. "You haven't said anything, but I can tell."

"I'm fine, Colton." She gazed up at him, then crumpled like a rag doll into his arms.

CHAPTER TWENTY-ONE

The doctor coiled the stethoscope and stowed it away in his black bag. "Keep her quiet. At least for the rest of the night. She should be feeling better by morning."

Colton rubbed the back of his neck, unable to lift his gaze from Hannah, lying in their bed in the faint glow of the single lamp. "She's been working too hard. She seems to think she should help with the horses."

"Hannah Kincaid is a determined woman, no doubt about it. But some changes are in order." Doc Gable ambled toward the door. "She'll have to give up some of her work from now on. I'm not saying there's anything wrong, but considering her history it might be best for her to take it easy. Not to overtire herself. And no heavy lifting."

Colton stepped out into the hall. His heart began to hammer. "Something's wrong with her. She hasn't been looking well."

"Or eating much in the mornings, I bet." The doc grinned. "Pregnant women tend to do that. And they cry easier, too."

"Pregnant?" The word felt strange on his tongue. "But Hannah can't—"

"Apparently she can." The doc shrugged. "When she lost her baby, there were no serious complications. She just never conceived again. Maybe the problem wasn't with her. It takes two."

Colton tried to swallow. Pregnant. A baby. Another child. Another adorable son. Or maybe this time a sweet daughter. His knees rocked, and he felt changed. So very changed.

"How—" He stopped. "How far along is she?"

"Come September you'll be a papa for the second time." The doctor's footsteps tapped on the steps. "I'll let myself out."

"Colton?" Her voice, muffled from beneath the covers.

He stepped into the room, heart racing. There she was, his wife, her angel's face so pale, her gold hair fanning the pillow like a halo. His beautiful angel. "You're supposed to be sleeping," he scolded softly.

"You promised to stay by the bed." Her voice wobbled. "I opened my eyes and you were gone."

"Just in the hallway talking with the doc." He eased down on the edge of the bed, afraid to disturb her, aching to hold her in his arms, to never let her go.

"Did he tell you?" Big tears filled her eyes.

"Yep." He watched those tears spill down her pale cheeks. "Looks like that night of wild abandon in the mountain shanty paid off."

More tears. "It sure did."

He rubbed the wetness from her cheeks with his fingers. So much tenderness filled his heart, for this woman he loved, for this new chance at life he'd been given.

"I've never been this happy." She gazed up at him. "I'm afraid it can't last. It never has."

"That doesn't mean it won't." He pulled the covers back. "I give you my word, Hannah Kincaid. I will do everything in my power to keep all of us safe from harm. And that includes our child you're carrying."

She nodded, so much vulnerability. There was so much to lose in life. He knew first hand. Life, birth, and death so closely related, so easy for one to become the other.

Yet she trusted him to protect her. To make sure everything worked out fine.

He lay down beside her, wrapped her in his arms, against his heart, and pressed a kiss to her forehead.

Rain tapped at the window and he held her the rest of the night.

The angry rattle of the windowpane tore Tom from sweet dreams. The visions of the ranch, the scent of hay and horse, the feeling of freedom in the air died like a blow to his head.

Pa.

There was no mistaking that shadow on the other side of the drapes. Nervous fear filled his blood. Tom, a grown man, blinked tears from his eyes. His dreams of starting anew, free of his past, shattered. There would be no pretty wife, no ranch, no barns to clean, no horses to train.

Defeated, he pulled back the curtain. Opened the window. Told his old man to be quiet. The innkeepers were light sleepers.

As his father guzzled whiskey and asked questions, made plans for tomorrow's job, Tom wished he had the strength to say no. But he couldn't. He couldn't endure one more beating.

Tears burned in his eyes, in his throat. Tom hated his father. But like the Devil, the old man had a hold on his soul. There was no escape.

He wished there was. He thought of what Pa wanted to do to that nice lady, and black anger raged in his heart But to go against Pa...there was no way. He felt sorry for poor Mrs. Kincaid.

* * *

The knock on the back door came early, before dawn lightened the sky. Hannah didn't turn from the washbasin. She already knew who'd come.

"I'd best get to work." Colton's chair scooted against the wood floor as he stood from the table.

She heard his footsteps knell closer, and she faced him. "I'll bring out some coffee later."

"I don't want you waiting on me." He brushed back the curls from her eyes as if she were a child, a tender gesture. Love sparkled bright and unmistakable in his dark eyes. "Promise me you'll take it easy."

"Promise." His kiss was quick but loving. She hated to see him go. Since the doctor's visit, so much had changed. There was suddenly so much to do, to look forward to. "I feel fine. Just tired."

"No more fainting. Want anything in town?"

"More coffee."

"Sure thing." He brushed a kiss to her cheek before he walked away.

Zac, seated at the table, tipped back his head for his own good-bye kiss.

Tom Varney waited outside, shy and timid. Well, he did look like a nice man, eager to learn. Hannah made a decision. She quickly fixed a big plate of eggs and potatoes and handed it to him.

He looked down, troubled, but managed a polite thanks. She wondered if something was wrong. Wondered if it had to do with Abby. Young love didn't run smooth, according to Rose and Paula's gossip.

"Mama?" The little boy leaned against her knee. "We goin' ridin'?"

"We can ride after it warms up a bit." Hannah set the plate to dry on the rack and lifted the soapy washbasins. "Where's Fiddle?"

"Sleepin'." Zac toddled after her through the door and down the steps.

She tossed the water well out of the worn pathway and

hurried back into the warm kitchen. Once the basins were set out to dry, she held out her hand. "Come with me."

"Train?"

"Yes, you can bring your train." She smiled as his sticky fingers curled into hers.

Zac granted her a smacking kiss on the cheek before he settled down on the floor of his room to play, busy with plans for his railroad. She watched him for a spell, so in love with everything about him. The pucker between his brows when he thought. The frustrated sigh when the latch between the cars stuck a bit. The chugging choo-choo sounds he made as he pushed the clattering train along the wooden floor, his knees banging against the wood.

Another child. She laid her hand on her stomach, still flat. She'd never thought such a blessing could happen to her. Not ever again. That was probably why she didn't recognize the early signs of pregnancy.

Through the bay window of the third bedroom upstairs, closed off and cold, she caught sight of Colton in the south field. He was exercising the stallion he'd bought from Paula's husband. The black was long and lean, beautifully lined. His gait was smooth. Colton urged him into a full gallop, man and animal moving as one.

Her heart filled with love for him. He'd given her more than she'd dared to hope for.

She knelt down before the small cedar chest, the one she'd bought long ago with the rocking horse carved into the wood, set aside the pink cushion she'd made, and drew open the lid. Inside, wrapped in paper with tiny satchels of dried flower petals to keep the contents scented, she withdrew so many treasures. Lovingly made and tucked away long ago in hopes there would some day be another baby.

Knit afghans and a garden basket quilt. Tiny pink gowns. Little lace and ruffled dresses. Knit hats and socks, sweaters and jumpers. All embroidered with flowers and hearts, kitties and ponies. Precious infant clothing for the girl she'd once known she was carrying.

And now there would be a baby to wear these tiny things she'd made with her hands and with her heart and so much love. For she'd decided she would give birth to a daughter.

That way she'd have one of each—a little boy and a little girl, two treasures she never thought she'd have.

A squeak rose up through the floorboards. The back door. Colton must have forgotten something. She hurried down the back stairs, eager to catch him. She had thought of something he could bring her from the mercantile. Five skeins of baby pink yarn.

She crossed into the empty kitchen. The back door stood open, but no Colton. A chill skittled along her spine. Something was wrong. Zac. She had to get to Zac.

Hannah turned, but a hand grabbed her arm. She stepped back in time to feel the impact of the two-by-four against her temple. Then nothing. Nothing at all.

* * *

The ranch spread out along the valley below—fresh green pastures, sturdy fences and sparkling stables, and the log house well-lit against the darkening afternoon. Storm clouds rolled in from the north and rain scented the mountain air.

A sense of pride filled him. He'd worked hard for his wife and son. Look where it had gotten them—a fine, prosperous ranch, a happy life. He thought of Hannah at home, maybe replenishing the cookie supply. Those gingerbread men hadn't lasted long at all. He thought of Zac, safe and happy, thriving in the light of Hannah's love.

It was more than he could have dared to dream of on the cold, snowy day he'd first driven into town.

The barn stirred with sounds of life. The horses knew him well now and stretched out their necks as he walked past, noses eager for a pat or two.

"Tom?" The young man ought to be around

somewhere.

But the horses were not disturbed. Nothing outside was amiss.

Except for the thin, wilting line of smoke from the chimney. Hannah ought to be in the house, feeding the fire. Unless...perhaps she wasn't feeling well.

Or worse.

Cold fear spurred him forward. He noticed small things out of place—the abandoned pitchfork in the aisle, a speckle of tobacco juice on the grass between the house and the barns, a strange bootprint—bigger than Varney's, and a different tread.

He dug his revolver out of the tack room and loaded the chambers. He cursed himself for being too damn careless. He cursed himself for thinking the worst.

The back door stood wide open. He listened—not one sound. No threatening voices. No footsteps knelling from inside. He watched the window—no shadow, no face, no aimed gun.

Hannah. It was all he could think about. Battling the tide of rushing emotions and fear as he stepped through the threshold, revolvers cocked and ready.

Emptiness echoed around him. No sign of life. No sign of his wife or son. Just a small puddle of blood on the floor. And the note next to it.

Dread pounded through his chest as he reached for the paper. Unfolded it. *Leave five thousand dollars by midnight tomorrow by the big rock at No Man's Bluff or they die, bounty hunter.*

His throat closed. Fear, anger, self-condemnation warred within him. Colton fisted his hands. He didn't know whose tracks and tobacco juice marked the rain-soft earth outside. But he would find out. He would not leave Hannah and Zac to perish by violent hands.

He'd lost one wife. He would not bury another.

CHAPTER TWENTY-TWO

"**M**ax Varney wanted for robbery and murder. This could be the one. Has the same last name." Colton tipped the yellowed paper toward the light. "Two years ago I brought in an Al Varney. He was a scary son of a bitch."

"From Arizona." Baker leaned back in his chair. "It's a long way from Montana."

"Not far for men bent on revenge." Colton had questions—but at least now he knew why they'd changed from robbery to kidnapping. "How's Drummond coming?"

"He'll be along soon." Baker stood and crossed the cramped little sheriff's office. "Probably counting out his money. You know he's a happier man now that you increased the mortgage on the ranch. And sold him your stock and your contract. He'll turn that around for a tenfold profit."

"Nothing matters but seeing my wife and son safe." If they were still alive. Bitterness filled his mouth, twisted in his guts. He'd been a fool to think anywhere was safe.

He'd failed Hannah. Guilt and fear pounded through

him with a blood-cold fury. His real concern now was making damn sure she and Zac stayed alive.

The storm had washed out all sign of Varney's tracks. Colton's stomach turned. He'd been stupid to trust anyone, even someone who seemed to want to ranch like he had, who had wanted a new start.

Now Colton knew why. His throat ached. He'd grown soft in this country, setting aside his gun for home and hearth. At a great cost.

"I've got an area mapped where it's logical they would be hiding." Colton pushed the paper into the puddle of lamplight. "The mountains are too dangerous. What I need is to find out how many abandoned cabins and homesteads there are in these forests."

"Too damn many." Baker rubbed his brow.

"My boys and I can start looking." Hank, leaning against the back wall by the door, grabbed his hat. "Figure we can start rulin' out some of the cabins one by one. Sneak in, look for smoke—they gotta have a fire to keep warm this time of year, it's too damn cold and damp. If we find nothin', we keep searchin'."

"It's a hell of a better idea than sitting and waiting." Colton thought of the money the banker was gathering for him—hell, he'd mortgaged everything but his soul. If Varney got away with the money, then Colton would be flat broke. But he would have his family. His wife and his son were everything.

He stood. "I'll go with you. Baker, what are you going to do? Sit here and wait?"

"I'm with you, Kincaid." Baker holstered his Peacemaker. "We can't trust that varmint ain't going to kill your wife and child anyway."

"Exactly." Colton gritted his teeth. He'd learned it the hard way. "There's no better way to make a man suffer than to threaten his loved ones. Let's go hunting."

* * *

Hannah felt cold. A hammering pain echoed through her head. Her mouth tasted dry as dirt. Her eyes felt gritty when she tried to open them. The sound of a child's muffled, heartbroken sobs forced her to sit up despite the pain.

Zac knelt at her side, tears staining his button face.

"Are you hurt?" She saw blood on him, but after a quick inspection she saw it was her own. Thank God. Relief whispered through her. She held the crying boy to her, but he stayed rigid, crying, "Mama" inconsolably.

Her heart ached, and she cuddled him more tightly. Her vision was a little blurry. She rocked him gently, kissing his brow; finally, when he quieted, she looked around.

They were in a cabin. An abandoned one. Probably up in the mountains somewhere. The wallboards were weathered. A few had broken away to leave gaping glimpses of the forest beyond. Rain blew in through the cracks in the western wall and tapped through the decaying roof. There was a door, but it was closed. And they were alone.

What about Colton? Was he dead? Hurt? Looking for them? All her love for him ached in her heart. He had to be all right. She held tight to that hope.

"Come with me, Zac." She took his hand and tried to stand. Dizziness washed over her in crashing waves. She wobbled, then hit the floor hard. Sat there, trying to get her bearings. She covered her stomach with one hand and thought of the baby within, a life dependent on her.

"Mama." Zac sniffed. Another dependent child.

She brushed her hand against his tear-stained cheek. "I'm all right"

He tilted his face against her palm. So sweet. He'd cried so over her. Her heart ached, wishing he'd never had to go through such an ordeal, a helpless little boy afraid for his unconscious mother. She patted his hand. "Let's try that again."

This time she remained standing. The world tilted when she took a step, but she waited, caught her breath, and kept going.

Where were they? Not the shanty where she'd spent the night with Colton. Not in any cabin she knew of. She breathed deep and smelled pine, rain, and mountain air.

Voices sounded through the door, muffled and close. Hannah froze, listening.

"Figure he'll try to find her first before he hands over that kind of money." Colton. They were talking about Colton. That meant he was alive. "That means the bastard may try to jump us without a penny in his pocket."

"Pa, I'm not so sure this is right."

"And what happened to my Al was right?"

"Well, no." This voice sounded familiar.

Tom Varney. Why would— Oh, her head hurt when she tried to think. She was far too weak to try to escape, especially with a small child. She felt sick. The painful lump near her ear beneath her blood-matted hair began to throb. Dizziness blurred her vision. Her stomach roiled, and she fought to keep from being sick.

She could hardly walk. But what could she do? She had to protect Zac from these men. She had to protect her unborn baby.

"Let's go back and sit down," Hannah whispered.

Obediently, Zac clung to her.

She had to try to think. The men outside blocked the door. Even if she were strong enough to push past them with Zac in her arms, she couldn't outrun them.

The door flew open, banging hard against the wall. Hannah jumped. Zac hid his face. She laid a protective hand on his back.

"Cook this." A skinned rabbit carcass hit the dirty floor in front of her.

Hannah looked up into the mud-and-rain-streaked face of a gray-haired, cold-eyed man. He was unkempt, and violence hung around him like a cloud. His height made her feel small and vulnerable. He wore two holstered revolvers and a knife in his belt

"I'll need a fire and s-some water." She heard the fear in her voice and hated that it showed. "And a blanket for my son."

"You cook, first." The cruel bark of his voice made her jump again.

She thought of Charles. Of the same way he used to speak to her when he was drunk. The stale scent of alcohol clung to this man, too.

"All right." She stood, keeping a tight hold on Zac's hand. She picked up the skinned and gutted carcass, the meat still warm but wet from the rain. "Is there any dry wood?"

"Tom!" He leaned out the door. "Bring in some of that wood."

"We can't light a fire, Pa." Tom stepped into the room, avoiding Hannah's gaze. He looked sad. Blood speckled his face. A bruise puffed out his left eye. "Someone will spot the smoke."

"I ain't gonna eat raw rabbit for supper." The old man slammed his beefy fist against the wall, cracking the wood plank. "Do as I say or this will be your head."

"Yes, Pa." Head down, Tom left the shack.

Zac hid in her skirts. She hugged his trembling little body to her. How vicious was the man who watched her now? Was he capable of hitting a child? He was certainly the one who'd struck her unconscious. Well, he'd better not try to hurt her son.

Hannah bent to work. Where was Colton? She felt cold inside. She feared none of them would make it out of this alive.

* * *

Night set in, hampering their efforts. The heavy beat of rain and wind only made riding more difficult. His horse was exhausted, he was bone-cold and wet all the way through, but he couldn't stop.

He could never stop. Nightmare images haunted his thoughts. Pictures he tried to purge from his mind of Hannah dead, Zac vanished.

He would kill the bastards when he found them.

"Colton?" Hank Mullen drew up beside him. "I'm going to send one of the boys home to check with my wife and make sure nothing new has happened in town."

"Fine." Colton pulled down the brim of his hat. Rain dripped off, slapping against his oiled canvas slicker. "Where do you think we should head?"

"My guts say north, but—" Hank sighed, torn.

"The avalanche danger. My guts say the same thing."

"Mine, too." Arnie Sutcliff gathered his reins. "Paula would have my hide if I came home because I was afraid of a little snow. Wouldn't let me sleep if I wasn't out here helping to find her good friend."

Colton nodded. "Then let's move north. Are you comin', Sheriff?"

"You can count on me, Kincaid."

Hannah was alone with a wanted felon. A man who'd killed before to get what he wanted. A man with a price on his head.

Colton reined the mare north, toward the mountain country. Determination to find the bastard fueled him. He gritted his teeth, ready to taste justice and revenge.

The truth beat cold and hard in his chest. He'd been a fool, wanting a new start in this country, believing in the peace and tranquility of this mountain paradise. He was a danger to those around him, to those who claimed to love him. And it would cost another woman her life, maybe this time his son's.

The past was alive. He was a bounty hunter, a man who lived by his gun. It beat in his blood, lived in his soul. There was no escape. He could never be anything else. Not a mild-mannered rancher who could trust a stranger. Not a husband able to spend warm evenings at the hearth with his family.

He was a dark man capable of great violence.
Anything else about him was just a lie.

* * *

Hannah watched Tom stuff his hands in his trouser pockets, avoiding her gaze as he approached his father. "You don't have to kill him, Pa. We can just take the money."

"I don't want the money. I want him to suffer. I want him to pay."

Cold fear shivered through her. She knelt before the crumbling fireplace and held out a hand to check the temperature of the fire. Not hot enough. She added two small sticks of wood.

"But you aren't going to hurt them, are you?" Tom's voice wobbled.

"Killing women is the fun part." Max chuckled. "Then again, you were always a soft, weak bastard. No guts. Maybe I'll make you do it. I've got to toughen you up."

"No, Pa. I can't."

Max uncapped his whiskey flask. "Yep, you're gonna do his little wife. I want to make Kincaid watch her die."

"What are you gonna do with the little boy, Pa? It ain't right to harm a child."

"That bastard Kincaid made Al suffer." Max took a long swig of whiskey. "Taking him to rot in that jail. Poor Al hanged himself after what happened in his cell, being beaten and...I can't even talk about it without wanting to kill her here and now."

"Pa, don't do that."

This was about a bounty Colton had collected. The hard truth struck her like a blow. Her hand shook as she turned the spit. Fat sizzled and popped in the fire.

"I know Al suffered, but I don't want to do this anymore, Pa. I want to start a ranch and live my own life."

"You and your stupid wants." Max's punch resounded in the shanty.

Zac whimpered, and Hannah pulled him close.

Tom hit the floor, his hand to his jaw.

"When the hell are you gonna be done with the friggin' rabbit?" Max's voice hammered.

"It needs ten more minutes." She held Zac more tightly.

Max spit a stream of tobacco juice at the floor. A brown stain spattered her skirt. "Tom didn't tell me you were so pretty. Maybe I won't kill you right away."

She tried not to shiver at the naked lust glinting in his eyes, bright and triumphant, a gleam of twisted victory on the man's face.

She eyed the gun Max had left on the floor. If only she could get to it. She had a feeling Tom wouldn't try to stop her.

"What the hell was that?" Max swung around.

Tom, cradling his jaw, shook his head.

"Go check anyway. I want to be alone with the lady."

Hannah cringed at the yellow-toothed grin. She thought of how much this big man could hurt her, and without a weapon of her own, she was powerless to stop him. She thought of the baby growing inside her. She pushed Zac behind her into the corner, determined to protect him.

"I'm not handsome like your bounty hunter. But at least I know how to treat a lady." He pulled his lips back. He wanted to hurt her. He liked hurting people. She could read it in those glittering, soulless eyes.

"Remember, you have your husband to thank for this." Max threw her against the fireplace. Hot stone gouged her spine and ribcage. His rancid breath fanned her face. "I'm going to make him pay. Starting with you."

The door flew open in the wind.

"Visitors?" Max asked.

Tom nodded.

Every bit of hope drained from Hannah's heart. Cotlon. They were going to kill him, ambush him in the dark.

Max tossed her and she broke most of her fall, but her teeth rattled when she hit the floor. Her baby! Immediately she laid her hand to her stomach, willing the life within her to stay safe.

"Kincaid's trickier than I thought." Max unholstered both revolvers. "But he's still a dead man. You guard the woman and child. If he makes it past me, shoot to kill, you weakling. Because if you don't, you're dead. They'll never believe anything you have to say."

Shoot to kill. Hannah shivered as the violent man dashed from the room, confident and lethal. She thought of Colton out there in the dark.

She had to warn him. But first she had to escape. But how?

Tom's jaw was broken. He held it in one hand, pain glassy in his apologetic eyes. She knew how it was to be beaten, how that could break a person. How much worse it must be for a little boy growing up, dominated by such a violent man.

But Tom Varney wasn't violent. It was there on his face, in the kind way he'd treated her at the ranch. In the way he looked at her now.

He gestured toward the door, his revolver drawn, but not aimed. Then she knew. He would protect her from his father. He would make certain she escaped safely.

"Thank you, Tom." She took Zac by the hand. "I won't forget this."

His eyes teared and ashamed, he bowed his head.

There was more she wanted to say. How wrong his father was. It was a strong man who didn't harm another, a strong man who protected the helpless.

But she didn't have time. So she pressed a kiss to his forehead, then stepped out into the night. Rain battered her face, blurring her vision, making it hard to breathe. Wet branches slapped her face. Her toe caught on a root. A rock smacked against her shin. Zac began to cry. She kept running.

Only the single gunshot, ringing in the still mountain air stopped her.

Colton.

CHAPTER TWENTY-THREE

Colton squeezed off another shot, his gaze riveted to Max Varney, even as he slipped from the saddle. Hannah's well-trained mustang stood still as he hit the ground.

His only satisfaction as blood spilled between his fingers was that Varney's dead body stared back at him.

"They got Colton!" A voice. Sutcliff's.

Someone's boots. The horse stepped over him and was led away.

"Damn it! He's getting away." Mullen's shout.

Another set of boots. Then the sheriff's face, frowning. Even in the faint light, Colton could read the look in the lawman's eyes. It was a mortal wound. Or close enough. Colton had known it the instant the bullet slammed into his chest.

"The bastard ambushed us." Colton drew breath, but sputtered blood.

"The nerve of those outlaws, when we were plannin' on ambushin' them." The sheriff untied his bandanna, then lifted Colton's hand to press the cloth to the bleeding wound.

"Hannah." He'd failed her. It was all he could think of. He'd failed the wife and son he'd sworn to protect.

What kind of man brought death and danger to his family?

Colton blinked back tears. They weren't for himself. He knew he was beyond saving. Frankly, he didn't care about his life. The tears, hot and blinding, were for Hannah, for the image of her suffering, for the pain he hadn't been man enough to prevent

"There he goes!" Mullen's voice. "That bastard's got Colton's mount."

"And the money." The sheriff jumped to his feet. Horses charged past.

Alone in the rain, Colton struggled to breathe. To pray to a God he didn't believe in that the men caught Varney. Would make him pay for whatever had happened to Hannah.

He knew. She was already dead. Nightmares painted bloody images across his brain.

Splashes of puddled water. Someone running. Someone light and... Hannah. Her shoes, the muddied hem of her dress. Her rain-streaked hair hanging in wet tangles around her face.

He must be dead. Cold like a devil's grip encircled him. He couldn't breathe. The taste of blood bubbled across his lips. Colton gazed up into the face of his precious Hannah even as the darkness took him away from her.

There would be no light in his afterlife. Only an eternity without the angel who tried to save him.

* * *

Hannah thought of nothing else but Colton. Zac was safe—crying and afraid, but safe. Blanche Mullen took the small boy from her arms and carried him to the kitchen for a nice hot bath.

Hank Mullen laid Colton on the quilt covering their bed. One of his sons had galloped ahead for the doctor. Hannah fell to her knees at the dark hearth. She had to light the fire. Colton was far too cold. His skin was clammy and ashen.

Her fingers trembled. Damn it, she couldn't light the match.

Hank Mullen's hand closed over hers. "Let me."

With a nod, she handed over the tin of matches. She hugged herself, trying to stop shaking as Hank lit the fire. The room was so cold.

And Colton was wet to his skin. She tugged off his boots first, peeled off his socks. Fear drove her and she worked quickly. Blood stained his clothes. She eased off his shirt and wetness fell in red drips to the floor.

"Best not to wait for the doctor." Hannah brushed the damp hair from Colton's forehead. "Hank, would you fetch a basin of hot water from Blanche? And I keep a bottle of whiskey in the top shelf of the pantry. For medicinal purposes."

He nodded, leaving the room with a competent step.

Hannah opened the wardrobe and pulled out an old set of sheets from the bottom shelf. She began ripping bandage strips as fast as she could.

Hank returned and she drew closer to inspect the wound. She had to stop the bleeding. At least try to curb it until the doctor arrived.

The wound was a nickel-sized tear in his skin, the edges gaping and raw, burned and tattered. Just two inches to the right of his breastbone. She washed it with whiskey and applied pressure. She didn't dare try to remove the bullet without the doctor.

Tears welled in her eyes. Colton was dying and she couldn't stop it.

Everything she stood to lose felt ready to break apart. She loved this man. Loved him like nothing else in her life, unlike anything she'd ever known. She never wanted to care for him this way, never meant to.

He was a dangerous man, far too at odds with her dreams, with her heart. He had a violent past. If one hateful man could track him down to this forgotten part of Montana Territory, then others could. And destroy everything dear to her, take from her the family and the children she'd always wanted.

To a girl growing up without family all those painful years, to the woman married to brutal Charles Sawyer with empty arms, this life Colton had given her was more precious than gold. He'd filled her heart with his love and her arms with his son and chased away her loneliness, given her love and happiness and a baby, come autumn.

And all these things, she'd nearly lost last night. Could still lose.

The door banged open; the doctor strode in, and she stepped aside, ready to assist him.

Colton felt so cold. So very cold.

* * *

"I can't make any promises. I wish I could." The doc rubbed his weary eyes against the too-bright morning light.

"I wish you could, too." Exhausted, Hannah set the steaming coffee cup on the nightstand, then offered the doctor a plate heaped with fried eggs, bacon, and browned potatoes.

He accepted with hungry eyes. "I've seen men hurt worse than this and live. I've seen men hurt less than this and die. I think it all comes down to whether or not it's his time. It's a bad wound, Hannah. He's still bleeding."

"I know." She stepped away, her head bowed.

"Tastes great." The young man's eyes dimmed, concern darkening his brow. "How are you doing?"

"Fine." She laid a hand on her swollen stomach. The baby within was safe. Zac was safe. Colton was still alive.

These were the things that mattered. "I'll rest plenty when I know Colton is better. I promise."

"That's a promise I'm going to make you keep. Right now." His fork scraped on the plate as he sampled the butter-fried potatoes. "Go lie down for a spell. I'll stay at his side."

"No, I can't leave him." Hannah eased down into the chair by the fire, closest to the bed. Her heart felt cold and empty.

Her Colton. How she loved him. She couldn't lose him. Not now. Not ever.

* * *

Pain kicked through his chest with each thud of his pulse. Colton opened his eyes. Slowly, the ceiling stopped spinning, his vision cleared. He was in his own bed, in his home.

Hannah. The bastards. He launched up off the mattress, but still found himself lying helpless on his back. Pain exploded in his chest.

"Lie still," the doctor instructed. "Don't go tearing out those stitches."

"T-tell me." He fought for breath. "Han—"

"Colton." She breezed into the room, alive. Beautiful and dazzling, still his angel.

He blinked against the images in his head, the nightmares of death, the memories of finding Ella, the visions of discovering Hannah the same way. Those fears twisted in his mind as they hunted down the Varneys' hideout Of Hannah dead. Zac forever gone. Sweat broke out on his brow as he realized where he was. Safe. In Hannah's bed. In their home. Those things hadn't happened. They weren't real.

But he was still a bounty hunter.

"Hannah." He choked out her name, tears hot on his cheeks. He'd thought... He'd been so terrified he'd lost her, that he would find her dead like Ella, having suffered horribly at the hands of a brutal man. One shot from a gun, that's all it took to end a life. One hate-filled man without a conscience, hungry for revenge.

Her hand brushed his cheek.

"We're all safe, Colton."

It was too good to be true, too much to ask for. He

277

could never put her life—so precious to him—at risk
again. He could never—

He didn't belong here. He knew it down deep in his
heart.

"Let me get you some broth. You need your strength
to get well. The doctor says you're not over this yet." His
heart filled, watching her smile. That beautiful angel's smile
that warmed her eyes and touched his cold soul.

He loved her. How he loved her.

* * *

Hannah's troubles felt lighter as she left Colton's
side. He had some color in his face. His fever was
broken. The worst was over.

She opened the front door before the sheriff could
knock again. She opened her mouth to tell him
immediately how well Colton was doing, but the sorrow in
Baker's eyes told her the news wasn't good.

"You didn't find Tom?"

Baker slid out of his rain-dotted slicker. "It's worse
than that."

"Do you mean it's just a matter of finding Tom and the
money?" Hannah took his coat and gestured toward the
wing chair by the fire.

Baker nodded as he crossed the room, hands
outstretched toward the heat. "This time of year my
arthritis bothers me something terrible." He settled down
by the fire.

He was stalling. And Hannah knew why. She hung up
the dripping slicker. The news was bad. Her hands felt
cold and she moved to the fire. "Tom got away, didn't he?"

"Not exactly." The sheriff gazed up at her, eyes
pinched in the corners. "We found him dead, Hannah.
Well, at least we think it's him."

"Tom helped me escape. I don't think he meant to take
the money. He probably didn't know—" She remembered
the injured man, torn into shreds by his brutal father,
struggling to do the right thing. "He didn't think anyone

would believe him. I think he was ashamed."

The sheriff rubbed the back of his neck. "Hank and Robert Mullen helped me track him once dawn came. The rain had washed away most sign of him, but we found your mare. She must have heard our voices and came right up to us. It wasn't hard to retrace her steps to the mountain creek he must have tried to make her cross in the dark, just above that waterfall on No Man's Bluff. We think it was a mountain lion, although it could have been a bear. The tracks had washed away. There wasn't much left of the body. Not much at all."

"But if my mare was all right—"

"The mare got away, but the saddle came clean off her. We searched the river, Hannah. Even downstream from the waterfall. The money's gone. Every last dollar. We didn't find a single piece of it, and we've been searching all day."

Gone. Hannah pressed her fingertips to her forehead. A rushing sound filled her ears, pounded through her head.

It was over. All their dreams. All their security. She tried to tell herself it was all right. She would rather have Colton alive and safe. He and Zac and the baby were all that mattered. They would make do. They would be all right as long as they were together.

But her heart felt cold. Maybe it was the way Colton had refused to look at her as he lay so helpless, so hurt. She fought the ugly, icy feeling that this happiness they'd built together had ended. Just as she'd once feared.

With the house so silent, Colton could hear the low rumble of the sheriff's voice through the floorboards. Gone. Everything he'd taken from Hannah and tried to make better. All they'd worked for together.

The doc checked the bandage. Colton didn't even feel the pain or the fever that raged through his body.

He'd failed Hannah. Worse, he'd failed his son, who always gazed up at him with those trusting brown eyes.

The cold, hard truth hurt him worse than the bullet wound in his chest: he loved his family, but his love put them at a great risk. The only way he could protect them, to keep them safe, was to leave. To forget they ever existed.

Yes, that was the answer. The only honor he had left. Colton grimaced against the pain.

He was a hunter, as ruthless as the mountain lion he'd fought, as rough and violent as the outlaws who'd taken Hannah.

A man like him didn't belong in paradise.

CHAPTER TWENTY-FOUR

Hannah ran the oiled rag over the rich cherry wood of the crib. So long unused. So many dreams to fill.

"Cookie." Zac toddled into the doorway and held up the oatmeal sweet with a grin. Fiddle trailed him, waiting to share.

"I see Blanche is spoiling you."

"Spoilin' me a lot." A big grin, then Zac scampered down the hall to his room. Fiddle loped after him.

Hannah heard the sounds of low, delighted laughter and imagined the little boy in his room, sharing that cookie with his beloved kitty.

A door opened. Footsteps knelled on the floor. She set down her rag. "Colton?"

He filled the threshold, all solid man. He wore a heavy flannel shirt and a pair of denim trousers. His dark hair was tousled and attractive, his jaw whiskered and set. The sight of him kicked through her. Every inch of her body reacted.

"You'd better get back in that bed, mister." She headed

toward him. "I'm not letting you out of that room just yet."

No smile. No flicker of light in those heartless eyes. That look stopped her cold. Something was wrong. A muscle jumped along his clenched jaw. "Are you working on the nursery?"

"Yes." With pride, Hannah looked around the small room tucked beneath the eaves. Everything would be fine. She couldn't believe otherwise. Colton's aloofness was normal after their ordeal. He was afraid. He was recovering from a life-threatening injury. That was all.

She brightened her voice, determined. "I think I'll have wallpaper put up. Maybe pink flowers. Or kitties or something. That will be a project for you when you're feeling better."

"No." He sounded so cold. So distant.

Her heart jumped. "I know we're broke, Colton. But surely we'll get by. I could take in work. I've done it before. I—"

"I will not have my wife working for others."

Her gaze fell to the satchel gripped tightly in his left hand, the knuckles white. Her pulse began to hammer in her ears. "You're leaving."

"Yes." Cold. Distant. So like the man who saved her life, who found it easy to kill. "There's no other way."

"Don't do this to me, Colton." A burning pain gathered behind her eyes. She leaned against the bureau for support.

"I have no choice."

"No choice?" Incredible. "You have a hundred choices. Every single one of them can keep you right here where you belong. With your family."

"I'm a danger. As long as I'm here." No emotion in those eyes, no waver to the hard set of his powerful jaw.

Her stomach tightened. "But I need you here."

"You'll be better off without me." He believed that. She could see it in his face, hear it in his voice.

"N-no." The word wobbled. She lifted her chin.

"You're injured, Colton. You're not thinking clearly. I know it seems as if we've lost everything, but we haven't. I've thought it over. We will be all right as long as we stay together. We're a family now."

The smallest trace of emotion glimmered in his eyes. He shook his head. "We're no family. We never will be. Men like me can't have families. To think otherwise is a fool's dream."

"But it's my dream, too." She ached to reach out and hold him. To wrap her arms around the iron-strong breadth of his back and hold him until the pain left his voice, until he could believe love was enough.

But he didn't want her touch.

"It could have been you." His voice broke. "Varney could have killed you."

"He didn't, Colton." She stepped forward, but hugged herself instead.

"Next time, maybe it will be different."

"Why would there be a next time?"

"Because a man like me doesn't have just one enemy." He tightened his grip on the satchel. "Is that how you want to live your life? Looking behind your back? Watching over your shoulder? Worrying about the children playing in the yard?"

"That won't happen." She believed it.

"What if it does? Tell me, Hannah. What would have happened to that baby you're carrying if I hadn't managed to kill Max Varney? What would have happened to Zac?"

Hannah shivered. The image burst through her mind. Max Varney would have killed them.

"If the Varneys found me, then anyone can." Sorrow stood in his eyes. "You're not safe, Hannah. And that life inside you will never be safe."

"We live in the middle of nowhere. We're not on the beaten path. No one is going to find you."

"The Varneys did." Determination shaped his face. "What kind of man puts his innocent son and pregnant wife in danger? What kind of man would I be if I stayed?"

He was leaving her. Hannah's eyes began to burn. "That doesn't mean you should walk away from us, from our life together."

"It does." He fastened his gaze on hers, unblinking, cold as stone.

"You're wrong. Don't leave me, Colton. I don't think I can stand that. Not after you've made me love you."

"You shouldn't love a man like me." His voice broke, but no other sign of emotion betrayed him, not the hard set of his wide shoulders, not the solid line of his square jaw, not the power tensed in his iron-hard body. "There was a bounty on Max Varney's head. It will see you through the next mortgage payment."

"Don't leave, Colton." Her heart wrenched. "I need you."

"You need to be alive." His eyes flashed. "I'll send you money. You never have to worry about that. I'll provide for you and the children."

Even though he didn't say it, she knew. He was going back to hunting bounties.

"Thank you for everything, Hannah." Colton turned so she couldn't see his face. "I'm going to say good-bye to my son."

"Colton—" She ran after him.

He held out one hand, his gaze snaring hers with a cold, brutal warning. He walked away, leaving her alone in the room filled with her dreams. With the newly polished crib and the bureau drawers filled with the freshly washed little dresses and socks and gowns and diapers. The pink afghan hung on the back of the rocking chair. The colorful flower quilt already covering the mattress. There were sheets to make and ruffly curtains to sew. And books to buy so she could read to Zac and the baby.

She loved Colton. She'd given him all of her love. She didn't know how to make him stay. How to make him try to love again. Her heart began to break piece by piece into tiny shards that could never be repaired.

He'd made her believe in love, stolen her heart with his strength and honor and goodness. But love couldn't last. Ever. She'd been afraid of that awful truth all along.

She heard Colton amble down the stairs and close the front door. He walked away from her love and their family as if it meant nothing.

And maybe to him, it did.

* * *

He felt her gaze on him as he checked the saddle. Cold and accusing. No, she wouldn't understand. A woman didn't have the same responsibilities, the same demands in life.

Yet she had to see how he'd failed them. How he'd failed himself.

He checked the bedroll and satchel tied tight behind the saddle. On the way through town he would stop at the mercantile, put a pair of saddlebags on credit, and have Baker see that Hannah received Varney's bounty. Then he'd ask the old man to keep an eye on her, a promise he'd already received from Hank Mullen.

Well, there was nothing left to do but leave. With a heavy heart, Colton slipped his boot in the stirrup and eased up into the saddle. His bay shifted to his weight— he'd only take one mare, leaving the other for Hannah's use. The barn was otherwise empty.

All his dreams and plans for the future were gone, too.

As he rode away from his family, he hoped he was doing the right thing—placing his honor to the ones he loved above his own heart-deep needs. To keep them safe.

Cold rain plopped in great droplets from the leaden sky, striking off his hat, thudding off his jacket. Colton shivered deep inside. The world would be hopeless without the warm light of his Hannah's smile, without the sweet comfort he'd found in her arms.

He would never know love like that again.

CHAPTER TWENTY-FIVE

His footsteps rose above the snap of the fire and the moaning of the wind outside. Awareness shivered along Hannah's spine as he circled toward her.

She heard his every movement. Felt his every breath. She ached to touch him, to pull him close and kiss him until he swore never to leave her again. Heart filling, she reached out to touch him but he disappeared, became as diffuse as fog, then disappeared the moment her hand brushed his.

Gone.

She woke with a start. The dream, the warmth of Colton's presence, faded against the reality of night. Moonbeams played against the curtains, finding their way inside to brush the corner of the room with silver shadows enough for her to know the room was empty, that she was alone.

Pain tore through her and she squeezed her eyes against the tears. Life went on without Colton, but it wasn't the same.

Zac cried for his papa. It was only the two of them to

eat meals, to read cuddled together before the parlor hearth, to decorate and eat gingerbread men.

Seth Mullen came twice a day to feed and water the mare and the cow, to muck out the stalls. He hauled in wood and gratefully accepted invitations to join in the meal, but she hated to depend on him. She didn't want to need anyone again.

Once, she'd asked him not to come, saying she couldn't afford to pay him, but he would smile shyly and refuse. Colton was taking care of it.

Alone in her bed, Hannah turned on her side and stared at the wall. She vowed never to dream of Colton Kincaid's broad shoulders and tender touch. Not ever again.

* * *

Colton unrolled the wool blanket in the light of the campfire. Alone, he'd cooked his supper. Washed his dishes. Now he settled down to lie on the ground, alone.

He steeled his mind against memories of home, of Zac and how Hannah would have read him to sleep, of his pregnant wife nestled in the big, soft bed in their room. No, in hers.

They were not his family. Not now. Not ever. That was the only thing that could keep them safe. He was certain of it.

At least, that's what he told the searing pain in his heart.

* *

"Hannah, you're looking too damn peaked," Rose announced as she fished for more straight pins in her sewing basket. "Are you sleeping?"

"Of course I am." It wasn't exactly a lie. "Holly, how are the wedding plans coming along?"

The young woman blushed with pleasure. "Just fine. My dress is arriving all the way from Missoula on the next stage."

"Wonderful," Abby breathed.

"Exciting." Paula smiled.

"I bet it's beautiful." Hannah managed a true smile. "Are you nervous?"

"Very."

"Especially about the wedding night." Rose winked. "That young man you're marrying is such a hunk of a man. A real handful, I'll bet."

Laughter rang in the air.

"He is a handful," Holly admitted.

More rowdy laughter.

Hannah felt a little lightheaded, although she tried to chuckle along with the others.

"Are you telling me the white wedding dress is a lie?" Paula asked in a shocked tone, her eyes merry.

"An absolute and total lie?" Abby leaned forward.

"And here I thought my Robert was a gentleman," Blanche's disapproval at her son's behavior rang out.

The talk dissolved into total laughter.

"I wouldn't wait, either," Rose reassured Holly with a gentle pat to the back of her hand. "In fact, I didn't. Sherman and I still burn up the sheets twenty-three years later."

"Arnie and I didn't wait," Paula confessed. "Although my brother the minister gave a sermon the week before my wedding on the virtue of self-control, so I knew he'd figured it out."

"Probably came upon you and Arnie alone in that buggy," Hannah teased.

After the party broke up, after needles, scissors, and spools of thread were stashed in sewing baskets, the women headed out into the warm spring day. Leaves filtered the sunlight in Rose's backyard. Hannah reached for her cloak.

"Please stay a spell." Rose touched her sleeve.

"I'd love to." She left her cloak and sat back down. In

truth, she wasn't feeling well.

"How about some coffee?" Rose headed toward the stove. "I've got some fresh cinnamon rolls hidden."

"No, just the coffee. Thanks." Hannah rubbed her forehead.

"Paula and I are making plans for Holly's wedding shower next Friday." Rose set two steaming cups on the table. "Can you make it?"

"I wouldn't miss it." Hannah reached for the sugar.

"And next we ought to start a baby quilt." Rose poured cream into her coffee, then paused. "This can't be easy for you, Hannah. I know Colton loved you."

She swallowed hard against the ball of tears rising in her throat "If he could leave, it wasn't love."

"You don't believe that."

Hannah dared to gaze into Rose's eyes. Her heart twisted. "I have to."

"Oh, my dear friend." Rose reached out. "I hate to see you hurting like this. Is there something I can do?"

"You're doing it." Hannah tried to smile.

"I'm going to make sure your hired girl comes every day from now on." Rose's eyes glistened. "You've got a gift Colton left you and we have to see it safely delivered."

"Yes." She already loved her baby. At night she could feel flutters of movement and knew the little one thrived. Her abdomen cramped a little. She laid her hand there and sat up, hoping to ease the ache in her lower back.

"Hannah?" Rose touched her face.

She looked up and read the concern in her friend's eyes. "I'm fine. It's just been very hard with Colton gone."

"I know." So much sympathy. "Would you like to lie down for a bit before you head back home?"

"Maybe that would be a good idea." Another cramp, this one sharp, tore through her.

"Here. Lean on me." Rose took Hannah's arm.

Grateful tears filled her eyes. She tried to stand, but the room spun. All the light drained from her head. She looked into darkness and felt her knees buckle, then weightlessness as she fell.

Hannah knew it beyond a doubt. She was losing her baby.

"We're going to keep your head below your knees and hope the bleeding stops." The doctor took off his spectacles, stared at them with regret, then carefully wiped one lens on his shirt. Then the other. "There's no guarantee."

"I know." It hurt too much to cry. Hannah bit her bottom lip. She couldn't. She just couldn't lose this baby. Not this time.

"You need to do your part." The doc couldn't look at her as he slipped his spectacles onto his nose. "No upset, no moving, no anything. You have to relax, Hannah. Even though I know this is very difficult emotionally."

Tears pooled in her eyes, blurred her vision, yet she wasn't crying.

The doc's warm hand, patient and caring, covered hers. "I just want you to rest for now. Close your eyes and sleep. It's the best thing for you."

It was in his voice. She would miscarry.

Hannah closed her eyes against the tears, but not the pain. How could she shut off such despair?

The room echoed around her, sterile and cold despite the heat radiating from the black potbellied stove. Or maybe it was her heart that felt empty and cold, lonely for the love and support she needed.

Colton. She didn't want to need him. Couldn't let herself need him. He'd left her, as if her love meant nothing to him. She wanted nothing to do with him. She didn't miss his wonderfully strong arms holding her, powerful enough to protect her from harm and danger and the loneliness of a lifetime. She really didn't.

A sob shuddered through her chest. Oh, she had to calm down. Had to relax. But how could she?

Her love for Colton, however shattered, still beat

within her heart. She needed him now. She needed his warm hand in hers. The capable solidness of his presence. The strength and honor she so admired.

Yet she knew he would not be there. That perhaps that had been his plan all along. To find a mother for Zac. Hadn't Colton made her promise to care for the child no matter what happened? Had he known he would leave one day? Had she been a fool to fall in love with such a man?

Tears beat at her eyes, burned in her throat. She could taste the bitterness of lost dreams and lost love. Colton would never come for her, even if he knew she was losing his baby.

Well, she didn't need him. She still had her son and she would raise him and provide for him and love him. And she would teach Zac to be a man of tenderness and gentle strength. To be a man who could love.

Unlike Colton.

"Got a telegraph for you," Sheriff Potter growled, his voice low and rough from too many years puffing on cigarettes, swilling whiskey, and eating dust.

"Can't be for me." Colton grabbed his hat, spurs jangling on the floor as he strode toward the door.

"You're Colton Kincaid and you're a bounty hunter, ain't ye?" Potter quirked one bushy brow.

"Guess I am." Colton held out one hand. "What do you want me to do with the prisoner? I've got him outside."

"Dead?"

"Handcuffed and hog-tied." Colton unfolded the telegraph. "Got a two-thousand-dollar bounty on him. Nasty son of a bitch."

"I'll send for the marshal. He's over at the saloon and got nothing better to do but suck down tequila juice. He can deal with the varmint." Potter gestured for his deputy, then spoke to him in gruff tones.

Colton looked down at the telegram. Baker's name was

on the page. He started to read, but he couldn't look past the words *will probably lose the baby.*

His knees shook. He had to sit down. No, he had to get back to her, to hold her hand. He didn't want her to bear that pain and grief alone.

"Sheriff?"

"Thought you was gonna bring in that convict."

Colton managed to stand. "I will." It would only take a few minutes to do his job. Then he was leaving. Heading back to Montana. Home to Hannah.

Yet he remembered the look on her face when he'd refused her touch. When he told her he was leaving for good. He'd destroyed her belief in him.

Whatever loving feelings she had were gone. He knew that. He knew he could not reclaim that idyllic life he had with her. He didn't have the right. He wasn't the man she needed him to be.

When Colton headed his mare north, it was without hope. He knew damn well Hannah had lost the baby. The new life that bound them, the only proof of their love was dead and buried in another little grave.

His lonely life stretched out before him, a life of hunting and looking over his shoulder. Of drawing faster, aiming better, being tougher than the criminals he hunted. Only that would keep him alive. But he wasn't living.

He hated his life. He hated his job. Nothing was the same, would ever be the same, without Hannah's love.

A love Colton knew he didn't deserve.

He wouldn't fool himself now. No, his vow remained. He would make damn sure she was all right, that she'd survived the miscarriage, and then he would be on his way.

It was for the best.

CHAPTER TWENTY-SIX

C olton reined in his horse at the crest of the hill.
Trepidation skidded through him, cold and sharp.
The peaceful town lay below, nestled amid the
mountain foothills painted a vivid spring green.
Wildflowers waved their purple, white, and yellow faces as
he kicked his mare into a steady lope.

He feared that with the baby lost, Hannah would hate
him. Would despise him for leaving her to face such grief
alone. But he had to see her. He had to know she was safe
And it would be good to see his son again. Even for a few
moments. How he'd missed that little boy's happy smile.

Colton rode into the quiet town. Familiar faces
conveyed silent surprise as they turned to greet him. He
halted his mount outside the doctor's neat little clinic and
walked through the door.

The doc looked up from his paperwork. Behind those
spectacles, his eyes widened and he stood. "Kincaid."

"Gable." He took off his hat. "Where's Hannah?"

"First room on your right." The doctor gestured down
the hall. "Colton, she's—"

"I know." He held up one hand. At least she was alive.

He didn't need to hear any explanations. Didn't have the stomach. Couldn't bear to hear the words.

He didn't knock on the closed door. He just turned the knob, then knuckled the door open.

"Colton." Hannah's ashen face stared back at him, eyes wide, disbelieving. She clutched a blanket to her middle and stared at him as if he were a ghost.

She didn't want him, he knew. And he didn't blame her. Months of loneliness fled at the sight of her dear face, and he fought the urge to wrap her in his arms.

He knew he ought to turn around and leave. "You look pale."

"I'm feeling a little better." No beautiful smile.

The dreams they'd lost. The future buried. Colton's throat filled with grief. He never should have intruded into her life.

"I'm glad." He choked out the words and stamped down the wave of emotion rising like the tide through his chest.

"Are you?" The hard line of her mouth didn't soften. She hated him. Blamed him. And she had the right.

He hated what he had to do. But it was for her. For his son. He'd vowed to keep them safe and he would. He was a man of his word.

A satchel sat on the foot of the bed. She was packed. That meant he could do something for her, try to take care of her one last time. "Let me take you home."

"I don't need you. I can make it to my house just fine." She finished folding a wool blanket and laid it on the bed, revealing the curve of her stomach. Her pregnant stomach.

"The b-baby—" His knees rocked. His jaw fell. The world quaked beneath his feet. He couldn't believe his eyes.

"Is still alive." Hannah's chin jutted. She looked so distant in her coolness. "The doctor is hopeful. It looks like the worst is over."

"You and the baby are out of danger?"

"Yes. I'll need to rest and stay off my feet."

Relief struck him like a brick. The baby lived. The love between them, the hopes and dreams he'd once dared to believe in, still existed.

Mind spinning, he ran his fingers through his hair. He'd been prepared for the worst. And it hadn't happened. He'd been prepared to find the baby lost, maybe even Hannah dead. It could have happened. There were complications sometimes...

"I was afraid." Tears filled his eyes. "I care so much, Hannah."

"You left me."

"I did what was right."

"For you, maybe." She lifted her chin. There was no compromise. No forgiveness. Just grief and shadow in those heavenly blue eyes. "You found out what you wanted. The baby will be fine. You can go back to wherever you came from."

"That's what I'm going to do."

"Good."

Her words tore at his empty, lonely heart. Couldn't she see how he ached for her? "Fine. I'll take care of the doctor's bill."

"Don't bother." Her eyes flashed. "I don't want your money, Colton. I don't want anything more from you."

Tears glimmered in her eyes. Lord, he'd hurt her. He never thought, he never imagined...

She'd honestly loved him. The enormity jolted him like a lightning bolt. And he knew what he'd done in leaving her. Knew what he'd done from the moment he'd asked her to be his wife.

She'd believed in his honor, in his promises. And he'd broken them all to hell.

Colton headed for the door. It was for the best that she didn't need him. Even if he felt torn between his duty to keep her safe and the memories of the loving warmth of their life together.

"Don't come back," she said as he opened the door. "And I don't want you visiting Zac. He was brokenhearted when you walked out on us." Vulnerability trembled along her bottom lip. She wasn't mean, he realized, she was hurt. Trying to protect both her heart and her son's. "We've been hurt enough."

"I understand." And he did. His life wasn't here. It could never be again.

He walked out of her life without a good-bye.

* * *

Hannah listened to the ring of his boots on the floor as he strode down the hall, walking away from her again. Forever, this time. She knew.

He would not be back.

Cold, black pain ripped through her chest. A grief so huge she felt dwarfed by it. She wanted to run after him, to beg him to stay with them, to renew the joy and love they used to know.

But both her pride and her fear stopped her. It had been his decision to leave in the first place, not hers. She feared his love for her had never existed.

Still, he'd come. He'd come to make sure she was all right. She'd seen the grief on his face when he thought she'd miscarried.

Hannah didn't know what to think, what to believe. But one thing was clear: Colton was leaving. Whatever love he had for her, it wasn't enough to keep him here. It wasn't enough for him to love her in return.

Even if she needed him to.

Colton stood outside the inn's front door. Lamplight, warm and cozy, shone in the window. He knew without asking Zac was somewhere inside with Rose. Hannah's words echoed in his head. I don't want you visiting Zac. He thought of his son's broken heart. Of how the boy must have suffered because of his father's abandonment.

It was for the best. It was. Colton turned away, tears aching in his eyes and crossed the muddy street. He untied his mare from the hitching post and tried to think of nothing, nothing at all.

There were men he wanted to see. The Mullens. Eaton Baker. Arnie Sutcliff. Friends. It had been a long lime, since before his prison term, that he'd had real friends.

Colton mounted the mare, comforted by the familiar creak of the leather saddle. His gaze drifted to Doc Gable's front door.

Hannah. His heart twisted. If he thought of her, he couldn't leave. And he had to. He had to keep her safe.

He wheeled the mare south. He passed the mercantile. The tannery. The houses on the edge of town. He thought of the empty nights, of the lonely days stretching out before him without Zac's merry smile, without the warm love shining in Hannah's eyes.

He drew the bay to a halt, then spun her around and stared back at the town, at the only life he'd ever loved.

He couldn't leave. He just couldn't do it. There had to be a solution. A way for him to stay and keep Hannah and their children safe.

But how?

His past stretched out behind him, lonely and desolate. But the road before him led home.

Hannah felt the baby's kick and laid her hand across the high curve of her stomach. The little one sure had strong legs.

"Papa!" Zac cried as he turned from the window. "Papa ridin'."

Zac's constant chatter about his father made her heart ache for both of them. For what could never be.

"I know, your papa promised he'd teach you to ride." Hannah rubbed her forehead, irritable from keeping her feet up all day. She hated being idle.

"Papa ridin' fast!" Zac clapped his hands. "Papa comin'."

"What?" Hannah hiked herself up in the chair and

turned toward the window.

"Papa!" Zac dashed to the front door and yanked back the bolt so fast, she couldn't hop to her feet in time.

"Come back here, cowboy," she called, chasing after him as fast as she dared.

"It's Papa!" was Zac's only answer.

Hannah looked up to see the man flanking the small herd of horses, waving his brown felt hat in greeting. She scooped up the little boy before he could get in the way of the galloping animals.

Hank Mullen pulled open the south corral's gate and the horses dashed into the large enclosure in a haze of flying manes and tails, of blacks and whites and browns and reds. One of the Mullen boys brought up the rear. There had to be thirty, maybe forty, horses. Young, strong, and beautiful.

"Do you like "em?" Colton's voice. Colton's smile. His dimpled, lopsided, sexy-as-sin smile.

"No. I don't." Her heart thudded even though she didn't want to respond to him, didn't want to acknowledge the beat of desire within her. "What are you doing here?"

"I see I'm still in trouble." He sidestepped the bay up to her and reached to take Zac from her arms.

"Papa!" Both little hands clasped around Colton's neck. The boy snuggled against his father's chest, so ready to love, so ready to forgive the long, lonely months.

Well, she wasn't. She wouldn't. Her heart couldn't take the grief when he decided to leave again.

"I figured this place felt pretty empty without a herd grazing in those pastures." Colton's gaze fastened on hers.

"Those empty pastures aren't your concern." She refused to give in to her softer, needier feelings. "This isn't your ranch. Not anymore."

"My name is on the mortgage. I guess that makes it mine."

"Your name on a scrap of paper doesn't mean anything to me."

He'd hurt her. She had to remember that. As soon as he'd begged her forgiveness or whatever it was he wanted, he would ride back off toward the horizon. He made it clear there was nothing here to keep him. Even if she wanted him to stay.

"But it means everything to me." He settled Zac on his lap. "You're mad."

"You bet I am."

"And you have every right." A lightness breezed through his rumbling words. An easiness that made her look.

His dark eyes were smiling, twinkling just so to catch all the light. Like temptation himself, he sat there on his mount, his identical son in his lap, the wind tangling the dark locks of hair at his shoulder, at his iron strong shoulders.

Oh, she had a weakness for Colton Kincaid. A very big, very bad weakness. "I told you in the beginning, I was never going to let a man have control over my life or my heart. And you've managed to do both. And look how it's turned out."

"You tell me, Hannah."

Tears balled in her throat. "Look what you've done to my ranch. My heart."

"I know." His big hand laid against her cheek, cradling her jaw.

Those tears burned in her eyes, blurred her vision. "What you do, the decisions you make, affect us. I can't have you here, Colton, breezing in, bringing us money or horses or whatever it is you want. Go away and stay there."

"I'm not going back. I have a choice, Hannah. I didn't understand that before."

"It seems to me you have all the choices."

Colton set Zac in the saddle, then dismounted. A fluid movement of male power and grace. A ripple of muscles beneath the cotton shirt and trousers. "We both do. What happens next, what our future holds, it's all up to you and me. It's our choice."

"Sure." What did he think she would do, hand over her heart only to have it broken again? "As far as I can tell, you've made all the decisions around here—when to sell what horses, who to hire, and then to walk away from us."

"Surely you know I never wanted to leave." He brushed back the curls at the side of her face. How she'd missed his gentle touch. "I've never left you, Hannah. Every step I took, every mile I traveled, you were right here, tucked away in my heart. You were all I thought about. This love you've given me. This beautiful life I had with you." Sincerity burned in his eyes, bright as the sun, twice as sustaining.

"We've been miserable and lonely without you, Colton. And we will be again when you decide someone might harm us and you're gone."

"I'm never leaving. I swear it." His thumb brushed the curve of her jaw. His fingers curled around the side of her neck. "I'm not going to let some outlaw, some criminal, chase me away from your love, Hannah. It's not fair to you or Zac. And it's not what I want."

"And what do you want?" She set her chin, ready to keep her heart protected, ready to keep from making the same mistake.

"You." His eyes sizzled. "I want you, Hannah. If you will have me. If you will accept me as I am—past, present, and future."

"How do I know I can trust you?" She felt the pieces of her heart, still broken and hurting.

His hand closed over hers. "Because I'm giving you my word of honor. Because I'm not alone anymore. I have friends and neighbors who will help me keep my family safe. And I have you. You are my heart, Hannah. You are my life. I am nothing without you. Don't make me leave."

"You're leaving the decision up to me?"

"Yes."

Her eyes filled, her throat too full to speak. His iron-strong arms enfolded her. She leaned against the solid heat of his chest, breathed in the wonderful feel of him.

"Looky me!" Zac's gleeful voice rang, fracturing the peace of the valley. "I'm ridin'."

Hannah turned to see her son sitting astride Colton's bay, who'd given up waiting patiently for grain and was heading to the barn on her own.

"I think he's going to grow up to be quite a man one day," Colton said tenderly, holding her close.

"Just like his papa." Hannah thought of everything she'd nearly lost, of everything Colton had done for her, of how much she needed him to be happy, to be fulfilled. She knew she could trust him. He'd always kept his word to her, always honored his vows.

And she could cherish this man, her husband, forever.

"So, am I staying?"

"Maybe." She tipped her head back and smiled. "I guess it all depends."

"On what?"

"On whether or not you want to go back to shoveling out those barns. I guess we're keeping these horses."

"I guess we are." He pulled her into his arms, so sweet and light, her familiar honeysuckle scent filling him up. He breathed her in, grateful for this chance. This second chance at happiness. This second chance at everything. "I don't mind shoveling."

"A true man of honor." She laughed, but the love shone through her words and didn't fool him.

He laid his cheek against her forehead, felt the curve of her abdomen against him. Their baby. Made from their love. "Should we go fetch our son?"

"We'd better. If he's anything like his father he's headed off into the mountains."

"Do you forgive me for leaving, Hannah?"

"I already have." Her love shone from the depth of her heart, glimmered in her eyes. It was so strong that it hadn't ended with his departure, with the threat of the Varneys, with the anger and hopelessness she must have felt all these lonely months.

His heart hurt with all he didn't know how to say. Of the cold nights, of life without her touch, how he felt empty without the beauty of her smile. Only she could fill him up, make him whole, make him new.

"I'm a cowboy!" Zac's merry voice called out loudly enough to scatter birds from the meadows. "Mama, Papa, come ride!"

"I could make a picnic." Hannah's gaze met his, warm and inviting, a tentative question.

"I'll saddle the horses." Colton's mouth caught hers, his heart thumping at the sizzling heat as their lips met.

Horses. Children. A picnic in the meadow. It was too good to be true.

They were a family again.

EPILOGUE

Despite the long labor, Hannah's exhaustion faded at the look of dazed wonder and relief on Colton's face. He stood in the threshold, as if afraid to step into their bedroom where they'd made their marriage and this new baby and nearly a year of love together.

"Come see your daughter," she invited, happiness so huge and shimmering in her chest she could hardly say the words. "This warm little bundle in my arms is really something."

He took one step forward. "Are you sure you're all right?"

"I'm perfect." She held out one hand, her other arm cradling her very own baby. A round pink face, squished up adorably in that brand new baby way, tight little fists, and the soft down of blond curls. The newborn opened her tiny mouth into a big yawn and Hannah's heart melted with a powerful love. "She has your nose."

"No, I think that's your nose." He peered down at the new little girl, minutes old, her tiny eyes scrunched tight against the new sensation of light.

Joy shivered through Hannah. She had never known such happiness. "Colton, you look overwhelmed."

"I am. I don't know a thing about little girls." Awe shone in his eyes, as dark as dreams and lit with love. He knelt down, gazing at his new child. "She's as beautiful as her mother."

"I would say she's the most beautiful girl in this world." Hannah felt the burn of tears in her eyes and she didn't bother to hide them. "Thank you for giving me this baby. My arms are no longer empty."

"Never. Not as long as you have me."

If she ever had the slightest doubt about his love for her, just looking into his eyes would have silenced those fears, erased those aching months he'd left her alone with a broken heart. All things mend and are often stronger for the healing. As was their love.

Footsteps thudded on the wood floor, echoing in the rafters. The new baby blinked in surprise at the noise and cried out, then punched one tight fist into her bow-shaped mouth. Hannah turned to comfort the newborn.

A cat dashed into the room and skidded to a stop, followed by Zac, cowboy hat askew, dirt stained from head to toe. "Is that my baby?"

Colton reached out for his son. "Yep, this is your new sister. What do you think?"

"She's kinda wrinkly." Zac climbed onto Colton's lap and studied the newborn intently. "She gonna stay like that?"

"She's going to be as big as you one day." Hannah brushed a wayward lock of curls from her son's eyes.

"She's awful little." Zac sighed, uncertain.

"She will get bigger. You wait and see."

Colton's heart ached simply watching his wife. Hannah gazed up at him, fatigue shadowing her face, tired and spent from a long labor, but how beautiful. How endlessly beautiful.

Months ago, there had been much uncertainty when he

returned from hunting bounties, intent to stay. But no trouble from his past returned with him, and hard work had resulted in prosperity for the ranch and for his family. His throat filled, grateful beyond words for this life Hannah had given him.

"We're going to have to name this little girl," she said with a smile.

"I'm sure you have a few suggestions."

Merry laughter lit her face and sparkled in her eyes. Once they had feared this baby would never be born, and now here she was, cradled against her mother's side. "I want to name her Hope. Because that's what you've given me."

"Sounds like a fine name." Colton's chest filled with pride. He'd become a father for the second time, and nothing could be finer. Hannah had a baby in her arms, just as she'd always wanted. Their world was as it should be, full of love, hope and prosperity, but most of all, love.

AN EXCERPT FROM

A Candle in The Window

CHAPTER ONE

*D*on't think you're getting out of this alive, McKenna.

The bounty hunter's threat haunted him, as Luke McKenna gritted his teeth and took another stumbling step head-on into the howling fury of a mean Montana blizzard. The frigid wind knifed through the layers of wool and flannel, cutting to his bones with ease. The snow plunged in a gray-white gale that cut off the world from his sight.

The one good thing about this storm was that if he couldn't see his way through it, then neither could Moss.

"P-Pa? I'm c-cold."

"I know, darlin'. Just hold on tight to me."

"Okay." Beth's thin voice sounded tiny and frail compared to the howling fury of the wind. Tiny arms clenched around his neck as she burrowed against his chest. She might be safely buttoned inside his coat, but she was shivering hard.

He had to find shelter and soon. Beth couldn't stand this cold much longer, and neither could he, not with the way his bullet wound was bleeding.

He'd survived ten years as a Texas Ranger; he'd fought

Indians and renegades and the toughest outlaws in three territories, and by God, he'd survive this storm, too. He'd survived what he couldn't bear to live through, and he wasn't about to fail now, not when all he had to fight was a blizzard. His child depended on him, and he wouldn't let her down. Not ever again.

A boom exploded behind him. Gunfire? Had Moss tracked him in this storm? Luke clutched Beth tightly and ran, kicking hard in the deep, unpacked snow. He sank up to his thighs but kept going. Then lightning flashed, and another boom pealed overhead, eerily muffled by the gale-force snowfall.

Thunder. Not gunfire. Relief burst through him in an icy wave, and Luke slumped to his knees, breathing hard. The child cradled against his chest began shaking with sobs.

"P-Pa? I'm really, really c-cold."

"I know." It tore him apart. "We're going to be warm and safe soon."

"You promise?"

"You can count on it." He'd go to hell and back for his daughter. He pressed his hand against the growing stain on his jacket. The blood was freezing solid and turning the ice driven into the fabric a bright red.

He stumbled forward and stared at the snow at his feet. The shod half circles of horse tracks were fresh and deep. *Moss.* That black-hearted killer had followed him into the storm after all.

Black fury roared through him. The child tucked against his heart sobbed again, her cries pitiful. Torn apart, he knew he'd gone as far as he could. His hopes of getting Beth out of this territory to someplace safe had ended. Moss had proven relentless, and now, cloaked by the storm, Luke could walk straight into the bounty hunter's sites and not know it until it was too late.

Hide and wait. It was the only solution. *That, and hope Moss doesn't hunt you down.* Luke pressed his lips to his daughter's brow, and the layers of wool didn't diminish the sweet love he harbored for his child, helpless and innocent, or his fierce vow to protect her from ruthless men.

"It won't be much longer," he whispered, backtracking as the storm shoved him forward. He stumbled, pain shooting through his side, and he felt the hot, wet glide of blood on his skin.

He had to keep going; he had to keep his daughter safe.

A shadow jumped up out of the darkness. Then, quick as it appeared, it vanished. Luke tore the Colt .45 from its holster and aimed, thumbing back the hammer. Lightning cracked overhead, and thunder rumbled, eerily muted by the thick blanket of falling snow.

Where was Moss? Where had that bastard gone? The winds shifted, and there it was again—a dark splash of gold in the unrelenting gray-white world of wind and snow. A horse. It wasn't the bounty hunter's black gelding. The pretty palomino disappeared again behind the veil of white. There was a road ahead, and he could follow the tracks to shelter.

"Hold on, darlin'." Relief gave him strength, for they were no longer lost in the storm. He found the horse's tracks, and marveled at the force of wind already trying to wipe them clean. "It won't be long now."

"Do I getta have hot cocoa?"

"Absolutely." He pressed his lips to her brow and took off after the blur of gold that disappeared and then reappeared again much farther away, taunting him. Running with the last of his strength, he felt his wound tear wider. Hot, sticky blood warmed his skin from waist to hip.

He lost sight of the golden horse in the thick curtain of snow and wind. His vision blurred, and he couldn't seem to find the tracks he'd just been following.

Beth. He had to keep going for her sake. She was all that mattered. He couldn't control the weather and he couldn't control the forces driving evil men in this world, but he would find a way to get his daughter to safety.

Or at least he'd die trying. His knees buckled, and he hit the snow with bone-rattling force. The howling fury of the storm filled his ears, and he breathed in icy snow. The bitter cold wrapped around him and hurt like a knife paring through every inch of his body.

He was lost and losing hope, but the child buttoned inside his coat, next to his heart, kept him going. He stumbled until he couldn't walk, and then he crawled until the light faded from his eyes and there was only darkness—until not even his body responded to his driving will to survive.

Then there was only Beth's sorrowful cry and nothing, nothing but cold and death.

* * *

Molly Lambert shook the snow from her coat, shivering from the bitter storm. The house was cold and dark, but not as cold as the trepidation filling her at the unopened letter in her pocket

Her hound danced around her in excited circles as Molly hung her cloak to thaw. Iced snow tumbled like shards of glass and *plinked* against the wood floor. She patted her dog and hurried to stir the banked embers in the kitchen stove.

The hinges squeaked slightly as she opened the door. The unread letter felt like a lead weight in her pocket. She hadn't wanted to open it in town, and then a storm blew up on the road home and she'd barely made it to the stable before the blizzard struck with full force.

The scent of cured pine tickled her nose as she fed the weak coals. The dog nudged her; the wind howled against the north wall, and soon the flames snapped greedily as they grew in strength. All the while the letter felt heavier, as if it were dragging her skirt pocket down to her knees.

She wasn't ready to read it, not yet—good news or bad. The letter was from her mother, a woman whose heart was distant and cold and growing bitter as life passed her by. Molly didn't feel strong enough for more heartache, not today. Maybe she wouldn't read it. Maybe she would tuck it into the flames and watch the words burn.

The dog shot through the kitchen and lunged with both front paws at the back door, barking high and sharp.

"What is it, girl?" Molly opened the damper wide. The metal hinges squeaked and iron *clunked* against iron as she shut the door tight. "I'll let you out in just a second."

The dog whined louder and scratched harder.

"All right, all right. I'm coming." Maybe the white-tailed deer had returned, taking shelter in the lee side of her stable, knowing she would fork out bales of sweet alfalfa for them. "Is it time to feed the deer?"

Lady barked high and sharp—the animals must be close.

"Don't chase them," she ordered as she shrugged back into her icy cloak.

Lady didn't seem to be making any promises this time. Molly opened the door to the blast of ice and wind and stepped out into the harsh Montana blizzard. The dog loped on ahead, already lost in the gale-force snowfall.

This was her first Montana Rockies winter—she'd heard from Aunt Aggie how cold and hard they were. Well, Aunt Aggie was right, Molly thought as she struggled through the thigh-high drifts and kept her hand on the clothesline, which was tied from the back door to the stable so she wouldn't become lost in a storm.

Montana was a rugged place, but it was free, too. Free from the past, free from her mistakes. She was proud of this new life she'd made for herself—and this beautiful land she'd homesteaded.

Lady's sharp bark of alarm penetrated the howling wind and driving snow. Something was wrong—the dog didn't sound anywhere near the barn, and she'd never bark like that at the deer. Molly didn't dare let go of the rope; many a person had been blown off course by the wind and blinding snow and froze to death, but alarm beat through her, hot as flame.

Then she heard it, the painful rasp of a child's sob, faint and small when compared to the storm's mighty fury. Molly let go of the clothesline and tried hard to follow the sound of that sob and Lady's intermittent barking. The powerful wind tossed her around, and she wasn't certain she was making any progress at all.

Then all of a sudden there was the corner post of her split-rail fence. High drifts nearly hid it from sight, but a dark splash of color marked the snow.

Lady leaped up, grabbing hold of Molly's jacket hem to tug her along. The dark color became navy blue, then the shadow of a man's unbuttoned coat. He lay slack and unmoving, and the dark stain in the snow surrounding him looked like blood.

"Pa's dead," the little girl sobbed. "Just like my ma. He's all dead."

Lady reached the child first. The girl's eyes widened, but before she could react, the dog swiped at her freezing tears with a warm tongue. She buried her face in the dog's silky coat and cried.

"Come here, sweetheart." Molly reached out her arms, and the little girl moved from the dog's warmth to hers, wordlessly, her wrenching sobs of loss and grief heart-breaking.

Why, the child felt as fragile as a bird and shook from head to toe with those sobs. Molly cradled her tight, chest filling with sympathy. She pulled off one glove and laid two fingers against the father's throat.

A faint pulse beat against his cold skin. Relief shivered through her. He was alive, but with so much blood lost, how could she save him? He looked like such a big man. How on earth was she going to get him into her house?

"He's dead," the little girl sobbed.

"No, he's still alive."

Lady nudged her hand, and Molly knew she had to act

fast. The temperature was dipping as the blizzard grew stronger. There was no way she could fetch the doctor in this weather. Chest tight with regret, she carried the child back toward the house, but the storm confused her. Where was the clothesline? All she could see was the white-gray swirl of snow, but then Lady's bark led her to the safety of the clothesline. Fighting the winds, Molly ran as fast as she could until the faintest glow from the window told her she was almost home.

"My papa," the child sobbed.

"I'll go back for him, but you have to be a big girl and help me. Can you do that?" Molly tumbled through the door and into the warming kitchen. "You have to stay right here by the fire and keep warm, so I can take care of your pa. Can you do that? Lady will stay with you."

"I want my papa." The child shook with terror and grief, and Molly held her tight, wishing she knew how to soothe away such deep, genuine pain. With every second that passed, she knew the child's father was closer to death.

Molly thanked heaven for the hound that nosed the child gently, intent on washing away those half-frozen tears.

The girl began to cry harder, filled with need, and it was all Molly could do to walk away. Again, she thought of the unconscious man bleeding and freezing in her backyard. Leaving the child safe and snug here was the father's best chance.

Suddenly Lady leaped away from the girl, snarling. The door smacked open, driven by the wind, and a shadow broke from the curtain of snow.

A man stumbled through her threshold, gun in hand and blood staining the front of his coat like a wide patch of crimson paint.

"Papa!" the girl cried just as Lady lunged, and the shadowed man tumbled to the floor, unconscious, his blood pooling on the snow-covered floorboards, his gun clattering to a stop beneath her lace-covered table.

Faster than lightning, the girl darted to her father's side and knelt, fingers curling into his coat. "Don't die, Papa. Please."

Molly pushed the door closed against the bitter wind and knelt at the big man's side. His face looked haggard and gray. His breathing came in short, struggling gasps. He was dying right in front of her. Right in front of his daughter.

She tore at his jacket buttons and ripped open the garment. Both dried and new blood stained his shirt and trousers, and the single charred hole in the fabric gave a clear indication of his injury—he'd been shot. By whom? And in this peaceful part of Montana?

"Papa, wake up." Heartbreak in those words. "Please wake up."

Lady did her best to comfort the distraught child while Molly's heart broke. She didn't know if she could save the man's life. There was so much blood, and since the skin around the charred wound was raw and torn, she figured that the bullet was still inside him.

What was she going to do? She knew nothing about treating a serious wound like this, and there was no way she'd be able to make it through the blizzard to town. Even if she could, this man wouldn't live that long without treatment.

Just use your common sense, Molly. She grabbed a clean dishcloth from the counter and pressed it against the flow of blood. She'd need to take out the bullet and sew up the wound, and her stomach dropped, suddenly nauseous.

Don't think about it. Just do it. The dish towel was soaking red. The man was running out of time.

"Lady, fetch my sewing box." The dog looked at her with pleading eyes, standing protectively over the sobbing child, not wanting to leave her. But when Molly repeated her command, the hound darted off.

"What's your name, sweetie?" She hopped up to fill a

kettle with water.

"Beth." The little girl turned frightened blue eyes upward. "Are you one of the bad people?"

Bad people? "No. My name is Molly." She set the kettle on the stove, then knelt to drain the water from the reservoir. "Can you feel your fingers and toes?"

"They're cold." Beth swiped at her eyes with both fisted hands. "Is my papa gonna die?"

"I don't know." Molly knew the pain of being lied to— she wasn't going to make promises she couldn't keep. "I'm going to do my best to help him."

She sent the child into the kitchen to warm by the stove, and when Lady returned, carting her sewing basket by the handle, she sent the dog to watch over the child. Beth didn't argue, but continued to sob quietly in the warm corner.

Wishing she had more time to comfort the girl, Molly moved fast. She brought two lamps to the floor beside the stranger and lit them, then fetched a flask of whiskey from the pantry. Heart pounding, she knelt down beside her patient, this handsome stranger with a rugged face made of sharp angles and even planes. She couldn't help noticing his straight nose and his chiseled chin.

She pulled down his gun belt and trousers enough to expose the span of his hip and startled at the lean muscular make of him. Dark hair fanned across his stomach in a soft downward swirl toward his groin. Blushing, Molly vowed not to think about that any further. But his hard male body was a mystery, and she couldn't help wondering...

No, that wasn't a decent thought at all. Blushing harder, she moved the lamp closer to the bullet wound in his lower side, just above his left hip. She ran her littlest pair of sewing scissors through the bright flame, then knelt over him.

His skin was hot, and her heart thundered with fear of what she was about to do and the awareness of the man. *Breathe deep, and do this right.* She gathered her courage, then pulled the soaked dishcloth aside. The blood was slowing, surely that was a good sign. She nosed the tip of her scissors into the wound.

"Beth," he murmured, his voice slurred by dream and shock, and his head thrashed to one side and then stilled. The tension drained from his big body; the pain eased from his clenched jaw.

The scissors hit something hard. Molly gritted her teeth, steeled her stomach, and dug out the bullet as gently as she could. Blood welled up fresh and fast, and her gut clenched hard.

Don't faint, she ordered, even though her entire body was shaking. She applied pressure to the wound, then reached for the whiskey and splashed it across his abdomen. The hard roped muscles beneath his bronzed skin clenched in pain, and he groaned low in his throat, a sound of agony even though he was unconscious.

Beth started sobbing again on the other side of the cabinets, a sound as hopeless as a lonely winter wind.

Tension gathered at the nape of Molly's neck as she kept working—she couldn't stop now. As she threaded her needle, she spoke softly to the girl, and the crying stopped. Beth talked in a low voice to Lady, who was no doubt offering the girl her own brand of comfort.

Molly caught the edge of the ragged flesh with her needle. She winced, knowing it caused pain. Her stomach clenched again, and she felt her head start to swirl. Fighting for air, she pulled the knot through the skin and knotted it again to make sure it would stay and not pull through.

More blood sluiced from the wound, faster than she could stem it. She edged the needle into his flesh again and tugged the thread taut. The yawning wound closed a fraction, and she kept working, bringing the skin together, trying to make the seam she sewed tight enough.

She knotted her thread well and slumped against the back wall, breathing heavily. Sweat soaked her, and she felt shaky. Exhaustion gathered like an ache in the tensed muscles of her shoulders, neck, and back. She felt so weak, she didn't think she could stand.

But she'd done it—the wound was sewn tight. Gazing at the man, who was both shivering and sweating at the same time, she feared he wouldn't live, feared that her best was, once again, not good enough.

* * *

Beth gazed up over the bowl of steaming stew, watching Molly's every move with wide eyes. Even though she was warm, bathed, and dry, the child still looked peaked. Exhaustion bruised her delicate skin and hung on her slim shoulders. She sat as silent as a ghost at the table and didn't touch her food.

"Are you going to eat that?"

Beth shook her head, her dark hair brushing the shoulders of Molly's warmest sweater, which was draped over her reed-thin body. The sleeves were rolled up in fat cuffs, and the garment engulfed her. She looked forlorn, as if she were losing her entire world.

"It's early, but you look like you need your rest." Molly held out her hand.

Silently, Beth nodded, and her fingers closed around Molly's, tight with need and fear.

Molly tucked the child into her spare bed, safe and warm, and left the door ajar, just enough to be able to check on her. No more sounds came from the room.

The poor child. She understood how seriously her father was wounded. Molly ached for her, and when she next peered through the nearly closed door, she saw that Beth had fallen into an exhausted sleep. Maybe her dreams would be sweet, without cold, injury, or fear. Lady had curled up on the foot of the bed, keeping watch.

The hinges in her door squeaked, and she set the steaming basin on the nightstand. The man on her bed remained unmoving except for the barely perceptible rise and fall of his wide chest. He still lived.

317

Pulse drumming, she turned up the wick. Her knuckles jarred the lamp's crystal teardrops, and they tinkled like chimes, tossing glimmering fragments of rainbows across the embroidered pillow slip and the man's pallid face.

He was handsome; there was no denying that. Her heart tripped as she pulled the blanket down the breadth of his chest. Roughly textured skin stretched taut over well-defined muscles. He was a strong man, one who worked for a living; anyone could see that. His hands bore old calluses across his palms, and his skin was rich with the deep bronze from many summers spent beneath the sun.

As she wet and soaped the washcloth, she couldn't help wondering why he was wandering on foot through a dangerous blizzard with a child so young. Was he homeless? A drifter? But he had so many guns. He'd dropped one on her floor. She'd found one in his shirt pocket when she'd removed it, after stitching his wound. Now two more were strapped into holsters tied snug to both powerful thighs.

Four guns. She tried not to think about that. Tried not to think about what kind of man he might be. He was injured and she would help him, but she wouldn't trust him. No, she *couldn't* trust him.

This man bore a hard-set face, handsome but powerful, even in his sleep. She could feel his masculinity, like heat radiating from his well-made body. What was she doing noticing? She was a decent woman, a *schoolteacher*, for heaven's sake. She didn't go around gaping at men's handsome bodies.

She set the soapy cloth to his face and gently scrubbed over the proud blade of his nose, the ridges of each high cheekbone, the soft slope of his cheeks, and the unyielding line of his jaw. She felt the shape of him through the cloth and again as she rinsed off the soap and dried him.

The rough stubble of several days' growth rasped against her fingertips and caught on the terry towel. He smelled like winter wind and man, and as she laid the cloth to the base of his throat and caressed the width of his broad chest, heat licked through her. Like kindling to flame, she felt engulfed from toes to brow, from inside out.

What was wrong with her? This was an injured man, a stranger, hewn of muscle and danger, who looked as hard as stone fast asleep on her ruffled, pink and green sheets.

Wringing the cloth out in the steaming basin, she took deep breaths, filling her lungs with fresh air, trying to drive out the heat. Awareness tingled through her body, leaving a fine trembling that radiated straight through her abdomen.

Her gaze drifted back to him. She couldn't remember ever seeing a man's bare chest before, unless she counted her neighbor who'd worked out in his fields the past summer shirtless beneath the glare of the bright sun. And even from a distance, she'd been prudent enough to keep her gaze averted.

But *this* man, he drew her like a moth to light, and she couldn't help being fascinated by the sight and feel of him. Bronzed skin gleamed in the lamplight, dusted with soft hair that fanned across his chest and gathered in the center of his ridged abdomen, where it arrowed down beneath the edge of his denim trousers.

Her gaze lingered there, where the sheet curved mysteriously over that part of him. She blushed even thinking of it, and approached the foot of the bed, not sure what to do. The very thought of washing his...his... Heat flamed her face, and she turned to the basin, to soap the cloth.

He was asleep, not unconscious. Although weak from losing so much blood, he wouldn't be helpless when he woke. Maybe he ought to take care of such a personal task. The white bandage that wrapped in a tight band just above his hips contrasted against the black sheen of dried blood, and she knew she couldn't leave him like this. He had to be cared for, and there was no one but her to do it.

She reached for his gun belt and loosened the buckle at his hips. He stirred, his head thrashing from side to side against the pillow and a moan tearing from his throat. Her knuckles brushed the hot skin and soft fur on his abdomen as she began slipping the leather strap through the plain silver buckle.

Lady's bark echoed in the parlor, sharp against the wood walls and alarming even above the constant roar of the blizzard. The dog barked again, and Molly left the stranger, dashing into the lit parlor. The Regulator clock on the wall chimed the hour as she grabbed the Winchester from its pegs above the fireplace.

"What is it, girl? What's wrong?"

The dog lunged at the door with both front paws, teeth bared.

The rifle's wooden stock felt clammy against her palms. Maybe the bear was back, determined to try to break in her door this time. Or maybe he was trying to get at the horse in the stable.

She eased back the corner of a lace-edged curtain. Even though it was late afternoon, the world was nearly dark from the storm. The gale-force wind drove the snow to the ground like bullets, making the swirling grayness so dense she couldn't see past her top porch step. The hairs on the back of her neck stood on end, and warning prickled down her spine.

The hinges squeaked behind her. She turned to see a tall, broad shadow lurch out of the dark, avoiding the light. Molly grabbed Lady by the collar and ordered her to be quiet as the nose of a revolver glinted for a flash of a second, reflecting the lamplight. His step, uneven and halting, knelled on the puncheon floors as he approached, shadowed face set, broad shoulders tensed into a steely line.

Molly shrank, and the gun she clutched so tightly felt useless against his overwhelming male power, predatory and territorial, as uncompromising as death. He pushed past her and nudged the barrel of her rifle toward the floor. Lady went wild.

"Lock her in the bedroom."

Molly took one look at the fresh bandage already stained crimson and went to do as he asked, but she was shaking from head to toe. He'd looked dangerous asleep but awake he was lethal, and although he didn't stand straight, he radiated power and not weakness, strength and not injury.

Molly remembered the guns she'd found and eyed the one he held. "It's not a bear out there at all. What kind of trouble have you brought to my house?"

"Too much, and I'm sorry, ma'am." He said no more and offered no further explanation.

The rumble of his voice, resonate and cello-deep, echoed inside her. She stepped back, not sure what to do. He towered over her and the lamplight, barely touching him, gleamed darkly off his skin. Like a knight of old, like myth and legend, he braced his broad shoulders and lifted one arm, gazing out through the dark window.

"Are your doors locked?"

His gaze latched on hers, and although she couldn't see anything more than his shadow, she felt his gaze probing straight through to her heart, as if he could read all her secrets. Exactly how dangerous was he?

"Bar the front and back doors." His shadowed jaw clenched as he stared out at the storm. "Hurry."

She hated it when a man thought he could tell her what to do, but with the way Lady's hair bristled around her neck and tail, she knew the danger outside was greater than the one inside her house. But she couldn't stop the spark of anger as she shut her dog in the bedroom, then grabbed the bar from the corner and laid it across the metal brackets on either side of the stout pine door.

A boom rumbled through the thick walls; the muffled crash could be either thunder or gunfire. Luke leaned one shoulder against the window casing, gritting his teeth against the pain that burned in his left side just above his hip. Weakness radiated down his left leg and washed through every muscle in his battered body.

He listened to the tap of the woman's step through the house and the scratch of the dog's nails against the closed bedroom door. The storm outside roared like the devil himself, and if Moss followed him here, then the storm camouflaged him well. Luke swore, anger building. If Moss was out there, then Beth still wasn't safe.

Damn. He couldn't see anything but darkness and the harsh veil of swirling snow washed with black now that night had fallen. Moss could be out there, no more than three feet away, and Luke wouldn't know it, couldn't see him. Fury tore through him like the swift edge of night.

He hadn't come this far to fail Beth.

The dog's startled bark split through the dark. He let the curtain fall, the lace feminine and soft against his knuckles, and charged around the perimeter of the room. His left foot dragged just enough to catch his toe on the edge of a braided carpet. Pain jolted up his leg and into the wound.

He gritted his teeth and kept running. The distance across the parlor seemed like a mile. He heard the crack of a door breaking, the slam of wood striking wood, and a woman screaming.

His adrenaline pumped, and he tore around the corner, revolver steady, calm from the years of working behind a gun. He saw it in a flash—the rifle on the floor, the re-flected glint off a revolver's nose, the swing of that revolver straight toward Luke's heart—

Where is the woman? He dove behind the thick wood wall as a gun fired and a bullet bit into the curve of the log wall not an inch from his brow. He could hear the rasp of frightened breathing. Moss had her. The bounty hunter he'd been ducking since crossing into Montana Territory. The coldhearted bastard who'd put Beth's life in danger. He had the woman.

"I've got a gun to her head, McKenna," a man's voice—not Moss's—boomed above the howling wind and the barking dog. "Toss me your Colt and come out, hands up and empty, or I'll shoot her. You know I will."

Hammond. Moss's right-hand man. Luke leaned his brow against the wall, breathing hard, shaking from weakness and pain. He was in no position to fight. Hell, he couldn't even hold his gun steady, and he knew Hammond would kill the woman, either way. He couldn't surrender, even if he wanted to.

"What's it gonna be, McKenna?"

"I'm coming out, Hammond." There was no other solution. He tossed down one gun and listened to it slide across the polished floor, metal gliding on wood. "I've got Beth in the next room. I don't want a fight."

"Sure, McKenna. Anything you say. Just step out with your hands up. I'd hate to put a hole in this little lady, not before I'm finished with her." Cruelty glittered like a rare jewel in the dark, as heartless as the storm, as dark as the night.

"Is Moss with you?" Luke tugged his second revolver from his gun belt, speaking to hide the click as he thumbed back the hammer.

"Get the hell out here or I shoot."

Luke shook like a son of a bitch, but he took a deep breath, willing his right hand to be steady for just a few seconds, just long enough to squeeze off one shot. You can do this. He had to, for Beth's sake and for the woman's.

"You win, Hammond. I'm coming out."

Luke flew around the corner. Pain blurred his vision as he squeezed the trigger, and his aim was sure and true. He saw Hammond's look of surprise, saw his gun tumble out of his hand, firing wild. The woman, hazel eyes wide with terror, opened her mouth in a silent scream as she realized the bullet had whizzed right past her neck to lodge in the middle of the bounty hunter's heart.

Luke waited, revolver cocked, as the big man tumbled backward already dead, hitting the floor with a sickening, lifeless thud. He didn't so much as twitch.

Staggering, Luke leaned against the counter. Relief swept through him, cold as a north wind. "Are you all right, ma'am?"

She shook her head. She trembled so hard, her teeth rattled. Wide eyes locked on his, and she looked ready to faint. "You could have shot me. You could have killed me."

"No. I'm a sharpshooter. I never miss." Pain exploded with every step, and he pressed the flat of his palm to his left side, where fresh blood warmed his skin. "I'll take care of the body."

"The body," she repeated dully. "You killed a man. Right here in my kitchen."

"A man who had no problem playing with your life." Luke retrieved his Colt from the floor and holstered both weapons. "You don't want to think about what he was going to do to you."

"You killed a man in my kitchen," she repeated, her hands beginning to fist. "You brought violence here, to my home."

"I'm sorry about that." He grabbed Hammond by the wrist. He knew the bounty hunter was already dead but checking was old habit. The blizzard hurled cold and ice through the open door and sheered straight through him. He debated about hauling Hammond's body away now because the woman hugging herself and shaking looked ready to faint.

He pushed the door closed with a bang and stepped over Hammond's body. Her back was to him, and he could see the rage in her clenched fists, see her fear in her rigid spine, and hear it in the constant rustle of her skirt as she trembled.

"You saved my life and my daughter's." He lingered in the shadows not knowing if he should approach her. "I had no right bringing trouble to your doorstep. I owe you more than that."

Her chin shot up. She looked ready to fight. She looked ready to crumble. She was a gently raised woman, he could see that right off. In the soft curves of her face, classically beautiful, her complexion was as smooth as cream. She was tall and willowy, but when her gaze locked on his he saw no delicate blossom easily damaged.

He saw hurt, he saw fear, but mostly he saw strength.

"Keep your distance from me." She knelt to retrieve her rifle, the fragile curve of her neck white and vulnerable in the flickering lamplight. She straightened, fingers curled hard around the wooden stock, her knuckles white. "If it wasn't blizzarding outside, I would lock you out. Look what you've done."

"Aren't you going to thank me?"

"For what?"

"Saving your life." He laid one hand on her shoulder, the other on her elbow. "And now you have to thank me for keeping you from fainting. Come, sit down."

"I don't need any help." She twisted away from his grip, but he tightened his hold on her elbow. She felt like fine china, far too fine for a man like him to touch.

"I don't understand where he came from." She let him lead her to the table and chairs by the window. "There isn't another house for half a mile, and it's impossible to travel in this kind of storm."

"Not impossible for men like Hammond." He held out the chair and waited until she settled into the polished wooden seat, skirts rustling, before he released her. His fingertips sparked with awareness. "The devil can travel anywhere, ma'am. Lower your head and try to breathe deeply."

"I'm not going to faint." She didn't heed his advice, but propped her elbows on the table instead, setting the crystal teardrops on the lamp tingling, and buried her face in her hands.

It had been a long time since he'd been this close to a woman. He liked the way she smelled faintly of lilacs sweetened by spring sunshine, how her lace-edged petticoats whispered, and the feeling of gentility, of something soft and feminine in a world cold and unforgiving. She reminded him that there were places where life was valued and killing was seen as an unbelievable sin.

He shook with weakness, but managed to step away. What did she see when she looked at him? What did she think of the worn clothes and his four guns? Of the bounty hunter dead at his feet? Of the child he couldn't provide for? What did she see?

He grabbed the dead body by one ankle, opened the back door, and tugged him outside into the black howling storm. The wind's force nearly knocked him to his knees. Luke gritted his teeth and kept going. But not the frigid temperatures or the brutal wind could drive the despair from his heart. He was a wanted man, and the next time a bounty hunter fired on him, Luke knew he might not be lucky.

He had no future, but for Beth's sake he would make peace with the woman inside the house, haloed with lamplight, frightened and alone. He was at her mercy for his daughter's safety until the blizzard blew out and he was on the run again.

COMING SOON

ABOUT THE AUTHOR

Jillian Hart makes her home in Washington State, where she has lived most of her life. When Jillian is not writing away on her next book, she can be found reading, going to lunch with friends and spending quiet evenings at home with her family.

4679215R00192

Made in the USA
San Bernardino, CA
01 October 2013